Beautifully Forgotten

Beautifully Forgotten

L.A. Fiore

Montlake
Romance

Text copyright © 2014 L.A. Fiore

Published by Montlake Romance, Seattle

www.apub.com

Amazon, the Amazon logo, and Montlake Romance are trademarks of Amazon.com, Inc., or its affiliates.

ISBN-13: 9781477823965
ISBN-10: 1477823964

Cover design by Laura Klynstra

Library of Congress Control Number: 2014903117

Printed in the United States of America

For the fans of Beautifully Damaged:
*I am humbled by the response it's received; you have
made my dream come true. This book is for you.*

*For Lois: Gone but certainly not forgotten.
We miss you.*

———◆———

Author's Note

There have been extensive revisions to Beautifully Damaged, *particularly with the secondary characters and their associations with one another. An example of this is the character Trent is now named Kyle.* Beautifully Forgotten *follows these character changes. Check out L.A. Fiore's Facebook page for these character revisions.*
https://www.facebook.com/l.a.fiore.publishing

$\mathscr{P}$rologue

"A nother one. Goddamn it."

He was probably not even two and looked even smaller. Despite that, the clothes on his back seemed new and his recently trimmed mahogany strands shined from a shampooing and combing. He had been loved, this child, loved and left at the front door of the old orphanage.

Sister Margaret continued, "I really hate children." She turned in a swirl of black cloth and started back inside, sweeping past Sister Anne and calling to her from over her shoulder, "Bring the little beggar inside."

His little legs shook with fear, his eyes wide as Sister Anne knelt down in front of him. Those eyes—his most remarkable feature—were like the water off the coast of the Caribbean: not blue and not green, but a shade just in between. She reached for his hand and saw that his fingers were curled around something. It took a bit of effort, but she was able to pry open his grip to reveal a small square of paper that simply read, "His name is Lucien and he deserves more than I can give him."

Sister Anne looked down at the little boy who was so terrified, but trying desperately to be brave. His eyes locked on her.

She reached for his hand again and instantly his little fingers closed around her palm.

"Stop dillydallying and don't bother making friends with him. He'll end up like all the rest of them in ten years: dead or doing time."

Sister Anne looked down at the little boy, and though he was young, she knew he understood the Mother Superior's cruel words.

"Prove her wrong, little one. Fate is what you make it."

Lucien would hear her words for the next fifteen years—they stuck with him and unconsciously guided his every move. He had been abandoned, but he would make something of himself if for no other reason than to prove everyone wrong.

Sister Anne Black died right before Lucien's eighteenth birthday. So when he left the orphanage, heartbroken and alone, he took more than her words with him; he claimed her name, the name of the only mother he had ever known.

Chapter One

Lucien Black pulled off his tie and shoved it into his jacket pocket. If only the pomp and circumstance could be shed as easily. He was unaccustomed to being forced into the spotlight. The exit sign just across the room flickered like a goddamn beacon, but he was the guest of honor; so even as he sought freedom, he was stopped by countless people wishing to offer him congratulations.

Tonight the fine people of the state of New York honored him as a humanitarian—a feat for someone with his shady past—all because he'd donated to various charities to help children have a better time of it than he'd had. Who knew that all you had to do to get a golden statue and a fucking plaque was write a check?

And be willing to ignore the irony of attending a charity gala that cost enough to have provided food, clothes, shoes, and books for half of those very children. Not that there were any of those children in this room—the people in attendance were concerned for the children, but only at a distance.

He glanced at his watch; the time read close to eleven. He had somewhere else to be, so he walked with determined strides to the exit and, just when freedom was in his grasp, an all too familiar voice spoke up from behind him: Judge Jonathan Carmichael.

Lucien hadn't been completely forthcoming with his friends last year about his association with the Carmichaels. Dane was a partying jackass who didn't understand the meaning of the word no. The senator and DA he knew of only by reputation, but the same could not be said of the judge.

The judge had made it his business to meddle in Lucien's affairs, presumably to find something to hang him with. The judge wasn't having much luck, though, since Lucien had lots of well-paid lawyers, but it was a constant irritation. Lucien had been all too happy with the part he played in getting an ethics committee to look into the judge and DA after Dane's attack on Ember last year. He knew the committee wouldn't find any-thing—the Carmichaels were too smart for that—but he enjoyed watching them get a small taste of what he'd been dealing with from the judge on a regular basis.

A waiter passed by and Lucien reached for a glass of cham-pagne and deliberately took his time tasting it before he turned his attention to the judge. The color that bloomed on the older man's face at the snub was very gratifying to see.

"All the money in the world won't make you respectable," the judge spat by way of greeting.

"Respectable like you, you mean? What an aspiration," Lucien replied.

"Buying your way into society won't work."

Lucien's fingers tightened on the stem of the glass as he worked to control his anger at the arrogance of the man before him to presume to know anything about him. Unlike half of the people in this room, Lucien wasn't looking to enter society; he was only helping those who needed it. None of the people in here knew what it was like to be cold, to be hungry, to feel forgotten.

Having been there and having survived it, he would continue to do all he could to give those kids a fighting chance.

"I'd bet my bank account that if you scratched at the shiny exterior of the society you praise, you'd find that it's not all it's cracked up to be. Take you, for instance. Those black robes can't hide the skeletons in your closet. You have almost as many as I have in mine."

"What the hell do you mean by that?" It wasn't what the judge said, but how he said it; Lucien had hit a nerve. He was intrigued far more than he wanted to be. Was there really something that would give Lucien the leverage to get the judge off his back? He was going to damn well find out. More than eager to leave the man guessing and seething, Lucien changed the subject.

"As much as I would love to stand here and continue this riveting conversation, I've better things planned for my evening." His eyes moved to his date; she wasn't hard to spot since she looked like a porn star. The judge's startled breath almost made Lucien laugh with pleasure. Kelly or Kelsey—he never could remember her name—was currently talking up one of the judge's respectable colleagues: old enough to be her grandfather, but richer than the Queen. Even from their distance he could see the old coot staring at her rack.

It was with genuine pleasure and more than a little sarcasm that Lucien said, "To aspire to be as respectable as you and yours, a life mission."

And then Lucien turned and walked away, feeling the judge's glare burning holes into his back. He didn't stop for anyone else, offering his regrets as he moved with purpose to the door. Once he was outside, he took a few minutes just to breathe deeply.

"Where do you want to go now?" his date purred after magically appearing at his side to press her body up against his. He knew what she wanted, but what Lucien found disturbing was that he didn't want the same thing.

Probably frustrated since he hadn't answered her, she moved her hand down his body to drive the point home. It seemed unwise for the newly honored humanitarian to get a hand job right outside of the event, so he called for his car.

As soon as the car appeared, he pulled the back door open before the driver could and gestured for his date to get in. His eyes found the driver's.

"Take her home."

He heard her protest as the car drove away, but he just didn't care. He walked for a bit to clear his head before hailing a cab and heading to Sapphire, a local club. The place was packed when he arrived, but he easily moved through the crowds to Trace's table: being friends with the owner had its perks. Rafe, his friend since they were kids, and Kyle, Ember's best friend, were in the middle of a conversation when he settled into a chair across from them.

"Hey, Lucien. How did it go?" Rafe signaled to the waitress and pointed to Lucien.

"I think a root canal would have been more enjoyable."

"You didn't enjoy hobnobbing with the rich and powerful?" Kyle laughed because he knew damn well that Lucien detested all of it.

Lucien responded by flipping Kyle off. "Where are Trace and Ember?"

Kyle gestured to the dance floor and Lucien turned his attention to where their friends were dancing. Trace's head leaned against Ember's as he played with a lock of her hair that had fallen over her shoulder. They moved like one body: seamlessly and without thought.

He was happy for Trace even as jealousy twisted in his gut. Who would have thought the hard-as-nails player would lose his heart to the girl next door. He couldn't blame Trace; Ember was great.

Not generally a jealous kind of guy, Lucien did envy his friend and the peace he'd found. But it gave him hope that maybe he'd be as lucky one day. Settling down was never something he thought he'd ever want—well, not for a long time anyway—but seeing it firsthand, the happiness and contentment that came from marrying the right person, he was beginning to think he didn't know shit.

"Makes you jealous, doesn't it?" Rafe said, which shifted Lucien's attention across the table. His friend was watching Trace and Ember with a look on his face that he imagined matched his own.

"Yeah." If you couldn't be truthful with your friends . . .

The song ended and the two made their way back to the table. Lucien stood for a hug and noticed Trace's scowl as he did so. To be an ass, Lucien also pressed a kiss on Ember's lips, which earned him a growl.

"Troublemaker," she said, but laughter shone out of those big brown eyes.

"Guilty as charged."

"So how was it? Did you get a fancy award you can display on your desk?" Trace asked before he pulled out the chair next to Ember and folded himself into it.

"It was what I expected."

"That bad? I'm sorry to hear it."

"How's Carlos working out?" Lucien asked, looking to change the subject.

"Good, thanks for the recommendation. It's nice not being tied to the cooking school twenty-four seven"—Trace looked over at Ember—"so I can spend more time with my wife."

Lucien didn't miss the look Ember gave Trace. The fact that he didn't pull her into a private corner right then proved that Trace had far more willpower than he.

She ran her fingers over the tat on his arm and said, "Sweet talker."

Trace abruptly stood and pulled her to her feet. "Dance with me, beautiful."

But they didn't head in the direction of the dance floor. Lucien grinned to himself and thought maybe he won in the will-power department after all.

"Lucky bastard," Rafe muttered before he reached for his beer and downed the rest of it. "I need to go. I've got to get up early to deliver a few pieces to a client in the morning."

"I'll leave with you. I'm beat," Kyle said.

"I'm going to stay and have another drink." What Lucien didn't add was that the idea of going back to his empty apartment was completely unappealing.

"All right, see you later." Rafe and Kyle disappeared into the mass of bodies.

Lucien signaled for another beer before he leaned back in his chair and idly glanced around. He didn't miss the looks he was getting from several of the women at the bar, but he was just not interested. It should concern him, his total lack of enthusiasm, but caring was too much effort.

Maybe he needed to find a hobby. Or join a cult. He took a pull from his beer, but it had lost its taste. Jesus, he was in some serious shit when he couldn't even enjoy a simple fucking beer.

He dropped some money on the table before heading to the bar where he signaled the bartender, Luke.

"Hey, what's up?"

"If you see Trace and Ember, will you let them know they're on their own?"

Lucien understood the smile that tugged at Luke's mouth— eight months married and they were still acting like newlyweds.

"You got it," Luke said before he moved down the bar to take an order.

Lucien stepped out into the balmy night and hailed a cab. When it stopped in front of his building on the Upper East Side, the doorman greeted him.

"Evening, Mr. Black."

"Johnny, how are the kids?"

"Good, we have the grandkids for the month, but they're in camp this week, which gives me and the missus some time to ourselves."

Lucien grinned because Johnny was pushing seventy and his wife was just behind him in age. The most they were likely to do with time alone was watch *Jeopardy* while holding hands. He pulled a fifty from his wallet and passed it to Johnny, knowing both Johnny and his wife had a preference for fine Scotch. "To keep from getting parched."

Johnny didn't hesitate to take the offered gift. "You are a fine young man."

Lucien laughed as he made his way up to his apartment. He dropped the keys in the Baccarat dish that one of his girlfriends insisted he had to have. His apartment had become a point of pride for him, especially coming from beginnings like his. The floors were bamboo, the walls were painted a dark tan with thick crown moldings, and he'd mixed several priceless old pieces with modern ones. A stand-alone linear fireplace separated the living room from the dining room and a massive kitchen took up the one entire wall. He didn't cook often, since he was a single man living alone, but he could if he needed to.

He moved to the kitchen, grabbed a beer, and popped the top before he settled on his sofa and took a long drink. Yeah, he'd come a long way since being a gravedigger sharing a studio with five other guys. Of course, he didn't realize at the time that the graveyard was really a front and that most of the caskets were filled with guns instead of bodies. Trafficking in firearms using a cemetery was both twisted and fucking clever. The only bodies buried in that graveyard were ones that were better off never being found. At eighteen, Lucien had been blissfully unaware and at thirty-one, he really didn't give a shit because that job helped him to get to where he was now. Of course, looking around his spacious apartment and seeing only his reflection in a mirror, where he was now wasn't all that great. He thought bitterly, *I need to get a fucking life.*

He switched on the television and when a picture of Horace Carmichael, the DA, flashed on the screen, he turned up the volume.

". . . a crack in the case against the Grimaldi crime syndicate. District Attorney Horace Carmichael has testimony from a source close to the Grimaldi family that conclusively links them with several arson cases, racketeering, and the cold murder case of Elizabeth Spano, the NYU theater major found strangled thirty-two years ago in Central Park. That case has been kept in the public eye by the tireless efforts of the victim's father, Anthony Spano. More to follow."

Darcy MacBride climbed from the cab and wiped her sweaty hands on her skirt. She was nervous, but then, this was Lucien Black, whom she hadn't seen in fourteen years. She remembered the first time they met at the orphanage. Even at sixteen, he was the most beautiful boy she had ever seen. And his eyes, God, she could have happily drowned in them; but he was so serious, as if he bore the weight of the world.

She had been scared when she'd first arrived at fourteen, given up by her mom because she hadn't wanted a kid anymore. She couldn't lie, it had hurt to be cast off like an unwanted puppy, but she hid the pain behind humor and sarcasm. Only Lucien seemed to see beyond that and offered her the one thing she always secretly longed for: a place to belong. And she did. She belonged with him and they both knew it. For those two years they were inseparable, and she gave him her young heart with the reckless abandon of youth.

The day Sister Anne died was forever burned into Darcy's memory. Even though Lucien loved Sister Anne, he tried so hard to not show how much her death hurt him. And when he did finally give in to his pain, he mourned so silently that watching his grief was even more heartbreaking than seeing Sister Anne waste away. It was that same night that Darcy gave him her virginity. Even at sixteen she knew that he was it for her.

When he said he was leaving the orphanage, he told her he wouldn't go without her. But her fairy tale died before it had ever even had a chance to start. Not leaving with him was her most profound regret.

When her headhunter told her about the position he was looking to fill, part of her didn't want to take the interview—some scars still hurt no matter how long they'd had to heal. But she missed him—had spent half her life missing him—and even if she didn't get the job, the opportunity to see him again wasn't one she could pass up.

She moved her hands down her black pencil skirt and absentmindedly touched her hand to her French twist before she reached for the door of Allegro. She had followed his successes through the years and knew that this was the first club he had ever opened. It looked like he kept his offices here too.

The bar and tables inside were as scarred as the floor. Of course those who came here were coming for the music, not the atmosphere. Darcy loved it. A woman at the bar looked up from washing glasses.

"Can I help you?"

"I'm here for an interview with Mr. Black."

"Oh right, he mentioned it. Please follow me."

She came from around the bar and led Darcy down a hallway. "Lucien's office is back here," she said from over her shoulder, but Darcy couldn't hear her words over the roaring in her ears. Her pulse pounded so hard she was surprised the other woman couldn't hear it. If she didn't calm down, she was very likely going to faint, which was not at all how she imagined their first meeting after all these years.

She heard his voice coming from down the hall, the cadence and pitch of it exactly as she remembered. When they reached the open door, she could see him behind his desk with his head down, working while he talked to someone on speakerphone.

He had been beautiful at sixteen, and at thirty-one he was simply gorgeous. His slightly longer hair brushed shoulders twice the size they'd been in high school. He wasn't a boy anymore, but a full-grown man, and the reality of that hurt.

"Lucien, your interview is here."

"Thanks, Tara," he said without looking up as he finished his call. "Let me know what you find out. Yeah, thanks."

His head lifted and Darcy found herself holding her breath when those teal eyes bore right into hers. Memories slammed into her, a mental collage of the two years they had spent together. The emotions they evoked made her almost throw herself into his arms.

She was so lost in her own thoughts that she didn't realize until he'd spoken that he didn't remember her.

"Please sit, Ms. MacBride."

And with those four words he gutted her, the pain slicing her open and leaving her empty. All the years she wished she could have gone back and done things differently—pained over the fact that she had hurt him—were all for nothing because he had forgotten her just like her mother had taunted.

She wanted to run from the room and him and the memories that were even now crumbling to dust, but her feet wouldn't obey.

The idea of working for him, of being the only one to remember their young love, made her feel sick. She felt the tears and cursed them.

"Are you unwell?" There was genuine concern in his voice, and in that moment she hated him.

"I'm sorry. This was a mistake." Somewhere she found the strength to turn from him and walk away, eager to put as much distance between them as possible. If only she could run from her memories as easily. She had hurt him once upon a time and now she had a taste of just how much.

———◆◦◆———

Darcy stepped off the subway and made the short trip to her mother's apartment in Queens. Her mother had come back for her; it had taken her three years, but as she was forever saying, she'd come back. Darcy wasn't the same girl her mother had dropped off at St. Agnes, though, because she had lived a lifetime of regret in that time.

She had been young, scared, and so deeply in love—the kind of love that you couldn't imagine would be reciprocated. And when her doubts were spoken back to her, she'd panicked. It was that doubt that brought the end to Lucien and her.

Her mom came for her almost a year after Lucien had left, and being alone and heartbroken at seventeen, Darcy went with her, especially since St. Agnes only served to remind her of what she'd lost. How her mother had been able to take her away from St. Agnes as easily as she had, considering it was a state-funded orphanage and not a hotel, had always baffled Darcy. More strange was the fact that her mother had given her up because of her drinking and the violent jealousy she felt toward her own daughter while drunk. And yet her mother hadn't had a change of heart, nor had she stopped drinking. If anything, the woman drank even more. Darcy also hadn't known that going with her mom meant selling herself into servitude.

She never understood how her mom had learned of Lucien and all that happened between them, but her mom took great delight in rubbing salt into the wound. While she worked her way through a bottle of vodka, she'd philosophize on how men were fickle and love didn't last and what a fool Darcy had been to give herself so completely to someone when she was so utterly forgettable.

Over the next year her mother's words had chipped away at Darcy's confidence, but what kept her from breaking was the belief that what she and Lucien had shared had meant as much to him as it had to her.

She was stronger now, because she'd learned to depend on herself, so the reality that her mother had been right all those years ago wasn't going to break her, but it did hurt like hell.

She pushed open the door to her mom's apartment and was immediately greeted by the smell of alcohol and rotting food. She moved through the littered living room to the kitchen where take-out boxes spilled off the counters and onto the floor near the trash can.

Her mom was forty-seven, but looked seventy. Her drinking was going to kill her. The doctors had already said this, but the woman couldn't stop. Darcy had tried—instead of sending her cash, she started having groceries delivered, but she couldn't take the phone calls, her mom raging one minute and crying the next. In the end Darcy decided if her mom wasn't interested in saving herself, then why the hell should *she* bother?

"Is that you, Darcy? It's about fucking time. Get in here. I can't find the remote."

Darcy stepped into the bedroom and gagged as the smell worsened. Her mother was sprawled out on the bed wearing only her bra and panties. Dirty clothes covered every surface and mixed in with them were the empty bottles of vodka. A naked man lay passed out on the bed next to her, just one of the many nameless, faceless men she picked up.

"You do have legs," Darcy said, and her mom sliced her with a look. The very same look she received as a child just before her mom hit her. Even now, as a grown woman, that look brought fear.

"Careful, little girl. I'm still your mama. Now change the channel and get me something to drink."

Darcy turned for the kitchen; disgust filled her that she could so easily turn back into that terrified little girl simply by crossing over that threshold. She hated herself for coming back here every month instead of just cutting the cord and being free. But what kept her coming was that, thirteen years ago, her mother had come for her. Yes, it had taken her longer than it should have, but in the end she had brought her home and, for better or worse, she was her mom.

Lucien didn't know how long he stood staring at the empty doorway. Darcy MacBride. Talk about a fucking kick in the gut. He had recognized the name immediately when the headhunter mentioned her, but he didn't believe it could possibly be the same person. And if it were, why was she resurfacing now after all these years? His curiosity about *that* answer was the major reason he'd agreed to the interview. But if he was being completely truthful, he had hoped it was her. He'd wanted to see her again. And even with the anger he always felt when he thought of her, he couldn't deny that he had soaked up the sight of her.

His Darcy had always been beautiful, and she was exquisite as a grown woman. There had been a time when he couldn't keep his fingers from her hair, those onyx strands feeling like silk between his fingers. And her eyes, as blue as a sapphire, formed the windows to her soul.

He had loved her with the intensity of first love, but he'd believed that love was strong enough to last forever. He had never felt as close to another person as he did the night Darcy had given him her virginity. She was so innocent and sweet, so eager to love him, so eager to be loved by him. He would have given it all to her, but then she ripped him into shreds and left him broken and alone.

He knew he hurt her by pretending he didn't know her. He had done it intentionally, trying to make her feel his pain. Unfortunately, he didn't derive any pleasure from seeing pain cloud her beautiful eyes.

Why the hell would she come here? Did she think he had forgotten having his heart ripped out by the only girl he would ever love? Her rejection sent his life in a direction he had never expected.

He moved to the cabinet in the corner of his office and poured himself a Scotch as he remembered.

──────◆──────

Fourteen years earlier . . .

"Keep your head down and your ears open. Mr. Santucci doesn't like people appearing too interested in his business. He needs another runner. I already told him about you," Jimmy cautioned.

"Are you sure this is legal?" Lucien knew it wasn't, but he couldn't help asking anyway.

"Legal enough. Look, all you have to do is take the purse from one place to the other. Don't ask questions; just do as you're told. You get paid when you deliver the purse."

"Why would he trust me?"

"Because I've vouched for you, so don't fuck up, Lucien. It ain't every day an eighteen-year-old gets five Benjamins for a simple walk. You do it good and he'll assign you four or five runs a week."

It seemed to Lucien a bad business practice to trust some unknown kid to carry a night's worth of profits. Five hundred bucks was probably a fraction of what the purse held. What was keeping Lucien from taking off with the purse besides the sheer fear of getting caught? Santucci had the reputation of being very smart, but this didn't seem smart unless there was more to the story. Either way, Lucien was greedy for the money because he was tired of living hand to mouth. He had only left St. Agnes two months before and he was coming to learn that making it on your own was hard.

They walked into the club where they were meeting Mr. Santucci, and Lucien's eyes nearly popped out of his head. He had never been in a gentlemen's club before. There were women everywhere—bare tits, G-strings—women shaking their wares for all to see. A large stage with two poles occupied the front of the place. The music played softly as the two women on stage worked the poles. A section of the stage jutted out into the middle of the room with rows of chairs flanking it. In the middle of that was another woman, on her back, her legs spread, but she looked zoned out: probably doped up on something. Far in the back, where he could only assume the customer lap dances were done, were a few more girls, but they were doing an entirely different kind of lap dance. Despite his disgust, he felt himself growing hard.

He heard Jimmy laugh, which pulled his attention.

"You gonna wanna take care of that, boy."

"What do you mean?"

"Take one and do her. It's one of the perks of the job."

"Are you kidding?"

"No man. Pay them and they'll do anything you want." As if to prove his point, Jimmy reached for the first girl who'd made her way over to him. He disappeared with her behind the red velvet curtain.

Lucien should take one; maybe by fucking her he'd forget the softness of Darcy's skin, the silkiness of her hair, the way she made small love noises when he sank into her the countless times they'd made love in those few incredible weeks before she'd ripped out his fucking heart. Maybe he'd forget how he had given her everything he had to give and it wasn't enough. The fact that he still thought of her disgusted him and it was that more than anything that made him walk behind the curtain to find Jimmy with the girl kneeling in front of him, his hands fisted in her hair. Lucien watched them with a detached callousness.

When Jimmy came, he grunted as he continued to push into her mouth, and then he pulled from her, wiped himself on her shoulder, and zipped up. He reached into his pocket and flicked a few twenties from his pile at the girl. Without a word to either of them, he turned and walked away. The girl didn't seem to care as she stuffed the cash into her G-string before she stood up.

She moved her hands up her body and squeezed her own tits before lifting one to her mouth and wrapping her lips around the nipple. Her eyes stayed on Lucien as she started sucking, then she purred, "Want a turn?"

Darcy's face filled his mind, and, wanting to rid himself of her, he took the two steps to the girl. His hand slipped between her legs where he pushed one finger roughly inside her. When he added a second finger to the first, she moaned and bit her lip. He worked her with his fingers as his mouth closed over her other tit, sucking that peak deep as he fought to exorcise the one who haunted him.

He pushed the girl down on her knees, almost insane with the need to be free of his memories.

"Take it out," he demanded, and she didn't hesitate as her fingers nimbly undid his fly. When her hand wrapped around his dick, he growled, "Open your mouth."

She was practically panting as her mouth opened for him. He stifled a moan when her lips closed around him and she pulled him in deep. She worked him, her tongue running up the length of him before she sucked him halfway down her throat. He grabbed her hair as his hips rocked back and forth, but instead of losing himself in the moment, all he could see was Darcy. When he came, the experience left him empty. The girl licked her lips before she stood; despite the fact that the encounter was unsatisfying, he reached for his wallet.

She touched his arm and smiled. "That was a freebie for the new kid."

And then she sauntered off. He watched as she walked away with an emotion he wasn't too eager to examine roiling in his gut. If you lie down with dogs, you get up with fleas. One of Sister Anne's favorite expressions. Trouble was, he was beginning to think that he was the dog. He silently cursed Darcy as he made his way to the owner's office.

Mr. Santucci looked like a cliché of an Italian mob boss. He was big, tall, and thick, and hairy as hell. As soon as Lucien entered, Mr. Santucci looked up from his desk, a stogie clenched in his teeth.

"You the new kid?"

"Yeah."

"You know the deal?"

"Yeah."

"Good. You get pinched, you keep your fucking mouth shut, feel me?"

"Yeah."

"I'll spring you, we're a family, but only if you keep your mouth shut."

"Got it."

"You get a trial run. If that works, I'll expand your route. Stay loyal to me and I'll be loyal to you. We got a deal?" He reached his big, meaty hand across his desk, nodding at his bodyguards as if to indicate Lucien could approach without being shot. Lucien didn't hesitate to step up and shake the older man's hand.

"We got a deal."

Lucien did his runs, got paid, and put a nice chunk of change away, and, though this wasn't where he thought he'd be, he wasn't alone anymore. That bubble burst about a year later when he got nicked by the cops. He did as instructed and kept his mouth shut, but he was soon to learn that Santucci wouldn't be true to his word.

Jimmy came to see him on the day he was being transported to juvie.

"Jimmy, man, what the fuck took you so long?"

"Got bad news. Boss man is going to let you hang."

"What the fuck are you talking about?" Lucien demanded.

"Too much heat, dude. He's got to cut you loose. You're on your own."

"Are you fucking kidding me? What happened to the 'we're a family' shit?"

"Sorry, dude."

And without another word, Jimmy turned and walked away.

Lucien spent only two weeks in juvenile detention, and on the day he was released, he stood on the curb outside the building, planning to check on his money when the banks opened. He had been smart enough to open an account, because had he left it in a coffee can like Jimmy did, he knew it wouldn't still be there. Yet his room at the club had been a perk of the job and, without that job, he was homeless—again.

His mind drifted to Darcy. He had a constant emotional tug-of-war over her—one minute he wanted to forget her and the next he missed her like hell.

He was bitter, yes, but it was Darcy, and all the bitterness in the world couldn't turn his heart from her. He loved that girl and probably always would.

"Hey, you Lucien?"

As he turned, he moved up onto the balls of his feet just in case he needed to get away quickly. He eyed the kid—a couple years older than himself, dressed nicely, good haircut, fancy shoes, but there was no denying he had that hardness that only came from living on the streets. You could polish them up all you wanted, but underneath, he, like Lucien, was still a kid from the wrong zip code.

He gestured to the building behind Lucien before he said, "Did six months a few years back. Not too bad as long as you keep one eye open."

"Shit, if that ain't true."

"I'm Dominic. I've been asked to offer you a job."

Lucien was immediately skeptical—random people didn't just stroll up to you and offer you a job. Not to mention that his timing was impeccable.

"You caught the eye of my boss and he's feeling generous."

"Who's your boss?"

"If he wants you to know that, he'll tell you."

"Fair enough. What's the job?"

"Oldest job there is."

Immediately Lucien thought Dominic was talking about pros-titution and getting paid to fuck and forget. Sign him up. Dominic

*clearly could tell what he was thinking. A grin cracked over his face.
"Not that old. Grave digging."*

*Lucien was sure he didn't hear the guy right, because who the
fuck dug graves anymore? "Say again?"*

*"My reaction too, but there are a few graveyards where the
owner believes in a more personal touch. You would work mostly
at night, you get paid a hundred fifty dollars a week, meals are
included, and there's housing—nothing fancy, but at least it's not
the streets. You interested?"*

"Yeah."

"Cool, let's walk and I'll fill you in."

Chapter Two

Fourteen years earlier . . .

*D*arcy sighed and tightened her arms around Lucien as he brushed his lips across the tender skin under her jaw. He moved slowly, building up the tension so that desire curled in her belly. Her hips tilted to take him deeper and her mouth pressed to his. The kiss grew a bit desperate as Darcy poured all her fears and hopes into it. She wanted it to always be like this between them, but change was coming. Lucien was turning eighteen, and with Sister Anne gone, he was leaving. Reality was a harsh truth and one that left her feeling adrift because she was unsure of what came next for them.

His head lifted and Darcy saw the concern in his eyes, even as lust made them glaze over. He gripped her hips and pulled her close as he moved deeper and faster. The orgasm rippled through her and brought tears to her eyes seconds before Lucien called out her name and emptied himself deep inside of her.

Afterward, he would hold her; and sometimes it seemed to Darcy that he liked the holding as much as the lovemaking. It was like he was seeking the same feeling of connection that she was.

"What's wrong?" His soft voice interrupted her thoughts.

"Nothing."

He leaned up on his elbow. "Come with me."

Her heart leaped. "What do you mean?"

"When I leave, come with me."

"Do you mean it?"

"I love you, Darcy, and I want you in my life. I don't know where we'll live or how we'll get on, but I do know that I don't want to go without you."

She threw her arms around him, and he chuckled as he fell onto his back, his arms tightening around her. "I'll take that as a yes."

Words wouldn't come, so Darcy responded by holding him even more tightly.

"You thought I was going to leave without you, didn't you?" His voice was whisper soft.

She nodded her head.

"Why?"

Her eyes were bright when she looked at him. "I never understood why someone like you would choose to hang out with someone like me."

He rolled so that she was pinned underneath him and he looked almost angry. "Why do you do that? Why do you always think so little of yourself? Never mind, I know it's because of your fucking mother. I shouldn't need to say this, but I will: I never had any intentions of leaving here without you. How could you possibly think I could?"

"I was trying to be realistic. You're moving on. It isn't unreasonable to believe that you'd forget me in time."

"Forget you? How the hell could I ever forget you?"

Darcy was yanked from the dream when her alarm went off, but it took a minute for the memory of it to fade. She climbed from bed and shut the buzzer off. Lucien had forgotten her; just how soon after he'd left had she slipped from his mind? It wasn't a question she needed an answer to.

She splashed some water on her face and reached for her toothbrush, her eyes falling on her Manhattan College mug on the counter. Her life had definitely gone in a direction she had never seen coming.

At sixteen, she'd planned to run away with Lucien. As an adult, she now understood the flaws in their plans; he'd been almost eighteen, so he could have left with no problem, but would she have escaped so easily? Probably not, but the idea of it had been so romantic that she hadn't seen the pitfalls in their plan, only the happily-ever-after they would have had.

But the day they'd planned to leave, fate stepped in. She didn't know the man who came to see her, but he'd confirmed her secret fear that though Lucien wanted to take her with him now, when they were out in the real world he would grow tired of her. She wavered in her intent to go. Her worry wasn't for herself, but for Lucien. The man knew all the right things to say, held the mirror to her face, so to speak, and her sixteen-year-old self wasn't strong enough in her convictions to fight for Lucien. She'd let him go, and what hurt more was how easily Lucien had walked away.

The year after Lucien had left was the hardest of her life. Darcy had hounded Sister Margaret for any news about him, and when she'd learned how much he was struggling, it had enraged her. The man who had promised her he'd look out for Lucien had been lying. She wanted to seek Lucien out and beg him to forgive her, to take her back, but then her life took another turn: one that left her broken.

She'd struggled to get through each day, and then a year after she left St. Agnes she got a summons from Sister Margaret. Seeing St. Agnes again after being away for so long had left her with the same feeling of awe she had felt the first time she had seen it. The old brownstone looked its age and yet dignity and charm exuded from the place. And the grounds were unbelievable considering it was located in the city; looking out the windows you saw green grass and trees. The sight almost didn't seem real. It was as if the building had been there long before the city, and the city built itself around it.

Darcy vividly remembered the day, a year after her mom had taken her back, that had changed her life *again*, even down to how Sister Margaret had looked sitting behind the desk in the small room that acted as her office.

—•—

Twelve years earlier . . .

"Darcy, sit."

Sister Margaret was not one for unnecessary words. Darcy settled into the old vinyl chair.

"You've been offered a scholarship to Manhattan College."

Darcy had no reaction to the statement—she wasn't quite sure she'd heard the words correctly.

"Did you hear me? You are getting an opportunity to go to college."

"How?"

Sister Margaret waved off her question. "It's not important."
Sincerity drifted into her expression when she added, "You've had

a tough time of it, but you have your whole life ahead of you. This is a chance for you to take control."

"But I can't afford to go to school."

"Tuition and housing are all covered in the scholarship. Look, I dedicated my life to the church, so I called in a few favors and made this happen. The least you can do is accept it."

"But why are you helping me?"

"You have had more than your share of pain, and sometimes the helping hand of another can make all the difference. I know this isn't where you hoped to be, but maybe you'll find you like the direction this takes you."

Darcy couldn't help but think there was more to it. Sister Margaret was not the warm and thoughtful type and yet here she was offering her a chance.

"Do you want to stay under the control of your mother or do you want to get away from your mom and be the master of your own destiny?"

Those were the magic words: away from your mom. Darcy couldn't help but feel that this offer was penance of some kind for Sister Margaret, but penance for what, Darcy didn't know. She couldn't lie—she wanted to take it. Wanted to run from her past and never look back.

"How will I ever repay you?"

Sister Margaret leaned back in her chair. "Don't squander the opportunity. Make something of yourself and we'll call it even."

<hr />

Darcy rinsed her mouth and put her toothbrush back. The day she'd signed the lease on her little apartment in Times Square was a wonderful affirmation that she was making it on her own. Her degree in business administration had landed her a job managing

Sookie's, a family-owned catering company, and that's where she'd found her niche. She loved the work and she was good at it.

She moved into her living room, taking a moment to stare at the print of Gustav Klimt's *Three Ages of Woman*. The painting had moved her the first time she'd seen it in Sister Anne's room, but the meaning behind it had grown exponentially for her after she'd left St. Agnes because it was a reminder of her past and how no one stayed the same. Every time she looked at it she appreciated just how far she had come and what she had lost along the way.

Even without the print, Lucien was never far from her thoughts. She had looked into the man who had come to see her, even recruited Sister Margaret's help, but they were never able to figure out who he was. He definitely had someone on the inside of St. Agnes who had gotten him in under the radar so that there was no record of him ever being there.

When Darcy had found herself in need of a job after leaving Sookie's, she had given specific instructions to her headhunter that if a job became available in any of Lucien Black's organizations, that she wanted to know of it. It had been fanciful and, she realized after the reality of their disastrous reunion, foolish, but she had hoped that he would recognize her name and they would take up where they left off. He hadn't recognized her name, though; he hadn't remembered her at all. And that reality was unimaginably painful.

<hr />

Lucien returned his sax to its case. The jam session had helped keep his mind occupied, but now thoughts of *her* crowded out everything else. He thought about getting drunk, but that would only be effective if he stayed drunk, and becoming an alcoholic was not on his bucket list. When he heard his name, he was relieved to have the distraction. He turned to see Kyle walking toward him.

He and Kyle shared a love of music and, after Ember had introduced them, they often found themselves at the same clubs, jamming. Lucien had no delusions about his skill and played only as an escape, but Kyle and his band were a different story. They had the kind of stage presence that sucked an audience in. It was a crime that they were only playing the small venues that they were.

"That was amazing," Kyle said in way of greeting.

"Thanks. Have you played?"

"I'm up later. You want to get a drink?"

"Yeah," Lucien replied.

Halfway to the bar, Kyle stopped abruptly, which made Lucien look in the direction that he was staring.

"Kyle?"

"What the hell is he doing here?"

"Who is that?" Lucien asked.

"Todd Samuels. An acquaintance of Ember's."

"Ah, the gambler. There's a back room here, poker mostly."

Kyle responded by shaking his head in disgust before he continued on to the bar. "Two beers," he called to the bartender.

"So how's the music? Getting any new gigs?" Lucien asked.

"Yeah, we have a few more, but we still aren't at the stage where I can give up my bartending job and focus completely on the music. We're working on it, though."

Lucien studied the other man for a minute. He knew how hard it was to get a break; even talented musicians like Kyle struggled for that one gig that could change everything. Someone once gave him a nudge in the right direction, and it was time for him to pay that forward. "I have some friends in the industry. I could give them a call."

"Are you serious?"

"Absolutely."

"Man, that would be awesome. Anytime and anywhere. We'll drop everything for the chance." Kyle's excitement was almost palpable.

"Let me see what I can do."

A ruckus broke out in the back of the place. Lucien turned to see Todd being physically removed from the club.

Kyle had noticed Todd too. "What the hell was that all about?"

"My guess—he was caught cheating. He must be pretty desperate to take the risk of cheating these card sharks," Lucien added almost absently.

Kyle replied to that with a snort. "He made his bed."

Chapter Three

The heat of the summer sun never seemed to warm this place. Nature continually attempted to reclaim the stone paths that guided visitors through the maze of stone memorials. Lucien walked in long, unhurried strides through the overgrown tangles. The small stone angel was centered in a colorful garden—each season the plants reflected the time of year. He didn't know who planted the garden and kept it, probably someone from St. Agnes, but he knew that Sister Anne would really have appreciated it.

He knelt down in front of her grave and rested his hand on the base of the angel where only four words were carved into the stone, "Gone, but not forgotten." She hadn't wanted a tombstone at all. She'd said the money should be used for the children. He'd wanted to honor her request, but he had to have something that he could visit, a place where he felt her.

He absentmindedly pulled the weeds that were poking through the bright-colored flowers as he remembered the day Sister Anne had died and how Darcy had known exactly what he'd needed. She hadn't cried, nor had she offered condolences; she'd just sat quietly at his side holding his hand in hers. That was the day he fell irrevocably in love with her. To think that only a few weeks later she would take his heart and squash it under her foot.

Coming here was a double-edged sword, because as much as he craved the connection to Sister Anne, it was here more than anywhere that his past came back to haunt him.

———•◦•———

Fourteen years earlier . . .

He checked his watch for the sixth time while he continued to pace, but he was excited because he and Darcy were leaving here together. He didn't really care where they ended up as long as she was with him.

He opened his palm to the little silver cross that Sister Anne had left for him, a necklace she was never without. He was going to give it to Darcy. He wanted her to know how he felt about her and this was the only thing of value he had.

A half hour later, his excitement had started to fade. Darcy was never late. Was she having second thoughts? He looked in the direction of the orphanage, wondering if they had gotten their signals crossed. He was about to walk up the hill to find her when someone came up behind him and wrapped their arms around him. He grinned.

"I thought you were having second thoughts." He turned into Darcy to kiss her only to realize it wasn't Darcy, but Heidi—the creepy girl who followed after his friend Trace like a lost puppy. He didn't understand why she continued to come around. She had been moved to different housing after she had given birth. Nor did he understand why the nuns were seemingly okay with her hanging around all the time. Before he could push her away, she kissed him. It took him a minute to react, but when he finally did, he pushed her hard enough to knock her to the ground.

"What the fuck are you doing?"

Her pale eyes always freaked him out. She tilted her head and smiled like a snake. "I just wanted a taste."

He turned from her without a second thought and went in search of Darcy, but when he reached her room, she wasn't there. Her roommates were sitting on the floor playing cards.

"Where's Darcy?"

The smallest of the girls looked up at him through her smudged glasses. "She left."

"What? Where?"

He noticed that she couldn't keep eye contact when she said, "She said she was leaving with her mom. Oh, she left you something." She stood and grabbed a note off the dresser and handed it to him.

His feet moved him out of the room as he looked blindly down at the note. It took him a while to work up the nerve to read it.

Lucien,
I can't go with you. I'm sorry. You'll thank me one day for not tying you down, maybe you already do.
Be happy. I wish only good things for you.
Darcy

His vision blurred from the tears that filled his eyes at how callously she'd discarded all the plans they had made. He crumpled up the note before pushing it into his pocket, and then he walked away and never looked back.

Darcy sat across from her headhunter, Michelle, trying desperately to keep from biting her nails. After the pain had subsided from the epic failure that was their reunion, she realized that it wasn't possible for Lucien not to remember her. If for no other reason than that she was there when Sister Anne died and that woman had meant everything to him.

If he wanted to pretend he didn't know her, she was fine with that. Really, she couldn't blame him, but she needed the job and having a chance to be near him again was just too tempting. She was surprised when Michelle called her and said that Lucien had requested rescheduling the interview. Maybe part of him did want to see her. It was why she was sitting here with her head-hunter, who was even now making excuses to the man himself for Darcy's ridiculous behavior.

Michelle smiled at her and gave her the thumbs-up.

"Yes, even without one? That's wonderful. I'll pass that along. Yes, eight o'clock Monday morning. Fabulous. Thank you."

She hung up on a sigh. "He didn't want an interview; he hired you. You start on Monday."

Excitement struck Darcy first, but then she sobered. If Lucien had loved her the way she believed he had, after what she'd done, he had to hate her. Maybe this was her penance. Lord knew she deserved it. Maybe she could make amends and right the wrong she had done him. Losing him as a lover had been hard, but losing him as a friend had been devastating.

———◆———

On her first day of work, Darcy took an extra hour getting ready. Silly, probably, but the last time she'd seen Lucien, aside from her disastrous display from the other day, she'd been sixteen and a bit awkward in her own skin. It was vanity, yes, but she wanted him to see her looking her best.

She showered, moisturized, plucked, tweezed, applied enough makeup to enhance, but not distract, and pulled her black hair up into a twist. She then stood for a half an hour in just her bra and panties, looking in her closet.

She settled on her formfitting but conservative black wrap dress. She slipped on her pumps before grabbing her purse and bag. The day had gotten hot by the time she stepped out of her apartment building and started walking toward the corner.

He had looked incredible. The few minutes she'd seen him, it was clear that he was even more beautiful than he had been as a kid, but there was a hardness about his features that he hadn't had at seventeen: the slant of his brow, the line between his eyes, the down tilt of his mouth, and the coldness in those eyes that were still as beautiful. She remembered when those eyes had looked at her with passion, desire, even love. It was her own fault that they no longer did. Even with the passing of time, her regret was just as great now as it had been then.

She hailed a cab because it was just too hot and she didn't want to deal with the subway. After the cab dropped her off, she stood at the doors of the bar for a minute, catching her breath. Allegro looked sort of sad in the daylight. It wasn't a remarkable building: simple brick with a portico for cabs to pull up out of the elements, and glass doors with the name etched into them. Inside was just as bleak during the day, looking almost like a fighter who binds up his wounds so he can fight another day. Melancholy . . . she was feeling entirely too melancholy.

She didn't want this meeting to go as calamitously as the last. Whatever he thought of her, he'd hired her, so maybe he wasn't holding a grudge. Maybe he really had put what was between them in the past and it was only she who was still harboring feelings about what they shared.

She pulled her shoulders back and lifted her chin, but butterflies were going berserk in her belly. The hall to the office was dark, so she searched for the switch and turned on the lights. By the time she was halfway down the hallway, she knew that he wasn't in yet. She was grateful for that; she could get herself settled and then be calmer when he did arrive to show her the ropes.

Twenty minutes later, she heard footsteps down the hall, and her stomach squeezed with nerves as she stood to greet Lucien. But it wasn't him. Instead it was the woman from the other day, Tara.

"Hi. You're Darcy, right?"

"Yes."

"Sorry, I must have been in the back when you arrived. I'm Tara. Lucien asked me to give you the quick rundown. Your desk is that one." She pointed to the receptionist's desk that sat in a small alcove. "There are files on the desk that will bring you up to speed. If you have any questions, I'll be setting up in the bar area."

Darcy was confused as to why Lucien wasn't here doing the introduction himself. He was the boss.

"Is Lucien coming in later, then?"

Tara had already started down the hall, and she answered from over her shoulder.

"No, he took the day off."

That shouldn't have hurt, but it did. Darcy walked to her desk and settled in before pulling open a file. It was Lucien's calendar. The other file was a supply list for the office and contact numbers for the printer and computer guys. Darcy immediately buried herself in work. Three hours later, she had the office completely organized, files alphabetized, supplies that were running low reordered, and she'd even cleaned the place.

At five she shut down her computer, but instead of leaving, she decided on a drink. She settled at the bar and Tara slid a napkin in front of her.

"How was the first day?"

"Good. I got a lot done."

"What can I get you?"

"Glass of pinot grigio, please."

Darcy watched as Tara poured the wine before placing the glass in front of her.

"On the house. Welcome to the team, Darcy."

The burning behind her eyes surprised her and she said, "Thank you, Tara."

———◆———

Later that night, Darcy returned home, dropped her keys on her table, kicked off her shoes, and went in search of another glass of wine. All in all, it could have been a worse first day. The job was interesting, even more so because she got an insight into what Lucien had accomplished since she'd last seen him.

She poured the ruby-red wine into a glass and took a long sip as she pondered Lucien's absence. Was it intentional? Probably, but then she had been expecting some kind of retaliation from him. She had it coming. She had the sense that he was testing her, but she was made of stronger stuff than she used to be. She would stick with it if for no other reason than to remind him that she could. She had before, had been there to offer him the comfort he had needed so desperately.

———◆———

Fourteen years earlier . . .

He had walked the length of the garden countless times with his head down and his shoulders slumped, and she knew he was hurting. A part of him was gone. It wasn't even a conscious thought that made her go to him. When she reached him, she took his hand into hers. His head lifted to show his teal eyes filled with tears.

She couldn't take the pain away, but she could show him that he wasn't alone, that he was still loved. He didn't argue when she led him back inside and up the stairs to the one place they were sure to have privacy. He stood silently at the door of the attic while she spread the blankets on the floor, watched her as she pulled her hair down. His eyes fixed on hers when she bridged the distance between them and pressed her mouth to his. They'd kissed countless times, but this kiss was different. He didn't move at first, frozen as if he wasn't sure she was real, and then his arms wrapped around her and pulled her so close. She framed his face and kissed him again, her tongue touching the corner of his mouth before running slowly along the seam of his lips. His hand cradled the back of her head and his mouth opened so his tongue could touch hers. Desire shot down to her toes. His skin was so warm as her hands moved over the muscles of his back, trailing down the deep groove of his spine and following the curve of his ass.

She took a step back from him and reached for her shirt; his eyes were hungry as he watched her lift it up over her head. His gaze moved over her possessively before his eyes returned to hers and, knowing what she was offering, he reached for the back of his shirt and pulled it forward over his head. He stepped to her, his fingers running down along her arms, across her collarbone, down between her breasts. His fingers flipped the clasp on her bra and his hands moved the silk, exposing her to his hot gaze. He touched her, his fingers brushing over her taut nipple before following the curve of her breast. He palmed her breasts and gently squeezed before he lowered his head and touched his tongue to her nipple. Moisture wet her panties as a throbbing started between her legs, and then he pulled her breast into his mouth and a sound of pure pleasure rumbled low in her throat and she moved her hands to his head to hold him there. He teased and sucked on her, taking turns with each breast, before he kissed down her belly until he was kneeling in front of her. He looked up as if he was asking for permission before he unbuttoned her jeans and moved them down her legs. A light touch on her hips made goose bumps rise on her skin as her panties followed her jeans. As soon as she stepped out of them, he looked up at her with fire in his eyes.

"Spread your legs for me."

Nerves, lust, and love made her feel edgy, so she braced herself on his bare shoulders and did as he asked.

He was gentle; his finger moved through the curls between her legs, opening her and finding her aching pulse. He ran his finger over her, back and forth, his eyes hungry again, and then he leaned into her and touched her with his tongue. Her knees gave out, but his arms were strong as he gently lowered her to the floor in front of him, spreading her legs wide, and touched her again. He watched her face as he moved his finger over the nub, her hips moving in time to his stroking. When he lowered his head, she held her breath, and then his mouth replaced his fingers. He licked her, teasing before moving through her folds to her center. She wasn't prepared for his tongue to push into her and she cried out while her hips lifted and her thighs tightened to hold him there.

She thought she was going to splinter apart from all the emotions that were coursing through her. And then he stopped and stood, and she was fascinated by the large bulge between his legs. Fascination turned into a touch of fear when he pulled his jeans off and she saw him thick and hard. He settled between her legs, his mouth covering hers as he kissed her almost reverently. He moved to her ear, his tongue tracing the curve of her lobe, dipping in and causing chills, before moving lower and taking her breast into his mouth again. She felt him, right where his tongue had been; he moved, rubbing himself against her until she almost begged. His head lifted and his eyes stayed on hers as he slowly pushed into her. She tensed at the intrusion, her body almost rejecting him, and then she felt a sharp pain, but he continued to move until he was fully inside her. Her legs were shaking, her heart pounding, but he held himself very still so she could adjust to him. And then his mouth found her breast and suddenly she wanted to feel him move, wanted him to push harder and deeper. She lifted her hips, and that was all he needed as he slowly moved in and out with his hips. Feeling him between her legs, moving with such care, made her ache again until she was nearly mindless with the need to reach whatever it was they were working toward. Her arms wrapped around his neck, her mouth sought his, and she kissed him hungrily. He moved faster, reached deeper, and for a moment she thought she was on some precipice as her stomach tightened and her entire body seemed to freeze—and then she shattered, the force of the orgasm ripping a scream from her throat.

He continued to move, prolonging the exquisite sensation, and then he tensed as his body spasmed his own release. He dropped down, cradled in her body, and pressed a kiss on her shoulder.

They fell asleep just like that.

<hr />

Darcy sat at her desk at work the next morning, the memory from last night still haunting her. She actually didn't mind the memory; there was comfort in remembering what had been between them, but she could do without the constant state of arousal she found herself in. Maybe it hadn't been such a good idea reconnecting with Lucien, because being turned on by a ghost was both twisted and pathetic. Of course, she jumped into this with both feet, so unless she wanted to be a loser on top of being pathetic and bail after only one day, she was going to need to suck it up.

She heard him before she saw him, and her body ached as if on command. He was walking down the hallway, talking on his phone. Sadly, it wasn't just her body that longed for him as her heart skipped a beat. He looked up and those eyes landed on her and she felt her heart drop into her stomach.

"Let me call you back."

He stopped just in front of her desk.

"Darcy."

"Mr. Black." She just couldn't bring herself to say his name. Did she have the right to be so informal with him anymore? He didn't correct her. She had often thought about what he would say to her if they were to ever meet again. Clearly, their first meeting he'd chosen to stay silent about their shared history, but she wondered if he would continue to do so. Her body leaned forward a bit on its own as she waited in anticipation. Maybe he'd welcome her and mean it, or say, why the fuck did you break my heart, you bitch? But she didn't get any of that; instead he looked through her and then he disappeared into his office.

His anger she could handle, but she hadn't prepared herself for indifference. She reminded herself that she had made her bed, and tried to put the look on his face out of her mind as she busied herself with work.

———◆———

Lucien paced in his office—concentrating was impossible with Darcy MacBride sitting outside his door. She'd blossomed, surpassing the beauty of her youth. He had half a mind to seduce her so he could rid himself of her ghost, because—damn, if she wasn't always in the back of his mind. She shouldn't be—it was so long ago—but she lingered like the scent of a favorite perfume.

How could he be just as captivated by her as he had been when they were teenagers? She had lured him in once, but she wouldn't be doing it again. He had learned that lesson the hard way. He needed to make sure the boundaries were firmly established. He probably shouldn't have hired her, but the truth was that he wanted her close almost as much as he wanted to push her away—probably more so.

"Darcy, a minute."

She entered the room and immediately the air felt like it was being sucked from it. His temper stirred.

"Working hours are eight thirty to five. I do not tolerate tardiness, Ms. MacBride." He let that comment linger in the air, a subtle dig to her that he hadn't forgotten that she was late fourteen years ago.

"If you have questions, ask them in a clear and concise manner. I have no tolerance for babbling. It is your responsibility to run this office. I won't be pleased if I need a binder and am unable to locate one. There is alcohol on the premises, but if you indulge in it during working hours you'll be terminated immediately. Personal calls are made on your own time, not during working hours. My calendar is to be maintained perfectly on all of my devices, and I will require both your home and cell numbers because my job is not just a nine-to-five and I may need to get in touch with you."

He stopped pacing and turned to her. "Any questions?"

"No."

"You're dismissed."

She left as meekly as she'd entered, without a single comment. The Darcy he knew, the one he at times still ached for, would have flayed a layer of skin from him. Maybe she wasn't the same girl she had been, which would make his life much less complicated.

———◆———

Darcy returned to her desk as her blood boiled. She gave herself a few minutes to envision the voodoo doll she was going to make of Lucien. Picturing stabbing him repeatedly put a smile on her face. Maybe riches had gone to his head. If so, it would make her life much less complicated.

That night after work, Darcy sat at a table in Allegro nursing a glass of wine and listening to a band with a very mellow sound. Lucien was mingling and chatting nearby. The room was dark enough that he wouldn't know she was staring, so she looked, really looked, at the man the boy she had loved had grown into. He was taller, but not much, since he had already been over six feet at sixteen. Definitely more muscles, particularly in the chest and arms. She remembered his body at seventeen; she couldn't get enough of that body. She'd tasted every inch of him, knew every muscle, every hard line. They had only had five weeks of loving before it all fell apart, but they didn't waste that time. They had sex two, sometimes three, times a day, thanks to the intensity of young love and a lack of the cynicism that comes when you get older and learn the hard way that not everything is possible.

Through the years, she often thought about how things would have been had she met him under that tree.

Would he be where he was now if she had left with him? Would he have lacked the drive to have accomplished all the incredible things that he had if he had had someone who loved him at his side? Would he have been content with a simpler life? And would it have mattered? In her heart she always believed that had they stayed together, regardless of where they ended up, they would have been happy.

But reality had shattered their fairy tale: the prince had staggered off into the sunset and the princess had stayed in her tower—no happily-ever-after for either of them.

———◆———

Every morning for a week, Darcy arrived at work with the hopes that that day would be the day the old Lucien would appear and would say more to her than her name: his form of greeting in the morning. And every day she was disappointed. It hurt that he wasn't even curious enough about her to ask how she'd been for the past fourteen years. She was tempted to walk into his office and bridge the gap herself, but to do that she would need to tell him everything that had happened after he left. She'd have to share her painful secret.

To relive that pain, when he seemed perfectly content with the distance between them, was not something she was prepared to do. Despite the harshness of her current reality, it didn't keep her from having dreams where Lucien pined for her as she had for him.

After work she decided to treat herself to dinner at a restaurant she'd heard Tara talking about. It was a small Italian place and the line to get in was ridiculous, but because she was eating alone, they found a spot for her in a dark corner. She was feasting on the best chicken marsala she had ever tasted when she heard a bit of a commotion coming from the entrance and looked up to see Lucien. He wasn't alone. Did she know he was coming here tonight? She mentally went through his calendar and no, there was nothing scheduled for this evening.

The woman he was with was—of course—gorgeous and knew it too. Her body had curves in all the right places and her curly brown hair hung halfway down her back. Lucien had changed into a black suit with a mist-green shirt and tie. She understood why people looked—the pair was stunning: the kind of elegant beauty rarely seen in real life.

She turned her eyes down. Watching him was too painful—a nasty reality check, but one she really needed. When she looked at Lucien she saw the boy he had been—*that* boy she had a chance with—but he wasn't that boy anymore. He was so far out of her league it was almost comical that she could still harbor hopes.

Fifteen years earlier . . .

"I've been looking all over for you. What are you doing down here?"

Darcy turned to see Lucien walking down the hill in that way of his. He was only sixteen and yet he moved with such confidence.

"Just thinking."

"Under your tree, I see," he said with a smile.

"Yeah, I like this tree. I feel almost at peace here."

He turned serious before he reached for her hand. "I heard about the other girls teasing you. You aren't upset about that, are you? They're just jealous."

"I know, because for some reason you hang with me and not them."

"That's not what I was talking about. They're jealous because you're funny and smart." He moved closer to her and reached for her other hand. "They're jealous because when you enter a room, I can't keep my eyes off of you."

"Afraid I'll trip and embarrass myself?"

He cradled her cheek in his palm, his thumb brushing over her cheekbone. "Afraid I'll embarrass myself with trying to get to you before anyone else does. They're jealous, Darcy, because you are beautiful."

"Have you had your eye exam lately? I think there might be a problem."

"Shut up. I'm going to kiss you now."

"I still won't be any good."

He flashed her a grin. "We'll learn together."

Before she could speak another word, his lips sealed over hers. He didn't take the kiss deep—he just brushed his lips lightly over hers—but it was the most amazing kiss ever.

"That wasn't so bad, was it?" he asked when he stepped away from her.

Her eyes were not yet open because she was still savoring the tingling her lips were doing. "No, not bad at all."

"Darcy?"

She opened her eyes to see Lucien looking very serious. "You're mine," he said.

"I know."

"Miss, would you like another glass of wine?"

Darcy looked up at the waiter, a little embarrassed to have been caught daydreaming. "No, thank you. I'll take the check, please."

She glanced over at Lucien's table. He was engaged in quiet conversation with his date, but it was the look of him all grown-up and important . . . Nope, he definitely wasn't the boy he used to be. She paid her bill, but as she left the restaurant, she was certain she felt Lucien's stare follow her out.

"A group of us are going to an improv club tonight. Do you want to come?" asked Tara. Darcy was surprised to see her because this was Tara's first day off in the two weeks since Darcy had started.

Something feeling remarkably like gratitude moved through Darcy at being included. "Yeah, that sounds great."

"We'll grab a bite before, say around six thirty?"

"I'll be ready."

Peacock was a little hole in the wall where the drinks were watered down, but the music was incredible. Darcy sat at a table with Tara, and Chloe and Tommy who waited tables at Allegro. They'd had dinner at a vegan diner, sitting in a booth eating veggie burgers and drinking "milk" shakes while gossiping about everything; nothing was off-limits. Now they were more mellow, tuned in to the band.

Darcy listened to the music while she looked around the place. It was during her sweep that she saw the tall man in the corner, his back to her. Her heart immediately moved into her throat and her body started to pulse with excitement.

Lucien wasn't dressed in his normal work clothes, but in faded jeans and a tee; the sight of him made her mouth water. His hair was pulled back into a ponytail and the stage lights were pulling out the red highlights. She hadn't yet seen his arms because he was always wearing long-sleeved shirts to work, but now she could see his well-defined triceps and biceps bulging underneath the black tee that was stretched taut across his muscled back. Her eyes moved lower to his denim-covered ass and thighs, and she had to catch herself from whistling in appreciation.

And then he moved enough for her to see that he was talking with a woman, a beautiful woman who was eying him like a piece of candy. Darcy should have turned her eyes from them, but she couldn't. It was like a train wreck—brutal and disarming—but she was morbidly curious.

Their heads were close, and though she had no idea what they were talking about, she saw a lot of smiling and touching.

"He's up next," Tara said, making Darcy turn pink from the embarrassment of getting caught staring like a drooling moron at her boss. And then she realized what Tara said.

"Who's next?"

"Lucien."

Darcy had no idea what Tara was talking about, but it wasn't necessary to ask her to clarify because in the next minute, Lucien was climbing onto the stage with a saxophone to join a band that was just setting up. The woman he had been talking to settled behind the piano.

And then the music started and Darcy sat transfixed. They were good, fantastic even, but that was not why she couldn't pull her eyes from the stage. Her eyes were completely on Lucien as she discovered yet another part of him. He was so comfortable and clearly doing something he really enjoyed because, even from her distance, she saw the sheer contentment on his face.

"They're fantastic, aren't they? People can't get enough of them," Tara said from her side, which made Darcy look from the stage toward the audience, and sure enough, they were captivated. She couldn't blame them because she was just as guilty.

In that moment the magnitude of what she had walked away from came crashing down on her. She tried to convince herself that they might not have worked out and so she hadn't missed out on as much as she feared, but she knew the words didn't ring true even as she thought them. Had she met him that day, they would have had fourteen years of memories, of smiles, of touches, and of love. Instead she got to sit and watch the life he had made for himself without her.

Darcy stood.

"Where are you going?" Tara asked.

"I need a drink."

Darcy wasn't a big drinker, limiting herself to a glass or two of wine, but she wanted numbness. She took a stool at the bar and flagged down the bartender.

"Patrón, straight up."

It burned all the way down her throat. She was pretty sure it was even now disintegrating her stomach lining and yet it didn't stop her from ordering another one. After two, she felt a lightness she hadn't felt in a long time. After three, she was smiling for no particular reason, and after four, she was downright happy.

She didn't realize the band had stopped playing and that music was being pumped in over the speakers until she recognized "Rhythm Of Love" by the Plain White T's. A group of people formed a sort of dance floor, so Darcy stood—almost losing her balance and grabbing the stool until she was steady—then walked over to join them.

The words of the song poured over her; she'd never realized how accurate the lyrics were to her own life. She had had more than a night of loving, she had had weeks, and for that time she was his and he was hers alone. And like the song, even after he was gone she remembered him; boy, did she remember him.

She felt him before she saw him, walking toward her in that sexy way of his. She couldn't read his expression and at that moment she didn't really care to. He pulled her into his arms without saying a word. And being in his arms again almost made her sigh.

Her hands moved over his back, relearning his body, the muscles and contours now unfamiliar. Her eyes closed and she rested her cheek against his heart and listened to the strong, even beat of it. His fingers trailed down her neck, lingering at her nape before he threaded them through her hair, and the memory of him doing that so many years ago made her tilt her head into his hand.

The song came to an end, and he separated them, waiting a minute to make sure she was steady, before he turned without a word and walked away. She was tempted to follow him, until he stopped at the side of the woman he had been talking to earlier. She looked pissed that he had danced with Darcy, but then Lucien leaned into her and pressed his mouth to hers. She obviously wasn't so pissed that she couldn't immediately drape her arms around his neck to pull him closer.

The alcohol had blessedly numbed her, so his cruelty was going to take a while to sink in. She just stood there watching and knowing that this was payback. She wanted to hate him for being so deliberate and, maybe when she wasn't numb from the alcohol, she would.

Somehow she watched as he disengaged from the succubus who was trying to swallow him whole, and his eyes turned to Darcy. For a moment it was like they were the only two in the room. She nodded her head at him, acknowledging that his slight had hit its desired target. She turned and headed to the table and grabbed her purse. She offered her good-byes and then left the club.

Chapter Four

The cab pulled up in front of Trace's cooking school, Everything, which pulled Ember from her thoughts on Lena, her onetime best friend. They hadn't spoken in over a year, but that didn't keep Ember from thinking about her sometimes. She climbed from the cab and took a minute to study the building. Had someone told her that the man she first saw in all of his sexy beauty two years ago would now be teaching people how to make homemade pasta, she would have thought they were on drugs, but Trace loved it.

He had come a long way from the tormented, lost soul trying to deal with the life he'd been dealt. There were times when she saw that lost look buried in his expression, but it was occurring less and less and that must be looked upon as progress.

Ember loved sneaking in and getting a seat in the back, so she could watch Trace, unnoticed, but somehow he always knew she was there.

As soon as she stepped inside, she heard the deep voice that still had the power to make butterflies take off in her stomach. When she entered the main section of the school, she saw him immediately. Standing at six feet four, he towered over everyone else in the room. He was walking around the various kitchens as his students worked on the day's lesson. Dressed in his favorite outfit of faded jeans, tee, and boots, he had added one of those chef's jackets in black. He'd been wearing his hair shorter lately, and the inky black strands were spiky around his wonderful face.

It didn't pass Ember's notice that most of his students were young women who spent a good portion of the class looking at him adoringly. But she couldn't blame them for their interest. Had she not been married to him, she'd be here for every class he taught too. That was not to say that she didn't have the occasional bout of jealousy since she was, after all, only human. And then, like right now, those steel-blue eyes looked right at her and she realized how silly she was being.

Ember watched as a smile spread over his face before he excused himself and started over to her; but the closer he got the less he was smiling, until he was downright frowning as he stood before her.

"What's wrong? You don't look so good."

"That is just what every wife wants to hear from her husband. Thank you for that."

She didn't miss the twitching of his lips. "Seriously, Em, what's wrong?"

The truth was, she was exhausted. She had given up her hours waitressing at Clover, but she'd been putting in long hours on writing her book and working as a correspondent at Trace's uncle, Charles Michaels's, campaign headquarters twenty hours a week. She was coming to realize that five hours of sleep a night wasn't enough. "I'm tired."

"I'm guessing you're on your way home. If you wait for a few minutes, I can take you because this class is almost over."

"I'd like that, but aren't you worried about disappointing your students? Several of whom are not looking too thrilled that you're over here talking to me. I guess it sort of bursts the illusion when you chat with your wife."

"What illusion?"

"That you're available and interested."

In a blur of movement he wrapped her in his arms and lifted her off her feet seconds before his mouth claimed hers. She pulled her hands through his hair and gave back as good as she was getting. She could feel the grin on his lips as his mouth lingered just above hers.

"Not interested and not available."

She was still reeling from that kiss, so the best she was able to offer was, "Yeah, I get that."

"Good. Give me ten and I'll see you home."

"Okay."

He dropped her to her feet before he kissed her hard one last time and then he turned and started back over to his students.

"Let's wrap this up."

"It stops now, Dane, or we cut you off completely."

Dane Carmichael shifted in his seat as he glared at his persecutors. His father, a senator; his uncle, the district attorney for New York; and his grandfather, the circuit court judge.

"You get high and you lose control."

"What the hell does that mean?" Dane demanded.

Irritation met his gaze as his dad continued, "You've had three women this year alone claim you raped them."

The women in question, except for one, never reported him to the cops. They only shared their "stories" with his family. Why his dad and grandfather refused to acknowledge the shakedown always baffled and annoyed Dane. Rape, like hell. He liked it rough and they wanted it the same way, flaunting their assets and teasing him. Besides, when he was balls to the wall inside them, it was too late to say no. Funny that he needed to explain his behavior to his father, affectionately termed the playboy senator—handsome, charming, and a total hound dog. "It's not rape," Dane said to his relatives. He pointed at his dad. "He is no different than me."

"His dates don't scream rape." The condemnation in the judge's voice made Dane grind his teeth.

"Funny coming from the man who has always told me that women are only good for one thing."

The judge leaned up as his hard eyes speared Dane from across the expanse of his walnut desk. "Willing women. There's a difference."

"And I'm supposed to know the difference when you claim my own mother was a whore."

The judge didn't miss a beat. "She was a whore. Pimped herself out and got pregnant so that she had a legal claim to the Carmichael name and fortune." Dane turned from his grandfather to see his dad, whose attention was on the floor, his jaw clenched—but whether that was for his dad's father or wife, Dane didn't know. What enraged Dane was that his father had never defended her, not once.

"You're going to let him defile my mother's name?"

His father remained silent, his face completely unreadable.

"Am I supposed to follow in his footsteps"—Dane gestured to his uncle—"and not date at all?"

"Horace works hard and maintains the good name of this family. He may lack social skills, but he doesn't bring shame."

Dane's eyes met his uncle's to see something close to hate sweep his face. He moved from his spot near the fireplace to loom over Dane. His uncle cut an imposing figure, but it was the violence behind his eyes that always stirred fear in Dane. "Your latest stunt came back on me. You want to screw up your life, that's your business, but I've worked too hard to get where I am to have it taken away because of a little worthless shit like you. These two are more forgiving than I. You fuck with me again, boy, and they won't find you, ever."

Dane stifled his gulp—his uncle meant every word. The encounter they were referring to was not something he liked to think about. Ember Walsh, a year ago. He didn't know how it had gotten so out of control. His friend Todd had promised him a good time. Dane had spent the evening just thinking about her wrapped around him, and when he was denied, yeah, he was pissed, but he'd been so high he didn't really even remember the night he attacked her. He didn't expect to get his face rearranged by her Neanderthal boyfriend, or their gangster friend to get all up into his family's business. Replaying the scene sober, it wasn't his proudest moment. His head started to pound.

"Enough, Horace. No point in having the boy shit his pants. Lydia has enough work to do around here." His grandfather stood and moved from behind his desk.

"Boys will be boys, but be more discreet."

And then he was dismissed and the three of them filed out of the room. Did they not see how contradictory they were? One minute he's a complete degenerate and the next it's "boys will be boys." It was no wonder that he was so fucked up—raised by that group of narcissistic sociopaths. It took a few minutes for his legs to steady before he moved across the room to the bar and poured himself a stiff drink. The alcohol calmed his wildly beating heart, but he needed to get high and then laid. He walked with determined strides from the study to do just that.

⬥

Trace moved quietly through the apartment, stopping when he reached their bedroom. Ember lay curled up into a ball, sleeping. She was working too hard—juggling writing her second book, which kept her up late most nights, and working for *In Step*, the online periodical she wrote a column for. The long hours were definitely taking a toll on her. Telling her to slow down was pointless since she acted much like a dog with a bone when she wanted something. Obstacles be damned. She had proven her tenacity with him, fighting for him, for them, even when he was doing everything he could to push her away.

He walked over to her and settled on the edge of the bed and ran his fingers lightly up and down her bare arm.

"Ember, sweetheart."

She turned and those guileless brown eyes opened; when she saw him, a smile spread over her face. It was like a sucker punch every time and he fucking craved it.

"Trace, hi."

"How are you feeling?"

"Sleepy."

"I have one more class tonight, but I can have Carlos take it if you want me to stay home."

"No, you should go."

"You sure?"

"Yeah."

She looked so soft and sweet that he was seriously tempted to ditch class, strip her out of those pajamas, wrap her legs around his waist, and sink himself deep into her. Yeah, the more he thought about it, the better and better it sounded, but when he really looked at her, she looked more than tired.

Knowing him as well as she did, she reached for his hand to entwine his fingers with her own. "Really, I just need sleep. Don't worry about me. Maybe later when you get home again you'll tell me, or better yet show me, whatever it was you were just thinking about."

A grin cracked over his face as he brushed his finger along her jaw. It was stupid, but the thought of something happening to her, of losing her, was his greatest fear. "You know me so well."

"Um." She settled more deeply into the blankets. "Wake me up when you get home."

He brushed his lips over hers and watched as her heavy lids closed over her eyes. "Sweet dreams, beautiful."

Later in the evening, Ember stirred awake as soon as he climbed into bed. She turned into him and pressed her lips to the skeleton key tattoo over his heart that had her name written along the blade. A shudder went through him as she touched him. "How was class?"

"Packed."

Ember lifted her head onto her hand as her fingers ran over the muscles of his chest and abs.

"What class was it tonight?"

He answered without conscious thought. "Sauces."

"Like gravy?"

Was she serious? "Ember, you don't really want to talk about sauces." He moved to pin her under him as he held himself up on his elbows. "Because there are so many other things that I'd rather do with you than talk about sauces."

She gave him a coy little smile. "Really, like what?"

His hand moved down her body to her stomach, his fingers

toying with her tank top, before he lowered his head to press a kiss on her bare belly. His eyes stayed on her as his tongue dipped into her navel before his hands moved her tank up her body, his mouth following the path. He loved it when she touched him, her hands so eager to feel him under her fingertips as she moved them along his body, claiming every inch she touched. He needed to taste her. His tongue flicked her nipple before he lightly bit it and then he lapped at the sensitive bud with his tongue. She moaned in pleasure, and he pulled her breast into his mouth and sucked on it hard. She actually cried out and—fuck if that wasn't hot. He was surprised and seriously turned on when her hands grabbed at his head and she arched her back.

"Oh God, Trace, I'm going to come."

Fuck yeah. He slipped his hand into her pants until he found the part of her that he so wanted to claim. She was so ready and as soon as he slipped two fingers inside her, her body spasmed around him as she climaxed. Her reaction fueled him as he yanked off her drawstring pants, lifted her hips and settled himself between her legs. Their eyes locked when he sank deep into her. He wrapped her legs around his waist, lifted her hips higher, and then started to move. He was never going to get enough of her. He moved slowly at first, savoring the feel of her body, but when she started to tighten around him, he lost control and moved harder and faster; when she came again, he did too.

"Holy hell," she whispered.

She looked sated as her lids closed over her eyes again.

He settled down next to her and wrapped her into his arms. He wasn't long to follow her into sleep.

In the morning, Trace climbed from bed and pulled on a pair of jeans before heading down the hall to the kitchen. He started the coffee and, as soon as the aroma filled the air, he heard Ember starting to stir. She was a complete caffeine junkie.

He turned toward the door just as she appeared looking all soft and sleepy.

"Morning," he said, but he knew she wasn't awake and wouldn't be until her first cup of coffee. Instead, as was her habit, she moved to him and settled herself right at his side.

There was another far more enjoyable way to wake her; he touched his mouth to the spot just behind her ear that made her weak. His hand moved under her shirt to cup her breast. Her reaction was a sharp inhale as her nipple turned hard. So did he.

He moved his lips along her jaw until they rested over hers. "Just my mouth—that was a first last night."

Embarrassment tinged her cheeks pink. "I know."

He knew she wanted to reprimand him for embarrassing her, but he distracted her when he moved the tee of his that she was wearing up her body before lifting her onto the counter. He bent forward and closed his mouth over her nipple.

"Oh God."

He chuckled and then got down to business. He brushed his finger between her legs and watched as she bit her lip to keep from whimpering. He felt her fingers on his fly and his dick twitched eagerly. When she wrapped her hand around him and pulled him free, it was his turn to moan.

"Impatient?" he teased in a gruff voice.

"To feel you inside me, hell yes."

He grabbed her ass and brought her hard against him, burying himself to the hilt, but instead of moving, he stayed completely immobile, just loving the way it felt to be sheathed in her beautiful body.

"What are you doing?" she demanded.

"You're never going to look at this counter the same way again."

"Teasing me now—oh my God, just move!"

"Yes, ma'am."

And as he complied, he knew neither of them was going to look at the counter the same way.

———————

Darcy stepped into the small garden center located in the middle of concrete and steel and smiled. Color and scents surrounded her. This was one of her most favorite places in the city. Her fire escape was in need of some color, so she grabbed a cart and started down the aisle.

"You're back. We just got in some climbing geraniums that are exquisite," the sales associate called to her.

"Thanks, I'll have to take a look at them."

"The pots are all forty percent off too."

"More pots, just what my fire escape needs." The sales associate laughed in reply before she turned to help another customer.

Darcy wasn't sure when she developed a love of gardening, but her world had been gray for so long that she craved the brilliance of color around her. Her fingers trailed over the soft petals of a petunia in the palest of pinks. It was a bit sad that her longest relationship was with the flower lady, but living with the revolving door that was her mother's house, Darcy had come to crave the solitude. She had made a few friends in college, but Darcy kept them at a distance because of the embarrassment and shame of where she came from. Lucien was the only person whose company she had ever wanted.

Sister Anne had shared her love of gardening. Every week, Darcy had brought an arrangement to her sick room to bring a little of the outdoors inside. And even now, Darcy still brought flowers to brighten her grave. It was something small she could do, but it comforted her, even though the walk down memory lane was always bittersweet. Memories were likely all she was ever going to have when it came to Lucien Black—and where better to reminiscence than with the one person who loved him as much as she did?

———•••———

Fourteen years earlier . . .

The room smelled like death. Darcy had heard that expression before, but never appreciated the meaning until now. The staleness in the air and the subtle scent of decay lingered and clung to everything. Sister Anne had lost so much weight that she was almost unrecognizable. Lucien was retrieving her lunch tray from the kitchen, not that Sister Anne was going to eat it.

Darcy walked to her dresser and placed the vase of freshly cut yellow and pink snapdragons where Sister Anne would see them.

"They're beautiful, thank you, Darcy."

"Oh, I thought you were asleep."

"Please join me. I like the company."

Darcy settled on the chair next to Sister Anne's bed and tried not to show her discomfort, but it was hard to look at her; she was so different from the vital woman she had been. "Lucien's getting your lunch."

Tenderness washed over her face. "He's been so wonderful." Sister Anne's bony hand reached for Darcy's and held it with surprising force.

"He loves you."

Embarrassment turned Darcy's cheeks pink before she replied, "I love him."

"He'll need you when I'm gone."

"I'm not going anywhere."

An exhale that sounded more like a death rattle escaped Sister Anne's throat. "Good. The road ahead isn't going to be easy for either of you, but anything is possible when there's love." Sister Anne's eyes moved from Darcy to the flowers.

"So simple and yet so comforting. If He can create something so beautiful in this life, then how can I fear what He has in store for me in the next?" Her gaze turned back to Darcy. *"Thank you for the reminder."*

Lucien entered with Sister Anne's tray and placed it on the table near her bed.

"Thank you, Lucien. I'm tired, but I promise I will eat something when I wake."

"I'll check on you later." He leaned over and pressed a kiss on her forehead before he turned and reached for Darcy's hand. She allowed him to pull her from the room and down the hall. When they reached a dark corner, he turned into her and wrapped her tightly into his arms. He buried his face in her neck and, though he said nothing, she could feel the tension in his body. They stood like that for quite some time before his head lifted to hers. She saw his pain reflected in his eyes.

"When she's gone, you will be all I have left." His words were a harsh whisper.

"You are all that I have."

His strong hands cradled her face as he stared at her intently. *"Your mother is an asshole, but I will be forever grateful that she dropped an angel into my life. You and me, Darcy, always."*

The emotion behind his words made her eyes sting. Someone who always seemed so strong and in control had a weakness, and to know that she was his weakness was humbling.

"Always," she vowed.

"Can I help you find anything else?" the flower lady snapped Darcy back to the present. Living in the past was dangerous. She seriously needed to move on. Lucien had.

Lucien sat across from his accountant, but he hadn't heard a single word the man said. Ever since Darcy had come back into his life, he couldn't seem to pull his thoughts from the past, which was infuriating, because he was a firm believer that what was done was done. He really shouldn't be all that surprised that he was acting so out of character—Darcy had always had some kind of strange influence over him. When they were younger, he had thought it was love, but now he was leaning more toward dark magic. Regardless, seeing her again had him constantly looking back for answers he suspected he would never find.

His mind drifted back even further to when he was dumped at St. Agnes. He remembered the fear and the loneliness that had been so overwhelming that at times it had threatened to consume him. Sister Anne was the only one to see how difficult the adjustment was for him, and she stepped up. She became his teacher, his disciplinarian, his friend, and his protector. She had made the intolerable tolerable and gave a lost boy hope that someday it would get better.

Twenty-three years earlier . . .

"Sissy boy. Are you gonna cry, baby?"

He tried to not listen, tried to ignore them like Sister Anne was forever encouraging him to do, but the fury that was always simmering just below the surface started to boil. He wasn't even aware that he had balled his hands into fists, or that he had taken a few steps closer to his taunter, until he pulled back his hand, stepped into the punch, and nailed the bully in the face.

Stars sparked in his vision and his hand throbbed like a mother, but seeing the look of shock and just a touch of fear on the face of the jerk he punched—yeah, it was worth it.

Sister Anne appeared, as she had a habit of doing, but it was the look of disappointment on her face that gave Lucien a moment of guilt. He wanted to please her but sometimes it was just too hard to rise above.

"Take Jake to the nurse, Billie. And don't for a second think that this is over, Jacob. I know you started this and we will have words."

Lucien watched as Jake was helped away; the sight of his blood dripping down his face drew a smile.

"That's nothing to be proud of, Lucien."

He knew the look on her face, the one that said far more than mere words ever could. He didn't want to look, but he also didn't want to be a coward. He braced himself before he turned his attention to her. He was not disappointed.

"Hitting is not the answer. Any animal can hit. Rise above it. Use your words, Lucien, not your fists."

"Sometimes that is easier said than done," he muttered.

Tenderness swept her face before she said, "I know, but in life you have to find solutions without using your fists."

"Maybe I'll be a fighter." He knew, even to his eight-year-old ears, that he sounded like a baby.

"Be a fighter—but for the love of the sport. Fighting for any other reason is just a cop-out."

She knelt down in front of him and gently took his hand into her own and studied the broken skin and blood.

"Let's get this cleaned up."

He knew his shoulders were slumped in defeat, because as much as he had wanted to hit Jake, he was upset that he had disappointed Sister Anne. She stood to lead him away, but drew him close to her side in a half hug.

"With that all being said, I think I would have hit him too." She winked at him before she led him to the infirmary. Inside his little chest, his heart swelled with love.

"Mr. Black?" Lucien focused back on his accountant. "Should we reschedule?"

If the older man was annoyed about the sudden change of plans, he remained professional about it.

"Thanks for being so accommodating. I'm a bit distracted," Lucien said in the way of an apology before he saw the man out. He closed his door and poured himself three fingers of Scotch. He wasn't one for drinking during the day, but he needed a drink now. It hadn't taken long for him to realize the gift that had been bestowed on him when Darcy arrived at St. Agnes. For those two years as he watched Sister Anne slowly lose her battle with cancer, he'd had Darcy. With everything that Sister Anne had been to him, it was Darcy who became his salvation.

Sixteen years earlier . . .

Lucien didn't cry, hadn't shed a tear in years, but he was damn close to it now. Sister Anne was dying. There weren't even words to express the desolation that filled him. He wanted to rage at the world, but what was the point?

She moved so soundlessly that he didn't hear her until she spoke from behind him. Darcy.

"I just heard about Sister Anne. I am so sorry, Lucien."

He wasn't able to answer and Darcy seemed to understand that when she continued. "A bird fell out of its nest once outside our building. The superintendent took it in, but he said he was too old to care for it. He asked if I would help and immediately I jumped at the opportunity. Every day I would visit, offering it food and company. It was so thin, you could see his bones and he had no feathers yet. He looked pathetic, but I loved that bird. For weeks I would run home from school and head straight to the super's office to look after my little bird.

"One day, when I arrived, the box was empty. He told me the bird miraculously grew very strong and flew off. I wanted to believe that, but I knew he was only trying to make it easier for me. My bird had died, not because he wasn't loved and offered the nourishment he needed, but because sometimes we can't stop the inevitable. Though I was heartbroken, there was a large part of me that was grateful. For that short time in my life, I found a reason to get up in the morning. For those few weeks, I had a purpose and felt pride in what I was doing. Even losing my bird, I wouldn't have traded that time for anything."

She reached for Lucien's hand. "You can't stop what's coming, but you were and are so lucky to have her in your life. We aren't all that fortunate."

Lucien lowered his head so she wouldn't see the brightness of tears in his eyes.

She graciously changed the subject. "Join me for dinner?"

His head lifted and his gaze met hers. "Yeah."

A slight smile touched her lips. "Don't worry, Lucien. When you fall, I'll be there."

"Why?"

"Because you gave me a purpose again."

He didn't want charity and his voice reflected that. "And what purpose is that?"

"To make you happy—when you're happy, so am I."

Her answer rendered him speechless. And then she added with a grin, "Feeding you is a good place to start."

And just like that, he lost a bit of his heart to her.

———◆———

Lucien was holding his Scotch glass so tightly he feared he was going to shatter it. She'd left him. Not long after Sister Anne died, she'd abandoned him too. It was no wonder that he was so conflicted about having her back in his life. That one woman had the power to make him feel both profound joy and gut-wrenching agony. What the hell was he supposed to do about that?

———◆———

For eighteen months Ember had been working in some capacity with Charles Michaels. This last year, Michaels had been mapping out the nuances of his campaign strategy to run against Nathaniel Carmichael, who had held the post of senator for three consecutive terms. It wasn't just about the politics, but the need to make his name and face a household name. With the election in November, it was crunch time.

She might not like the man, but working with him for as long as she had, she'd learned he was an excellent politician. He stood behind what he believed in. She had to give him credit for that. He didn't talk out of both sides of his mouth, and when he made commitments, he followed through. It was a damn shame he couldn't have shown that kind of character when Trace and Chelsea were younger and had needed someone in their corner when their father was abusing them.

Her most recent article on Charles was with Stanley, her manager at *In Step*, for review, so while she waited to hear back from him, she was jotting down ideas for her next article that she wanted to review with her editor. Caitlin, an intern working the campaign as part of a night school poli-sci class, stopped by.

"Ember, would you mind keeping Brandon company? I have to get to class."

"Sure."

"I'm back tomorrow afternoon, so I can go over his instruction then."

"Don't worry about it." Ember turned to Brandon and extended her hand. "I'm Ember. Nice to meet you, Brandon."

"Hey."

"Okay, so I'll see you both tomorrow. Thanks, Ember."

Brandon watched Caitlin until she disappeared, so Ember took the opportunity to study the boy. He had dark-brown hair and greenish-gray eyes. And he was tall, close to six feet, and surprisingly muscled for a teenager.

His eyes suddenly turned back to Ember and she blushed at getting caught staring. He grinned, and Ember couldn't help but think that this boy was going to be trouble when he got older.

"What brings you here? Charles doesn't often get volunteers that are still in high school. Are you interested in politics?"

All traces of humor left Brandon's expression before he said, "Didn't really have a choice."

"Your parents?"

"Don't have any. I live in a group home."

"Oh, sorry."

"It's cool. I got in some trouble so it was either this or juvie."

As arrogant as Charles was, Ember was surprised he was okay with the arrangement. Brandon seemed to read her thoughts and added, "Mr. Michaels is cool with it."

Ember thought that was an interesting tidbit on Charles. Was it possible there was another side to him? The thought had just entered her head when the door to his office slammed open and out came Heidi Moore, red-faced. At first Ember thought she was seeing things, but no, it was definitely Heidi. She had been so infatuated with Trace for a time that she'd actually stalked him.

A knot formed in Ember's stomach since she knew there was more to Trace and Heidi's relationship than Heidi's unrequited love; Trace had also once used her to try to drive Ember away. She tried to ignore her reaction to that fact and focused instead on the scene before her. What the hell was Heidi doing here? And how did she know Charles?

"I'm not kidding. Don't fuck with me or you'll regret it," Heidi yelled.

"What the . . . ?" Charles grabbed her by the arm and pulled her from the office and Ember shamelessly strained her neck looking out the window to see him haul her down the street.

"What was that all about?" Brandon said.

"Politics," Ember answered, but she knew even as she spoke the words that politics had very little to do with that scene. What the hell *was* that all about?

Ember returned home later in the day and, based on the incredible smell wafting down the hall from the kitchen, Trace had beaten her home. As if on cue, her stomach growled. Dropping her keys on the table, she walked into the kitchen.

"Hello, beautiful."

"Hi. What are you making?"

"My sister was in the mood for mac and cheese."

"Sounds good, smells better. Chelsea has good taste."

He looked at Ember from over his shoulder, but whatever was on the tip of his tongue was replaced with a look of concern. He moved to the table and pulled out a chair.

"You should sit. You look exhausted."

She dropped down into the chair just as he knelt down next to her. "Can I get you anything?" he asked her.

"Some of that mac and cheese when it's done."

"You got it."

"So guess who I saw today at campaign headquarters?"

"No idea."

"Heidi."

For just a second, Ember saw rage sweep Trace's expression before he pulled it under control. He lowered himself so that they were eye level and then he kissed her. It started out as a chaste kiss, but his tongue sought and was granted access into her mouth. He cradled the back of her head to take the kiss deeper. In the next minute, he lifted her into his arms. He turned the heat off on the stove and carried her down the hall to their bedroom. Ember barely heard the click of the lock before Trace had her on the bed where he slowly undressed her. Exhaustion took a backseat to desire as tingles burned through her. Edginess made her reach for him, but her hands came away empty. Her eyes opened to find Trace reaching for the covers to pull them up over her.

"What are you doing?"

"You should sleep."

"But I'm not tired."

His grin was devilish. "You are and dinner won't be ready for another hour, so take the hour and sleep."

"I don't want to sleep, I want you naked and in this bed with me."

Lust darkened his eyes, but he didn't waver. "I want that too, but you have dark circles under your eyes." He pressed a kiss to her forehead that was very chaste before he turned and started from the room. "I'll wake you."

He gave her one last look and then closed the door. Words wouldn't come—Trace had never turned down sex before.

In the morning Ember woke to find herself completely wrapped in Trace. His arm was draped over her stomach, his legs entwined with her own, and her back was pressed up against his chest. He'd never woken her.

"Trace?"

"Hmm?"

"You didn't wake me."

He waited a beat too long to reply and she knew he was hedging, but why? "You needed your sleep."

Somehow she knew there was more to it than her need for sleep and she was about to pry it out of him, but before she could speak, he moved and she felt him, hard and thick, pressing into her butt. She wiggled and he instinctively started moving his hips, rubbing himself against her. His hand found her breast and he fondled her as he pressed a kiss behind her ear.

"Morning," he whispered.

He moved over her as his clever fingers worked off her panties, and he found her so ready. He pushed his leg between her thighs so he could touch and tease that sensitive nub and, all the while, his hips continued to grind against her. When his finger slipped inside of her, she spread her legs even wider and pressed back into his hard length. He growled low in his throat just as his hands circled her hips and lifted her ass in the air. He was naked and hard when he settled between her legs. His caress was gentle as he moved his fingers over her moist heat before slipping inside her. His other hand moved up her stomach to cup her breast, massaging her aching peak. He rolled her nipple and tugged while his fingers sought deeper penetration. The small part of her brain that was still working couldn't shake the feeling that he was distracting her, but he was playing her body like a seasoned maestro, which prevented her from forming any coherent reasons for why he wanted her distracted. She felt him pressing against her ass as he ground his hips against her. He worked her until her body was so sensitive, and then he gripped her hips and pushed into her in one long, hard thrust. She cried out as her body spasmed, every nerve ending firing off to send electric jolts racing over her. Her body was still clenching around him when he pulled out of her, and a second later, his tongue was driving into her folds.

"On my God, Trace."

His grip on her hips tightened as his tongue plunged deep, her hips instinctively moving against him. His finger worked the nub between her legs and she was helpless to stop the second orgasm that ripped through her. Her head fell against the pillow, her body went weak with exhaustion. His hands were gentle when he flipped her onto her back, lifted her hips, and sunk deep into her again.

"Stay with me, Ember."

Her eyes opened, and in his, she saw something that looked an awful lot like guilt, but it was quickly replaced with lust as his hips started to rock back and forth.

"One more time, sweetheart."

He moved slowly and deliberately; she marveled over how he could control his own release, but he did, working her until she felt her body start that upward spiral again. And when she splintered apart, his body jerked and he roared her name, spilling himself deep inside her.

She couldn't move and couldn't think. He had loved her nearly to death.

"Was that too much?"

She couldn't deny her suspicion that he had intentionally loved her stupid, but she was too exhausted to call him on it and so she replied with a simple, "It was incredible."

He lifted her from the bed and started to the bathroom.

"What are you doing?"

"I need a shower." He wiggled his eyebrows. "Thought we could conserve resources."

"My legs don't work, you're going to have to hold me up."

He looked positively wicked when he replied, "That's the whole idea."

Chapter Five

Lucien reread the same sentence for the hundredth time and still he had no idea what was on the page because his concentration was shot. Damn it. He was acting like a fucking adolescent with Darcy constantly on his mind. From the moment she'd stepped into his office, she was all he could think about. How he managed indifference, when what he was feeling was quite the opposite, surprised him. Remembering how it had been between them made him ridiculously curious to know just what she had been doing with her life. Was she happy? Was she where she hoped she would be? Did she regret not meeting him that day? He couldn't bring himself to ask her, though; there was a part of him that wanted revenge even though her offense had happened long ago. But if he was being completely truthful, there was an even larger part of him that didn't think he would like her answers.

When Darcy's headhunter called him about the job, voicing her name, there was no way he wouldn't have agreed to the interview. Of course, he hadn't handled their first meeting very well because there was still bitterness there. He imagined that meant something, that he still harbored animosity toward her. People say there's a fine line between love and hate—he was living it.

His mind drifted to the night at Peacock. Watching her dancing with that secret smile on her face had driven him crazy with the need to touch her. He hadn't realized his feet had propelled him across the club until he was pulling her into his arms. She was the same and yet different and still her body fit against his as if they were two parts of a whole.

He felt guilty about kissing Cassandra in front of her, but he had done it on purpose. Holding Darcy made him remember, and remembering made him angry. The look she had given him from across the club, as if she was acknowledging that she deserved the slight, twisted in his gut. Though he wanted her to take the insult, he was angry that she hadn't stood up for herself and told him to fuck off. He thought about Darcy's mother and how Darcy was also looking for the good in the ugly there. He didn't like how that made him feel.

Seeing her again, all the memories he had pushed into the farthest reaches of his brain came rushing back like a fucking tidal wave. She'd been so awkward when she'd first arrived at the orphanage, a girl who was clearly neglected; but it had been her eyes that first caught his attention, because the twinkle in them hinted at an extraordinary person.

Her arrival coincided with Sister Anne telling him that she was seriously ill, and there was a part of him that believed Darcy was sent to him to help him get through what would be the worst and best two years of his life.

—◆—

Sixteen years earlier . . .

Lucien sat in the dark corner of the room that served as the dining hall. Meals at St. Agnes were often quiet affairs since food was so efficiently handed out. Just like any good prison, you were given three squares, and if you missed mealtime, you went without. He was grateful for the silence—hearing laughter, when he felt so empty inside, made the anger that was always just under the surface break free from the tenuous hold he had on it.

Sister Anne was sick, apparently had been for some time, but now she was no longer responding to treatments. She was dying. How long she had, he didn't know, but there was going to come a time when she would be gone.

He didn't understand how the God that she worshiped could be so cruel. She gave her life to Him and, in return, she got an early death. And what would happen to him? He'd leave, because with her gone there was nothing there for him. He felt the tears, hated feeling weak, and tried to push Sister Anne from his head.

He felt eyes on him; he had for most of the meal, and turned to see a girl staring at him from across the room. Her long black hair was pulled back from her face in a ponytail, she wore no makeup, and her clothes seemed to be a size too big, hanging loosely from her thin frame.

He watched as she stood and he was tempted to follow her out of the hall, but then she started toward him. When she was close enough for him to touch her, he noticed she held a small cup of chocolate pudding.

She sat down without being invited and pushed the pudding across the table to him. That act of kindness took him completely by surprise and he responded by being more curt than he intended.

"What are you doing?"

"You like pudding, so I'm giving you mine."

"How do you know I like pudding?"

"I've been watching you."

"What?"

She just smiled at him in response.

"Don't you like it?" he asked.

"It is the most delicious thing I ever tasted."

That wasn't the answer he was expecting. "So why don't you eat it?"

"Because I thought if you had an extra, it would make you smile. I've been here two weeks and I have not seen you smile once." *She touched her finger to his hand. "Why are you so sad?"*

He didn't mean to yell, but what did she know? "What the hell is there to smile about?"

A sadness swept her face and Lucien wished he could take back his words. And then she spoke and what she said sliced through him.

"Sometimes it seems like there's nothing, like when my mom hits me or when I used to have to hide in the basement of our apartment building so that my mom's friends didn't come for me when they were done with her. But then every once in a while I'll see a butterfly soaring through the sky. The idea of that being me— to be free—makes me smile."

He didn't understand the feelings this girl evoked in him—a rage that was nearly palpable, but at the same time a tenderness that nearly brought him to his knees. His need to protect her, the caterpillar who was waiting to become a butterfly, was overwhelming.

"What happened to your mom?"

"Nothing. She has a new boyfriend that was paying me more attention than her, so she sent me here."

Lucien had some choice words for her mom, but instead reached for his spoon.

"I won't be able to eat all of this. Maybe we could share."

Her smile took up her whole face. "You're a terrible liar, but I'd like to share it with you."

He handed her the spoon with an answering smile. "Thanks, Caterpillar."

——•—•——

Darcy sat at her desk, but as hard as she tried to forget the scene at Peacock a few nights ago, it was right there. She had been right. She had half a mind to walk into his office and tell him to fuck off, but that wasn't the professional way to handle a conflict. She was pondering drafting a harshly worded e-mail when he appeared in his doorway.

"Darcy, could you come in here, please?"

Shock rendered her mute for a minute. It was almost three weeks since she had started and the only time he'd asked her into his office was the day he spouted off instructions at her like she was a willful child. What pearls of wisdom would he impart today? It was curiosity that made her get to her feet and follow him into his office.

Lucien decided he needed to start acting his fucking age. Darcy was his employee, really way overqualified for the assistant position he'd offered her, and he owed her common courtesy. And while he could feed that bullshit to himself all he wanted, the real reason he wanted to reach out was because he missed her. She had sought him out and maybe she was fourteen years late, but she was here and she was trying.

He sat across from her and he took a minute to study her, knowing his scrutiny would serve two purposes: it would give him a minute to enjoy the view and, at the same time, his blatant staring would piss her off. Yes, he was going to try to make an effort, but he was only human after all, and the dig was a small one, but a very gratifying one when he saw her eyes narrow ever so slightly at him.

"I was a bit of prick the first time I called you in here. Hours are flexible as long as you're putting in eight and that includes an hour for lunch."

He didn't miss her look of surprise, nor did he miss the skepticism burning in her gaze. He couldn't blame her for it. How to lighten the mood? And then, remembering their banter as kids, he tried to think of the most absurd instructions to show her he'd been rude. "When you arrive, I expect the coffee to be started since there's nothing I like more than a nice cup of steaming hot coffee in the morning." He hated coffee, and he suspected she remembered that. Seeing the humor in her eyes, he continued on with his list of completely bogus instructions.

Darcy sat back and listened to the litany of bullshit coming out of his mouth and had to stifle the need to laugh. She couldn't lie; it was nice seeing this side of him again. She thought he had lost it. Had he felt guilty for his actions at Peacock or was it possible that he felt something besides indifference toward her? Either way, she intended to enjoy this lighter side of Lucien.

When he wasn't brooding, he was even more beautiful. She half listened and used the opportunity to just stare. She remembered those lips. Even at seventeen, he'd known what he was doing. Jealousy churned in her gut over all the women he'd later used those lips on, even realizing it was she who had pushed him away. Karma was vicious.

"Are you listening, Ms. MacBride?"

"Yes, Mr. Black, the stapler should always be on the left of the desk and the tape dispenser on the right. Though I would like to point out that I am left-handed and so it'll be a bit awkward for me to be constantly reaching across myself to get to the tape."

His lips curved ever so slightly and the sight of it was like a hit from a defibrillator. He looked at her rather magnanimously before he said, "Well, I suppose I can give you some leeway regarding the tape."

"They should throw a parade in your honor," Darcy countered with the same generosity.

"Do you think this is a joke, Ms. MacBride?"

"Not at all, Mr. Black. I assure you I am giving your instructions all the attention they deserve."

She saw him bite his tongue and knew he was trying to keep himself from laughing. His tone sounded mildly disinterested when he asked, "You know how to type, yes?"

She lifted her two pointer fingers and wiggled them at him. "Taught myself."

"Touché. There's a file of correspondence that needs to be typed up. Once you're done with that, we'll take it from there. That's all."

Darcy stood and started from the room when Lucien added, "Welcome to the team, Darcy."

She turned to find him staring at her, and the look in his eyes made her heart move into her throat. It wasn't Mr. Black welcoming Ms. MacBride; it was Lucien welcoming Darcy.

"Thank you . . ." She almost added "Lucien" but couldn't bring herself to do it. She turned and walked out of his office with his name left unspoken between them.

———⬥———

At lunchtime, Darcy decided to slice up an apple to go with her sandwich, but she wasn't paying attention because her thoughts were on that small smile that Lucien had given her. She hadn't expected humor; she'd been prepared for him to be harsh and cruel, but not silly, decreeing where the tape dispenser should be placed on her desk. She chuckled and the knife slipped, slicing into her finger.

It didn't hurt and she thought she must have just nicked it, but with one look she knew she was wrong. It was deep, almost to the bone, and she reacted by cursing like a sailor.

"Fuck!"

Lucien appeared in the threshold of the kitchen. "I don't know the type of place you are used to working, but here we don't use that kind of . . ."

And then he saw the blood dripping down her arm.

"What the fuck did you do?" he roared as he reached for a towel to wrap her hand in.

She was feeling stupid enough already and his bellowing, regardless of cause, set her off. "I was attacked by a vampire. What the hell does it look like happened? I was cutting up my apple and the knife slipped." Some of the anger gave way to fear, and she added more softly, "I think it went to the bone. I may need stitches."

"If you can see the bone, then you definitely need stitches." He reached for his phone as he started to guide her to the sofa in his office.

Despite her best efforts, her next words came out as more of a plea: "I don't want to go to the hospital." She knew stitches meant the hospital, but her fear of them was illogical and crippling.

Darcy felt Lucien tense at her words. "Okay. I'll call a friend, but I want you to sit. You look like a ghost."

She took two steps and felt her legs giving out from under her. "I'm going to . . ." But the rest of the sentence was cut short by blackness.

When she came to, she was lying on the sofa in Lucien's office with her hand wrapped in a white bandage. Humiliation burned through her that she had not only nearly cut her finger off and fainted, but that she had succumbed to a fear she had spent a long time learning how to control.

"Sleeping Beauty awakes." He was trying to be funny, but Darcy heard the odd note in his words. She tried to sit up and he moved quickly to her side to help.

"What happened?"

He stared at her so intensely—like he thought she was going to disappear or something. And then he said, "You fainted."

When she felt out of control, she fell back on what she knew: humor. "With grace though, right?"

"You went down like a sack of bricks. You're lucky I'm as fast as I am or you'd have a concussion to go along with the severed hand."

"It was a paper cut."

"Right, a paper cut that required six stitches."

"Who stitched me up?"

"A friend. He usually works on dead animals, but he made an exception for you."

"Not funny."

He sobered. "It wasn't funny at all. Seeing you as pale as a ghost and then having you faint on me. Jesus, that scared the shit out of me. Never do that again or I'll dock your pay."

"I can see now why you won the humanitarian award."

Some emotion passed through his expression, but Darcy couldn't make out what it was. He said, "Perhaps you should take the rest of the day off."

She moved to stand and Lucien's strong hands wrapped around her upper arms to steady her. He added, "Maybe I should take you home."

"No!" The idea of bringing him into her sanctuary would be her hell. She hadn't meant to bark out that answer, however, and saw by the way Lucien was clenching his jaw that he had taken offense.

"I'm sorry, it's just that I've been a big enough pain in the ass for one day. I'll catch a cab, but thank you"—she looked down at her hand, seeking the strength to finish the apology she was choking on, then lifted her eyes to his to find his focus on her—"for not taking me to the hospital. My fear of them is ridiculous, but very real."

———•———

Lucien stood on the curb a long time after the cab disappeared from sight, thinking about Darcy. He thought about her comment regarding his award. He couldn't shake his suspicion about her motives, particularly having discovered she had been keeping tabs on him over the years. She'd walked away from him and never looked back, so what changed? Was she just curious or was she really after something? Not to mention he knew the kind of woman Darcy's mother was. Yet hadn't Darcy voluntarily gone back with that woman instead of coming away with him? Why? He had tried not to put too much thought into what had happened between them, because he had just wanted to forget her. But was it possible that there was more to the story?

He spent the rest of the day trying not to think of Darcy and failing miserably. The sound of his phone was a welcome distraction.

"Hey, it's Josh." Ember's uncle happened to be a damn fine private investigator. "Is this a bad time?" he asked.

"No, not at all."

"Sorry it's taken me so long to get back to you, but work has been keeping me really busy. You called?"

"I did. Have you found any dirt on the Carmichaels?"

"Nothing that throws up any flags, but I did learn that Dane has a serious drug problem."

"Really?"

"Yeah, pretty hard stuff too. It's entirely likely that he wasn't even in his right state of mind when he attacked Ember. Doesn't change the fact that he needs help, but it's a very revealing tidbit."

"Agreed."

"His family is an interesting lot. His grandfather, the judge, rules that family with an iron fist. So why he hasn't made Dane stop, I've no idea. But I'm guessing now that you've upped the stakes with the ethics committee, he may be forced to do something."

Lucien almost snorted at that. Josh continued, "Dane's father, the senator, is too busy running his campaign to bother with Dane since he has true competition for his seat for the first time in twelve years."

An uneasy feeling moved through Lucien before he said, "Charles Michaels."

"Exactly. From what I've been able to uncover, the judge, DA, and senator are all clean."

"And Dane? Has anyone besides Ember come forward to report him?"

"No, but I did uncover something interesting about Sabrina Douglas. Dane wasn't the first man she claimed had raped her."

Sabrina was a woman who had worked for Lucien and was someone who Dane had allegedly raped. She couldn't handle what Dane had done and escaped it by killing herself. This news about her completely took Lucien by surprise. "What?"

"Yeah, she filed against two other guys. One in her hometown of Oklahoma City and another here in Manhattan a few months before she met Dane."

"Wait, Sabrina was from Iowa."

"No, she wasn't."

"What the hell?" Lucien stood and started to pace around his office. "Why would she lie about that, of all things?"

"Because she was a guest of their state mental facility for several years."

"Jesus, so it's entirely likely that Dane didn't rape her."

"Afraid so. Doesn't change what he tried with Ember, but as far as Sabrina Douglas is concerned, I'm guessing that of the two, Dane wasn't the unstable one. There was one other thing that I found odd. The way the senator's wife, Dane's mother, left seems suspect."

"Meaning?"

"I didn't want to probe too much and raise anyone's suspicions, but I did talk with the woman at the salon Belinda Carmichael always frequented, her yoga instructor, and some other people on the outskirts of her social circle. They were all completely surprised by her leaving. According to them, she was very happily married."

Lucien stopped pacing. "That is interesting and even more so after my conversation with the judge a few weeks ago. I hinted that I knew of the skeletons in his closet. It was a total bluff, but he reacted like a guilty man."

"That *is* interesting. So maybe the daughter-in-law learned a dirty little secret and he made her an offer she couldn't refuse."

"Paid her off to leave? Seems thin, don't you think? Particularly since she's never tried to contact her family," Lucien said.

"True, unless what she learned was reason enough to stay away. The cold murder case in the news—Elizabeth Spano—that's Belinda's sister."

"Really? Well that is interesting. Have you located Belinda?"

"It wasn't easy. Someone did a really good job of covering their trail."

"But you're better."

Josh sounded almost cocky in reply. "She's living in Maryland with her other sister. You want me to contact her and find out what made her leave?"

"Do you think she'll talk?" Lucien asked.

"I can be very persuasive."

Lucien laughed. "I bet. Let me know what you find out."

"Sure thing."

"There's something else, but this needs to be handled with great care."

"Okay."

"I would like you to look into a Darcy MacBride. Namely what she's been up to for the past fourteen years."

"Sure. Who is she?"

How did Lucien answer that? He tried to be as vague as possible. "We lived at the same orphanage and now she's working for me."

"Ah, an ex. You sure you want me digging into her past? If there's something you want to know, shouldn't you just ask her?"

"It's complicated."

"Well, son, it'll get even more complicated if she learns that you're invading her privacy."

Lucien knew he was right, but his need to fill in all the missing pieces so he could make sense of what had happened between them was just too strong. "I know, but could you do it anyway?"

It was the only time that Josh didn't jump on an assignment, but he was a professional and so after a few minutes he said, "I'll get right on it."

"Thanks."

Lucien felt guilty about what he was doing, but not guilty enough to not do it. Besides, *she* was the one at fault. He had a right to know what had happened.

———◆———

Dane hated coming to the estate. He was out of blow, though, and knew where there was a stash. The irony behind the lectures on family and appearances and how Dane was a lowlife was that one of his family members, probably his uncle, snorted lines just the same as him.

He moved across the floor, hoping like hell that his grandfather wasn't home.

The shout, when it came, was unexpected. Not to mention, not his grandfather's. So who was in his office? He moved closer to peek through the crack in the door and caught part of the conversation.

"... not worth the price I've paid. You'd think you had a golden pussy. I'm done, but if you want to continue, you'll learn firsthand the convenience of a rich and well-connected family."

Dane's gasp was audible, loud enough for his dad to turn in his direction. He didn't stick around to have a father-son chat. He walked out the door without even bothering to get what he'd come for. The man on the phone looked like his dad, but he sure as hell didn't act like him. And what did the voice on the phone have on him?

He always wondered why his mother, a seemingly loving parent and wife, up and left one day, never to return. He hadn't been much more than a baby, but he had heard the story of her betrayal from his grandfather more times than he could count. He always believed she met with foul play, particularly given his grandfather used the past tense when he spoke of her.

He never thought too hard on it. In truth, he was scared. He didn't put anything past his family. But maybe her leaving was no mystery. The man who the public knew as a charming ladies' man seemed something quite different behind closed doors.

———⋅•⋅———

Dane returned home and was still unnerved by his father's behavior from earlier. He called Lena since she was always a good distraction, and she came over. As he prepared them a drink, he heard a knock at the door followed quickly by Lena calling, "I'll get it." As she moved to the door and pulled it open, Dane could tell that whoever was on the other side of it put Lena on edge.

"Can I help you?"

"I need to see Dane." He knew that voice. Heidi.

"May I ask what you want?"

"As if it is any of your business."

Outrage made Lena's cheeks burn, which earned her a laugh from Heidi. "Relax, I don't want to fuck him, I just need to talk to him."

Dane stepped into view and glared at Heidi. "What the hell are you doing here?"

"I've got some news to share."

"No. I told you already I'm out. It was fun for a while, but you're going too far. I'm done. Don't come around here anymore."

"Coward."

"You should be a bit more cowardly."

Heidi dismissed his comment with a wave of her hand before she started for the door. "Whatever. Don't come to me when you see how much you lost out on."

"Believe me, I won't."

Dane closed the door at her back and leaned up against it.

"What was that all about?" Lena asked.

"You don't want to know, trust me."

------◆------

Trace watched Ember talking with her father and uncle.

They were having their monthly dinner party, an event that Trace found he actually enjoyed. His focus moved to the older men's faces and knew it wasn't going to be long before both of them made their way over to him. Hugging was something he still hadn't gotten accustomed to, but Ember and her family did it often.

She laughed and brushed a rogue lock of hair from her face, her wedding rings sparkling on her finger. Possession filled him and he started over to her just as his cell phone buzzed with an incoming call. He was about to let it go to voice mail, determined to pull his wife into his office for a few minutes of privacy, but something made him reach for it.

"Trace," he said.

"We need to talk."

Anger surged in him even as apprehension filled him. It was Heidi, and this was the fourth time she'd called him this week.

He moved down the hall to his office and shut the door behind him. "I told you to stop calling me."

"I need money."

Trace's heart stopped as a moment of guilt twisted his gut. He hardened his tone. "Not my problem."

"It will be if you don't help me."

"How exactly?"

"How's Ember?"

Rage burned through him, but his voice was controlled when he said, "You are playing a very dangerous game, Heidi. Stay the fuck out of my life and away from my wife."

"You've never told her about us. Why?" Her voice turned pouty before she said, "I think there's a part of you that misses me."

"Don't flatter yourself."

"I need money and you'll give it to me or I'll tell her everything."

"You tell my wife anything and I'll make sure they never find the body. You hear me?"

She was silent for a moment, but when Heidi finally spoke up her voice was less sure. "Two thousand by next Friday."

She hung up, but she knew damn well that he'd pay it. He had deluded himself into believing that his past was finally in the past. Since he'd married Ember, everything seemed to have settled. But Heidi was never going to go away and so once again his past was staring him in the fucking face.

He took a few minutes to calm down. Hearing a light knock on the door, he tried to school his expression just as Ember appeared.

"Hey, are you okay?"

"Yeah, sorry, a business thing."

She studied him a moment before she asked, "You sure everything is okay?"

"Everything's fine." And then to change the subject, he said, "You look beautiful tonight."

He touched her hair, needed to feel those silky strands beneath his fingers. Even after everything they'd been through, she blushed over a compliment.

"Thank you."

She smiled and pressed her mouth to his. His arms tightened around her just as she said, "Our guests are going to start talking."

"Let them fucking talk," he said as he pulled her in for another kiss. He was tempted to push her up against the wall and sink himself into her, but the thought of her father and uncle in the other room dampened his ardor. She knew where his thoughts were, and not just because he was as hard as a pike.

"I'm feeling the need for a back washing later," she whispered.

"Oh hell yeah." He kissed her hard and then put some distance between them before he threw caution to the wind.

He started for the door. "A back washing, a front washing . . ." He looked back at her, only to see her blushing.

"Don't do that, sweetheart, or we aren't leaving this room."

"How do you do that?"

"What?" he asked.

"Turn it on so fast."

"It's not fast, Ember, I want you twenty-four seven."

"Now I need to splash my face with cold water."

"You do that and I'll go stick my head in the freezer." He was halfway out the door when he looked back at her and winked before disappearing down the corridor.

Trace was talking with Rafe when Ember reappeared, and based on her lack of makeup, she really had splashed her face with water. He was about to walk over and whisper something suggestive in her ear when the doorbell sounded. He changed course and answered the door to see Lucien, carrying a present wrapped in silver with a white bow. The oddness of the picture made Trace ask almost harshly, "What the hell is that?"

"My laundry. What the hell do you mean what's that? It's a hostess gift, you moron."

Ember appeared then, pulling the door open wider as she bestowed a smile on Lucien. Trace's jaw clenched.

"Lucien, hi. Please ignore this lug and come in. Can I take that?"

"Let the lug take it." Lucien didn't even bother waiting for his friend's reply before he thrust the gift into Trace's hands. To be a dick, he reached for Ember's hand, and brushed his lips across her knuckles before lacing her hand through the crook of his arm. He looked at Trace over Ember's head and was happy to see that his flirting had hit its mark. A smug grin played over his mouth. Trace would get him back later for that, but it had been so worth it.

Ember walked him to her father just as Trace appeared and deftly inserted himself between Lucien and Ember.

"Lucien, how are you, son?"

Lucien grinned at Shawn, ignoring Trace, and extended his hand. "I'm good, sir, and you?"

"Wonderful."

Lucien watched as Trace drew Ember back against his chest and wrapped his arms around her waist. For a moment, they weren't Trace and Ember, but him and Darcy, a vision of what could have been had their lives gone differently. It was in that moment he was able to admit to himself that he never dated seriously because none of the women in his life were Darcy. He didn't know what to do with that knowledge, but thankfully he didn't have to think too long on it, because Chelsea appeared and took his hand and said, "Come and see my room. I painted it purple."

The following morning, Trace walked up the two floors to the small apartment in the Village that he'd bought five years earlier. He rarely came here; he didn't see a need to twist the knife in any more than necessary, but Heidi had gone too far. He had been willing to take on the responsibility he found dumped at his feet, but he wasn't willing to do so at the cost of his wife. No fucking way.

He unlocked the apartment and wasn't surprised to see the ice princess lying on the sofa watching television. Her pale eyes found him and she sat up as a purely sexual smile curved her lips. Trace's stomach turned.

"Where's the boy?"

"Out," she purred as she moved from the sofa, her dress barely covering her thighs. "Can you stay a while?" The implication was clear.

"This shit stops now, Heidi."

She came to stop just in front of him, her lips pouting in an expression he supposed was meant to be a turn-on, but he felt his breakfast lurching up his throat. When her hands found his chest, he grabbed her wrists.

"I agreed to help, but you threaten me and we're done. The only one who stands to get hurt in all of this is the boy. I would think that as his mother, you'd be more motherly."

She pulled from him and hissed, "I never wanted the little beggar, but he comes from a wealthy family. You don't toss that kind of good fortune away."

"You fucking bitch."

"I'm serious, Trace. You might not like that, or me, but you don't have a choice. We're family, whether you want to admit it or not." She sat on the arm of the sofa and spread her legs, her thong barely covering her assets. "Besides, you took us on."

"I don't know what it is you think you stand to gain from this, but I promise you it will not end the way you hope."

"Oh Trace. Don't worry about me. As long as those checks keep coming regularly, we're good." She ran her finger up her thigh. "If you wanted to take some of the money out in trade, I'm always up for that."

"Never going to fucking happen."

"Whatever."

At that moment the door opened as a boy of about sixteen entered. Every time Trace saw him, he felt a searing pain in his chest. The black hair and blue eyes . . . the boy was almost his mirror image.

"Hey, Trace."

"Seth, how are you doing?"

"Good. Got to eat, though, and get to my homework."

Trace watched as Seth disappeared into his room. He never once looked at his mother and it was that, more than anything, that left Trace with a sour taste in his mouth. He knew how it felt to be neglected. Guilt twisted inside him just as Heidi said, "He looks just like you."

"Fuck off." Trace slammed the door behind him. What was that expression Lucien was forever saying? *Lie down with dogs and get up with fleas.* Fuck if that wasn't true.

Chapter Six

Darcy arrived to work at eight in the morning. It had been a week since Lucien had given his goofy instructions and since they seemed to be enjoying a truce, she decided he wouldn't object to a bit of humor. She'd stopped at one of the junk shops near her apartment and bought Lucien the biggest mug she could find. It said, "I ♥ Coffee."

She dropped her bag at her desk and headed to the kitchen. She set the coffee machine and then stood with mug in hand, tapping her foot, waiting for the coffee to finish. Not only did Lucien not like coffee, but the idea of it fixed with sugar and cream turned his stomach, so naturally she added four heaping tablespoons of sugar to the mug and filled it with enough cream to make it look like vanilla ice cream.

Trying very hard to keep the smile from her face, she knocked when she reached his office.

"Come in."

"Your coffee," she said in way of greeting.

He looked up, his eyes on her for a minute before they moved to the mug in her hand. He was trying, and she gave him points for a valid effort, but the grin cracked over his face nonetheless. He leaned back in his chair just as Darcy placed the mug in the middle of his desk.

"Thank you."

Her eyes met his and for just a second she saw her Lucien—the beautiful, serious boy with eyes that saw far more than they should. As if lured by a favorite tune, just looking into his unguarded expression swept her back to a time when she'd still believed in happily-ever-afters. But of course they weren't real, as she'd learned all too well. She started from his office.

"Darcy."

She closed her eyes for a moment, before she glanced at him over her shoulder.

"Yes?"

"I was reading through your resume—very impressive."

Pride rushed through her at his words since he was the only one whose opinion had ever mattered to her. Her voice wasn't quite steady in reply. "Thanks."

He studied her a minute before he asked, "Can I ask why you left Sookie's Catering?"

"Sookie retired because she was having a baby and handed the reins to her partner. We didn't see eye to eye, so I resigned."

"I've used them a few times—delicious food and outstanding service. The fact that it was you behind the scenes keeping it running so smoothly speaks volumes about your managerial skills."

She didn't want to smile at the compliment, but how could she not? "I enjoyed the work."

"This job doesn't have to just be typing, filing"—he grinned—"and making coffee. I have vendors for my various restaurants that need to be managed. If you're interested, the information is all in those files out there."

And just like that she was that fourteen-year-old girl again who believed that he hung the moon. "I'd really like that. Thank you for the opportunity." Before she slipped from the room, she added, "Enjoy the coffee."

Later that afternoon an e-mail pinged in her inbox, and seeing that it was from Lucien made her heart hammer in her chest.

```
Effective immediately, all vendor-related issues
should be brought to the attention of Darcy MacBride,
my new manager of vendor relations.
     Lucien
```

"Get ready for the phone calls."

Darcy was embarrassed to have been caught staring at his e-mail, but how like him to just leap in with both feet. It was like he knew what she was thinking when he said, "You're perfect for the job and overqualified as an assistant."

When she looked up at him, she knew what she was feeling was easy enough to read on her face. "Thank you."

"Besides, you make terrible coffee."

Her laugh was unexpected and as genuine as the smile he offered in return.

It was a good thing that Lucien had warned her to expect some calls. She soon found herself getting her ass reamed for an hour and a half by a vendor pissed that he'd been canned by the temperamental chef of Tapas.

Tapas was one of Lucien's properties in the Financial District. It catered mostly to those coming in after work for drinks and snacks.

Darcy could understand the chef's need for perfection, especially when it was his name associated with the food, but there were protocols to follow. By neglecting to bring his complaint to Darcy, she now had an earache from the outraged vendor ripping her a new one.

She did her best to smooth things over, and when she hung up, she started to dial Kenneth, the chef, but realized he didn't know her from Adam. This needed to be handled face-to-face. She would introduce herself and then smack him upside the head.

Lucien wasn't in his office so she left a Post-it on his monitor, grabbed her purse, and went in search of a cab—that she was damn well charging back to the office.

Kenneth's back was to her when she entered his domain.

"Excuse me?"

He ignored her and continued to talk to whoever was with him, most likely a member of the wait staff.

"Mr. Drake, my name is Darcy MacBride. I was recently hired by Mr. Black to handle vendor relations."

Nothing, not even a shrug of his head. Darcy gave up on being both professional and civil and just bellowed, "You can't just fire a vendor. We have contracts with all of them. Terminating them without following protocol could lead to lawsuits."

Kenneth turned, his huge form concealing the person he'd been speaking with as he returned her bellow with one of his own. "Who the hell are you?"

"I'm Darcy MacBride. I'm responsible for dealing with the vendors."

"Better you than me."

"Yes, well, you can't fire them without talking with me first."

"The hell I can't. Substandard produce is unacceptable."

"It's my job to get you what you need and it's your job to make the dishes that keep people coming back. Would you like it if I came in here and told you how to run your kitchen?"

Some of the bite left Kenneth before he said, "No."

"Then let me do what I'm being paid to do."

"I will not receive produce from that supplier again," Kenneth said, but it was really just for show and they both knew it.

"I agree. I have a list of other vendors that I have asked to bring a selection of fruits and vegetables for your inspection this afternoon."

"Fair enough." He studied her a minute before he asked, "How much work did I cause you?"

"A few phone calls, an earache, and a lot of ass-kissing, but it's handled."

"Sorry." Seeing contrition coming from such a large man was rather funny. And then the person with whom Kenneth had been speaking stood. Lucien. Ah hell. For just a fraction of a second, she thought about diving behind the prep counter, but that would be stupid because he had seen her.

"Darcy, I see you've met Kenneth. He has the worst temperament of my chefs, hotheaded to a fault, but that doesn't seem to be a problem for you."

"I'm sorry—"

"Don't apologize. He needs his head smacked every once in a while."

"I do, it's true," Kenneth agreed.

Lucien added, "But he makes a hell of a spicy orange beef wrap."

And as if on cue Kenneth moved to the stove and started spooning stuff onto a plate.

"You must try this. It just came to me in a dream."

Lucien pulled the stool out that he had been using.

It did smell heavenly, so though she tried to sound put out, she failed when she said, "Well, if you insist."

Brandon caught himself almost running as he made his way to the Michaels headquarters, so he forced himself to slow down. It was crazy—she was too old for him, but he had gone and developed a crush on Ember Montgomery. It was a death wish knowing who her husband was, but the heart wants what the heart wants.

She didn't realize that he had a crush on her; if she did, she didn't encourage him.

He stopped just outside and fixed his hair before he pulled the door open. His eyes zeroed in on Ember, but it was the giant next to her who had his total attention. It was her husband and he was looking at her like a hungry man staring at a steak dinner. Brandon straightened his spine. He felt short, which at six foot was ridiculous.

He started toward them, but hesitated when he saw the seriousness of their expressions. Then quite suddenly, Ember smiled and all the breath left his lungs. He noticed that the husband wasn't immune to her smile as his eyes softened right before his mouth lowered and captured hers. Lucky, lucky bastard.

He felt like a bit of a Peeping Tom, but Ember was clearly wildly in love with her husband and he was just as smitten. Figured. And then her head turned toward him and she smiled, not the same "we share a secret" one that she gave her husband, but still dazzling.

"Brandon. This is my husband, Trace."

When Trace turned to Brandon, he gulped loudly. It was the hardness in those eyes that surprised him, because he had just seen them soft and tender when Trace was looking at his wife. Brandon's legs refused to move him forward—fear that Trace would uncover his secret made his stomach knot. And then, as if he had said that out loud, he watched as Trace's eyebrow rose slightly. A smile spread over Trace's face and meaning dripped from that arrogant grin: poor bastard.

Ember, oblivious, said to Trace, "We're working until six and then we're going to catch a bite at a place not too far from here. I'll be home around eight."

Trace's eyes never left Brandon's. "You'll make sure my wife gets home safely."

His meaning—or threat, however you wanted to look at it—was very clear. "Yes, sir."

"Call me Trace. Nice to meet you, Brandon."

"Um, likewise."

"Ember, can you help with this?" Caitlin called from across the room.

"Sure, one second." Ember moved from her desk toward Trace. "I'll see you later." Brandon watched them as if he was witnessing a perfectly orchestrated dance move. Ember moved into her husband, fitting perfectly against his body, as he lowered his head for her kiss.

"Be safe," Trace whispered just as Ember pulled from him.

"Always."

Trace watched Ember a moment longer before he turned back to Brandon. Brandon almost squirmed at the very thorough inspection he was being given, and then Trace moved closer and said, "I can't fault you for your taste."

Brandon's jaw dropped.

"With that being said, she's my wife. You feel me?"

"Yes, sir."

"Good. Have fun tonight." And with that he strolled away.

By quitting time, Brandon had found his balance again. It was unnerving to come face-to-face with the competition for the one you loved—not that there was any competition for Ember's affections outside of his fantasies. They were going to dinner; he had her all to himself for the next two hours. Once she shut down her computer and grabbed her purse, they started for the door. They had reached the street when she asked, "You said your friend works where we're going?"

"Yeah, but he isn't working tonight."

A small brick tavern appeared before them. They had the best damn hamburgers in the city. "Here we are," Brandon said as he held the door for her. They found a spot in a quiet corner. After their orders were placed, Ember rested her arms on the table and asked, "You mentioned you lived in a group home. Do you mind me asking where?"

"In Hell's Kitchen—St. Agnes."

Surprise flashed across her expression before she said, "Really? My husband spent a year there as a child."

"Really?" Brandon perked up at that. "But isn't he rich?"

Ember laughed. "Yes, but he needed something money couldn't buy."

Brandon's curiosity had been truly piqued. "What?"

"Love."

Brandon pondered that answer for a moment before he changed the subject. "The place is really old, but there have been renovations lately that have made it so much cooler. We have Wii and Xboxes, pool tables, and better books. The attic is a bit creepy, but there's so much old stuff stored up there. The nuns asked if any of us kids wanted to make a few bucks and go through it for items the orphanage might be able to use, otherwise we're supposed to box it up for donations. I jumped on the opportunity because I like looking at old stuff."

"Really?"

"Yeah, maybe that's stupid, but I like understanding where

people come from. I suppose because I have no idea where I do. Maybe you'd like to see it sometime."

"I would really like that, Brandon."

———◦—◦———

Dane hated wearing a tuxedo, and hated having to socialize with the pompous asses who made up Manhattan's high society even more. He tugged on his collar, hoping to relieve the feeling of being strangled, and wished like hell he had gotten high first. He reached for a glass of champagne from a passing waiter's tray and downed the entire contents before taking another.

"It's wonderful. Don't you just love it?" Lena cooed.

He eyed her from over his glass and felt his dick twitch to life. Yeah, at least he'd be tapping that later. Dressed in a formfitting green gown with that fiery hair pulled up, she looked edible. Todd was an ass to let her slip through his fingers. He lowered his head and brushed his lips over her ear.

"What are you wearing under that?"

Her eyes widened a second before narrowing to sexy slits. Her voice lowered to a seductive purr. "Nothing."

"Good girl." His hand moved over her ass and squeezed. "Maybe we should find a closet."

Her reply was a pout. "Not yet. I haven't even met the man of the hour."

"And you're not going to. My dad is too busy schmoozing. Trust me, you aren't missing anything."

He noticed the line that formed between her brows, but he just wasn't interested in what was going on in her head. The idea of introducing her to his father was out of the question. He'd never hear the end of it until he dumped her and frankly, he liked her. She was a bit clingy, but she was smart and fun and very daring in the sack. He wasn't getting rid of her until he was ready to.

Lena linked her arm through his, and when he looked down at her, she smiled.

"Okay."

Her easy agreement was suspicious since Lena was anything but agreeable, but he was thankful that he didn't have to deal with her that evening as well.

"Let's get a drink," he suggested.

"I want to run to the powder room first. I'll be right back."

She moved through the crowd with grace, his eyes on her ass, which looked fantastic in that dress. Oh yeah, he definitely couldn't wait until later.

"Close your mouth, Dane."

He closed his eyes on a moan. "What the hell are you doing here, Heidi?"

"You know damn well why I'm here."

He thought he had finally gotten rid of her, because he hadn't heard from her since she'd come to his apartment, and that was over two weeks ago. His eyes looked down her body and he wasn't surprised to see her looking regal in her formfitting white gown, or that most of the men in the room were eying her. Heidi Moore knew how to play her looks to get what she wanted.

"Going for virginal, are we?"

She tossed her hair over her shoulder and eyed him coolly. "I have every right to be here."

"I suspect there are those here who would disagree with that," Dane countered.

"Whatever."

He grabbed her arm and lowered his voice in warning. "You have no idea who you're fucking with. I'd be very careful in this game. You've been warned," Dane said before he turned and walked away.

"Watch your step, Ember. There are more boxes just at the top of the stairs too," Brandon cautioned before he stepped into the darkness to turn on the light, bringing a soft glow to the dark attic. "Thanks for coming. I was surprised when you said yes."

"I love looking through old things and, with Trace off helping a friend deliver some of his pieces, I had the morning free." Ember reached the top and took a moment to look around. "You weren't kidding about there being a lot of stuff up here. I don't think I'd ever leave here until I'd uncovered everything."

"It is tempting. I've been through those boxes over there already: mostly old clothes and shoes that'll be washed and distributed among the kids. My friend and I are working on this part."

"Your friend?"

"Yeah, Seth. The one who works at that restaurant we went to the other day. He'll be here soon."

"Does he live here too?"

"No, he lives with his mom, but he's been here a few times with her. Not sure why she would come here, but on one of their visits I asked Seth to play video games with me while he waited. After that, he started coming on his own. He's cool. We've talked about getting a place together when we're older."

"I can't wait to meet him," Ember said. She settled down in front of a large cedar chest. There was a lock, but it wasn't secured because when she lifted the lid, it opened with ease. "Are you sure no one will mind us going through this?"

"I'm sure. They want it gone, so the more people helping the better."

She pushed the lid all the way back before she reached in and picked up a small blanket. The colors were fading, but outside of that it was in remarkably good condition. There was no mistaking that it had been handmade and Ember thought it strange that such a piece would find its way up here. Why would a child who had received such a loving gift be abandoned? She refolded it and placed it gently aside before she reached in for a small pair of shoes. With sparkly rhinestones on the top, she imagined they were once a little girl's prize possession.

There was a part of her that wondered if she might uncover anything of Trace's. A smaller wooden box was buried deep in the chest and opening it revealed letters tied together with a pink silk ribbon. She didn't have to read them to know they were love letters.

"Brandon, where did all of this come from?"

"Apparently, the Mother Superior who used to work here was a bit of a tag sale junky."

Well, that certainly explained the wooden box. It was sad that the letters were here, forgotten, when they had clearly meant a great deal to someone. She wanted to read them; though it would be an invasion of privacy, the temptation was too strong.

"Can I take these to read? I'll bring them back."

"Keep them. Stuff like that is going to be tossed."

Ember looked down at the letters, debating with herself.

"Just take them," Brandon insisted; that was all she needed to hear before she tucked them in her purse and continued her exploration of the chest. When she reached the bottom, she carefully put everything back. She stood and started over to the corner of the attic, but almost fell backward onto the boxes. Brandon was there to steady her.

"Are you okay?"

"Yeah, thanks. Just lost my footing." She looked down at the floorboard like it was at fault; but she'd really stumbled from the head rush from seeing a box labeled "Sister Anne."

She pulled it into the light and was so tempted to look in it—but she thought it should be Lucien who did so first.

"A friend of mine who grew up here should have this. Maybe I could talk with the Mother Superior and convince her to let me take it."

"I don't see why not. It gets the stuff out of here."

The sound of feet on the stairs made Brandon call out, "Good timing, Seth."

Ember was dusting off the box when Seth stepped into the attic. "Found someone else to help you go through all this junk?"

"It's not junk; it's memories, lost memories, right, Brandon?" Ember said.

"Seth, this is Ember. Ember, my friend Seth."

"Hey," Seth said, but Ember remained silent, which made Brandon turn his attention to her.

"Ember, what's wrong?"

"I'm sorry. I'm being very rude, it's just that you look so much like my husband that it's uncanny."

"It's cool." Seth gestured to the box. "What's that?"

"A box that a friend would very much like to see."

"I'll take it down for you," Seth offered.

"Thanks, I'm going to see if I can track down Mother Superior," Ember said before she started down the stairs.

Brandon walked up next to his friend and hissed, "I saw her first."

"Based on what you told me, I doubt it matters."

"Yeah, still."

"You're an idiot," Seth said and laughed when his friend flipped him off.

Ember continued down the stairs and, though she was flattered that Brandon had a crush on her, she was going to have to be very careful not to lead him on.

Chapter Seven

"Get both."

Darcy turned to see Lucien holding a shopping basket. The sight of him doing something so routine had a strange effect on her: it made her sad. She glanced in his basket and spotted the pudding, which caused a smile even as her heart ached.

"Still like pudding, I see."

If she wasn't standing there watching him, she would never have believed that Lucien Black looked embarrassed, but he recovered quickly. "It's an addiction." In the week since her run-in with Kenneth, Lucien was in the office more, and they were definitely making progress in the friendship department. Trouble was, being near him again only reinforced what she already knew. She didn't want to be just his friend.

In an attempt to ease the craving for something she couldn't have, she stopped off at the grocery store on her way home from work. Ice cream was a poor substitute, but beggars couldn't be choosers.

And it was while she stood in front of the freezer, trying to decide between New York Super Fudge Chunk and Half Baked, that the voice of the man she was trying to forget had popped up behind her.

"Do you shop here often?" As soon as the words were out, she wanted to slam her head against the freezer, repeatedly. Now *she* was embarrassed for being so lame.

He seemed to sense what she was feeling and answered, "It's convenient."

"Shopping for one?" That was it. She was really on a roll of stupidity now.

Something flashed in his eyes before they drifted to her basket. "Yeah, same as you."

He studied her for a few minutes, his thoughts his own, then he asked, "Have you had dinner?"

Nerves rippled down her spine as excitement made her heart beat faster. "No."

He lifted his basket. "I won't be able to eat all of this myself."

The memory hit so hard that she felt tears burning the back of her eyes. She knew he was feeling it too because, though he looked unconcerned, she saw his jaw clench.

"You're a terrible liar, but I'd love some."

She watched as the weight he seemed to always carry simply dropped from his shoulders before he reached for her hand.

"I know the perfect place."

<hr />

They sat under a tree in the park eating a dinner that consisted entirely of chocolate pudding. Darcy licked the spoon before handing it back to Lucien. "Have you ever switched it up and gotten vanilla?"

The grin he gave her was so boyish that for a moment she saw him at sixteen doing exactly what he was now. "No." When he offered her the spoon, she put up her hand.

"I couldn't eat another spoonful." She leaned back against the tree and watched him scrape the small cup to get every last bite. At that moment he reminded her so much of the boy she'd known, but he wasn't that boy anymore. One glance at his clothes, which cost more than she made in a week, was proof of that.

"Are you happy?" It was a question she'd been wanting to ask him, but had never had the nerve. But the shared memory of the pudding and the reminder of how good it had been between them once had the words tumbling from her mouth. She tensed, prepared for the anger she knew had to be in him. He studied her for a minute and then took a few more moments to throw the cup in the bag they were using for trash. She assumed that this was his way of not answering her, but then his head lifted and his eyes met hers.

"Are you?"

She took a minute to think about it, since it wasn't something she ever really delved into. "I've been content. Happy, I think, is too strong a word, but I haven't been *un*happy."

"How's your mom?"

Darcy rested her head against the tree to look up at the stars. "She's drinking herself to death and sleeping with anything that has a pulse. But I can't cut the cord because deep down I fear that I'll end up just like her, miserable and alone."

His question was so softly spoken she wasn't sure he even asked it. "Are you alone?"

Sitting on the grass, she turned to him. How natural that looked for him, and yet she knew he was equally comfortable in suits, socializing with the rich and famous. His question was not one she could answer honestly—every man who came into her life was always lacking something. She knew what that something was, even if she tried to ignore it. None of them were Lucien.

"Alone, but not always lonely." She was silent for a minute before she added, "I want to know what you've been up to for the last fourteen years, but I don't think I have a right to ask you that."

He silently watched her before the slightest of smiles pulled at one side of his mouth and he leaned over and tugged on a lock of her hair. "What do you want to know?"

"Have you forgiven me?"

She saw the flash of pain in response to her question before he asked, "For not showing up?"

"For not following my heart and for breaking yours."

The silence stretched out for so long it became awkward; Darcy was trying to find something to say to change the subject when Lucien abruptly stood. Darcy felt like kicking herself for bringing up the painful memory. The friendship they'd been trying to rebuild was about to go up in flames.

She'd just opened her mouth to apologize when he reached his hand down to her. She slipped her hand in his and felt the heat that always sparked when they touched burn up her arm. He pulled her to her feet, but didn't let go of her hand. They stood for a few minutes just staring at each other and then he said, "It's late. I'll hail you a cab."

Darcy had to stifle a sigh when she thought about Lucien and her dinner in the park. She never thought that he would ever again look at her as he did last night: affectionately. They might never get back what they'd had, but they were finding their way as friends, and that was far more than she'd ever hoped for. Worry churned in her belly because they were speaking regularly and so she really didn't have an excuse to not tell him her secret. Fear was keeping her silent now. Would he hate her like she hated herself? Would he turn from her again? The idea of losing him after just finding him again was enough to bring her to her knees.

She couldn't avoid telling him forever, but she didn't have to do so today.

She stood and walked to his door, knocking lightly.

"Come in."

Darcy pushed the door open and strolled to his desk, calendar in hand. She didn't waste time on pleasantries, but got right down to business.

"You've got lunch with Declan Grant at Savannah's at noon, a meeting at two o'clock with Kenneth to discuss the new menu for Tapas, and dinner with Candy or Sandy at Clover at seven."

Lucien looked up from his paperwork. "Well, is it Candy or Sandy?"

She rolled her eyes at him before she muttered, "Of course there would be a Candy *and* a Sandy. I don't know. Her voice was so high it was almost outside the range of human hearing."

Lucien leaned back in his chair as a smile pulled at his mouth. "Did you just crack a joke?"

The deadpan look she gave him in reply should have been answer enough. "No, merely stating a fact."

He studied her for a minute.

"What else are you thinking?"

"Me? Thinking independently? I will endeavor to squelch that unattractive trait immediately."

"Meaning?"

"Candy and/or Sandy? Do I have to spell it out? Oops, hopefully not in front of them or they'll be completely lost."

Instantly the humor fled from his expression and was replaced with anger. It was so sudden and so dramatic that Darcy felt her heart drop into her stomach. His next words were clipped with anger. "My personal life is none of your damn business."

It stung, but then again, she had crossed that line. They were friends, or working on it, but some topics just hit too close to home. She wasn't as quick to reply again, and when she did, her voice had lost the teasing quality it had held a moment before.

"I apologize. Do you need anything?"

"No."

She didn't hesitate to turn from him, pulling his office door closed behind her with a decided click.

By the time Lucien finally called it a night, it had grown late. He had canceled his dinner with Candy since she wasn't the one with whom he wanted to share the evening. He flicked off the lights to his office and looked down the hall to see that Darcy had already left for the day. He felt bad about earlier, but he couldn't seem to help the bitterness that sometimes came up out of nowhere and threatened to choke him. He should be over it, for Christ's sake. It was fucking fourteen years ago, but he wasn't and wondered if he ever would be.

Like his feelings over losing Sister Anne, a place in him would always be empty from losing Darcy; he was beginning to realize that Darcy had claimed a piece of his heart that would forever be hers.

Allegro was packed as he walked through the club, looking for Darcy to apologize for being such an ass. He knew she usually had a drink before she left for home, but when he found her, she wasn't alone. Her head was slightly turned so he could see the smile and the way her eyes were sparkling from too much alcohol.

The man was touching her, a light brush of his finger over the back of her hand, and he felt a primitive urge to rip the bastard into shreds for touching what was his. In the next minute, the brazen bastard reached for Darcy's hand and pulled her from the stool to the dance floor. Even though the music was upbeat, he pulled her close as he staked his claim that she, at least for the night, was his.

It should be his arms she was in and his body pressed up against hers. They belonged together, so why was he constantly pushing her away? That was an easy question to answer: he was an idiot.

He moved to the opposite end of the bar from where Darcy and her friend had been sitting, and signaled Tara.

"Hey, boss, what can I get you?"

"Dewar's neat."

"You got it."

Tara placed the glass in front of him and poured the Scotch. She noticed Lucien's eyes were on the dance floor. "Darcy made a friend. He's been watching her for the past few nights and finally worked up the nerve to make his move."

Lucien downed the whiskey and touched the rim of his glass, indicating he wanted another. "Know anything about him?"

"He's a regular. Seems to come mostly for the music, like Darcy. No worries, boss, we're watching out for her."

"Good."

———◆———

"Are you sure there's actually alcohol in this drink, Tara?" The buzz wasn't coming fast enough. Darcy hadn't set out to get drunk, but the buzz kept her from thinking about how she had fucked up earlier with Lucien.

"Double the alcohol, just like you asked." Darcy almost forgot she'd asked Tara the question. Her mind tended to wander when she drank too much.

"Can't taste it." And yet her tongue seemed almost too large for her mouth. The idea of her tongue growing exponentially until it hung to the floor brought on a bout of giggles.

"Where's your date?"

"Not my date. He's a nice man who wanted a drink and a dance. I think he's in the men's room."

"How are you getting home, Darcy?" Tara asked.

Darcy shrugged, which prompted Tara to say, "Don't leave alone, got it?"

Her salute turned into a solid whack to her nose, which turned her giggles into outright laughter.

"Maybe you should eat something. I'll get you a menu."

"Just pick something. I'll eat anything," Darcy said.

"You got it."

Her attention was on Tara, so she didn't know that Lucien had stepped up next to her until he said her name. She turned so fast in her stool, she almost went sailing right off it. Lucien's quick reflexes prevented a truly humiliating scene.

"You okay?" he asked, but Darcy was more focused on the fact that his hands were still on her. Yes, she knew it was because he didn't want her falling and suing him, but it felt really nice. She gave herself another minute to enjoy the feeling of his warm hands on her before she slapped her own hands down on the bar so hard she felt the impact all the way up to her shoulder joints.

"Darcy?"

"Hands are funny looking, don't you think? But not as funny as feet." She bent forward to look at her feet, which almost made her slide off the stool again. Lucien steadied her. Her gaze moved to his hands.

"Not yours," Darcy said.

Darcy saw the grin that twisted his beautiful mouth. She wanted to kiss him breathless and actually felt herself moving toward him.

"Not mine what?" There was humor in his tone.

His lips were moving, but she didn't hear what he said because she was too busy visualizing her tongue in his mouth.

"Darcy?"

"Um."

"Not mine what?"

Oh right, hands.

"Your hands are beautiful."

His expression turned his eyes darker, and the sight of it had the words that were always on the tip of her tongue just tumbling out of her mouth. "You are so fucking beautiful."

He moved into her so close that she felt the stir of his breath against her mouth. The moment faded fast when the man, Kevin, returned.

"Hey, Darcy."

She wanted to hit Kevin because she was fairly certain that had he not walked over, her tongue would now be in Lucien's mouth, but she controlled the urge and smiled. "Hi. Kevin, this is my boss, Lucien. Lucien, Kevin."

Darcy didn't see the look Lucien gave her at referring to him as her boss because she was too busy contemplating how else she could have introduced him.

"Are you ready to go home, Darcy? I'll take you if you are."

He was sweet, Kevin, and she should go with him, but that was a little difficult to do at the moment because Lucien's hands were still on her arms. Before she could come up with an excuse, Lucien said, "I'll take her home. It's on my way."

Kevin seemed to have the sense not to argue with her boss. She was fuzzy from the alcohol, but there was a touch of annoyance in her that Lucien was being so high-handed when he was the one who just that morning had drawn such a harsh line in the sand when it came to their relationship.

Kevin was looking at her expectantly, so she said, "Maybe I'll see you tomorrow. I'm usually here for a bit every night."

"It's a date." He looked at Lucien as he spoke, issuing a silent challenge. Darcy laughed out loud.

"Don't worry about him. He's just my boss. I'm not his type anymore. He can't forgive me for something I did fourteen years ago. I can't blame him, but talk about holding a grudge."

"I'll see you tomorrow then." Kevin leaned over and pressed a kiss on Darcy's lips despite the fact that Lucien was hovering over her like a protective mama. He turned and walked away and Darcy grinned.

"Let's go, Darcy." Lucien started to reach for her purse, but she stopped him.

"I have to get my bag from my office."

"I'll get it," Lucien said before he looked over at Tara. "Can you watch Darcy for a minute? I'll be right back."

"You got it, boss." She dropped a plate of nachos in front of Darcy.

"Eat this while you wait."

"Oh, good call." She was chowing down on chips smothered in cheese when Lucien returned.

"Are you ready?"

She popped the last chip into her mouth and licked her fingers. "Yep."

He reached for her hand and linked their fingers before calling to Tara. "See you tomorrow."

"Night, boss. Night, Darcy."

It was surprisingly cool when they stepped outside. Without having to ask, the valet ran to get Lucien's car and Darcy wondered what it felt like to have so many people ready to do your bidding.

"What are you thinking?"

She turned her head from him to hide her smile because she was one of those minions willing to do absolutely anything for this man. "Nothing."

"Are you feeling okay?"

"Yeah, I won't get sick in your car."

He touched her chin and turned her face to his. "That's not why I asked. I don't give a shit about the car."

"I've seen your car. You're lying."

He said nothing, but the look he was giving her made her blood boil. Clearly she was hallucinating. She was probably face-down in her bathroom dreaming this entire evening. The dream was very realistic; the sound of Lucien's car purring like a large wild cat reverberated down the street seconds before the sleek black car came to a stop in front of them.

"Sixty-nine Charger, right?" Darcy asked.

She didn't miss the flash of pride in his eyes before he said, "Sixty-eight."

"I imagine it costs a pretty penny to have this car in the city since I'm sure you don't street-park her."

He flashed her a smile. "Worth every penny."

Lucien reached for the door and helped Darcy in, going so far as to buckle her into her seat before coming around and folding himself into the driver's side. A moment later they were cruising down the street. She leaned her head against the window and closed her eyes. In her imagination, they were on a date and were on their way home to make love. The idea of it was so raw that Darcy felt lust sear her nerve endings. She must have made a sound because Lucien asked her what she was thinking.

She answered without thought: "About you."

When she realized what she'd said, she wanted to throw herself out of the moving car. What was wrong with her? It was for this reason that one should avoid drinking alcohol in excess. He was silent for the rest of the ride—he was probably afraid she was going to throw herself at him as soon as he helped her from the car.

She didn't, though. Tempting as the idea was, she kept her hands and her thoughts to herself. They reached her apartment building just off of Times Square and despite her sour mood, she was happy to be home. She loved it here: the crowds, the lights, and the general chaos. It was what had attracted her to this section of the city; it was hard to feel lonely when there was so much around you. They climbed the stairs to the third floor. When they reached her apartment door, he seemed in almost a hurry to be free of her. If he were in such a rush, then why the hell had he driven her home? She felt the anger again, but tried to bank it because, regardless of what motivated him, he had seen her home safely. She unlocked her door and stepped inside. Lucien made no move to follow her in.

"Are you going to be okay?" Even his voice sounded strained. She felt the tears and hated herself for them.

"I'm fine. Thanks for the ride home."

He silently studied her, his hands moving into the pockets of his trousers. She couldn't read him, but she guessed he was trying to determine the shortest amount of time he needed to stay without looking rude. She was about to put him out of his misery when he reached for the door.

"See you tomorrow."

He closed the door before she even had time to answer, the click of the door latch echoing like a gun blast in her quiet apartment. She leaned up against it and let the tears fall for being so fucking foolish when it came to Lucien.

Chapter Eight

Darcy wasn't sure how she managed to avoid Lucien for the next week. She hadn't asked him to interfere that night with Kevin, but he'd done so anyway, and now she suspected that he was avoiding her.

When he'd forwarded her an invitation to a function that she was to attend, her first thought was that he was asking her to go with him, but then sanity returned and she assumed she was to go in his place. She learned neither was true when she checked his calendar and saw he had the event penciled in. It was like a double slap in the face and because of it, she decided to take the rest of the day off and go shopping. She needed a dress, and even better, he wasn't there to tell her she couldn't. Childish, yes, but she wasn't above it. She might even buy dinner and charge it back to him, because if he had a problem with that he'd be forced to suck it up and talk to her. She was smiling as she shut down her computer.

The annual restaurateur guild gala was a huge event every year and was the perfect opportunity for Darcy to meet the vendors that she was working with on a daily basis. Lucien had been tempted to ask Darcy to come with him, but things between them had been off ever since that night a week ago when he'd driven her home, so he'd asked one of his countless lady friends. He always prided himself on being an even-tempered person, but ever since Darcy had returned, he'd been acting like a complete lunatic.

He could be honest with himself and acknowledge that he was acting like a mental patient because despite everything that had happened between them, he still wanted Darcy as wildly as he had when they were teenagers. But being a contrary son of a bitch, every time he entertained the idea of going down that road with her again, his self-preservation kicked in to remind him of how callously she had walked away from everything they had planned.

He was just getting a drink for his date when he lifted his head and almost dropped the glass of wine he was holding. His heart took off in a gallop. Darcy. She was a vision in white, the flowing dress hinting at the small but toned body under it. She looked ethereal: like an angel who had just fallen from the heavens. She was exquisite.

And then his eyes landed on the man who'd followed her in. He was interrupted from spearing the man with his glare when his date stepped up next to him.

"Lucien?" His jaw clenched, but he pulled his attention from Darcy and turned to his date.

To his surprise, his voice didn't betray what he was really feeling: jealousy so severe it twisted his gut. "Let's go find a corner."

———◆———

It was like she was in one of those nightmares where she was standing in the middle of the school cafeteria naked. In reality, no one was staring at her. She wasn't getting pointed at while people whispered behind their hands, but hell if it didn't feel that way.

Darcy unconsciously ran her palms down the sides of her dress while she attempted to calm her wildly beating heart. She had never before been to an event like this. Sookie's had been successful, but it was a small family-run business. The people in this room ran 95 percent of the restaurants in the city—she had done a bit of research to prepare.

Despite her nerves, she took a minute to admire the room with its cloth-covered tables and exquisite place settings accented with huge fresh flower arrangements. The people in the room were dressed in labels she had only ever seen in magazines. She felt terrified and excited all at once.

"Want a drink?"

She turned to her date: Kevin. She enjoyed Kevin's company and as luck would have it, he also happened to own the Smoothie Hut—a chain of them, apparently—and was coming to the event anyway. It was childish but she was glad it was Kevin who was her date, what with how well he and Lucien had hit it off. It was a small dig, but a very gratifying one. Maybe his sea-green eyes didn't send her body into chaos with a look, but he definitely had potential. He was nice, funny, and sexy with his unruly chestnut-brown hair.

"Wine, please," she said.

"I'll be right back."

She scanned the room for Lucien because she was hoping to get him to make the introductions, but she spotted him in a corner with his date and business seemed to be the last thing on his mind.

A table was set up with name tags, which was an enormous help, so she crossed the room and retrieved both hers and Kevin's. He returned with their drinks just as she spotted a vendor she had spoken to the other day, so she squared her shoulders and walked over to introduce herself.

"You did that very well. Have you spoken to everyone you were hoping to?" Kevin asked an hour later.

"I think so. It wasn't so bad after the first introduction." She squeezed his hand. "Thanks for being my wingman."

"My pleasure." He looked at her empty glass. "Dinner is going to start in a minute. Would you like another glass of wine?"

"Yes, please."

He hesitated for a moment before he brushed his lips over her cheek. "I'll be right back."

She watched him go, and her heart beat just a little bit faster.

"You're certainly making your way through the male population."

And then her heart stopped altogether before it lurched into a rapid rhythm. She turned to Lucien as his words settled over her and anger came to the fore. "As someone once so eloquently stated, my personal life is none of your damn business."

Her words had the desired effect as Lucien's eyes went dark with anger before he turned without another word and walked away. She wasn't sure what it said about her that she actually derived pleasure from that. And then she worked to put Lucien out of her mind before her date returned. But all through dinner she stewed. Not only had he not introduced her to *his* vendors, but he implied she was being a slut because she made the contacts on her own. She was so angry she finally sought him out. His date was draped over him like a fucking poncho. He eyed her coolly, and she was just as cold when she asked, "Can we talk?"

He removed his date easily and beckoned Darcy to a quiet corner.

"Yes?"

"Are you calling me a whore because I'm reaching out to the people you asked me to reach out to? Was this not why you asked me here tonight?"

She saw guilt flash in his eyes, but she was fucking done with his bullshit.

"I made a mistake almost half my life ago. I thought we were over this, but clearly you aren't, so let me offer you some advice: fucking get over it," she said.

"Maybe I can't."

"Then I'll quit, because I've put myself through enough regret and guilt over what happened and I let you get your digs in because I owed you that. But I'm not going to pay penance for the rest of my life for a decision I made when I was a scared kid. Fucking grow up, Lucien, because you're the one in the wrong now, but you are old enough to know better."

And then she turned with a sweep of white and walked away with her head held high.

———

Lucien paced his office, but his guilt just weighed him down. He couldn't believe he'd actually implied that Darcy was a whore last night. What the fuck? Maybe he had a brain tumor, but he knew that wasn't true. He'd only started acting like a complete douche the day Darcy came back into his life. He knew what provoked him, and as much as he'd like to say it was his anger or his need for self-preservation, it wasn't either. He was fucking jealous—so jealous of any man that touched her—so of course being the mature adult that he was, he called her a whore.

He hadn't slept a wink because he was trying to figure out how to apologize to her, really apologize. She was right. He was the one in the wrong and he did know better. He pulled a hand through his hair before he walked to the door and yanked it open. He had given her the office just next to his and he found her at her desk working.

"Could we talk for a minute?"

She looked up, and like it was programmed into her, she smiled, but damn if it didn't look genuine.

"Sure."

He walked into her office, but didn't sit because he was feeling too edgy.

"I'm sorry. I've been a dick."

Her response to that was to lean back in her chair and link her fingers. "Go on."

"You aren't going to make this easy, are you?"

"I don't think so, no."

He had to grin at her honesty. "I have forgiven you."

"Really? I'm not getting that. I think you want to forgive me, but you just can't. Any opportunity you have to knock me down, you take it. That isn't forgiveness, that's revenge. I get it. I hurt you, but that was fourteen years ago. We aren't those people anymore."

"You're right."

"I want to work here. I want to work for you. I want you in my life, Lucien, because you were my best friend once. I've never had, then or now, anyone who meant to me what you did."

He moved to sit on the edge of her desk as a grin tugged at his mouth. "I guess you are going to make this easy. You always did have a way of getting right to the heart of the matter and at the same time letting me off the hook."

"I can't continue to put myself in a position to get knocked down by you, particularly when my feet aren't steady enough on their own."

"I'm sorry, Darcy. I am really, truly sorry. I want you here. And you are right. That was then and this is now. Will you give me another chance?"

She rolled her eyes heavenward, something she'd often used to do when she forgave him, before she said, "Okay."

He started for the door, but looked at her over his shoulder. "Lunch?"

"Sorry, I already have plans."

———◦———

Darcy sat in Allegro listening to Kevin tell her about his day when she felt a sizzling down her spine and just knew that Lucien had arrived. It was a sad state of affairs when her body reacted more to someone clear across the room than the very nice man sitting next to her.

Darcy had been out with Kevin four times in the past week and she so wanted to feel that spark, wanted to move on with her life. He was such a good guy. But it wasn't him her mind turned to, even when he was talking to her like he was now. She was pathetic, truly pathetic.

And then she saw Lucien doing his walk-through, and immediately her body was vibrating with excitement. She knew Lucien's eyes were on her, so she kept her gaze on Kevin. Yet her nipples had grown hard and she refused to acknowledge the ache between her legs was due to Lucien undressing her with his eyes from across the room. And then she looked over at Lucien. The sexy, smug bastard winked at her. Winked!

Yep, she was pathetic. Kevin never stood a chance.

———◦———

It was after her near orgasm from a simple look a week ago that the sexual banter between her and Lucien began. He knew she had been responsive. All too often he would stand just a touch too close, his arm would brush her, or his finger would trail a line down her neck. But it was the looks, the ones that said, "I've seen you naked before and I want to again," that were the hardest for her. Every time he gave her that look she wanted to tackle him to the floor and devour him. She suspected, but didn't know for certain, that he was battling the same feelings. She hoped so, because it wasn't right for only her to suffer, even if it were an exquisite torture.

That same day Lucien watched as Darcy struggled to get the printer working. Even from his distance he could hear the cursing, which made him smile. It had been a week since their relationship had taken a very pleasant turn. She was still just as feisty as he remembered and it wasn't hard for him to recall why he had fallen for her in the first place. Their sparring was verbal foreplay and he fucking craved it.

His eyes moved over her. Her body was nothing like the one he had known, with curves that his hands itched to touch. Her hair was up, though he preferred it down, and tendrils were falling out of the twist. He remembered vividly the sight of it spread out over his pillow.

He had to admit that she was still just as interesting to him as she had been at fourteen. Despite everything, she was still his Darcy—sweet, witty, and guileless, except at the moment. She looked about ready to torch the printer, so he moved to help her. As he approached, she was actually staring into the paper tray, yelling at the creatures that lived inside it.

He chuckled, which must have taken her by surprise, because she leaped backward and landed on his foot.

"Fuck!" he cursed.

"Sorry."

He looked down at her strappy sandals with heels high enough to stake a vampire and had a vision of those legs draped over his shoulders. Instantly, he was hard.

"I was going to offer to help you. The printer can be temperamental, but now I'm bleeding out from a stab wound."

She didn't miss a beat. "It probably didn't even break the skin. What is it you guys say? Rub some dirt into it."

He eyed her shoes. "Those things should be listed as lethal weapons."

"Hardly. There are far cheaper ways to kill someone." She bent to stare into the printer again and Lucien took the opportunity to check out the curve of her ass in the little black skirt she wore.

"Stop checking out my ass and help me."

Not at all repentant for getting caught staring, he replied easily, "It's a paper jam."

He thought he was being helpful and when she straightened slowly, he entertained the notion that she was struggling with the need to throw herself into his arms in gratitude.

One look at her face, though, and he knew he wasn't going to be copping a feel.

"Your powers of deduction are astounding. Seriously, you should give a seminar on mastering the obvious."

He tried not to laugh, but he lost that battle. And she responded by flaying a layer of skin off him with her sharp tongue. "I know it's a paper jam, Sherlock, I just can't find it."

"It's usually in the back," Lucien said as he reached for the back of the printer, his arm brushing up against her on purpose. Darcy's inhaled breath in response had his balls tightening. He dislodged the paper and pulled it free.

He turned to her with a smug smile, which she returned with uncanny accuracy before she said, "Thanks. I almost lost my cool."

"Almost?"

A slight smile touched her lips. "I should go restart my print job."

"Probably, unless you can get the little men in the printer to do it."

"Brownies."

"What?"

She laughed. "Not the baked goods, the little mischievous mystical creatures."

"They live in my printer?"

"Maybe." She started away, but stopped and turned to him. "Thanks."

"Have dinner with me tonight."

She eyed him through her lashes before she said, "You're on." And then she turned and disappeared into her office.

———◆———

He took her to a greasy spoon where they ate pancakes and meat loaf. It was the most ridiculous dinner she had ever had and the most enjoyable.

When they were on the curb outside the diner, Darcy turned to Lucien and asked, "Do you do that often—have breakfast and dinner together?"

"Sometimes I can't decide what I want, so I have both."

Remembering how food was so limited in the orphanage, she couldn't really blame him. He must have noticed the change in her, because his voice softened. "Would you take a walk with me?"

Emotion moved up her throat to choke her as she remembered just how many times they'd escaped by going for long walks.

He pushed his hands into the front pockets of his trousers, but held his elbow out to her. She slipped her arm through it before they started along. The night was hot, but the humidity had dropped. It could have been a thousand degrees and she would have absolutely loved it.

"Times Square." His head turned in her direction and the impact of those eyes made her heart flip over in her chest. "What's it like living there? It must be madness on New Year's Eve."

"The first few, I loved it; now I make sure I'm elsewhere in the city."

She could tell he wanted to ask something, but seemed to be debating with himself if he should.

"What do you want to know?" she asked.

"How long have you lived there?"

"I moved in right after college."

She knew what he was thinking, as clearly as if he were speaking the words out loud: What had happened in her life during the years that had separated them? How had she managed college? He didn't ask, though, and his silence in response hurt. She moved on. "Where do you live?"

"The Upper East Side."

"I bet it's beautiful."

"Maybe you'll come and see it sometime."

And in that moment he wasn't the successful and confident man he had become, but the seventeen-year-old boy wishing to share a piece of his present with a part of his past. She needed him to know she understood that this was a form of affirmation, so she said, "I'll bring the pudding."

She couldn't read what he was thinking, but she knew that he was working very hard to maintain his control. His voice sounded almost strained.

"It's late; I'll get you a cab." But before he did so, he kissed her and she responded out of instinct. His lips moved over hers, molding to her own, and then he licked the seam of her lips before his tongue swept her mouth. He sucked her tongue into his mouth as his arms moved around her to hold her close. Before she wanted him to, he drew away from her, but his fingers lifted to trace the line of her jaw.

A cab appeared as if conjured and Lucien opened the back door for her.

"See you in the morning, Caterpillar." He closed the door before she could reply. She turned to look back at him standing on the curb watching her, his hands in the front pockets of his trousers and his expression so serious. They were older now, but he was still her Lucien and she was still his Caterpillar. She smiled all the way home.

———◆———

The following morning Lucien paced in his office. He was fairly certain that he had lost his mind; it was the only explanation for why he'd kissed her when they were still working on being friends. But he liked her—hell, he was able to admit to himself that he loved her. He always had. Being around her again brought it all back, and not just the bad stuff. Even as kids they'd had a connection that so few ever experienced and despite everything it was just as strong.

He wanted to take her out, wanted her on his arm, wanted to claim her. It sounded barbaric, but the need to make her his own was as strong now as it had been in that orphanage.

He heard her arrive and gave her a few minutes to get settled. Once he reached her office he could tell just by looking at her that she had been having the same argument with herself over the wisdom of traveling down that road again. And he knew she was going to come to the same conclusion that he had—they could fight it all they wanted, but it was a battle they wouldn't win.

Her eyes lifted to his and she smiled like she'd used to, so effortlessly and sincere. "Good morning."

"I have a fund-raiser tonight. Will you come with me?"

If possible, her smile grew even warmer. "I would love to." And then it looked as if she remembered something, adding, "I'll have to meet you there because I have a prior engagement."

He didn't like that at all. He snarled at her, "What engagement?"

"It's just a commitment I've made, but I'll be yours for the rest of the evening."

Some of his ire left him. A man could dream.

"It starts at seven at the New York Public Library on Fifth. I'll meet you inside at the entrance to Astor Hall."

"I'll be there."

He started out of her office, but peered at her from the door. "Oh, and it's black tie," he said with a smile.

"Of course it is."

The cemetery was empty and Darcy was thankful for that, since she liked her time alone with Sister Anne. She carried with her a tray of plants and her shovel and gloves. This was her way to remember not only Sister Anne, but Lucien too. She felt closer to him here, touching the same stone he did countless times throughout the year, walking the same path that he walked.

She'd had only two years with Sister Anne—and, sadly, for much of that time the nun had been battling cancer—but the woman had left her mark. In a world where even the clergy were caught up in appearances and politics, Sister Anne had been a refreshing change because she was more interested in what was on the inside of a person.

Lucien often referred to her as his mother and, having witnessed their relationship, it was a beautiful thing to see. Darcy envied him that even as she felt happy for him to have found it. Sister Anne was more a mother to Lucien than her own mother had ever been to her.

Darcy settled in front of the grave and pulled the dying plants from the soil before she started to plant the new ones: yellow lantana, purple heliotrope, pale pink petunias, and white stock. As was her habit, she filled Sister Anne in on current events.

"It's funny, but it doesn't feel like fourteen years have passed. It's not the same as it was, but I think it has the potential to be even better." She reached for the small watering can and watched as the water beaded on the flower petals.

"I think he's happy, in his way, and I know you would be happy with the man he has become. You did a fine job with him, Sister Anne." She checked her watch, prompting Darcy to rise. "I should go. I'm going to be late to this function and Mr. Black doesn't tolerate tardiness." A smile touched her lips at the memory.

She kissed the gravestone in farewell before she gathered her things and headed from the cemetery.

Lucien paced the entrance of Astor Hall, checking his watch every few minutes. He was going to wear a trench in the marble floor. She was late, which was completely out of character for Darcy. He wondered what was keeping her. Whatever it was must be very important to her. The fact that he didn't know what that something was, particularly whether it involved a man, made him clench his jaw.

Ten minutes passed; just as he was reaching for his phone, the door opened and in she walked. He had planned on lecturing her about tardiness, but the words fled at the sight of her. She was breathtaking. Her black gown hung low in the front and dipped in the back, hugging her curves and sweeping the ground; but it was the slit up the left leg that made his mouth go dry. With her hair up, her delicate neck was exposed and suddenly he wanted his mouth right where her neck and shoulder met. He knew how it drove her wild.

The sight of her was like getting sucker punched, so to help regain his balance, he decided to throw her off hers. Instead of telling her how beautiful she looked, he furrowed his brow and said, "You're late." He brought her hand to his lips and pressed a kiss in her palm. "I forgive you, though, because you look absolutely stunning."

A softness entered her expression and her smile hit him right in the middle of his chest. He didn't want to let her go, so he kept her hand in his.

"Shall we?"

They walked to the third floor where the fund-raiser was being held in an astonishingly ornate room with murals painted on the stucco walls that were made to look like wood panels. As they moved through the crowd toward the bar, Lucien was stopped by an older gentleman. He had to be pushing seventy, and yet he was fit and rather handsome in a distinguished way; but it was the way that Lucien tensed when the man stepped into their path that clued Darcy in that this was no friend.

"Lucien Black."

"Judge."

"I'm surprised to see you here; I would have thought for sure you had more entertaining pursuits than supporting the arts."

"Which goes to show you know nothing about me." Lucien tightened his hold on Darcy's hand and she could practically feel the anger pulsing from him.

"Who is your friend? She's not really your type, is she?"

Darcy stepped in at that moment because she had the sense that Lucien was about to punch the older man in the face.

"Darcy MacBride, and you are?"

He didn't seem to hear her, because he simply stared with an odd look on his face. And then, as if his brain kick-started again, a smile spread over his face, but it was far from warm as he reached for her hand and brought it to his lips.

"And what is such a beautiful creature doing with the likes of him?"

Darcy pulled her hand away and her voice turned cold. "Lucien, I'd like a drink."

Not missing a beat, Lucien pulled her from the judge.

"Nicely done, Darcy," he whispered in her ear, and she looked up at him, surprised to see humor had already replaced his anger.

"What a jackass," she said in reply.

A short while later, Darcy sipped her wine and watched Lucien talk with someone important across the room. She hadn't been able to move her thoughts from their greeting earlier. It wasn't so much what he'd said, but how he'd looked at her, like she was a tall glass of water and he was a thirsty man.

His head turned in her direction and he smiled, a secret little smile that made desire stir in her gut. In the next minute he was walking toward her, and his determined look made her body pulse. He reached her and grabbed her hand before leading her away from the crowd. He found an empty room and pulled her into it before closing the door behind them.

"If you don't stop looking at me like that, I'm going to give in, Darcy, and to hell with the consequences."

Even though she already knew the answer, she heard herself ask, "Looking like what?"

He moved so close that their bodies were practically touching. His breath fanned out along her skin as his scent filled her. "Like you want to devour me."

She did. Heaven help her, but she did.

"Tell me I'm wrong," he demanded.

The words wouldn't come and she even went so far as to lick her lips in anticipation. His eyes moved to her mouth and she saw how hard he was fighting it.

"Kiss me," she said.

He needed no other encouragement and yanked her up against him before settling his mouth over hers. She was like a junkie, craving his taste. He licked her lips and when she sighed, he plunged in, tasting her with a thoroughness that left her weak. His hands moved over her bare back, claiming her as hers moved under his jacket to roam over the corded muscles of his back.

He wanted to push her up against the wall, lift her skirt, and sink into her, but self-preservation made him pull back. Her eyes were still closed and desire had brought a rosy hue to her cheeks. She was so fucking beautiful, so goddamn edible, but sex was the easy part; it was all the rest they'd had trouble with.

"I shouldn't have done that."

"I wanted you to," she said simply.

"I wanted to too, but—"

Darcy finished what he intended to say.

"Not a good idea."

"I'm glad you feel the same way." But he wasn't glad. He was actually pissed that she could even suggest that something as explosive as that kiss could be a bad idea. He ignored the fact that he had been about to say that very same thing to her.

"We should probably get back out there. There are still elbows to rub," she said, and though she sounded like she was trying for funny, it fell flat.

Regret, that was what he felt—but it was for the best. He reached for her hand, which had grown cold, and linked their fingers.

"I'm sorry."

She turned those eyes on him and he saw a brightness there, as if from tears, but she smiled and squeezed his hand. "Me too."

Chapter Nine

"Lucien, are you here?"

Darcy was in the middle of finding a file in the cabinet, but looked up to see a woman unlike Lucien's usual preference: wholesome, kindergarten-teacher sweet, with dark hair and eyes. And after Lucien had withdrawn from her the other night, the thought that this woman was involved with him made Darcy feel suddenly sick; unlike the others, Darcy could see herself liking this woman. When the woman turned and saw Darcy, she seemed genuinely surprised.

"Oh, hi. Is Lucien here?"

"No, sorry, he had a lunch meeting."

"Right. I should have called first. I'm Ember. Are you new?"

"Yes, I started a few months ago. I'm Darcy."

Mischief sparkled in the other woman's eyes before she asked, "What's it like working for Lucien?"

"He's actually a pretty fair boss."

"I bet. Well, I don't want to keep you. Could you let him know I stopped by?"

"I will."

She smiled and started away, but stopped and looked back over her shoulder. "Have you had lunch?"

"I was about to."

"Alone?"

"Yeah."

"Would you like company?"

Darcy was completely thrown. It had been a long time since she was on the receiving end of such genuine friendliness.

"I mean, unless you prefer eating alone. I completely understand that."

"No, I'd like to have lunch."

"Oh cool. I know a great little place that's close."

<hr />

The restaurant Ember picked was in the Village, a café that served organic sandwiches and smoothies. It looked a little grassroots, beatnik, and just up Darcy's alley. They checked the blackboard of offerings for the day before grabbing a little bistro table with an umbrella to keep them cool in the bright afternoon sun. Once they were settled, a waitress came over and took their drink orders.

"Those planter boxes are beautiful. What an arrangement. I'm going to try to copy that for my fire escape," Darcy said almost absently.

Ember followed her gaze to the large terra-cotta planters spilling over with color. "You're a gardener."

"I work with what I have."

Ember smiled in reply before she changed the subject. "I didn't realize that Lucien was hiring, though I completely see his need for help. The man is constantly trying to do everything and somehow manages to do so successfully. Me, if I had that many balls in the air, it would be a disaster."

"Can I ask how you know him?" Darcy asked.

"He's good friends with my husband, Trace."

"Trace Montgomery?"

The other woman gave Darcy a questioning look. "Yes. Do you know him?"

"Not really."

Darcy wasn't sure if it was a trick of the sunlight, but it looked as if some of the easy kindness faded from Ember's gaze as she studied her, so Darcy changed the subject.

"Have you lived in Manhattan long?"

"Close to four years. It's expensive, crowded, noisy, dirty, and I love it."

"I agree; there's something about it here that just feels a bit magical."

The waitress stepped up to them to take their order, but something across the street caught Darcy's attention. She barely heard Ember telling the waitress they needed a few more minutes, or ask, "Darcy, what's wrong?"

She was seeing a ghost.

As Ember turned her attention to see what Darcy was staring at, Darcy didn't expect to hear her gasp. She turned to see that Ember had turned pale.

"Do you know her?" Darcy asked.

"That's Heidi Moore, and the man with her is my husband."

Darcy looked back at the couple across the street who were obviously in the middle of an argument. Ember asked after a minute, "How do you know her?"

"Don't you want to walk over there and find out what the hell is going on?"

"I do, but I trust him. His past is riddled with shit and she's a part of that. I'll find out, but not in the middle of day with all these eyes watching."

"That's very . . . wow, I don't think I could do that."

Ember turned her attention to Darcy. "Maybe you just haven't found the right man. So, tell me, how do you know Heidi?"

It wasn't a story she ever told, but there was something about Ember that made Darcy want to unload the burden she'd carried for so long. "This is a conversation best had with wine and lots of it."

Darcy signaled for the waitress, and after their wine was set before them, she took a long sip before she started.

"When I was fourteen, my mom dropped me off at an orphan-age."

Ember caught on immediately. "St. Agnes."

"Yeah, that's how I know of Trace. We were there together for a short time. Anyway, Lucien and I hit it off immediately. For two years we were inseparable and we planned on running away together."

There was sympathy in Ember's eyes when Darcy looked at her; clearly their plans had never come to fruition. "But as you can guess, it didn't work out and part of the reason was that woman."

"I don't understand."

Darcy had given it a lot of thought over the years and con-cluded that someone had to have been watching Lucien and her at St. Agnes and passing on what they were seeing. That would explain the visit from the stranger and how he'd known so much. There had been one person who'd made it her job to know every-one's business and that was the woman currently standing across the street.

Darcy said, "She was instrumental in breaking Lucien and me up."

"How?"

"The day I was supposed to leave with Lucien, a man came to see me. He knew things he couldn't possibly have known. He played on all of my sixteen-year-old insecurities and convinced me that it was in Lucien's best interest to not have me in his life. I listened."

"Oh my God. Who was he?"

"I don't know. I never saw him again, but all the promises he made were lies. I broke Lucien's heart and my own for nothing."

"Have you told Lucien? I mean, now that you're older."

Darcy fiddled with her glass. "I don't know how to have that conversation. How to tell him that I turned my back on everything we'd planned based on the words of a complete stranger." She looked up at Ember. "I hurt him, Ember, really hurt him, and he repaid me by giving me a job. He is better off without me, but while I can say that a thousand times, I just can't seem to let him go."

Ember was silent for a moment, as if in hesitation, so Darcy asked, "What?"

"It seems to me that whether you are good for him or not should be Lucien's call to make. Enough time has passed that maybe you should just talk to him. At the very least you'll be able to put it to rest, but maybe he'll surprise you."

"To what end?"

"Being a woman madly in love with her husband, I recognize the signs in others. You're crazy about him. You owe it to yourself and to him to put the past in the past."

Darcy chuckled and reached for her wine. "Are you always so free with advice?"

"Sorry, it's a problem; I get it from my dad."

"I think I'd like your dad."

After lunch Darcy walked back to the office, but her mind flitted back to the day that had changed everything.

Fourteen years earlier . . .

Darcy was packing, but her hands were shaking from excitement, which was making the job take that much longer. She had a surprise for Lucien and she couldn't think of a better time to tell him than today, the day they were going to start their lives together. She looked over at her clock—she was running late.

Hearing a knock, she called for the person to enter as she checked under her bed to make sure she hadn't left anything.

A man she had never seen before walked in, and with her only experience of men being her mom's friends, fear shot down her spine. He wasn't dressed like her mom's friends, though. He looked fancy—the kind of fancy reserved for holidays and church.

"Darcy?"

"Um, yeah."

"Are you going somewhere?"

Running off with Lucien was still a secret, so Darcy lied. "No."

"No point in lying. I can see for myself that you are packing. You're running away with Lucien, aren't you?"

Even through her fear, Darcy was suspicious of how he knew of them and their plans. Who had told him? And who was he? How did he get in to the building? Who helped him?

The man walked into her room as if he owned it and sat down on her roommate's bed.

"Have you told him about the baby?"

Her body went numb, even as anger burned through her. "How do you know about that?" And then she remembered the day she'd found out she was pregnant. Someone had come into the bathroom when she was waiting for the pregnancy test to show. She'd left the box on the counter while she was in the stall, and when she exited, Heidi had been lurking in the hallway.

"Not important. Do you really think he's going to be happy? He wants to get away from here so he can make something of him-self. How easy do you think that will be when he has to care for you and a baby? I know you know him well enough to know that he'll work whatever job he can to do just that, but is that what

you want for him? Dead-end jobs, all because you wanted a family at your age?"

Darcy felt the tears start—as much as she didn't want to listen, the man was voicing her own thoughts.

"I'm asking you to think of Lucien. If you love him as much as I believe you do, let him go. I will take care of him, look out for him, and make sure he achieves all that he wishes, but I'll only do it if you step out of his life."

"No! Don't ask me to do that. I love him; he's my family. Who are you to him?"

"Someone with his best interests at heart, and I seem to be the only one. You are more concerned about yourself than what's best for Lucien. Will you consider not being so selfish by stepping away and giving him a real chance at happiness?"

"He's happy with me."

"Young love is very fickle. Once he learns about the baby and how his freedom is about to be snatched away, his love will fade—and quickly. Trust me."

Darcy's heart broke as he spoke aloud her greatest fear. She loved Lucien so much, loved him enough to let him go. Yet just thinking of not seeing him again nearly brought her to her knees.

"He's waiting for me. I need to tell him. I have to say good-bye."

"Do you think that's wise?"

She was incredulous and outraged when she accused correctly, "You want him to think I forgot him."

"Yes, his anger will let him break from his past and move on to his future. Do we have a deal?"

Her answer was barely audible, but it was all the man needed before he turned and walked out. Darcy dropped onto her bed. She felt dead inside, but each painful beat of her heart only served to remind her that she wasn't that lucky.

That night Lucien walked around Allegro doing his normal routine check, but there was a part of him that was hoping to find Darcy. He found her sitting in a corner, drinking a glass of wine, completely absorbed in the music. He liked that she appeared to like music as much as he did. Her eyes moved to him as if she knew he was there and a small smile touched her lips.

"Hi."

"Do you mind if I join you?"

She gestured to the free chair across from her. "Please."

"They're great, aren't they?"

Her attention had already turned back to the band when she replied, "Yes." She looked over at him. "Where did you learn to play?"

"There was this guy who played at a club where I was a bouncer. He was brilliant and so content. I think that was what first caught my notice, the peace about him when he played. He told me that music could give me the escape I was looking for. He taught me, and every free moment I had, I practiced."

"You're wonderful—that night at Peacock. I could listen to you all night."

He knew he was staring, but he couldn't help it. She was older and more confident, but even so he could still see the caterpillar she had been. He saw the corner of her mouth lift before she said, "I'll send you a picture."

"You turned into a butterfly."

The sight of the pain that swept her face made his heart twist in his chest. She lowered her eyes. "No, I just traded one cage for another."

"What does that mean?"

She lifted her sad eyes to his. "I made a choice that I have regretted from the very moment I made it. I hurt the only person I ever loved. I'll regret not meeting you that day for the rest of my life."

Pain and anger turned his voice hard. "Why didn't you?"

"Believe it or not, I did it for you. I thought you would be better off without me."

He hadn't meant to grab her arm so hard, but to think she could use such a lame excuse as the reason for breaking his heart just fucking pissed him off. "Why the hell would you think that?"

"He told me he would look out for you, that he would make sure all your dreams came true, but only if I stepped out of your life. I shouldn't have believed him; I shouldn't have been such a fool."

"Who are you talking about?"

Tears filled her eyes. "That's just it, I don't know."

He was so confused at her words that he made no move to stop her when she stood and walked away.

※

Lucien spent a few days at home, stewing. He damn well was going to get answers from Darcy, whether she liked it or not, but he needed to cool off or he was liable to say something that he couldn't take back.

Tara called him on the third day of his absence because a band notorious for causing a ruckus was playing the club and he had completely forgotten. That night he was talking with one of the band members while he scanned the crowd for potential trouble and he found it, though not in the form he'd been expecting.

"Excuse me."

He moved through the dance floor with the skill of someone who spent a lot of time in crowds, but his eyes were totally focused on Darcy, who was dancing up against some guy. Her hair was down, the thick black strands shone like silk, and the man was touching it, fisting it as he moved his hips against her. Her eyes were closed and she seemed lost in the music or the man. Her body swayed in time to the beat. He felt fury, as expected, but also a punch of lust that almost knocked him to his knees.

Darcy loved dancing and she had to admit it felt nice having someone touch her. The man she was currently dancing with was a bit too touchy, but she had learned how to defend herself if needed, thanks to her mother's motley crew of losers.

The music filled her head and wrapped around her as her body moved to it. A tranquility settled over her, like a dream that was just a bit out of focus; real, but illusive. The calm shattered when strong fingers wrapped around her arm, and she knew before she even opened her eyes that it was Lucien. He didn't look happy; in fact, he looked as if he wanted to murder her, slowly. Before she could object to his macho idiocy, the man she was dancing with stepped closer and puffed his chest up like a baboon.

"Hey, man, wait your turn."

The look Lucien leveled on him could have melted steel, but the man didn't take a hint and moved up into Lucien's space. Without a word, Lucien pulled Darcy behind him just before the man threw a punch that landed quite solidly on his jaw.

A red haze filled Darcy's vision and rage consumed her as Lucien's head snapped back from the blow. She started around him, but she had no idea what she intended to do. She didn't get far before Lucien turned his head and gave her a look that froze her in her tracks. He moved with a speed she'd never seen in him, and seconds later, the man was flat on the ground.

Lucien, it seemed, had only one thing in mind next and that was screaming at her until she was deaf. He reached for her hand and pulled her from the dance floor, dragging her across the club and down the hall to their offices. He pushed her into his, then closed and locked the door and glared at her.

She could admit to herself that his stare was very unnerving as sweat dripped down between her breasts. When he only continued to stare, she found her own temper stirring.

"What the hell is your problem?" she demanded.

"What the hell were you doing out there?" She actually felt her hair blow back from her face by the force of his bellow.

"I was dancing."

"Dancing? No, that wasn't dancing."

"Oh really, so what would you call it?"

"If you want to fuck, there are more private places for you to do so. Unless, of course, you want an audience."

Shit. He wanted to take it back as soon as it came out of his mouth. Her reaction was immediate: the color drained from her face and her eyes grew wide with hurt and then hate.

"Consider this my resignation." She flipped him off and then strode from the room.

It took him a minute to react because he couldn't believe what had just come out of his mouth. When he realized she was clear down the hall, he ran after her. "I'm sorry. Jesus, I'm sorry, Darcy."

Rage filled her as she turned on him and pushed him with both hands, and it was only because she caught him off guard that he slammed back into the wall.

"Who the fuck do you think you are? I don't see you for fourteen years and you call me a whore, twice! I may be a lot of things, but I'm not a whore." She turned from him, but hadn't gotten far when he grabbed for her and pulled her to him.

"What the fuck does that mean?" he demanded.

"I hurt you, I get it. You want payback, but you hurt me too."

"How?" he spat.

"You believed that I went with my mother, my fucking mother. You knew what it was like for me there, but you believed without question. I didn't show up, sure, but you didn't even try to find out why. You knew how I felt about you. You knew what we had was real, but you never demanded to know why I didn't come." Darcy was surprised at the level of her pain. She had been the one in the wrong, but Lucien had been wrong too.

"You loved me, but not enough to fight for me. If it had been you who didn't show, I would have hunted you down and forced you to tell me why to my face. You gave up without a fight."

And then she was gone, but all Lucien could do was stand there and watch her go because his mind was still trying to understand what he had just heard.

For two days Lucien tried to make sense of Darcy's cryptic words before he decided to visit Sister Margaret. Voluntarily, no less. Darcy regretted not meeting him that day, and had been encouraged not to by someone, but who? There was one person at St. Agnes who knew everything and saw everything: Sister Margaret, the evil bitch.

He pulled up in front of the nursing home near the West Side Highway and climbed from his car. He had called ahead as a courtesy and was surprised that visiting turned out to be fairly easy. A volunteer escorted him down the dingy hallway and for a moment he had a pang of sympathy that Sister Margaret was to spend her final days in such a hole. This thought was immediately dismissed when he heard that all too familiar screeching coming from a room clear down the corridor.

"Charming, isn't she?" Lucien muttered, earning him a smile from the volunteer.

As soon as he saw her, a flood of memories slammed into him, none of which were good. Her beady eyes looked from the orderly she was reprimanding to him, and recognition showed on her face.

"Lucien Black. What the hell are you doing here?"

"Nice to see you too."

"Don't back talk me, boy. I may be old, but you'll show me respect."

Lucien bit his tongue; he refused to take the bait and instead tried to suffocate her with kindness.

"You're looking well." For a soul-sucking demon.

"I look like shit and you damn well know it. What do you want?"

Right to the point. He had to like that about the old bird. "Do you remember Darcy MacBride?"

"The girl that thought you walked on water."

His anger turned his voice very cold. "I thought *she* walked on water."

Sister Margaret waved her hand in dismissal. "Whatever. So what do you want to know?"

"The day I left, someone came to see her. Do you know who?"

An odd look passed over her face before she turned her attention to the volunteer who had escorted Lucien and said, "Fetch us some iced tea, sweetened, and cookies."

And just as regally, she dismissed both the volunteer and the orderly before looking back at Lucien. He was surprised by her request since the place really wasn't very nice, but he knew they would bring the tea and cookies because they were afraid not to.

"Well, sit down. I'm going to get a neck cramp."

He eyed the pillow and thought how very easy it would be to suffocate the old bitch, but then he wouldn't learn what he had come seeking. He sat.

"A man came to St. Agnes that day, but he was a sneaky bastard. Someone let him in, so he bypassed the check-in. My guess is he didn't want anyone to know he was there."

"How do you know, then?"

"Darcy came to my office afterward. She didn't go into detail, but the sight of her was heartbreaking and coming from me, you know that means something."

"What the fuck did he say to her?"

"Do not use that language with me, boy. Did you learn nothing from Sister Anne?" She waited for the volunteer who had returned with a plate of cookies and reached for one before turning her beady eyes back on him. "But to answer your question, I don't know."

"And you never saw him?"

"No, I didn't, but like I said, someone must have snuck him in."

"Any ideas who?"

"The same girl who conveniently distracted you at the same exact time the man was visiting with Darcy."

Realization that he and Darcy had been played was a bitter fucking pill. "Heidi."

And then guilt quickly followed like a kick in the gut. All this time he'd blamed Darcy, but she was just a pawn, someone hurt as much if not more than he had been. Knowing how insecure Darcy had been at sixteen—to be confronted by an adult would have made her question herself. Her words from the other night were still hammering in his head because she was right. He hadn't fought for her.

"Thanks," was about all Lucien felt compelled to say, but the next words from Sister Margaret stopped him as he made to leave.

"I think Sister Anne would be proud to see the man you've become."

Lucien was already experiencing an odd tightness in his chest thinking about Darcy and then a burning started behind his eyes as he glanced back at Sister Margaret. She looked as uncomfortable as he felt.

"I'll deny I ever said that. Now get lost."

He needed a drink, but first he needed to make a call. He waited until he was in his car before he dialed Josh.

"Hey, Lucien. Sorry I haven't gotten back to you, but I am looking into Darcy."

"That's not why I'm calling. How do you feel about puzzles?"

There was humor over the line when Josh replied, "I like them. It's part of the PI gig. Why? You got one for me?"

"Yeah, I need you to find a man who visited Darcy at St. Agnes fourteen years ago, but I've got next to nothing for you to go on."

"Sounds like a challenge."

Lucien started at the beginning and told him everything he knew.

"Ember, could I have a moment?" Charles turned for his office without waiting for a response. He had just settled at his desk as Ember appeared.

"Yes?"

"Please have a seat. I asked you in here because I know of the situation with Dane Carmichael from last year and I wanted to make sure he wasn't still bothering you."

Ember was surprised by his question as well as the sincerity she saw in his expression.

"No, Dane hasn't bothered me since that night."

"Good." Charles's grin was both charming and contrite. "I have made a lot of mistakes in my life and have failed my family countless times. I'm trying to change that."

Ember was speechless and a bit uncomfortable with the direction of their conversation. Charles was obviously feeling it too when he hurriedly added, "That's all I wanted to say."

Ember had just reached the door when he said, "The woman who was here some time back, Heidi Moore, I believe she's an acquaintance of my nephew's. Be careful; she's trouble."

Ember waited until she was back at her desk before she let out a shaky breath. She had the feeling that there was more than concern coming from Charles. He was trying to tell her something, but what? Ember remembered vividly when Dane and Heidi had come to see her at Clover last year. What was their connection? Ember was going to find out.

<hr />

Lucien had drunk his body weight in Scotch over the past two days and still he couldn't make the guilt or the pain fade. He had blamed Darcy for breaking his heart, and yet the truth was that he hadn't had enough faith in them and let things lie for too long.

Who the hell was the man who had talked to Darcy fourteen years ago, and why had he been so determined to keep Darcy away? The idea of beating a confession out of Heidi almost put a smile on his face.

An hour later he tracked Heidi down at her apartment in the Village. He wasn't surprised that he only needed to ring the bell and she buzzed him in without bothering to find out who he was. She was the reckless type. In the stairwell on the way up, he passed Todd on his way down. He wondered briefly if Todd lived in the building, but then he reached Heidi's door and immediately dismissed Todd from his thoughts.

She looked genuinely surprised when she opened the door. Who was it she had been expecting? But then, looking in the face of the bitch who'd helped to break him and Darcy up sent his temper soaring.

"Lucien Black, what a pleasant surprise."

"Heidi, you're looking as slutty as ever. Still chasing after what you can't have?"

Her eyes flashed hot, but her voice remained even when she said, "No, I get what I want now."

"I bet." He moved into her apartment and noticed that, though it was nicely furnished, the place was filthy.

"Looks a bit like a pig pen. I guess you're spending too much time in the bedroom." He looked back at her and eyed her from head to toe before he added, "Probably not making much these days. You're getting a bit tired around the eyes."

She snapped. "What the hell do you want?"

"Who put you up to kissing me?"

It took her a minute to understand what he was asking, but then an evil smile curved her lips. "Wouldn't you like to know?"

"I'm only going to ask you once more."

She laughed. "Or what?"

He kept his voice even and soft, making the threat all the more frightening. "I'll find another way to get you to talk. I've had a very colorful past and I've learned a lot about how to persuade people to tell their secrets. To me you are simply someone who has information I want and I will get it from you in any way necessary." He stepped closer to her before he added, "With what you cost me, painfully would be preferable."

Heidi's eyes widened with fear before she caught herself. He could see the wheels turning in her head and he suspected that telling him what he wanted to know would jeopardize her carefully constructed future plans. His gut knew what she said next would be a lie.

"I don't know. I never saw him before or since. He gave me a hundred bucks to hold the door open and keep you distracted."

"But you didn't live at St. Agnes then."

"I liked to visit."

That was bullshit, but he let it pass. "Why don't I believe you?"

"Because you're cynical."

He grabbed her arm so hard that he knew it was going to bruise, but rage fueled him. She wasn't going to give him what he wanted. "Hurt me if you must, but I don't know," she said.

The door to the apartment opened, which made Lucien release his hold on Heidi. He had been about to issue a threat when a boy walked in. Heidi had been pregnant when she'd first arrived at the orphanage and seeing the boy who was the spitting image of Trace had the threat dying on his tongue.

"Ah fuck."

"Looks just like his daddy, doesn't he?" Her words dripped with smugness.

Chapter Ten

You can't eat the raw dough, Chelsea."

"Why not? It's delicious."

"Don't you think it tastes better cooked?"

"I like it both ways."

Ember grinned in response because she happened to agree. The sound of the front door opening made Chelsea squeal before she took off into a run.

"Trace!" she screamed.

His laughter carried down the hall to Ember, as did the sound of his body crashing against the door. Moments later, Trace entered the kitchen.

"Hey, beautiful."

"Hey. Where's Chelsea?"

"Some movie caught her eye."

"I guess there goes my helper."

He pulled her into his arms and kissed her quite soundly. "What are you making?"

"Chicken pot pie."

"Nice. I'll be out to help you in a minute."

"Okay." He pressed his lips to hers once more and then turned and walked out of the kitchen. It had been a few days since Ember's talk with Charles, and over a week since she'd seen Trace with Heidi. She had hoped he would voluntarily share with her what was going on, but so far he hadn't.

It was more than a little disturbing to learn of the part that Heidi had played in Darcy and Lucien's past. It seemed that Heidi was an instigator. What was it she held over Trace that kept her on the periphery of his life?

Ten minutes later, Trace had still not returned, so Ember walked back to the bedroom to see what was taking him so long. She reached the office and heard his clipped, angry voice. She couldn't make out what he was saying, but he was definitely pissed. Not wanting to eavesdrop, she returned to the kitchen, but wondered if he was talking to Heidi.

Trace appeared a few minutes later and he looked completely at ease. Had she not heard his argument, she would never have believed he had just had one.

The question tumbled from her mouth. "What took you so long?"

Something passed over his face. "I needed to make a quick call. Can I help you?"

"Is something wrong? Is it Heidi?"

Surprise swept his face. "Why do you ask that?"

"Just something Charles said to me."

"What did he say?"

"He warned me that Heidi was trouble, so I just assumed that she was up to something."

"Charles warned you about Heidi?" Trace asked, genuinely surprised.

"Yeah, why?"

"I wasn't aware he knew her."

"Is it Heidi?"

He looked her right in the eyes. "No, Ember."

Her heart sank. It was on the tip of her tongue to tell him that she had seen him with Heidi, but the words just wouldn't come. She knew whatever was going on, he was trying to protect her from it. The fact that he had to lie to her to do that was something she had to overlook. "Okay."

He smiled, but it didn't quite reach his eyes. "What can I do?"

Ember woke in the morning to an empty bed. She quietly looked through the apartment, but Trace was not home. Chelsea was in the living room eating cereal and watching television.

"Good morning, Chelsea."

"Hi, Ember. Look, I made my own breakfast."

"Where's Trace?"

"He left a while ago. Said he had things to do before his fight tonight." Trace was an amateur fighter and, though he didn't fight as often as he used to, he still liked getting into the ring a few times a month.

"Oh, okay. I'm going to make some coffee."

"I want some."

"You bet."

She started for the kitchen when a wave of nausea hit out of nowhere. She hurried down the hall and just made it to the toilet. After she puked she went to the sink to splash some water on her face and caught the ghostly reflection looking back at her in the mirror. How long had it been since she'd had her period? When realization dawned, excitement almost made her call Trace immediately, but she decided it would be better to know for sure before she said anything. She called a drugstore and made arrangements to have several pregnancy tests delivered to the apartment. An hour later, she was looking at three positive results. She didn't trust it, though. She wanted to be absolutely certain, so she called her doctor.

She was lucky to get an appointment later that same day and she battled excitement as she sat in the waiting room. The sound of her name brought her to her feet and she followed the nurse to the scale where she was weighed. She was handed a paper robe.

"Undress, opening in front. Dr. Cole will be with you in a moment."

A few minutes after she'd climbed up onto the table, Dr. Cole entered. She'd been Ember's gynecologist for years.

"Ember, you look wonderful. Married life certainly agrees with you. So, you think you're pregnant. Let's take a look."

Ember's heart lodged into her throat because if she wasn't pregnant the disappointment that followed was going to be tough.

She lay back on the examination table as the doctor squeezed some cold goo onto Ember's stomach.

"Okay, let's see what we see. Normally we'd used a vaginal probe, but to confirm pregnancy, the old way works just as well and isn't as uncomfortable."

Dr. Cole moved the probe, but Ember's focus was completely on the screen. She couldn't tell what she was looking at until she saw a small little point that was fluttering. She pointed to it and asked, "Oh my God, is that the heart?"

"Sure is. Based on the size I would say you are about seven weeks along. It's important that you start taking prenatal vitamins. I'll prescribe them before you leave."

Ember was surprised that she was that far along, but then, her period had never been regular, so tracking her cycle was always a challenge. By the way Dr. Cole was looking at her, Ember realized that she was awaiting an answer. She quickly replied, "Okay."

Dr. Cole started moving the probe around again, but Ember's thoughts were already on Trace and telling him he was going to be a father. She knew at first it was going to terrify him—the thought that he could end up like his father—but he really wanted children. She was so lost in her thoughts that she didn't hear Dr. Cole until she laughed and handed her a towel to wipe off the goo.

"We need to schedule an internal ultrasound at your earliest convenience. Now, here's what you can expect in the next few months . . ."

<hr />

Ember stood outside the doctor's office and dialed Trace. She wanted to find out where he was so she could tell him the good news in person, but he didn't answer. For the rest of the afternoon, she was unable to get through to him. That night as she waited for Trace's fight to start, she felt almost restless with the need to tell him that he was going to be a dad. She didn't want to blow his concentration, but she couldn't bear to wait any longer. She glanced over at Lucien and knew something was up with him too, and took a moment to appreciate that she was coming to know him well enough to know his different levels of silence.

"Is everything okay, Ember? You've been awfully quiet."

His question surprised her and she answered him with the joy she was feeling. "Everything's wonderful. When is the fight starting?"

He looked at his watch. "In about ten minutes. Why?"

"I need to talk with Trace."

"Now?"

"Yeah."

"He's probably in the locker room. Come on, I'll get him for you." He reached for her hand as he battled his way through the bodies. "You know, you look like the cat that just ate the canary," he said over his shoulder.

She only grinned in reply. They'd just reached the back near the locker room when Lucien stopped abruptly and Ember slammed right into his back.

"You could have warned me you were stopping," she said jokingly, but when she saw the reason for the suddenness of their halt, all humor left her. Trace was standing in a dark corner, and he wasn't alone. Heidi was with him. As they spoke, their heads nearly touched. Ember knew he loved her and she knew that he wouldn't cheat on her, but he'd lied and, for some reason, seeing the proof of that lie hurt even more than the actual lie.

As if he knew she was there, Trace's head snapped in her direction and their eyes locked.

"Ember."

She knew he could see that she was hurt before she turned and started away. She didn't get far before his hand touched her arm. "I'm sorry."

"You lied to me." She couldn't bring herself to look at him.

"I know. I didn't want to pull you into it. You've been through enough shit because of me."

"What does she want?"

"Money. And I'm dealing with it."

She did turn at that. "How exactly? And why does she think you're the person who's going to give it to her?"

He pulled a hand through his hair. "It's a long story. I'll tell you everything tonight."

She wanted to demand to know what he had to tell her, but they were calling his fight.

"Wait for me." He kissed her hard on the mouth. She watched as he climbed into the ring and then his eyes landed on her and he winked. She couldn't help her smile, but it faltered when she saw Heidi and the boy with her. Seth. Her eyes moved to Heidi to find her already staring in Ember's direction, and the smug look on her face was confirmation. Seth was Trace's child.

She couldn't breathe, couldn't get air into her lungs. She didn't know how long she stood there, but when she could no longer see because of the tears in her eyes, she turned and fled. Lucien appeared just as she reached the door.

"Ember."

"I just need some air."

"I'll take you home."

"Okay, but I just want a few minutes alone." He obviously didn't like it, but he acquiesced. "Okay."

Outside the gym, a searing pain exploded in her chest. Seth, the boy that looked like her husband, *was* his son. No wonder Heidi was more than just one of the horde. What a fucking secret to keep. What made Ember feel really ill was wondering: Would he have told her about Seth if she hadn't seen him tonight?

Her tears fell harder because she thought they were going to be experiencing the pregnancy as a first together and he already had an almost full-grown son he'd never thought to mention: a son who had been in his life for over fifteen years. And was Heidi blackmailing him to keep the secret from Ember? That thought made her bend over and vomit.

Lucien appeared and took her by the arm. "I'm taking you home."

"I don't want to be there."

"Then I'll take you to my apartment."

The fight just drained out of her. "Okay."

Lucien could feel Ember's pain well across the room. He didn't know what the hell was going on, but he knew that Ember deserved some time away from Trace.

"Would you like something to drink?" It sounded lame, but he was a bit out of his depth here.

The sight of her tear-streaked face moved him across the room. He joined her on the sofa and took her hand in his.

"He loves you."

"I know, but it still hurts."

"Well, he is a man, and I've been told repeatedly that men are idiots."

Her slight smile in response encouraged him to continue. "He should have told you, but I understand why he didn't."

He could see the question in her eyes when she looked up at him. "He loves you. You've made a life together and the idea that a secret from the past could pull you away from him, well, that would make anyone hedge their bets." And he realized as he spoke the words how accurately they pertained to him as well. The lack of open communication between Darcy and him had certainly taken a toll on their relationship.

Ember shook her head. "He should know, especially after everything that we've been through, that his secrets don't have that kind of power. I love him and that means I love everything about him."

"Agreed, and that takes us back to him being an idiot." Lucien sobered a minute. "Seriously, I was in a situation similar to the one you are in now. The woman I loved hurt me and, instead of fighting for her, fighting for *us,* I made the easy choice and walked away. I've had to live with that ever since, and I know that if I had it to do over, I would have fought with everything I had. Life with her is messy and frustrating, but life without her isn't much of a life."

"Darcy?"

"Yeah, Darcy."

"I like her."

Surprise flashed over his face. "You met her?"

"I came to see you at Allegro, but you weren't there. We ended up going to lunch."

"And what did you talk about at this lunch?"

Ember's grin turned coy. "Wouldn't you like to know?" And then she squeezed his hand. "We talked enough for me to know that she feels the same way about you as you do about her. It isn't too late for you."

"And we are working on it. Not that I haven't had my own bouts of idiocy."

"Meaning?" Ember asked.

"Let's just say I keep letting my jealousy overrule common sense and have said things to Darcy that she really should slug me for."

"What did you say to her?"

"I called her a whore, twice."

"What! Oh, I would have slugged you."

Lucien's grin was wicked. "Of that I have no doubt." He turned serious. "I need her to know that I'm aware of just how much of an ass I've been."

"Then say that."

Lucien's raised his one brow in skepticism. "That simple?"

"Yup. And she likes flowers."

"Thanks, I'll keep that in mind." He could see that her thoughts had turned back to Trace as sadness washed over her expression. "Do you think that the boy is Trace's?"

"He looks a hell of a lot like him, but I can't believe that Trace would have kept that from you. I honestly don't know. Would it be a problem if he were?"

"No, of course not. I'm only hurt that he didn't tell me. It isn't Seth's fault."

"Seth? You know his name?"

"Yeah, he's friends with Brandon, the boy I met at the campaign office. Great kid."

"Small world," Lucien said just as Ember yawned. He stood and pulled her from the sofa.

"You need sleep."

"I don't want to be a bother."

He turned and looked at her as if she had three heads. "Friends can never be a bother."

He walked her to the guest room. She stepped into the room and turned to him. "Thank you, Lucien."

"Anytime, Ember."

———◆———

Three hours later, Lucien opened the door to a very worried Trace.

"Where is she?" Trace demanded.

"She's sleeping. Come in; I'll get you a beer." They hadn't even made it to the kitchen before Lucien asked, "Trace, who's the kid living with Heidi?"

"Why were you at Heidi's?"

"A long story that I'll share another time. Who is he? Because when I saw him, I thought he was yours and so did Ember."

"What?" And then realization slammed into Trace and suddenly his anger was replaced with fear, an emotion he wasn't accustomed to feeling. Ember was going to jump to the natural conclusion and hate him for keeping this from her.

"His mother is Heidi," Trace said in defeat.

Lucien's voice sounded like a gun blast. "It's bad enough Ember had to see you and Heidi together, but you didn't think it was important to tell your wife that you had a kid with her?"

Guilt churned in Trace's gut. "He isn't mine."

"What?" Lucien demanded.

"He isn't my kid. He's my half brother. He doesn't know who his father is because I'm trying to protect him from the reality of where he comes from. He suspects we're related since we look so much alike, so I've told him he's the son of a cousin of mine. I have to live with the knowledge of my father; I don't wish that on him. I didn't tell Ember or Chelsea; I was trying to protect them from it too."

"And now your wife thinks you fathered a child and never told her," Lucien said softly.

That reality twisted like a knife in Trace's gut. God, she must hate him. He hated himself in that minute for not telling her immediately. His intent was to spare the child, but not at the expense of his wife. When he saw Heidi again, he was going to wring her fucking neck. He needed to see Ember and, as if his friend had read his mind, Lucien said, "She's down the hall, last door on the left."

"Thank you, Lucien, for being there."

"Anytime."

Trace moved down the hall and was careful to be quiet when he pushed open the door. He approached the bed where Ember was curled into a ball, her typical sleeping position when he wasn't in bed with her. Her hands were tucked under her cheek, and he could tell by the puffiness of her eyes that she had spent a fair amount of time crying. His heart twisted in his chest. Settling on the edge of the bed, he touched her face, needing to feel her solid and warm under his fingers. She stirred, instinctively moving into him as if she knew he was there. He wanted to wake her, beg her forgiveness, make love to her, but instead he took a seat across the room and watched her sleep.

When Ember woke, it was dark outside. It took her a minute, but Trace watched as her body tensed, and he knew she knew he was there. She turned to him, and the kaleidoscope of emotions that passed over her face broke his heart, but he hadn't missed her look of joy when she'd initially seen him.

She climbed from the bed and put the distance of the room between them. "Lucien called you," she said without preamble.

"Yeah."

"You should have told me."

"He's not my son."

It took her a moment to register what he'd said before she exhaled on a sob, covering her mouth with her hand and turning from him. He moved to her and wrapped her in his arms. She stiffened under his embrace, but he responded by holding her closer.

"He's not my son, Ember. I should have told you about him, but I was trying to protect Seth. I didn't want him to have to feel the burden of being an offspring of my bastard father."

Teary eyes looked up in his. "Seth is your brother?"

"Half brother. Heidi is his mom."

Her response to that was to bury her face in his chest.

"Heidi's been extorting money from me and I've been paying her in an attempt to keep Seth from knowing who his real father is. I didn't tell you because it was just more shit from my past, but I'm sorry you had to learn about it the way you did. I can't even begin to imagine how you felt seeing Seth with Heidi."

He lifted her chin to force her gaze on him. "Forgive me."

"I need a minute," she whispered.

The coldness of her tone made icicles form in his blood. Was this just one drama too many? Was she finally going to come to her senses and kick his ass to the curb? She should—should have already—but fuck it, now he could never let her go. She pulled from him and he suddenly felt very empty inside.

"Is there anything else I need to know?"

"No."

"I can't take another surprise like that, Trace. You told me once you had a lot of shit in your past and I appreciate that, but another shocker like this one and I think it might just break me."

"There's nothing else."

Her head lowered but he heard her words clearly. "You took responsibility for Seth, didn't you?"

"Someone needed to. With a father and mother like his, he would have fallen through the cracks."

Bright eyes looked up at him. "And you're concerned about becoming your father? You're nothing like him."

"Tell me you forgive me, Ember."

"I do."

"I'm so sorry."

"I'm sorry I jumped to conclusions," she whispered.

"It was a fair conclusion to make." He walked to her and pulled her into his arms. He brushed his lips over hers, but one taste and he needed more. The kiss turned carnal and he ached to be inside her, to find the connection that only she could give him, but he wasn't a complete rutting bastard that he would take her after hurting her so badly. She apparently felt otherwise. She reached for his hand and moved it down her body. He was as hard as stone. At least in this he could show her how he felt. He slipped his hand in between their bodies to find and stroke the nub between her legs.

She responded with a breathless moan and spread her legs wider to give him better access.

Trace remembered when he'd first met Ember and how he had wished he'd been entertaining her that night in a similar manner, instead of the girl he'd been with. "Remember you said you wished it had been you I was with at Sapphire that first time? So did I."

Her soft sounds were driving him crazy. Her head dropped onto his shoulder while her hips moved against his hand. His thumb continued the assault on that pleasure point as he pushed two fingers inside her, her body moving silkily up and down as she rode him. He wanted to drop to his knees and take her in his mouth, taste her as she came, but she was so close. His lips brushed over her ear, "Ride it harder; come for me."

Her muscles spasmed and she bit his shoulder to stifle her cry as she climaxed. It was the fucking sexiest thing he'd ever seen. Her face was flushed and her eyes still warm with desire when she looked up at him. He held her gaze and brought his fingers to his mouth to lick off her taste.

"Fucking sweet."

Ember was suddenly quiet and he was about to ask her what she was thinking when her hand unconsciously moved to her stomach. "I went to see the doctor yesterday."

It took him a second or two and then his hand covered hers as what she didn't say slammed into him. "You're pregnant."

She linked their fingers. "We're pregnant."

He wasn't sure what emotion he felt more strongly, joy or fear. He held her gaze when he asked, "What's that look for?"

His heart twisted with love at the sudden tears in her eyes. "This is a good thing, right?"

His voice caught, but he answered honestly. "Incredible."

"But?"

They were pregnant. He couldn't lie, he was thrilled, but he was also terrified. What if he became his sick fuck of a father? Ember would leave him, he'd insist on it, and losing her would be the end of him.

"Trace."

A piece of him was growing inside of her and that thought brought on a surge of protectiveness in him.

"Penny for your thoughts?" She moved closer before she asked, "Tell me what's putting that look on your face."

"What if I'm like him? What if I'm really a sick son of a bitch like my father? What if I abuse our child?"

Ember reacted to that as if he'd slapped her. "How the hell can you even think that?"

"How the hell can I not?"

It was compassion that filled her voice when next she spoke. "You are nothing like your father, but I see I'll have to remind you of this repeatedly over the next seven months."

A reluctant smile tugged at his mouth. Her unwavering belief in him was fucking humbling. He moved to her and wrapped her in his arms. "Probably."

Looking down into those eyes, he knew she was his home. He'd do anything for her. "I want to go with you for your next prenatal visit."

"I would really like that."

"How far along are you?"

"Seven weeks. I hadn't even realized that I hadn't gotten my period. It has never been regular and being so happy, I honestly just didn't even think about it."

The fucking shit she said. He smiled and his heart beat faster in his chest.

He pulled her to him and sealed her perfect words with a kiss.

Chapter Eleven

✦

Darcy arrived to work very early on Monday. She couldn't lie—she was disappointed that Lucien had made no attempt to contact her over the weekend, and considering he'd called her a whore, twice, he should have. Her office door was closed, which was odd since she always left it open. As soon as she flicked on the lights, she gasped in delight. Her entire office was one colorful garden—vases filled with every color and variety of flower covered every horizontal surface.

One vase, filled with peonies in varying shades of pink, sat right in the middle of her desk. She reached for the card and couldn't help but laugh at Lucien's apology.

I was a dick. Forgive me.

"So?"

She turned, her heart in her throat, to see him leaning in the doorway of her office. He took her breath away, and to see him looking so contrite and sexy—damn, she'd forgive him anything. But she was going to make him work for it.

"The flowers are beautiful."

"Do you forgive me?"

"For calling me a whore because I was dancing? I'm still on the fence."

"I suppose I deserve that." He entered her office and stopped just in front of her. "I thought about what you said, how I didn't fight for you. You're right, I didn't. At the time I was so devastated, losing Sister Anne and then you, I guess I just shut down. I should have come for you."

She wanted to throw herself into his arms, but she held her ground. He needed to know that he couldn't keep throwing their past in her face.

"I'm sorry about Friday night." He looked down for a moment before he said, "I was jealous."

His words made her feel almost giddy, but she schooled her expression. "Jealous. Well, there was no need to be. I was just dancing."

"But not with me."

She tilted her head and smiled. "You didn't ask."

"And that's all I need to do? Ask?"

Her expression changed from teasing to sincere. "I've never denied you anything, you know that."

His fingers played with a lock of her hair and though she had the sense he was up to something, he said not a word before he turned and walked out of her office.

Around noon, Darcy went to get a bite to eat, but when she stepped out of her office, there was a sign on the wall just opposite her door that said, "Join me?"

Down the hall she could see another sign. This one had an arrow and she followed that to the next one, up the stairs, down a hall to a door with a sign that read, "Took you long enough."

It was the door to the roof and she pushed it open to see Lucien standing next to a small table with two large crystal bowls filled with pudding. When she reached him, he pulled her chair out and settled her napkin in her lap before he took the seat across from her. He lifted his spoon and waited for her to do the same, before he winked. Words weren't needed. It was, hands down, the best lunch ever.

Two nights later Darcy sat in her apartment with her thoughts entirely on Lucien. After their lunch of pudding, he'd walked her back to her office and kissed her hand before returning to his own office. The following morning there had been a small box on her desk. She'd been hoping there would be a follow-up to the flowers, but she didn't expect this type of gift. She opened the box to find a mug bearing Lucien's face. She'd laughed out loud at the ridiculous picture. It would, of course, sit prominently on her desk, just like he knew it would.

She threaded her fingers through her hair as worry tingled her spine. She had to tell him about the baby, but she didn't know how. She'd suffered with guilt for years over subsequently losing their child. Would he hold her responsible too? It was terrifying, and yet she knew they'd be unable to move forward until she overcame her fear and told him.

Darcy's morning was booked, so at lunchtime she went in search of Lucien. She'd take him to lunch and tell him everything. She stopped at his office door and took a minute to just look at him. He glanced up, saw her, and smiled.

"Would you like to go to lunch?" she asked.

"Yeah. What are you in the mood for?" he asked as he moved from his desk toward her.

"Chinese."

"I know a place."

Outside, the sun was bright in the blue sky. He reached for her hand, something so simple, and yet it made her feel as if she were on top of the world. She never thought that much about hand-holding, but holding Lucien's hand, when it was done so naturally, almost unconsciously—yep, she liked it a lot.

They reached a silver truck on the corner. "We're getting Chinese from a truck?" Darcy asked.

"No better place in the city, trust me."

He carried the white plastic bag while leading her to what was, according to him, the perfect place to eat it. They stopped in front of one of the horse drawn carriages and, after paying, he helped her up into it. He settled next to her and dealt out the cartons.

"I've never ridden in one of these before," she said.

"Me neither."

"Well then, how do you know it's the perfect place to have our lunch?"

His smile was slow to form, but breathtaking when complete. "We're moving, so if I say something stupid, you can't escape."

"You're an idiot." But inside she was grateful that he couldn't walk away after she told him her news.

He never took his eyes from her when he said, "I have been, but I'm working on that."

His words surprised her. And his lips were so close that if she leaned into him, she would feel them under hers.

"I'm going to kiss you," he said softly. And then those lips were on hers and she sighed, granting him full access to her mouth.

Minutes later, he leaned back as if he were trying to keep himself in check, but desire burned in his eyes when he looked at her.

"Tasty," he said, then grinned. "The Chinese, I mean."

Now was the time to tell him, but she couldn't get the words out. The thought of him never again looking at her with such tenderness was enough to make Darcy delay for just another day.

———◆———

"Ember, Trace, this is Dr. Lipton. If it's all right with you, he's going to sit in on your ultrasound today. He's a neonatal surgeon whom I asked for a consult," Dr. Cole said.

"Sure." Ember's voice sounded a bit strained, not surprisingly since she was nervous, a feeling Trace shared.

"Okay, let's get you ready."

Dr. Cole handed the paper gown to Ember before showing them to a room. "We'll be back in ten."

Trace turned to Ember once the doctor had left. She was looking at the ultrasound machine.

"That doesn't look very comfortable," she said.

Trace's eyes followed hers. "No, it doesn't." He took a step closer to her. "Are you okay?"

"Nervous."

"We should get you undressed."

"Normally, that statement from you makes me almost light-headed in anticipation, but not so much today."

"I'll be right here."

"I know."

Trace placed the gown on the table before reaching for the hem of Ember's shirt. "Arms up, sweetheart. When this is over, I'll buy you a cake pop."

She grinned. "Two cake pops."

"You got it."

A knock at the door signaled the arrival of the doctors. They took a few minutes to get everything set up. "Are you ready, Ember?"

"Yeah."

"I know it's a bit uncomfortable, but try to relax."

Trace felt a swell of love for her as she took a few calming breaths before she said, "I'm ready."

Ember tensed, her grip on his hand tightening as Dr. Cole inserted the probe.

"Okay, let's have a look." Dr. Cole's voice pulled Trace's attention to the screen. He saw it when Ember did since she squeezed his hand. The heart beating. He couldn't exactly say what emotion moved through him seeing the heartbeat of their child, but it was damn powerful.

Dr. Lipton moved forward to study something on the screen, which made Trace ask, "Is everything okay?"

"There seems to be a membrane that divides Ember's uterus." Dr. Cole pointed to a small, thin white line.

"Is that a problem?" Trace felt his heart constrict.

"The baby has room to grow, but enough room, I don't know," he said. "Right now, we look good. The baby's in a good position and the placenta looks fine. Let's monitor with ultrasounds, one every two weeks. The uterus is an incredible organ and has the ability to grow substantially, so we could all be worrying for nothing."

"And if it's not?" Trace asked.

"Well, depending on how far along the pregnancy is, we'll confine Ember to bed rest to get as many weeks as we can for the baby before we deliver. And if we have to deliver early, premature babies' chances are incredible with today's technology. But let's not worry about that now. Like I said, it may never come to that."

"I'll ask the nurse to schedule another ultrasound in two weeks. Take your vitamins, eat well, do some light exercise, and let's take it a day at a time," Dr. Cole encouraged.

"Okay, and thank you," Ember said.

"We'll see you in two weeks," Dr. Lipton said right before he and Dr. Cole left the room.

Ember moved to sit up as Trace reached for her clothes.

"Are you worried?" Ember asked as soon as the doctors left. Trace could tell that she was, her fear practically rolling off her in waves.

"Yes, but let's try not to worry. You heard the doctors. It could all be worry for nothing." He turned her face to his. "But promise me something."

"Anything."

"If it comes down to you or the baby, I want you."

"Trace."

"Ember, promise me."

He knew the words were hard for her to say, but he also knew that once she gave her word, she would honor it. "I promise."

He'd never survive losing her—no fucking way. He pushed the thought from his head and tried for levity when he said, "I can't believe I'm saying this, but let's get you dressed. We have cake pops to buy."

———

Darcy had started biting her nails. It was a terrible habit, but nerves did that to her. Two weeks after she vowed to tell Lucien about the baby, she still hadn't. And worse, he was off on a business trip to hear a band that he was considering sponsoring. What the hell was she doing? She knew very well what she was doing; she was procrastinating because she feared she was going to lose him so soon after getting him back in her life. There was a small part of her brain that thought she was being unreasonable, but she couldn't get herself to listen to that voice of reason. Her fingers were back in her mouth when there was a knock at her door.

She walked to the door, peering out the peephole to see Lucien standing there.

Her heart went into her throat.

She pulled the door open.

His eyes stared boldly into hers and then quite deliberately he moved his gaze down her body.

"When did you—" Her words were cut off when his mouth crushed down on hers. Every cell in her body exploded from the contact as her arms found their way around his neck, even without her conscious thought to do so. Strong arms wrapped around her waist and pulled her close so that their bodies were pressed tight, the softness of her body molding to the hard planes of his.

"Open your mouth for me," he demanded against her lips, and she was mindless to do anything but what he asked. As soon as she did, his tongue swept every inch of her mouth. He lifted her and pressed her up against the wall of her apartment, closing her door. She pulled her hands through his hair and wrapped her legs around his waist.

He wanted her, he wanted her naked underneath him. His need was so powerful he almost gave in to it, but they needed to take things slowly this time. With more will than he knew he possessed, he pulled his mouth away. She lowered her head to his shoulder, her breathing unsteady. Her heart pounded against his.

She lifted her head and her brilliant blue eyes were shining with love and desire, something Lucien hadn't seen in a really long time. His instinct was to hold her closer. A small smile played around her mouth, and the sight of it had him answering with a grin.

"I've missed you," she said.

"Understatement." And then he took her to the bedroom. When he reached her bed, he dropped her onto it.

"Lucien." He stopped in midmotion for the blanket and kissed her long and hard. He liked that it took her a few minutes to open her eyes after. He covered her with the blanket just as she asked, "What are you doing?"

He rubbed the back of his neck and looked thoughtful for a minute. "Taking things slowly." He wanted to be naked and in bed with her, but it was best to be more cautious this time around. And then he said, "I know your feelings for me are keeping you up at night, but you need sleep; you've got dark circles under your eyes."

"Presumptuous."

"But right."

"Arrogant."

"Still right."

"Cocky bastard."

He pressed his lips to hers. "And right." He turned serious and brushed her hair from her face. "I don't want to fuck this up again. I know we had help fucking it up, but we played a part in it too."

"I agree, but why did you come tonight if you're leaving already?"

"I got off the plane and found myself at your door."

"Good answer."

He kissed her again before he stood. "See you in the morning."

He turned, but then her soft voice came from behind him. "Sleep here."

He turned back. "No, we won't sleep."

She looked almost nervous when she said, "I have to tell you something."

Apprehension filled him. "It sounds important."

"It is."

"Can we talk tomorrow? I'm exhausted."

She worked her lower lip for a minute. "Okay."

He started from the room again, feeling tense. He knew she was tense too when she sought to ease it through teasing. He was happy to play along.

"You aren't going to forget my name, are you?" she said.

"No, Gwen."

"Get out."

"Leaving, Nancy."

She threw her pillow at him, which he dodged easily, and started from the room. "Sleep well, Bertha."

He closed the door to her room on the sound of her laughter.

Darcy woke in the morning and smelled coffee, so she padded down the hall to see Lucien sitting in her kitchen reading a paper. The memory of last night in all of its glory came rushing back to her and then that wonderful voice greeted her from across the room.

"Morning."

"You're here again."

He folded the paper and placed it on the table before he stood and walked over to her. He pulled her close.

"I never left. Struggled for over an hour with myself knowing you were in there and I could be too. I fell asleep on your sofa. I couldn't seem to get myself to leave." He kissed her and she felt his lips turning into a smile before he said, "I made you coffee."

She didn't want the coffee; she wanted to strip him out of his clothes and drink him down. His arms tightened around her as if he could read her mind.

"You wanted to talk."

"Yes, but I don't want to have that conversation at this particular moment."

Curiosity flashed in his eyes but he seemed to move past it and asked, "There's a party at Trace's tomorrow night. Will you come with me?"

"Yes."

He touched her hair, rubbing a few strands between his fingers, before he lifted his eyes to her. "I want to make love to you, Darcy, but first, I want to get to know you again."

"Okay."

"No arguments? That doesn't seem possible."

"When you make sense, I have no need to argue with you." Her teasing turned serious before she added, "I never thought we'd be here again, so I'll take you any way I can have you."

His eyes darkened. "Fuck waiting."

He lifted her off the floor and didn't release her when they reached her room, but let her slide down against him, pressing her tightly to him just before his mouth covered hers. Her hands moved around his back to learn the body of the man he had become. She slipped under his shirt to touch his warm skin, hard with muscle. His hands moved to frame her face as he deepened the kiss, his tongue exploring every part of her mouth before he sucked her tongue into his. He moved to her shoulders, pushing the loose shirt down her arms, pinning them to her side. His mouth pulled from her and he looked dangerous as his eyes moved down her body to her breasts.

"You're beautiful," he whispered before he closed his mouth over her nipple, sucking one of those peaks deep into his mouth. Lust shot straight between her legs. He moved to the other breast and the need to touch him was raw, but she couldn't because her arms were pinned.

"I want to touch you."

He guided her shirt down, freeing her arms before he lowered himself in front of her and pressed kisses down her belly. When he kissed her between her legs through the silk of her panties, she almost came. He slid the silk down her legs. "Spread your legs for me."

The memory of their first time teased her mind and she knew he remembered it too. He pressed a kiss on the inside of her knee, then up her thigh until he reached her center. He spread her with his fingers before his tongue tasted her, right on her aching nub.

"Oh God."

He looked up at her with a grin before he said, "Lucien. Oh Lucien."

"Tease," she whispered.

As if to confirm that statement, he ran a finger over her moist heat, teasing her as he played with the sensitive nub before circling her, but not entering. Her hips moved against his hand, eager for penetration, but not getting it.

The words came from her throat without conscious thought. "Oh Lucien."

He pushed a finger into her, deep and slow, before pulling out. He added another finger, sucking on her at the same time, and she came hard. His tongue moved to join his fingers to taste the evidence of her orgasm. He kissed his way up her body before settling his mouth over hers.

"I never forgot your taste."

She wrapped her arms around his neck and kissed him, tasting herself on his tongue. His arms wrapped around her before he lowered them both onto the bed. He settled between her legs and rubbed against her through his clothes.

"You're wearing too many clothes."

He smiled against her lips. "Agreed."

He moved with a grace that was mouthwatering. She greedily watched him lift his shirt up over his head. His chest was spectacular, tanned and ripped with muscle, his stomach was flat, and his eight-pack was so defined it looked airbrushed. And then her eyes saw the tattoo under his right arm. One word looking lonely, even a bit lost, which she was sure was the point: "Forgotten."

"Darcy?"

She moved to kneel in front of him and lifted his arm to trace the cursive lines of his tattoo. When her eyes found his again, there were tears in hers because he believed himself forgotten.

"Why are you crying?"

"You were never forgotten, Lucien. I thought of you every fucking day."

Her confession left Lucien speechless. There were no words that could do justice to what he was feeling, so he showed her. He moved between her legs and when he entered her, he did so slowly and watched her face as he claimed her inch by inch. When he was fully inside her, he moaned and then started to move. Her legs came around him, demanding that he go deeper. He felt her tighten around him and he shifted so that with each thrust he was hitting the part of her that would send her over. And when she did come, he lifted her hips and pulled her against him before he really started moving. He was losing himself in being inside her again, but when he came, he didn't roar her name, but whispered it almost reverently.

She was smiling up at him, and just like that he wanted her again.

Darcy stayed in bed, claiming she had lost the use of her legs. It was possible. Lucien had had her four times already today and he was itching to get back to her and make it five.

Her words to him—that he wasn't forgotten—had fucking gotten to him, especially since he knew she spoke the truth. He felt anger claw at him at the idea that someone had deliberately pulled them apart. Josh hadn't made any headway into the man who had come to see Darcy, but he had called to tell Lucien he had some information on her past. He seemed rather reluctant to discuss it over the phone. Curiosity, as well as guilt, washed over him that he had gone behind Darcy's back, but what was done was done.

Now wasn't the time to ponder the unpleasant. He suspected he knew why Trace and Ember were having a party.

Twenty minutes later he stood in the middle of a store that looked like a fairy tale gone horribly wrong. What the hell had possessed him? It wasn't so much the mini-kitchens and the gigantic cribs, but the mommies pushing around those Hummers for toddlers. If one more stroller nailed him in the back of the leg, he was very likely going to burn the place down.

His happy afterglow was fading quickly and then a rocking horse in the far corner of the store caught his attention. The wood looked to be oak and was the color of honey and real horsehair had been used to create the mane. Ember would love it.

A voice behind him shifted his attention from the chaos all around him. It took a moment for it to register that the leggy blond was a sales associate in the baby section, because she looked more like the star from the Van Halen's "Hot for Teacher" video: too short a skirt, fuck-me heels, and an oxford unbuttoned in an entirely unteacherly fashion. Who the hell was she trying to impress? And then he noticed a few dads across the room—tired, stressed, and clearly sex-deprived by the way their eyes were fixated on the sales associate's ass. Who knew that a baby department could be so carnal?

"Can I help you?" Honest to God, she purred at him, the question just laced with a double meaning.

"I'd like this horse."

"Sure thing. You see anything else that you like?"

The saleswoman was definitely a master of the double entendre, and there was a time that Lucien would have taken the sexy woman up on her offer. He'd have done her up against the wall in the family bathroom, but now he had Darcy. And the thought of her naked and in bed had him in a hurry to get back to her.

"No, just the horse."

"It'll only be a moment," she hissed.

———◆———

Darcy lay next to Lucien, running her fingers over the muscles of his abs. She had missed this almost more than the sex—the moments after when they just talked about anything and everything. It had always been like that for them, so easy and comfortable.

She'd been thinking more and more about the conversation she'd had with that man that day. He had told her that he'd look out for Lucien, but based on some of the stories she had heard, it didn't appear he had kept his word. But still, Lucien was a very wealthy man now, so maybe he had. She lifted up on her elbows.

"How did you get so rich?"

"You're only after my money, I see." He gave her a wink.

She pushed at him and laughed. "I fell in love with you when you didn't have a penny to your name."

Tenderness washed over his face and he leaned in and kissed her. "True." He tucked a lock of her hair behind her ear. "Why are you asking?"

"The man who came to me that day promised he'd help you as long as I stayed out of your life. I thought that was just another lie, but you can't argue with your success. Do you know if maybe he did keep his word? He could have been helping you along the way."

She saw his anger and couldn't fault him for it, but maybe the one they were looking for was right under their noses.

"I took any job I could find and saved most of what I made. When I had saved enough, I started investing in not very reputable businesses and before long I owned those businesses. Eventually I started investing in legitimate businesses. It wasn't easy. I put in my dues and did shit I'm not proud of." He touched her hair before running his finger along her jaw. "Hindsight being what it is, I'm glad you weren't there for that. That you weren't exposed to all that I was."

She saw the ah-ha moment right before he said, "But . . . yeah, there were a few times I didn't understand how I got some of the jobs I did. Why someone would trust a kid like me. Someone important behind the scenes could have pulled some strings. That would make sense. Even my juvenile record . . ."

Darcy sat up. "You have a criminal record?"

"Would that surprise you?"

She didn't even hesitate to answer, which made his heart pound a bit faster in his chest. "Yes, because the boy I knew was no criminal."

He kissed her cheek. "Well, rest easy, I don't have a *criminal* record and the few times I was incarcerated, it was only an overnight stay. I was never booked. What about you? Do you have any skeletons in your closet?"

He was joking, but she looked as if she were guilty. What was she hiding from him? He was tempted to pry a confession from her, but he didn't have the heart. She'd tell him when she was ready.

She met his eyes and pursed her lips thoughtfully. "So who's the man behind the curtain and what's his interest in you?"

He'd expected she'd change the subject. Time for something different. He rolled, pinning Darcy under him. "Good question, but I'm so not interested at the moment."

Her legs came around his waist and she rubbed herself against him. "Me neither."

Chapter Twelve

"A re you sure you're up for this?" Trace studied Ember from the doorway of their bedroom while she pulled her hair up into some kind of sexy knot thing. They'd decided to have a dinner party to announce the baby. Knowing she was pregnant, especially after the emotional roller coaster he'd put her through, he didn't want her pushing it.

Patience dominated the look she gave him. "I'm pregnant, not an invalid."

"A few weeks ago I put you through hell."

"Yes, and we've moved on."

"If you get tired, just say something and I will kick everyone out of the apartment."

She moved to him, wrapped her arms around his waist, and pressed her lips to his. "I'm fine, but I will tell you when I grow tired."

"Good." His hands moved down her body to her hips so he could press her closer, then his mouth settled firmly over hers. It was some time before he released her. Her eyes were still closed when she said, "Definitely finishing this conversation later."

His grin was cocky when she finally opened her eyes. The kiss was hard and quick. "See you out there," he said.

"'Kay."

An hour later, Trace asked for everyone's attention. "We're pregnant."

Ember's father lifted her right up off the floor and spun her around, causing her laughter to fill every corner of the apartment.

"I'm going to be an aunt," Chelsea yelled as she threw herself into Trace. "Auntie Chelsea."

"And a fine one you'll make too, little sister."

"Thanks for coming with me. When the crowd clears, I'll take you over and introduce you again to Trace. Ember mentioned that you and she already met," Lucien said to Darcy.

An odd look crossed over Darcy's face at his comment, and Lucien raised an eyebrow in curiosity. "I was jealous when I saw her."

"Of Ember—why?"

"She wasn't your usual type and the thought that you could be serious about her made me jealous."

"Ember has only ever had eyes for Trace. But I like knowing that you were jealous."

The eye roll was classic Darcy. "You're a clown."

Trace approached Lucien later while Ember talked with Darcy.

"Thanks for coming, and for the rocking horse. Ember actually cried when she saw it. Of course she cries at the drop of a hat these days. Just yesterday she broke down while watching a coffee commercial."

Lucien laughed. "Congratulations. You must be excited and terrified all at once."

"I am thrilled, but I don't know if I'm cut out for fatherhood."
The tone of Trace's voice revealed more than his actual words.

Lucien put his hand on his friend's shoulder.

"I've known you a long time, and I can say without question
that you are going to make an excellent father. Look at how you
care for Chelsea and Seth. You are not your father, Trace."

"That's what Ember keeps saying."

"Listen to her. She knows what she's talking about."

Trace's gaze moved to Ember just as Lucien's moved to Darcy.
"Darcy's your Caterpillar, isn't she?"

Even though the three of them had been at St. Agnes together,
Trace and Darcy had never really gotten to know each other. It
was years after St. Agnes that Lucien had gotten so drunk he
started babbling on about Darcy. He hadn't been drunk enough,
unfortunately, because he remembered his lovesick stupor and so
did Trace. "You remember that?"

"Yeah. So what happened?"

"She applied for a job at Allegro and one thing led to another.
Now is not the time, but later I'd like to talk with you about Heidi."

"Why the hell do you want to talk about her?"

"She played a part in what happened between Darcy and me.
She knows more than she's saying."

Something dark moved across Trace's face. "Heidi is a schem-
ing bitch, so I can believe just about anything when it comes to
her. If she saw an opportunity, she absolutely would take it. I'm
guessing since Darcy is here with you that you've worked it out."

"We're working on it."

Trace slapped his friend on the back. "I'm happy for you. I
always had the sense that she meant to you what Ember has come
to mean to me."

Lucien didn't even hesitate in his reply. "She does."

Later Josh approached Lucien. "Can we talk?"

"Sure."

They stepped into the office, which was empty, before Josh turned to Lucien. "The timing sucks, but you're here and this assignment is not sitting right with me." He looked down for a minute. "I looked into Darcy like you asked, but you're with her now so I think it would be best if you just talked with her."

Lucien was about to agree, but there was something in Josh's tone that made him pause.

"What did you learn?"

"Something that I think should come from Darcy."

Immediately Lucien was put on the defensive. Was she keeping something from him? Was she married? Had she been? After the weeks they had just shared, how could she keep anything from him?

"No, tell me."

"I really think you need to talk with Darcy."

"Just tell me!" Lucien demanded, his jealousy turning into a living thing.

"There was a baby."

She had had a baby. Someone else's baby? His baby? Was that why she'd sought him out? Was she looking for money? Jealousy turned into rage. Or did she give up his baby? And then he remembered her reaction to his question regarding skeletons. What a fucking secret to keep from him, especially considering their own childhoods.

His voice turned cold and hard. "Where is the child now?"

There was sympathy in Josh's expression when he said, "The baby died."

Suddenly Lucien felt ill. "How?"

"Apparently the pregnancy was a difficult one. One day Darcy got light-headed and fell down the stairs. She was rushed to the hospital, but the baby didn't make it, and she almost didn't either." Josh's voice softened when he added, "It *was* your child."

"Oh my God." Lucien was horrified, almost as much at himself for the conclusions he had jumped to as he was for the loss of their child. "Where is the baby buried?"

"Darcy's mother had the baby cremated with John and Jane Does while Darcy lay unconscious in her hospital bed. There were no ashes."

"What?" That word came out in a roar. Knowing Darcy as he did, she would have felt responsible for losing the baby; but having the decision on its resting place taken from her would have been devastating. She didn't even have a place to go to mourn their child.

Suspicion filled him at Darcy's mother's motives. She didn't give a shit about Darcy, so why get involved in the baby's burial? Why come for Darcy after the tragedy?

And Darcy had to deal with a pregnancy, the loss of her child, and almost dying herself—and did so alone. He needed her at that moment. He needed to feel her safe and warm, and then he was going to get on his knees and beg her to forgive him. And not just for the past, but because he had violated her trust by seeking out information that she obviously wasn't ready to share.

"Thanks, Josh."

"What are you going to do?"

"Beg for her forgiveness."

Josh's smile was slight before he said, "Sounds like a good place to start, son."

Darcy was on her way to the bathroom when she heard the sound of Lucien's voice. She stopped in time to hear Lucien yell, "Just tell me!"

"There was a baby."

She recognized that voice as Ember's uncle's. But Lucien's tone made her sick. He believed she had given their baby up. How could he believe that of her? But then Josh proceeded to detail her very own nightmare. She backed away from the door as numbness filled her. He had had her investigated, had violated her privacy and dug into her past and her pain. What the hell gave him the right to do that? She had to get out of there.

She reached the living room and spotted Ember. She thought about making some excuse for why she was leaving so suddenly, but she just didn't have it in her.

"I have to go."

The concern was clear in Ember's voice. "Is everything okay?"

She couldn't reply because the words wouldn't come. Instead she grabbed Ember's hand and squeezed before she practically ran from the apartment. Outside she started walking until she saw a cab and hailed it.

———•◆•———

When she arrived at the orphanage, it looked so different than it had when she'd called it home, but there was one place that still looked the same: her tree. The same gnarly tree that she and Lucien had agreed to meet at that day.

Her baby had already been cremated by the time she was conscious again—an open cremation with other nameless souls so that there were no ashes for Darcy. Her mom claimed it was the cheapest option, but why did her mom not wait for her? It was like her mom was purposely spiting her. So she lost her baby, never got to hold him or her, or say good-bye. There wasn't even anywhere for her to go to visit the baby she'd loved from the moment she'd found out she was pregnant.

Darcy had hated returning home with her mom after she'd lost the baby, but the woman had insisted and since Darcy had been underage, she didn't have a choice. And then as soon as they'd returned home, everything was exactly as it had been, except her mom's increased dependency on alcohol. Why had her mom wanted her home again?

Her mom spent her days drinking and her nights picking up strangers. How she paid the rent was beyond Darcy because the woman didn't work. Darcy had thought about leaving countless times, but the only place she had to go was St. Agnes. Two things kept her from escaping to there: her mom would only find her and bring her back and there were too many memories to haunt her.

She turned her thoughts from her mom. The pain of Lucien's betrayal was staggering. It was on her for not telling him sooner about the baby, she knew that. But he had had her investigated, which was bad enough, but it was unforgivable that he could jump to the conclusion that he had about the baby: that she had abandoned their child. Once again he believed the worst of her. He didn't question, didn't argue, but believed so easily that she could do something so horrendous: inflict on their child the type of childhood they both had suffered through. She had loved their baby, would have done anything for their child; in fact, she had already started looking into government aid and housing so she could keep her baby.

All these years she carried the guilt and responsibility of what had happened between her and Lucien, but for the first time her anger wasn't directed inwardly. Hearing the disgust in his voice, knowing he immediately believed the worst of her, left her with an emotion that felt an awful lot like hate.

Lucien walked out of Trace's office feeling like he'd just played chicken with an eighteen-wheeler. They had made a baby. He gave himself a moment to indulge in what-ifs. Their child would have been almost fourteen now had he or she lived. Was it a boy or a girl? Would he or she have had his nose and Darcy's mouth? Maybe her beautiful eyes.

The thought that Darcy had dealt with both the pregnancy and the loss alone while he was off being bitter and self-destructive sickened him. He needed to find her and tell her everything and then do as he told Josh he would, beg her to forgive him. When he reached the living room, he noticed that Darcy wasn't there, but Ember and Trace were and it looked as if they were waiting for him.

He asked, "Where's Darcy?"

"She left." Ember's voice held a note of pity.

Immediately he knew that Darcy overheard his discussion with Josh. "How long ago?"

"About ten minutes."

"Goddamn it."

"You want help finding her?" Trace asked.

Lucien stopped halfway to the door to look back at his friend. "Thanks, but I need to do this alone."

"Call if you change your mind."

By the time Darcy returned home it was close to three in the morning and she wasn't really surprised to see Lucien sitting in the hall outside of her apartment. As soon as he saw her, he stood up and started toward her. She stopped him from pulling her into his arms by stepping back and putting her hand up.

"I'm tired. This is going to have to wait."

"Damn it, Darcy, I've been sitting out here all fucking night."

She turned on him and all the anger she had been feeling for the past few hours just bubbled right out of her.

"Really, I'm so fucking sorry for that, but, just a thought, maybe if you hadn't gone behind my back and had me investigated, you wouldn't have had to sit out here."

"I was wrong." How simple and easily given those words were.

"I'm glad we agree on that point."

"I was wrong, Darcy. I know just how wrong I was, but I love you, damn it."

And the hits just kept coming—to hear those words from him now broke her heart. They weren't going to change what she needed to do.

"You have no idea how long I've waited to hear you say those words to me again, but it's too little, too late, Lucien."

"What the hell are you saying?"

She was surprised how calm she sounded when her heart was shattering. "I could have forgiven you for invading my privacy, can even understand what fueled your need to do so, but I can't forgive you for believing that I would have abandoned our child. Every time you are faced with a choice, you always end up believing the worst about me."

"Darcy, I was wrong."

"Yeah, you were, and the next time you are faced with believing in me or not, what's to keep you from doing what you always do? Judging me and finding me wanting." Angry tears burned her eyes and stained her cheeks. "You don't get to judge me. You weren't there"—her voice broke and her shoulders slumped in defeat—"through the devastation of loss and the years that followed. I don't need your judgment or your hate because I hate myself enough for both of us."

Lucien tried to take a step toward her but she pulled away from him. "Darcy."

"I can't do this." She turned and started for her door.

"And you get to decide that it's over between us? This second chance we've been given, you're just willing to walk away from it?"

Her eyes speared him from over her shoulder. "I'm following your lead."

The door closed in his face with a decided click.

The following morning Darcy wanted to call in sick, but she had never been a coward. As she pulled open the door of Allegro, she hoped that Lucien had taken the day—hell, the week—off. She wasn't that lucky; when she passed his office, she saw him behind his desk. His head lifted and he looked right at her, but his expression was completely blank.

She hurried to her office hoping to hide the day away, but she hadn't even sat down when a soft knock and a movement at the door caught her attention. Lucien stood in her doorway. Her mouth opened to ask that he please just leave it be, but he stopped her with his words:

"Hear what I have to say and then I'll leave you alone."

Pain laced through his words, and hearing it broke her heart. She wasn't the only one hurting and so she nodded her head in reply.

"I've only ever loved two people in my life. I lost Sister Anne and right on the heels of that, I lost you. Her loss was painful, but yours was devastating. You're right I didn't fight for you back then, because something inside me broke when you left me.

"I know you wouldn't have given up our child, my reaction was knee-jerk and it was wrong. I'm sorry I hurt you, but I'm not going to make the same mistake again. I want you in my life, Darcy, and I'm not going to let you turn away from me. I'll give you time because I owe you that, but I plan on fighting like hell for you."

Darcy watched him walk away before she pulled out her chair and dropped down into it. "Wow."

<hr />

"Do you have a minute?" Darcy looked up from her work later that day to see Ember in her doorway.

"Ember, hi."

"Sorry to just drop by, but . . ."

Darcy leaned back in her chair and studied the other woman. She wasn't at all hard to read. "You've come to see if I'm okay."

Humor moved across Ember's expression. "Am I really that expressive?"

"Yep."

"I'm not trying to pry, but you looked really upset yesterday and I know it's not my business, but if you need someone to talk to or a shoulder to cry on or just want to eat your body weight in chocolate and watch sappy movies, I'm here."

Darcy was surprised, not just by the offer but by the realization that she really wanted someone to talk to. "I'd like that. Are you free tonight?"

"I am. At the risk of meddling, I don't know what happened between you and Lucien, but I do know the man he is now. He's complicated and private, but he's the first to offer a hand when someone needs it."

"It sounds like he hasn't changed much at all."

"The ones we love can hurt us the most, and he does love you. It's written all over his face."

"Thanks for that. My place, tonight at seven. I'll text you the address."

"I'll be there."

———•——

Lucien nursed his Scotch and thought about Darcy. The memory slammed into him.

———•——

Fifteen years earlier . . .

"Have you thought about where you want to be in ten years?" Lucien asked Darcy as they walked the familiar neighborhood near St. Agnes.

"I have."

It was more how she answered that piqued his interest. "And?"

"I want a family: children and a husband who loves me to distraction. I want a place where I belong, where I don't feel like I'm wanting, where I can just be me."

Lucien stopped walking and turned into Darcy. "Do you feel that way around me?"

Her eyes couldn't quite meet his. "I do. In my dreams you're the husband who loves me to distraction."

He touched her chin to lift her gaze to his. "I'm well on my way to loving you to distraction." And then he wiggled his eyebrows. "Children . . . yeah, when we're older I can get behind that, particularly with how dedicated we would have to be in our quest for children. It's tireless work, but I do believe I am up to the task."

"You're a goofball."

His arm wrapped around her shoulders so he could pull her closer to kiss her head. "But I'm your goofball."

"What about you?" Darcy asked. "Have you thought about where you'll be in ten years?"

He met her gaze. "Surrounded by hordes of children with a wife whom I love to distraction."

Darcy tried to pull away from him. "You're making fun of me."

He drew her closer and wrapped his arms around her. "I want to make something of myself. How I'm going to do that, I don't know. When I look into my future, the only thing I see clearly is that you're with me."

"Are you teasing me?"

He framed her face with his hands. "I am being completely serious. You are my constant."

Lucien was jolted out of the memory when someone spoke his name. He looked up to see Kyle.

"Hey."

"Sorry, you looked deep in thought, but I wanted to thank you for hooking my band up with your friend. We're working on making a demo."

Lucien gestured to the chair across from him. "I heard. He called me right after he heard you play. He hasn't been this excited about a band in a really long time."

"Thanks for putting in the word and getting us a chance."

Lucien grinned. "Just remember me when you're accepting your Grammy."

"If we ever get that far, you can be damn sure of that." Kyle was silent for a moment. "You okay? You look like someone just kicked your dog."

"Do you have a girlfriend, Kyle?"

"Not at the moment; never met anyone I liked enough that I wanted to stick with after a fight. Why?"

"I've been profoundly stupid when it comes to the most important person in my life. I'm pulling her close one minute and pushing her away the next."

"That seems like a normal reaction to me."

Lucien didn't hide his confusion when he asked, "How so?"

"It's crap when people say you shouldn't try to change someone. The whole nature of a relationship is compromise, and compromise is change. It can be scary as hell changing what you know to fit with someone else, so I think you're entitled to drag your feet a bit."

Lucien chuckled with self-deprecation at Kyle's simple truth because damn if he didn't recognize himself. "That was remarkably insightful, Kyle."

"I'm a regular Dr. Phil." He leaned up and rested his elbows on the table. "I've never met anyone I was even willing to brood over, so the fact that you've found her . . . Don't drag your feet too long. It's not likely she'll come around again."

Lucien signaled the bartender before his gaze turned back to Kyle. "If your music career doesn't take off, you could always become a television shrink."

"Well, now that's comforting. Then you can buy rounds until my residuals start coming in."

"With pleasure, and thanks, Kyle."

Kyle's grin came in a flash. "One good turn deserves another."

Tears rolled down Darcy's face as she blew her nose into a tissue. Ember was sitting next to her, sobbing softly. The credits to *Beaches* were rolling on the screen, but Darcy couldn't see them through the tears in her eyes.

"Why the hell did you make us watch that?"

"Your troubles don't seem as bad now, do they?"

Darcy knew she was looking at Ember like she had sprouted wings, but she realized Ember wasn't wrong. "I guess not."

"We could watch *Bram Stoker's Dracula* next."

"Why?"

"Because that's a relationship to cry over."

Darcy laughed, but it came out in more of a gasp, and then she sobered. She didn't mean to blurt it out the way she did. "I lost Lucien and my baby when I was seventeen."

"Oh Darcy."

"Lucien found out about the baby and thought I had given our child up."

A look of disbelief crossed Ember's face. "That's quite a conclusion to jump to."

"Exactly."

"Of course, Lucien learned that he had fathered a child, so I imagine it was easier for him to accept that you gave up the baby than to take the leap that the baby he had just learned about had died."

Darcy felt ill. She hadn't even considered Lucien's feelings. He may have learned after the fact about their child, but it didn't make the pain of loss any less, even all these years later. Shame filled her that she could have been so selfish.

Ember seemed to be a mind reader. "Sometimes it's hard to see a situation clearly when you're in the middle of it."

Darcy felt the damn tears again. "I didn't even hold him, didn't commiserate with him about the loss of our child. I didn't think about him at all."

Ember's words had more impact because of how simple they were. "I think he'll understand that because he wasn't thinking about you either; or rather, he was thinking more about how the news affected him. But it's not too late."

———◆———

Darcy shut off the lights and moved into her bedroom after Ember left. After she got ready for bed she climbed under her covers and tried for sleep, but her mind remained restless. She was angry with Lucien for his reaction to the news about their baby, but it was his intensity that she loved. How could she hold what she loved most about him against him? When she fell asleep, she dreamt of him.

Fourteen years earlier . . .

She didn't hear him enter the common room until his hand wrapped around hers and he pulled her from it. He didn't say a word, but led her up to the attic. The door had barely closed behind her before his mouth was on hers. There was a wildness about him that left Darcy breathless and unimaginably turned on. He lifted her shirt up over her head and flicked off her bra a second before his mouth closed over her breast. Her jeans followed her shirt and then he was dragging her onto the floor, spreading her legs, and taking her into his mouth. His tongue was almost brutal as he penetrated her, and then his fingers replaced his tongue while he moved to flick the sensitive nub, teasing her until he worked her up to an orgasm that bordered on violent. Her body was still coming down when he stood and walked to the far side of the attic.

She felt exposed and vulnerable and though she wouldn't call it rape, there had been more to their lovemaking than love. Before she could say anything, his anguished voice filled the awkward silence.

"I'm sorry."

"What was that all about?"

He linked his fingers behind his head and she watched as he struggled to lift his gaze to hers. "I was thinking about you and I don't know. I'm constantly walking the line of insanity when it comes to you. It's about more than sex and even love: I need you. It scares the shit out of me that I could lose you like I did Sister Anne. I didn't mean to . . ." He turned from her. "I just needed you."

She stood and moved to him, her hands coming to rest on his back. "I'm here."

"Fuck. I practically raped you."

She forced him to face her. "It could never be rape with you. It was just slightly out of control."

"I'm sorry."

"Never apologize for loving me." Her fingers gripped his shirt and lifted it over his head. "Even when you're slightly out of control, I love every second." He was so tense and she knew of a way to relax him, but she had never done it before. Even so, she hoped that he couldn't see how badly her hands were shaking when she unbuttoned his jeans and moved his pants and briefs down his legs. She kneeled in front of him and looked up to see his eyes burning hot, but she saw guilt there too: that she would offer something so intimate after he had been so out of control with her.

"I want to," was all she said. Her eyes never left his as she took him into her mouth.

"Darcy, oh God . . ." His words ended on a groan as she sucked him deep into her throat. Her hands sought the hard curve of his ass as she worked him. He wasn't the one out of control this time as was evident when he moved from her and lowered himself to kneel on the floor, pulling her down with him. Their eyes were locked when she straddled his hips and took him deep inside her. Her legs wrapped around his waist as his hands cradled her ass.

The words came from her heart. "You and me always."

Her words hit their mark and he started to move her up and down his hard shaft. Their eyes never left each other and when she came, he was right there with her. He wrapped her in his arms and held her so close.

"Always. Remember that, Darcy."

<hr />

Trace stood in the doorway of the office and watched as Ember taped paint swatches to the wall. Rafe had helped him move the furniture to the storage unit in the basement earlier so that Ember could start working on the nursery. They had only announced the baby a week ago and Ember was already knee-deep in planning.

He hadn't been able to stop thinking about the doctor visit from earlier that day. They had had another positive ultrasound, but he felt conflicted. As incredible as it was to see the flutter that was their child's heartbeat, the thought of something going wrong and Ember being put in harm's way never left him. Ember's voice took him from his troubled thoughts.

"Do you want to know the gender?" she asked as she looked at him from over her shoulder.

He leaned against the doorjamb with his hands in the front pockets of his jeans. "I don't know. Do you?"

She turned to face him and a slight smile touched her lips as she said, "I think I do."

"Are you hoping for a boy or a girl?"

"Either, but I would love to have a little you walking around," she said.

He'd have thought he would be used to the stuff she said, but she always surprised him. He started toward her. "Is it too soon to find out?"

"We can ask Dr. Cole at the next ultrasound."

She walked right into him, wrapping her arms around his waist and resting her head on his chest.

"You should probably take a nap. You look exhausted," he said.

"I am."

"I'm sorry, Ember."

Confusion furrowed her brow when she asked, "For what?"

"Getting us pulled into this blackmailing shit with Heidi. You've been through enough and just when things settle down, we're faced with something else."

"It isn't your fault."

He held her close and pressed a kiss on her head. "Doesn't matter."

"We'll get through it."

The smile bloomed involuntarily as he looked down at her. "Looking for that silver lining, are you?"

"There always is one," she muttered.

He lifted her into his arms and started for their bedroom. "You really need to rest."

"Rest with me."

"If I join you, we won't be resting."

Her fingers danced along his jaw. "I know."

They reached the bed and he lowered her to her feet just as his mouth came down on hers. She sighed into his mouth and wrapped her arms around him to keep him close.

"Lift up your arms," he whispered. And as soon as she did, he lifted her shirt up and over her head. Her hands lowered to rest on his shoulders before she slowly moved them down his arms, her delicate touch making him feel almost primal. He deftly undid the clasp of her bra and slid the lace down her arms.

"My turn," she breathed against his mouth as her fingers found his tee and worked it up over his head. She pressed her lips over his heart, as she did every time she saw her name on his skin, and he felt the heat of her kiss clear down to his bones.

He rid them of the rest of their clothes before he wrapped his arm around her waist and pulled her onto the bed, settling himself between her thighs. She tilted her hips, rubbing herself against him, as his mouth crushed down on hers. She reached for his face, framing it with her hands as she pulled his tongue into her mouth, sucking on it before stroking it with her own. Her hands moved over him and everywhere she touched, it felt like fire was sizzling along his skin.

He shifted so he could look at her; her eyes were closed and desire had brought a blush to her cheeks. He didn't have the words like she did to express how he felt.

"Look at me, Ember."

Her eyes opened and there was that tenderness that he had come to crave seeing. She touched him, her fingers running a trail along his jaw to his chin. He moved, slowly sinking into her as he joined them, her legs spreading wider as her hips lifted, and then he held himself completely still. It was as close to heaven as he was ever going to get.

"My wife," he whispered reverently, and then he started to move. Her legs wrapped around his waist as he slowly brought her to the brink, and he watched her eyes glaze over as her orgasm took her. His was soon to follow, her body still spasming around him as he came. He lowered himself onto the bed and wrapped Ember into his arms. Protectiveness swelled in him as his arms unconsciously tightened around her. She settled her head against his chest, her arm coming to rest at his waist.

"That was beautiful." Her words were so softly spoken, as if she were feeling what he was: awe over what they just shared that was so much more than sex.

He pressed a kiss to her forehead since he had no words that would do justice to what he was feeling.

"Sleep, sweetheart."

"Stay with me."

"Forever."

She pressed another kiss to his heart and he felt a wetness there before she whispered, "I love you."

He fucking loved it when she said that to him. Before he could reply, she was sound asleep.

Trace woke four hours later with a start. He had never in his life taken a nap. It was dark out and a glance at the clock showed it was close to nine at night. Ember was still asleep, practically on top of him.

He gently rolled her off and slipped from the bed. In sleep, her hand reached for him and, when she came away empty, she curled into a ball on her side. He pulled the covers over her and kissed her head. He put on some jeans and ducked into the nursery. In under six months there would be a baby sleeping there. He grinned as he went to the kitchen for a beer, then settled in the living room with some files he wanted to read through.

The sound of the house phone startled him from his work. When he looked at the display he was surprised that it was after three in the morning. His surprise turned to annoyance when he saw Heidi's number.

Why the hell was she calling his home number?

"What the fuck do you want?"

"You have to help me." Her voice sounded odd.

"No, I don't."

He was about to hang up when she sobbed. "They're going to kill me."

"What the fuck are you talking about?"

"I underestimated them. Help me, Trace."

He was tempted to hang up on her, but the fear in her voice was genuine. And if she were in danger, then so was Seth. "Underestimated whom?"

"Not over the phone. Can you meet me at the twenty-four-hour diner near the apartment?"

"Now?"

"Please."

"If you're fucking around . . . I swear to God, Heidi."

"I'm not."

"I'll meet you in thirty." He hung up without waiting for a reply. He didn't want to wake Ember, but he didn't want her waking up and finding him gone, either. He walked into their room and settled on the edge of their bed.

"Ember, sweetheart."

It took her a few minutes for her eyes to open. When he saw she was mostly awake, he said, "I need to go out."

She looked past him to the clock and when she realized it was three in the morning, she was instantly wide awake. "Why?"

"Heidi called. She's in trouble and she's scared."

He saw her face darken in response, so he added, "I know what you're thinking, I'm with you on that, but she really sounded scared. If there is even the slightest chance that Seth could be in danger, I need to do what I can."

She sat up before she asked, "Did she say what or who scared her?"

"She wouldn't over the phone."

"Okay." Ember started climbing from the bed.

"What are you doing?"

"I'm coming with you."

"The hell you are," he snapped. "If there really is something to this, you're going to be as far from it as possible."

"And you, once again, are going to walk blindly into something. This is Heidi we're talking about."

He rubbed a hand over his head in frustration. "Believe me, I know, but it's late and you're pregnant."

"I don't want you going by yourself," she said softly.

The arrogant grin was instinctual. "I can handle Heidi."

"Trace."

He moved to her and wrapped her in his arms. "I'll be fine. Please get back into bed; you've circles under your eyes."

He knew she was more tired than she was letting on when she didn't argue further and slipped under the covers.

"Wake me when you get home."

"I will."

He was out the door ten minutes later and on his bike five minutes after that. An unsettling sensation twinged in his gut when he reached the corner where the diner was located and saw red-and-blue lights flashing. He pulled over, climbed off, and joined the crowd that had formed at the crime tape blocking the alley by the diner. One look and his stomach dropped because lying in a pool of blood, looking but not seeing, was Heidi.

"Oh fuck." Even he was surprised at his callousness when he didn't feel the slightest bit of remorse at her death, just irritation. Just like Heidi, even in death she brought him grief. Thank God Ember hadn't come and seen this. The sight of Heidi's pale hair soaked with blood was something he wasn't going to forget for a good long time. Where the hell was Seth? He looked around, but didn't see him and felt a wave of relief. At least he'd been spared this.

Trace sought out the officer in charge. The officer was older, maybe late forties, and stocky in build, but intelligence burned in his brown eyes as he looked at Trace.

"Can I help you?" he asked impatiently.

Trace exhaled in resignation before he said, "My name's Trace Montgomery. Heidi Moore is the victim and she called me and asked that I meet her here."

Immediately, impatience was replaced with interest. "Really? Well, the detectives are going to want to talk with you. They'll be here in twenty."

It was close to nine in the morning when Trace returned home. He keyed into the apartment and saw Ember standing in the living room with the phone in her hand. As soon as she saw him, she started toward him and there was worry and concern in her voice when she asked, "What happened?"

The sight of her so vibrant and alive made him silently move toward her and wrap her in his arms.

"Trace, you're scaring me."

"Heidi's dead."

Ember broke away from him. "What? Dead?"

"Murdered."

"Oh my God."

Her body started to shake, so he brought her back to him and held her close. "She was killed right outside of where we'd agreed to meet."

Her voice wasn't quite steady when she asked, "The cops don't think you had anything to do with it, do they?"

"I'm not sure. There seems to be some discrepancy regarding the timeline because they were hammering me about when she called. They're running our phone records to find out the exact time. I've been asked not to leave town."

"That's outrageous. Why would the timeline be of such interest to them?" She wasn't really asking him, just talking out loud as she tried to work it out.

"And you have no idea why she wanted to meet you?"

"Only that she was scared of someone, said someone was going to kill her, but I didn't push because I thought it was just another one of her games. Clearly it wasn't."

Her eyes went wide. "What about Seth? Where's he?"

"He's okay. He was home asleep. The police allowed me to come with them and I was surprised at how well he took the news. I realize there was no love between them, but she was still his mother."

Ember said, "I imagine the cops found his reaction interesting. He no doubt is being looked at as a potential suspect."

"They didn't say as much, but I got that impression, yeah."

"I don't think he did it," she said with fierceness.

"Neither do I."

"Poor Seth. Regardless of his relationship with Heidi, I couldn't imagine having to stay in that apartment where everything reminds him of her."

"I agree."

"Brandon mentioned that he and Seth were hoping to get an apartment together. Right now, he's living in the group home in Hell's Kitchen that you, Lucien, and Rafe stayed in," she said.

"Really? That's interesting. Next time you see Brandon, mention it to him. I'd help them cover the expenses."

Ember reached for his hand. "I think it's a wonderful idea and we can think about it later. Right now, you need to sleep."

He allowed her to lead him toward their bedroom because he was exhausted. They passed Chelsea's room and Ember looked back at him. "Are you going to tell her?"

"Not right now. She doesn't know who Seth is and I don't really want to burden her with it."

"Good choice."

When they reached their room, Ember turned to Trace and lifted his shirt over his head. Feeling her hands on the button of his jeans made him instantly wide-awake and he rose to greet her. She felt him as her hand moved lower to stroke his hard length through his jeans. Her nipples pebbled through the silk of her nightgown and he lowered his head to capture her breast in his mouth.

"You need to sleep."

"I need you more."

He took a step back and lifted her gown in one move. He devoured the sight of her as she worked his zipper to free him. He reached for her and tossed her onto the bed before removing the last of his clothes and pouncing, covering her body with his own. She was ready when his fingers found their way between her legs. His knees spread her further as he positioned himself and slowly entered her. His eyes stayed on hers as he claimed her inch by breathtakingly slow inch. It was about more than love: it was affirmation of life and living. When he was fully inside her, he held himself still, fucking loving being part of her, and then he started to move. His mouth closed over her breast and her hands grabbed his ass, urging him to go faster. He rolled, keeping her close, until she was astride him. She needed no further encouragement as she started to move, her hips driving him crazy. He felt her body squeezing him just as he found the spot that he knew would send her over the edge. She cried out as she came.

Trace was rock hard when he flipped her over and started to thrust into her again, deep and fast.

"Again," he demanded as his fingers found that nub and stroked her. He felt her spasming around him just as he came.

Her eyes were closed when she whispered, "I love when you lose your control with me."

He didn't answer with words, but took her mouth in a kiss that made him lose control again.

Chapter Thirteen

A dark cloud hung over the campaign headquarters when
Ember returned two days after Heidi's murder, though most
who worked there didn't know of Heidi or that she was dead. It
was probably Ember's own emotions causing the sensation. She
tried to focus her attention on her latest assignment from her
editor, reading about Nathaniel Carmichael.

It was strange reading about Dane's father. Nathaniel was
liked, well respected, and a successful politician, who had been
an even more successful investment banker before his aspirations
turned to politics. Though he had been described as a playboy,
he was respectful of women, unlike Dane. From all that she had
read, there were no skeletons in his closet, but she was sure the
same could not be said for his son.

His life seemed pretty cut-and-dried except for his marriage.
Dane's mom had been beautiful, and there were countless pictures of her, young and smiling on the arm of her husband. For
all intents and purposes, the two looked happily in love, but looks
could be deceiving, because she'd left them when Dane was just a

baby and had never looked back. To have a mother who chose to leave you actually explained a lot about Dane.

Yet Nathaniel had never filed for a divorce. Maybe she didn't love him, but it seemed that he loved her.

Ember's attention turned to Charles as he paced his office. He was acting strange, almost nervous. The memory of Heidi's visit to Charles flashed in her head. It was surprising to Ember that Charles had even known of Heidi, but even odder was the anger Heidi had shown that day. What had that been all about?

Heidi had been blackmailing Trace; maybe she had something on Charles too, but what?

Later that day, Ember returned home to find Trace sitting in the living room, staring at the wall.

"Hi, beautiful."

"Hey. Where's Chelsea?"

"I dropped her off at her friend's. She's going to spend the night."

"That's nice." She settled next to him, and he turned his focus from the wall to her.

"Charles seems to be taking Heidi's death hard," Ember said.

"Why do you say that?"

"He's off, acting edgy and nervous. He knew Heidi. I told you about the day she came to see him and they had words. Do you think he knew her when she was at St. Agnes?"

"Why's that important?"

"Just trying to figure out how far back their relationship goes."

Trace thought on her question. "I don't know how he would have known her then and I certainly never introduced them."

"She was there because she was pregnant, wasn't she?"

"Yeah."

Ember knew they were both thinking the same thing: what a disgusting human being his father had been. Abusing his children, drugging his wife, and knocking up sixteen-year-old girls.

"How the hell did your father even meet her?"

"Knowing my dad, he probably scoped out the high school, the sick fuck."

"You minimize it, but you took her under your wing, albeit begrudgingly, because she was a link to Seth." He looked at her funny and she added, "You didn't have to pay that ransom. I know you, and you could have found several ways to get her to keep quiet without paying her a cent."

His grin looked almost boyish. "You think so?"

"I know so."

"I paid her in the beginning because she and Seth needed it, despite the fact that she was blackmailing me. But after you came into my life, I paid her to keep quiet. Stupid, but done with the best intentions."

She reached for his hand. "And before?"

"I avoided her because she developed a crush on me and I wasn't at all interested. I didn't tell you much about her because she was just another one of my father's messes that I had to clean up. She never was anything more to me than that despite her efforts to change it."

Ember thought about the talk she and Heidi had had last year and how Heidi had stalked Trace to learn more about him, which had been odd then. But now, knowing what linked them, it only reinforced what he said. She really had meant nothing to him.

"Then why did you use her to try and drive me away?"

"Because unlike the other women of my acquaintance, Heidi wouldn't have misinterpreted my actions because she knew she meant nothing to me." He looked a little nervous before he asked, "We okay?"

She leaned into him and pressed her lips to his. "Always."

He moved quickly to bring her mouth back to his for a kiss that she felt all the way down to her toes. He was grinning when he leaned back.

"Why were you sitting here staring at the wall?"

The humor faded from his face. "The police called. They checked the phone records and I'm off the hook for Heidi's murder."

"But?"

"They wanted to go through our conversation again, word for word."

"Why?"

"The timeline again. Our phone records confirm that Heidi called here at three oh eight a.m. The call lasted two minutes. The medical examiner puts time of death at around quarter after to half past three."

A chill went through her. "Okay, that's creepy."

His eyes finally looked into hers. "It gets creepier. The nine-one-one call reporting the murder was made just before three."

"Holy shit."

"Yeah, the person who called nine-one-one about the murder was the actual murderer."

"I don't understand."

"I don't either, but the police have a few theories."

"And they shared these theories with you?"

"Yeah, I got the sense they were trying to trip me up. But based on what they told me, they think Heidi was blackmailing someone. She went too far and they pushed back. They think that the blackmailee contacted Heidi that night. There's a record of a call on her phone at two a.m. and I'm guessing it was from a burner phone so they can't trace it. They're working under the assumption that he was right in the area, watching Heidi's reaction to his call. Possibly hoping that if she was working with someone, she'd contact them."

"And that's where you come in."

"Exactly. Whether the police believe I'm involved in the blackmail plot is unclear, but if the murderer really was there, then they're going to think I was working with Heidi."

"Goddamn her, even in death she's fucking with us."

"Agreed."

"What's the other theory?" she asked.

"That she had an accomplice who she double-crossed and they sought payback."

Trace moved to wrap Ember in his arms. "There's one person even more affected by this shit than us."

Her heart stopped. "Seth."

"He was there in that apartment with no alibi. Based on the police's theory, he's their number one suspect."

Chapter Fourteen

D ane's head rested against the sofa while the drugs coursed through his blood. Lena was kneeling in front of him sucking him off, but surprisingly his thoughts were elsewhere.

Heidi was dead. And he had a feeling he knew by whose hand. That scared the shit out of him. He knew that Heidi had been blackmailing someone in his family, maybe even all of them. She'd believed she had them all wrapped around her little finger, but obviously the blackmailee disagreed. What concerned him was what Heidi had left behind. Could he be implicated in Heidi's scheme? If so, would the killer come after him?

He had no illusions that he'd been spared because he was a blood relation; in fact, most of the time he knew his biological link to his family only served to piss them all off, including dear ol' dad.

He'd been following the news and knew that the investigation was hovering over Heidi's son and he knew from Heidi herself the connection with Trace Montgomery. If he shared what he knew, maybe Trace would uncover who did it before they came looking for Dane.

He was so lost in thought he didn't realize that Lena had stopped working him and was watching him intently.

"What are you thinking?"

"I think I need you to reach out to Ember."

Lena stood. "No."

"I need you to call her."

"I was giving you a blow job and you were fucking thinking about Ember?" Her next words echoed off the walls. "Why her?"

"I have information that might help them uncover who killed Heidi."

"And we care about that why?"

"Because maybe they'll find the killer before he comes after me."

Confusion moved over her face and words didn't follow for a few minutes. "Why would the killer come after you?" she managed.

"Heidi and I shared in a little activity for a while and if it got out I was her accomplice, the killer may think I was still working with her when she died. If they killed her to keep their secret, there's no reason to believe they won't kill me."

The fight just drained out of her. "I'll call her."

———•———

Lucien was in the kitchen making lunch when his cell phone rang. Seeing it was Trace again, and knowing he had been off the grid for two days not taking calls or e-mails—hell, he wasn't even paying attention to current events—he answered it.

"Trace."

"I've been trying to call you for two days. I'm guessing things are not going well with Darcy?"

"She's pigheaded and stubborn, but so am I."

"Ain't that true. Listen, Heidi's been murdered."

"What?"

"Yeah, and right now they're looking at Seth as a suspect."

"That's bullshit."

"You don't have to tell me. You mentioned she fucked with you and Darcy back in the day?"

"Not just her. There was a man who came to see Darcy to get her out of my life. Whoever it was told her he'd watch out for me. Heidi helped get him past visitor sign-in and kept me distracted so he would have time to intimidate Darcy."

"What the fuck? Who was he?"

"That is what we're trying to figure out. I got Josh looking into it, but the man is like a fucking ghost."

"Why the interest?"

"Same question we're asking ourselves."

"Man, I'm sorry. Especially knowing what Darcy means to you, that's fucked up."

Lucien's voice was icy cold when he said, "Yeah, which will make bringing that fucker down oh-so enjoyable."

"Count me in. Do you ever recall Charles or Vivian coming to St. Agnes when I was there?"

"No, not that I recall, but Sister Margaret would know. Why?"

"Ember made me think about Charles and his connection to Heidi and how far back exactly they've known each other."

They had the thought at the same time: "You don't think Charles came to see Darcy?" Trace asked. "What would be the point?"

"I don't know, but it's easy enough to find out. I'll show her a picture of him."

"Even though she isn't speaking to you."

"I can be persuasive."

Trace was silent for a minute. "If it was him, you get first crack."

"And you'll finish him off."

"Fucking straight. He has a lot to atone for."

Darcy wiped her hands on her pants and stopped in the doorway of Lucien's office. He looked up and immediately rose.

"Darcy."

"Do you have a minute?"

"Yeah." He walked around the desk and gestured to the sofa. She settled herself on the edge while she worked out in her head what she wanted to say. Her eyes met his and she could see what she was feeling staring back at her: love.

"I shouldn't have walked out at the party."

"I understand why you did."

"It was just that hearing my nightmare being spoken out loud and hearing the censure in your voice . . . it was too much. I should have told you about the baby. I wanted to, but every time we were together, I found an excuse to delay because I was so happy and I didn't want to ruin that."

"Why would telling me ruin that?" he asked.

"Because I was afraid you would hold me responsible. If I hadn't fallen, our baby would be alive. I've lived with that guilt for so long."

"Jesus, Darcy. It was an accident. How the hell could I hold you responsible?"

Tears filled her eyes and she managed a small, sad smile. "Because I hold myself responsible and so I just assumed you would too."

"Will you tell me what happened?" he asked.

"I found out right before we were going to leave together that I was pregnant. I had planned to tell you that day. When I found myself alone and pregnant, I was terrified, but I was excited too, because I was going to have a family. I was pretty far along when I fell. I don't really remember much after the fall, except that it was Sister Margaret who took me to the hospital. The days that followed were like a blur and then I learned that our baby had died.

I died that day too. My mom came for me and demanded that I come home with her. I didn't understand why because nothing had changed, but I wasn't given a choice."

Darcy noticed the look that crossed Lucien's face. "What are you thinking?"

"People don't do things without a reason. I'd like to know what reason your mom had to get involved."

Darcy had never really thought about it that way. It was a question she was going to demand her mother answer.

"Did the man that came to see you know you were pregnant?"

Darcy nodded.

"Any idea how he knew that?"

"Heidi. She was in the bathroom the day I took the pregnancy test. I'd bet money she fished the test out of the trash. At the time I just thought she was being her typical creepy self, but later I realized she had to be the link to the man."

Anger turned Lucien's voice hard. "Makes sense."

"I'm sorry that you learned about our baby in the way that you did."

"I'm sorry I wasn't there at your side. If I had known, I would have been."

"I don't want to keep running from you. I'm so tired of running, Lucien."

He ran his finger along her jaw. "We've both been hurt and are way more cautious this time around. You said once that we aren't the same people we were. We're not, but I want to get to know the person you've become. I still want you in my life, Darcy."

"I want that too."

"I've no other secrets, do you?" he asked.

"No."

"Then let's take it day by day." He reached for her hand and pulled her to her feet. "Have you had lunch?"

"No."

"Good, then I'll whip something up in the kitchen and you can comment on my culinary skills."

"You can forgive me that easily?" she whispered.

"Can you?" he asked.

Her reply was immediate and heartfelt. "Yes."

He pressed a kiss on her forehead. "Me too. Come on. I'm starving."

⋯✦⋯

The following evening, Darcy sat across from Lucien at Tapas. They were doing exactly as Lucien had suggested, taking it a day at a time. She watched as he placed the order for their drinks before he turned his attention on her.

"There's something I've been wanting to ask you, but being a stubborn prick, I kept myself from doing so."

"What?"

"How did you manage college?"

Her reaction to that question surprised her. A lump formed in her throat and her eyes burned. Lucien noticed when he gently asked, "What's wrong?"

"I didn't think you cared."

"I've always cared."

She accepted those words with the same sincerity with which they were offered. She collected herself before she answered him.

"Sister Margaret arranged it."

His look of disbelief brought a chuckle from her. "How did that happen?"

"When I turned eighteen, she summoned me. Told me she had it all worked out and that all I needed to do was accept."

"Why? Not that I'm not glad she gave you the opportunity, but that isn't like her."

"That's exactly how I felt. She claimed it was because I had suffered through a lot, but I don't know. I always had the sense that it was penance for something."

"Why do you say that?"

"Like you said, she wasn't that kind of person, so why take the interest? People don't change overnight, and yet she did a complete one-eighty when she offered me a chance to change my life. And it did—going to college took my life in a direction it never would have gone."

It was the thoughtful look on his face that made her ask, "What are you thinking?"

The waitress returned in that moment and they waited for the wine to be served and for her to move on before he replied, "It just seems odd that two people in your life known for their disinterest suddenly take an interest in you. Why?"

"I don't know. I've thought about what could have motivated Sister Margaret and the only thing she seemed to care about was St. Agnes. Maybe she thought I was going to seek restitution because I fell there."

Lucien lifted his glass but Darcy could tell he was mulling over her words. "Maybe. Doesn't explain your mom."

"Unless Sister Margaret asked her to come for me, maybe compensating her to do so. My mom would do just about anything for money."

His response was barely audible. "Bitch."

And then he sobered. "I'm sorry you went through that alone. There were several times I almost came back during that first year just to see how you were doing. If I had, maybe you wouldn't have fallen."

"Maybe. And you would have stayed; I know you well enough to know that. We'd have our child, but I would never have known if you stayed because you wanted to or because you thought you had to. And I suspect you would have wondered yourself. It was a difficult time—everything happens for a reason."

He reached across the table for her hand. "No, there wouldn't have been any question. I would have stayed because, despite how much you'd hurt me, you're it for me. Always, Darcy. I meant that."

"Me too."

He squeezed her hand before he released it and reached for his menu. "Our waitress is circling."

——◆——

My dearest love,

It has been two weeks since I held you in my arms. I cannot bear this separation. I need to see you. I cannot focus on my work or my family because all of my thoughts are with you. You must put me out of my misery and agree to be my wife. Please, my love. I know what I ask, how much you would have to give up, but I am lost without you.

Yours always,

XX

Darling,

You must marry me now. Can you not see that? We will be happy, I promise. Please let me love you. Let me give you the world. I will devote all that I have to you. Give us a chance to have our happily-ever-after.

Love,

XX

You win. I will not write again and I will keep my promise. You are making a mistake, and one day I think you will come to realize what you gave up. I hope the life you chose

was worth it, worth losing something so absolute. I will
never stop loving you and I will watch over you.
As always, your devoted love,
    XX

Ember folded up the last letter and felt the tears stinging her eyes. It was heartbreaking, the agony of loving someone but being denied a lifetime with them. What had kept them apart? Clearly there was love on both sides; the fact that the letters were saved was proof that they meant a great deal to the recipient. They looked old, a few decades, she would guess by the discoloration. Whose were they?

She was so focused on the letters that she didn't notice Trace until he bent down and kissed her. He looked at the letters.

"What are they?"

"Old love letters that I found in the attic at St. Agnes. It's like a treasure trove. I can't imagine the number of secrets that attic is hiding."

She turned into him and pulled him down onto the floor with her. "What are you doing home? I thought you had a class."

"I asked Carlos to take it."

"Why?"

"I wanted to see you." His fingers raked through her hair and he seemed to be following the motion before he asked, "How's the writing?"

"Good, but I'm trying to decide on one of two directions." She was nervous when she asked, "Did you read what I sent you?"

"I did."

"And?"

"Well . . ."

She felt her heart start to pound with nerves.

"A story about two very unlikely people falling wildly in love."

His eyes looked right into hers and he looked so serious. "I think it's . . . a little farfetched."

A grin cracked over his face and humor burned in his eyes as he continued. "I mean, what's the likelihood that would ever happen? It seems to lack that realism your professor is so fond of."

Ember's jaw dropped and Trace touched his thumb to it to close her mouth.

"Holy shit, you're teasing me. Trace Montgomery has discovered a sense of humor. I need to write this down."

"I'm learning from you that there are other ways to express how I feel that don't require getting naked."

In response, her body clenched since she happened to like, a lot, that he expressed himself by getting naked. So much, in fact, that she was suddenly feeling really warm; but the sentiment was beautiful and she said as much.

And then those eyes went dark as he lowered her to the floor and covered her body with his own.

"That being said, I happen to be a great fan of expressing one's self naked."

His fingers were already moving her shirt up just before he pressed a kiss on her belly. He did that often and she loved that even though he was worried, he wanted the baby. He gripped her pants and moved them down her legs, then lifted her foot in his hands, rubbing the arch in a massage that felt so good.

He pressed a kiss where he was massaging before moving his lips slowly up her leg. He kissed the edge of her panties, just over her navel before moving up her body to pop her breasts from the top of her bra right before closing his mouth over one of them. She rubbed herself against his jean-clad body and reached for his button. He quickly yanked her panties off before he removed his clothes with an economy of moves that was very much appreciated. And then he took his good sweet time expressing himself.

Trace went back to the cooking school after their fabulous lunch break. Ember went to work on her book and was just getting into the scene when her phone rang. She wasn't going to answer it until she saw that it was Lena. Her stomach dropped, even as she felt joy that Lena was finally returning her calls.

"Hello."

"Ember, it's Lena." She paused for a moment, then said, "Look, I'm sorry I haven't called you, I've just been busy with my own stuff."

"I understand."

"How was the wedding?"

Maybe it was silly, but Ember couldn't help her smile. "It was beautiful."

"You're happy, right?"

"I am. How about you?"

"I'm getting there. You were right about Todd. I know that now and I'm sorry."

Progress, Ember thought. "Thanks for saying that."

There was a moment of silence. "I'm really calling you at Dane's request."

Ember totally didn't see that coming. "Dane?"

"I know. He was high and his judgment was seriously off. He's the first to admit it."

Ember couldn't help the anger she felt remembering the night he'd dragged her from Sapphire with the intention of . . . she didn't even want to think about it.

"You have every right to hate him, but he asked that I pass something on to you."

Only out of curiosity as to what Dane could possibly think she'd find interesting, Ember said, "Okay."

"He knows the cops are looking at Seth for Heidi's murder, but he knows for a fact that she was blackmailing someone in his family and, though he doesn't know who for sure, he thinks it was his dad."

Ember couldn't deny Dane's timing was impeccable, but why would he want her to know this? She asked Lena.

"Heidi and Dane had a little blackmailing deal going on. Small potatoes, pretty harmless stuff and not very big payouts, but Heidi escalated it. She wouldn't tell him how she'd come to know certain things. So when she took the blackmailing to the next level, Dane stepped back. He's concerned the killer doesn't know that."

"And he's worried the killer may come after him," Ember finished.

"Yeah, the more people looking into who stood to gain the most with Heidi's death, the sooner the killer will be caught."

"Why doesn't he just go to the cops?"

"Fear of his family. And since he knows from Heidi that you have a PI in your family, he figured you were the next best thing."

"I don't know how much we can help, but I'll pass the information along."

"I better go."

"Okay, thanks for the information and the call."

"Yeah. I'll talk to you later."

Lena hung up before Ember had a chance to reply. She stared at her phone for a long time in mild shock, wondering if perhaps that was a step toward them being friends again, and then she called her uncle and relayed the news.

Chapter Fifteen

❧

I contacted Belinda Carmichael, the senator's estranged wife. It took some time to get through to her. Her sister Lily is a hell of a guard dog and when I finally was able to speak to Belinda, she wasn't any more helpful. I suspect that was because of fear, but of what I am not sure," Josh said to Lucien at lunch. "She painted a picture of her husband as a serial adulterer, though I suspect she was exaggerating his affairs because there's a lot of bitterness there; but nothing she told me would be profitable for a blackmailer. She had threatened to leave, but it was the judge who objected because of how that would look to the public."

"And yet she left. How did that happen?" Lucien asked.

"Apparently she had something to use as leverage against him and he agreed to let her go. The cost of her leaving was giving up her son and maintaining her family's silence about whatever she had on him."

"So maybe Heidi learned whatever it was Belinda had on the judge," Lucien concluded.

"That's what I'm thinking."

"And we still don't know the connection between Heidi and Charles, but I'm guessing she was blackmailing him too," Lucien said.

Josh leaned forward. "So Heidi was blackmailing one or more of the Carmichaels and possibly Charles. That's an awful lot of people who wanted her dead and there were probably more that we don't know about."

"Undoubtedly," Lucien replied. "Trace is already looking into the connection between Heidi and Charles."

"I'll keep digging into the Carmichaels," Josh offered. "How are things with Darcy?"

"I was an ass and she called me on it. We're working it out."

"I'm glad to hear that."

"I should have listened to you," Lucien admitted with a self-deprecating smile.

"I'm not one for I told you so . . ." Lucien joined in as Josh laughed.

———◆———

Darcy was a bit early for her monthly visit to her mom, but she couldn't stop thinking about Lucien's comment. What had been in it for her mom? She stepped off the subway in Queens and walked to her mom's apartment.

When she arrived there was a man just leaving, and his uniform from a popular parcel place made Darcy stop him.

"Can I help you?" she asked.

"I was just dropping off, but it's all signed for."

"Dropping off what?"

"A case of vodka." And then clearly nervous that maybe he had gotten something wrong, he looked at the work order. "Yeah, every two weeks a case of Absolut."

"Can I see that?"

"Sure, but I left a copy on the kitchen counter."

"Thanks, I'll just look at that one."

Darcy entered her mom's apartment and, as always, the place smelled like death. She walked into the kitchen to see a box on the counter filled with bottles of vodka. She saw the receipt and pocketed it before she grabbed a bottle and marched into her mom's room. The woman was sprawled out on the bed, one eye closed as she attempted to watch something on television.

"Where the hell did this come from?" Darcy asked. Her mom ignored her, so she stepped in front of the television, which immediately made her mom bellow, "Move the fuck out of the way."

"Where did this come from?" Darcy demanded as she shook the bottle of vodka.

"Give me that, that's mine," her mom said and tried to grab at it, but her balance was way off and she missed by a mile.

"Tell me where it came from first."

"It's delivery day."

"Is this how you are spending the money I send you?"

Her mom laughed. "Right. What you send me would barely keep me happy for two days. No, I've got me a little arrangement."

"With whom?"

"Don't know."

"And what do they get out of this arrangement?"

"Nothing."

"So some stranger is sending you a case of vodka every two weeks and they want nothing in return?"

"Nope. They already got what they wanted."

"Which was?"

Her mom seemed to have a moment of lucidity and she immediately turned her eyes away and started fiddling with her sheets. "I don't remember."

"What the fuck did you do?"

Hatred stared back at her when her mom turned her focus on Darcy. She could see that her mom was just dying to tell her and even as a numbness filled her, Darcy somehow managed to get the words out again. "What did you do?"

"Nothing, really, just had to lie. You were too young anyway. I did you a favor."

Darcy threw the bottle against the wall and lunged at her mom, her face right up into hers.

"What the fuck did you do? I swear to God if you don't tell me, I will pour out every fucking bottle of vodka in this house."

Panic replaced hatred before the words just tumbled out of her mom's mouth. "Your baby didn't die, you were just supposed to think that it had."

"What? Who would do such a thing?"

"I don't know and I don't care."

Darcy took a few steps back, but her legs gave out and she fell to her knees. Her baby was alive. Tears burned her eyes and rolled down her cheeks.

"My baby's alive?"

"Not that you'll ever find it."

Her joy was tampered by the rising hatred she felt for the woman who called herself her mom.

"Is that why you came for me at St. Agnes?" Darcy's voice was barely audible.

"Yes."

"How could you?"

"Because you are my greatest regret."

Darcy hardly recognized her own voice when she said, "And you are the lowest form of life. Why did someone as beautiful as Sister Anne have to die when a complete waste of matter like you gets to live? You can go to hell, Mother. I hope you burn for what you did."

And then she walked right out the door, putting her mom and that part of her life out of her mind forever. She would never, ever, come back here.

Her baby was alive. She had to find him—or was it a her? She fumbled in her purse for her phone and called Lucien, but his phone went to voice mail. Her next call was to Ember.

"Hey, Darcy."

"Can I get your uncle's number?"

"Yeah. Is everything okay?"

"It will be."

Josh O'Donnell's office was in the Bronx. A simple green shingle hung over the door. Darcy saw him as soon as she entered and didn't miss the look of contrition in his gaze.

"Darcy." He gestured to a chair. "Please have a seat." He studied her a minute before he said, "I'm sorry about before. I tried—"

Darcy cut him off. "I need your help."

He saw how worked up she was and immediately switched gears. "What can I do?"

"My baby is alive."

His shock couldn't be feigned. "What? How do you know that?"

Anger toward her mom burned through her, but she reined in her temper. "My mom was paid off to lie to me. She doesn't know who it was, but she didn't care since the incentive was liquor. I'm guessing it was the same man who came to me that day." She reached into her purse for the vodka receipt. "I think this order was placed by whoever took my baby. I don't know if it will help, but . . ."

"Any information, no matter how small, is helpful. Do you think you would recognize the man who came to see you if you saw him again?" Josh asked.

"He ruined my life. You bet I'd fucking recognize him."

"Sorry again," Josh said, which immediately made Darcy feel repentant.

"No, I'm sorry. It isn't your fault."

"Yeah, well I was the messenger." He took out a notebook. "Give me all the details you can remember and I'll get on it immediately."

Tears filled her eyes and her breath hitched. "Thank you."

❖

Darcy went to Allegro to find Lucien. He wasn't answering his cell and she needed to tell him the news about their child. But a walk through the bar showed that he wasn't there. Tara was working, so Darcy stopped at the bar and waited to get her attention to find out how long ago Lucien had left and if he'd happened to mention where he was going.

A group of women entered and settled at the bar next to her.

"I wonder if he's here tonight. I haven't seen him in a while. I heard he has a girlfriend now."

"Lucien? He doesn't strike me as the monogamous type. Man, I hope he isn't, anyway. That man knows his way around a woman's body."

"Fucking straight."

"Hell, maybe his girlfriend is into threesomes."

Darcy felt her temper stir and jealousy burn through her.

"Hey, Darcy. You want a drink?"

"Do you know where Lucien is? He isn't answering his phone."

"He was heading home. His phone battery died, so he was going to stop on the way home to buy a new one."

When she reached his building, she suddenly felt out of her depth at the sight of the place because it was so posh. The cab door was opened by an elderly gentleman.

"Evening, miss."

"Hi."

He held the door open and silently waited for her to climb out.

"Who are you here to see?"

"Lucien Black."

"Please, this way."

He led her inside and Darcy was taken aback by the beauty of Lucien's apartment building. She stood by the marble concierge desk while the man who had escorted her into the building spoke to another man who sat behind the desk.

"He'll call Mr. Black for you," the elderly man said before he started back toward the door. "Have a nice evening, miss."

"Thank you." Darcy had just gotten the words from her mouth when the gentleman behind the desk lifted the receiver to his ear. A minute later he said, "Mr. Black. I have a . . ."

He looked at Darcy who immediately said, "Darcy MacBride."

"A Darcy MacBride to see you. Right away." He hung up the receiver. "Take that elevator there up to the top."

Darcy started away from him. "Thank you."

When the gilded, be-chandeliered elevator opened, she felt her confidence slipping further. She knew Lucien was a wealthy man, but she hadn't appreciated just how wealthy until that moment.

The elevator door opened into the penthouse, and standing in the private entrance hall was Lucien.

"Darcy."

"Lucien."

He gestured to the living room. "Do you want to sit?"

"Yes . . . no."

His eyebrow rose and he tilted his head in question.

She twisted her hands and tears filled her eyes as the words just tumbled from her mouth. "Our baby is alive."

His expression changed from patience to shock before settling on joy. He moved across the room and wrapped her in his arms. "How do you know?"

"My mother lied—was paid to lie to me."

She felt him tense with anger when she said, "We have to find our child, but I don't even know where to start. I've asked Ember's uncle to look into it."

He released her only to frame her face with his hands. "We will find him"—he grinned—"or her. What's that look for?"

She wanted to move closer to Lucien, but instead she took a step away from him. She looked around at his lofty and elegant apartment—she really didn't have anything in common with him anymore. It was almost comical to pretend that they did. "Why would someone like you even look twice at me: a nothing girl with no family? You could have anyone; no one is outside of your reach, so why me? Maybe you keep finding me wanting because I really am, at least to someone like you. I know we said we were going to take it a day at a time, but maybe you are motivated to do so because we have a history. I won't hold that against you, if you don't."

"Are you finished?"

She looked at him and, damn, but she loved him. "I think so."

"Well, now you'll shut up and let me talk."

"Excuse me. I was being very civil. There's no need to be such a dick."

"Really? You come into my home and tell me that you won't hold me to our past. Well, that just fucking pisses me off."

"Why?" she spat back.

He reached her in two strides. His mouth connected with hers a second later, tasting her with a thoroughness that was breathtaking. He tore his mouth from her, his eyes like blue fire when he said, "Because our past is the only thing in my life I'm fucking proud of. Because I was a jackass running away from the one thing I should have been running to. Because I've loved you almost my whole life and I'll go right on loving you and, damn it, you love me too."

Her words were so softly spoken that he almost didn't hear them. "I do."

A grin flashed over his mouth before he kissed her again. His hands moved to her hips where he shifted the fabric of her skirt up her legs and lifted her off the floor, her legs wrapping around his waist, and moved to the wall, pressing her up against it as he ground his hips against her.

Her hands were eager when they reached for his shirt and lifted it up over his head. She pressed her mouth to him before she'd even discarded it. Her tongue licked his smooth, hard skin while her fingers worked the button of his jeans.

His hand moved between her legs and slipped under the silk to find her wet and ready. He drew his thumb across her pleasure point repeatedly before he slipped a finger inside. She moaned when he added another.

Her hand wrapped around him and pulled him free as his mouth settled over her breast, sucking her nipple into his mouth through the silk of her shirt and bra. She moved her hand up the silky, hard shaft, matching his rhythm as his fingers moved in and out of her.

She felt him grow harder and then he was ripping her panties off and she was guiding him to where she wanted him most. He pushed into her slowly and, having expected hard and fast, she almost begged at his deliberate pace. His eyes moved to hers and he watched her as he claimed her. When he was fully inside her, he held himself still until her eyes opened.

"We belong together, you and I, we always have."

Love burned through her at his words and her fingers moved down his cheek in a sweet caress before she pressed her lips to his. His took the kiss deeper, pressed her up against the wall, and started to move. She held him closer with her arms and her legs and just let herself go.

His mouth was on her ear, his tongue running along the curve of her lobe. "Come for me, Darcy."

The orgasm ripped through her, and she cried out as he continued to thrust into her, hitting her in just the right spot to prolong it. He came with a growl, his eyes closed as pure pleasure washed over his features. He dropped his head on her shoulder, his rapid heartbeat matching her own, and when he lifted his face to her, he was smiling. "Let's try that again, but with a bed."

"Good idea."

They lay in bed an hour later completely spent. Lucien had Darcy tucked in his arms with her back to his chest, his fingers idly running up and down her stomach.

"I was coming to see you," he said.

"Really?"

"Yeah, I was being gentlemanly by suggesting we take it a day at a time, but I'm not much of a gentleman."

She looked back at him and his grin was boyish and wicked all at once.

While watching him, she saw his expression turn serious. "Tell me about the visit to your mom."

She turned into him. "Your comment about what was in it for her to get involved in my life again was rattling around in my brain. When I arrived at her apartment, there was a delivery man dropping off a case of vodka." Anger surged through her again just thinking about her mother, and Lucien, being so attuned to her, noticed it.

"What's that look for?" he asked.

"I think she was delighted to tell me about the role she played in what happened to our child; I think she actually got off on it."

She saw the fury burning in his eyes, but his voice was soft, almost tender, when he replied, "As sad as it is to say, I'm not surprised by her behavior. Are you?"

"No."

His arms tightened around her and he spoke with conviction. "We will find our child."

"I know."

"Do you think it's a boy or a girl?"

It was almost too much to bear, knowing their child was out there and they didn't know him or her. Lucien seemed to sense how painful it was for her when he added, "Too soon."

"Yeah."

She needed to lighten the mood because she was dangerously close to losing it. She rested her head on her hand. "I was at Allegro when your fan club arrived. They were talking about you like a piece of meat."

Seeming to sense what she needed, Lucien replied. "Really?" He wiggled his brows at her. "Do tell."

Her response to that was to elbow him in the stomach, which earned her a laugh.

"I didn't like hearing them talk about you as if you were public property. They even mentioned me and how they wouldn't mind a threesome."

Lucien leaned up a bit at that and Darcy thought he was going to say something provocative and was prepared to hit him again, but she was completely taken by surprise by what he did say.

"Sharing you? No way in hell."

"What?"

"It's not really my thing to begin with, but my focus is completely on you, now that you're back in my bed."

She straddled him at those words, taking him into her hand. She settled onto him, moving down his hard length, which earned her a moan of approval. His hands found her hips as she started to move, slowly, like he had done with her earlier. It started off as lazy and teasing, but as the orgasm tightened in her belly, she threw her head back and rode him hard until she came.

Lucien sat up to suck her breast into his mouth before he flipped them, lifted her hips, and started to really move until he followed her with his own release.

Darcy's eyes closed as complete contentment filled her. She felt herself slipping into sleep when Lucien rolled her nipple and tugged.

"Let's go out."

"What?" she answered, but couldn't bring herself to open her eyes.

"Come on, I've a need to take my lady out."

Darcy was tempted to roll onto her side, but she liked what he was doing to her and how her body was responding to it.

"Where do you want to go?"

"Allegro."

There was a note of something in his tone, which made her lift her heavy lids to look at him. "What are you up to?"

"Nothing. Come with me and then we'll come back and start round two."

"Let's skip the middle part and go right to round two."

He pressed a kiss on her belly before he climbed from bed. "Come on."

"I need a shower."

"No."

She sat up in time to see him pulling on his jeans, and knowing that he wasn't wearing anything under them was going to be very distracting.

"Why can't I shower?"

"Because I want my scent on you as a reminder of how it got there and how it'll get there again later."

"Oh my God."

"Now get dressed. The sooner we leave, the sooner we get back."

Darcy was turned on. She had been since Lucien decreed that she couldn't shower. Once they'd entered the club, Lucien made his usual rounds, keeping her at his side the whole time, before he ordered her a drink at the bar. His lips moved to her ear.

"Where are the ladies you were talking about?"

"Changed your mind?"

He smiled, but with an intensity that had the place between her legs throbbing in time with her heart.

"The table near the stage, the three blonds and a brunette."

He took her hand and guided her through the crowd, heading in the direction of his fan club.

"What are you doing?" Darcy hissed.

His hand tightened on hers, but he didn't answer. As soon as they saw him coming, they started fluffing their hair and batting their lashes. Darcy wanted to vomit.

"Ladies, are you enjoying your evening?"

"More so now," the tall blond, who had mentioned the threesome, purred. Darcy wanted to yank her hair, hard.

"We haven't seen you around. It's been too long." The brunette said, tilting her head and closing her lips around her finger. Darcy almost laughed; honestly, could she be any more obvious? Why didn't she just take off her dress, climb on the table, and spread her legs? On second thought, with the way she was eying Lucien, she might yet.

"Who's your friend?" the brunette somehow managed to ask around the finger she was sucking on.

Lucien leaned closer to the brunette. "She's everything."

And then he turned and drew Darcy onto the dance floor, wrapping her in his arms, and holding her close.

"Why did you do that?" Darcy asked, looking around him at the women who were watching them with dropped jaws. She wasn't certain, but she thought she might have seen tears in the brunette's eyes.

"Just making it even."

Darcy pushed at him, feeling her temper starting to stir again. "What does that mean?"

Humor turned to sincerity. "You claimed me at sixteen, so I claimed you right back. And with that group of gossiping divas, in under an hour the entire place is going to know that you aren't just some girl, but that you are my forever girl."

Her anger immediately fled. "Good answer."

His hands moved down her back to her ass and he pressed her close so she could feel the hard length of him. "Let's go home so I can claim you again."

———◆———

"Darcy, could you please come in here?" Lucien called from his office. A moment later she appeared in his doorway.

"Yes?"

"Close the door."

"Is something wrong?" she asked as he came from around his desk. He said not a word but took her mouth in a kiss. He'd been thinking about that mouth all morning. And she was actually breathless when his lips lifted from hers.

"Mr. Black. I'm not sure that is appropriate office etiquette." Her voice wasn't steady and her eyes were soft with desire.

"No?" He slid her skirt up over her hips and felt the lacy edge of her thigh-high stockings. "What the—" He'd never seen anything more sexy and instantly he was rock hard. His voice shook from raging lust. "You cannot wear these little skirts with these"—his finger ran along her thigh—"and not expect me to take you up against the wall at every opportunity."

The coy look in her eyes made him grow even harder as he said, "You little vixen. You *want* me to take you up against the wall."

She brushed her hair behind her shoulder and suddenly he wanted his fingers buried in those onyx strands. "I have no idea what you're talking about."

In the next minute, she was up against the wall with her legs wrapped around his waist as he worked his zipper. He moaned when he pushed into her and felt her body squeezing him. Her eyes glazed over and her thighs held him tightly as he moved deeply inside her. It was rough, fast, and so fucking good that he knew he was going to be thinking about it for the rest of the day.

He dropped his head on her shoulder. "I may have to fire you, otherwise we're never going to get any work done."

Her fingers raked through his hair. "I can behave if you can."

"That's a big if."

"Lucien."

He lifted his head at the seriousness of her voice.

"I want to know who took this away from us. I want to know who took our child and why. I want justice. Hell, I want revenge."

"You and me both. We will find out, I promise you."

Chapter Sixteen

Trace was at Everything when his phone rang.

"Yeah."

"It's Lucien. Can you meet me at Sapphire in about twenty minutes? I need your help."

"I'm leaving now."

When Trace arrived, he was surprised to see that Lucien had called Rafe and Kyle too. He reached them and pulled out a chair. "What's up?"

"I'm sorry to call you in the middle of the day, but I need help. Darcy was pregnant when I left St. Agnes. I've thought about this every moment since I found out about the baby. She was pregnant. Can you imagine how terrified she had to have been to be alone and pregnant at sixteen? What could that bastard have said to make her believe that it was better for me that she face pregnancy alone?"

"And the baby?" Kyle asked.

"She was told she lost it, but her mother finally confessed that she lied. That she was paid to lie, probably by the same bastard who came to see Darcy that day."

"What! What the fuck for?" Trace demanded.

"I don't know, but I want to find my child."

"Do you know if it's a boy or girl?" Rafe asked.

"No, but he or she would be almost fourteen now, growing up as we had, believing that they were forgotten. They deserve to know the truth, deserve to know they have a mother who has mourned their loss every day for fourteen years and a father who would move heaven and earth for them. I want to give them what we all were denied: a family."

"Fuck yeah. What do you need?" Trace said, which made Lucien smile.

"I can't be everywhere at once, but I need to find out who was on duty the night Darcy delivered the baby. Clearly it wasn't just her mother this man paid off. Josh is already looking into it, but he's going to need help; so much time has passed that there's going to be a lot of researching and legwork just to find everyone."

"Whatever you need, you've got it," Trace said, then asked, "And Darcy?"

Lucien's smile filled his face. Trace chuckled. "I'm guessing by that look you are working it out."

"Hell yeah."

————◆————

Later that day, Trace walked into Charles's campaign headquarters. He'd waited for a day when Ember wasn't working because he didn't want to upset her and he couldn't be sure how this conversation was going to go. Charles's secretary greeted him and stood.

"Please follow me. Your uncle is expecting you."

Charles was on the phone when they entered his office, but immediately ended the call.

"Trace, it's nice to see you." He stood and shook Trace's hand. "Please have a seat."

Trace didn't return the greeting and instead got right to the point. "What's your connection to Heidi?"

Trace noticed that, though the man paled slightly, he wasn't surprised by the question.

"The boy, Seth . . . he isn't your father's. He's mine."

"Come again?" Trace had definitely not been expecting that.

Charles walked to a cabinet and pulled out a bottle of Scotch and two glasses, before returning to his desk and pouring them each three fingers. He drank the entire glass before he poured another.

"Let me start from the beginning. When I met Vivian, she was like no one I had ever known. She came from nothing and yet held herself like a queen. Though my affection for her was genuine, it was my money and connections that she sought. I didn't mind because she was fun to be around and she did like me in her way. When we got together, she didn't hesitate to change her appearance, even going so far as to model her makeover on my sister . . ." He rubbed a hand over his head. "Hell, even her name Vivian was chosen because of how close it was to Victoria. Obviously there was a little hero worship there.

"For a time we were happy, but then Vivian really took to her new image and started focusing more on the social life her connection to me offered. I found myself alone often."

"And that's when you met Heidi," Trace concluded.

"Yeah, she was young, fresh, and sexy as hell and she was interested in me, a man pushing forty."

"And you didn't think that was odd, a girl falling for a man old enough to be her father?"

"There was a part of me that wondered, but it was heady to be desired by someone like her. Anyway, our brief affair ended almost as soon as it started."

"And then she drops the bomb that you're going to be a father."

"Yeah, but it was how methodical she was that made it clear to me that she had planned it." He pushed from his desk and walked to the window. "She was only sixteen."

Trace was incredulous because that was brazen even for Heidi. "Shit. She set you up for blackmail."

"She knew that if my affair with her got out, my career and life would have gone up in smoke, so she made her proposition." He turned to Trace. "If we paid her a monthly sum, she would keep quiet."

"And you agreed."

"Vivian wasn't about to give up the lifestyle she had become accustomed to and insisted that I agree. She didn't even care about the affair, only about the idea of losing her status in society. That was a hit, but one I should have seen coming."

"So why the hell did Heidi tell me that Seth was my father's?"

"She was fixated on you and even moved herself to St. Agnes to be closer to you. By claiming her child was your father's, it gave her a hold over you. I knew what she was doing but I didn't stop her; yet another opportunity I had to help you that I didn't take." He paused for a minute before he added, "I need you to know that I didn't help you when your father was alive because I was dealing with this shit with Heidi, but I should have, because nothing comes close to the horror that animal inflicted on you and your sister. I'll have to live with failing you and Chelsea for the rest of my life."

Charles sat back down, but there was conviction burning in his eyes. "I didn't kill her. I was willing to pay for my sins, but we weren't the only ones she was blackmailing."

"How do you know that?" Trace asked.

"She took delight in it. She made it her job to find dirt on people and exploit them with it. We were small potatoes compared to the others."

Trace's thoughts turned to Dane and how he believed Heidi had been blackmailing his family. But how had she met them, since Dane seemed too afraid to have made the introductions? "Do you know if Heidi knew the older Carmichaels?"

"Yeah, meeting them was part of her blackmail demands."

"What does that mean?"

"She wanted to be introduced to rich and powerful people, that family specifically. I wouldn't be surprised to learn that she was blackmailing them too. It was what she did."

He wasn't wrong, but Trace moved on. "You said you didn't kill her. Do you think Vivian could have?"

"And miss a gala because of a jail sentence? No. Vivian is many things, but she isn't a killer."

"It's going to come out about you and Heidi. You know that, right?"

"Yes."

"What are you going to do about Seth?"

"You mean, am I going to claim him as my son?"

"Yeah. He's at St. Agnes. Did you arrange that?" Trace asked.

"Yes, he's a ward of the state with Heidi gone, but at least at St. Agnes he has a friend. Seth deserves more than me. I've never been there for him and his life is in turmoil enough without adding me to the equation."

Trace studied the older man for a minute. It wasn't often that people took him by surprise, but it seemed that Charles Michaels wasn't as much of a selfish prick as he'd thought. "Would you consider making me his legal guardian?"

Surprised flashed over Charles's face. "You would do that?"

"I've sort of been doing it already. Might as well make it legal."

"I think Seth is very lucky to have you. I'll take care of it."

Trace stood. "Thank you for sharing that with me. It couldn't have been easy. It might get out about you and Heidi, but it won't be coming from me."

It was as close to absolution as Trace could offer before he turned and walked out.

———◆———

Trace walked into his apartment to see Chelsea in the living room watching television and eating ice cream. She turned to him and smiled, her lips covered in chocolate.

"Hey, Trace."

He walked over and knelt down in front of her. "Chocolate, chocolate chip, yum."

"You look sad. Why are you sad?"

"Not so much sad, but thankful. I love you, Chelsea."

"I know that."

He grinned before he pressed a kiss to her forehead and stood. "Where's Ember?"

"Sleeping."

He walked down the hall to their room and saw Ember curled up in a ball on their bed. He closed and locked their door before he kicked off his shoes and climbed in. He pulled her to him and held her close.

"Hi." Her voice was still soft with sleep.

"I'm sorry I woke you."

"I'm not." She looked up at him and immediately sat up. "What's wrong?"

He told her about his meeting with Charles and his talk with Lucien. He watched anger and sympathy play across her face.

"I couldn't imagine losing a child, but for someone to lie about it . . . To have lost all that time . . . Who would do such a vile thing?" she asked with tears in her eyes.

"I don't know, but that's what we're going to find out."

"I want to help."

"I knew that you would. I told Lucien that you could do the research into what nurses were on call the day Darcy delivered. Your uncle can give you the details, since Darcy's already hired him to start the search."

Trace was silent for a moment, prompting Ember to ask, "What?"

"I've asked to become Seth's legal guardian. I should have talked with you first before—"

She pressed her finger to his lips. "Absolutely."

"Are you sure?"

"You've already been acting like his legal guardian, so let's make it official."

He grinned. Ember asked, "What's that grin for?"

"That was the exact argument I used on Charles."

"Great minds think alike." Ember's expression turned serious. "What about Darcy and Lucien?"

"They're finding their way."

"How can you be so sure?"

"Because we did." And then he shifted and rolled, pinning her underneath him. "Please remember that you're pregnant."

"I will."

"You're showing; there's a little swell."

"I wasn't sure that you noticed."

"I know every inch of your body. Of course I noticed."

And then to prove his point, he lifted her nightshirt up and over her head and pressed a kiss at the base of her throat. He licked her along her collarbone before pressing kisses down the valley between her breasts to her navel. He palmed the small swell of her belly before he lowered his lips and kissed her right in the middle of it.

"I know I didn't have a great role model, but I promise you that this child will never doubt that he or she is loved."

Ember wrapped his face in her hands and lifted his gaze to hers. "I know."

Darcy was pacing outside of Lucien's office. She was trying very hard to keep her temper in check, but she had heard about the meeting Lucien had called with his friends and how a strategy had been hashed out to find their child—and she had not been included. She knew Lucien's intentions were in the right place, but she was not going to be forced to stand on the sidelines while he took control. Her head snapped up when she heard the heavy footfalls coming from the down the hall.

"Where have you been?" she said in way of greeting.

He tried to move into her, but she stepped away from him. "Lucien, you're keeping me out of the loop."

Determination moved across his face. "That's not my intention. I'm trying to keep you safe."

"I've kept myself safe for fourteen years."

She saw irritation in his expression. "Things are different. Our child is alive and we're actively searching for him or her, which is going to make the kidnapper nervous when they learn of it."

"That doesn't give you the right to be so high-handed. I will not be kept from this."

Anger replaced irritation. "We have no idea who the fuck we are dealing with, but based on what they've done to us so far, I'm betting there is very little this person wouldn't do to get whatever the hell it is they are after. If you think for a second that I am going to sit back and watch as you step into potential danger, you are out of your fucking mind."

Her anger rose to match his. "And if you think that I'm going to take a step back just because you and I are sleeping together and your inner caveman is coming to the fore, you are out of your fucking mind."

His voice turned icy. "If I were being a caveman, I would have already knocked you over the head with my club and put you over my shoulder. Not that the idea doesn't have some merit." She realized it wasn't just anger pouring off him, but hurt too. "I think I'll call it a day."

She watched his long strides carry him away from her as anger and remorse warred inside her.

Chapter Seventeen

Darcy paced her office. It had been over a week since she and Lucien had had their heated words. She knew, even without him needing to say it, that he was leaving her in the dark because he was trying to keep her safe. Despite the thoughtfulness behind his actions, it still pissed her off.

Darcy tried to run the scenario of the kidnapping in her head. There were quite a few people who had to be involved just to get the baby out of the hospital. She knew Ember was looking into the nurses, so she focused on her mom. How was she approached? The person had to have been watching her to know what would persuade her. Darcy had never paid attention to her mom's activities as long as she and her boyfriends had stayed away from her. The part of the entire mess that Darcy was hung up on was: Why would anyone care about two teenagers? Why meddle so much in their lives when they were literally nobodies?

The only link they had to their child was Darcy's mother, and as much as she didn't want to go back to Queens, she wanted to take a look around her mom's apartment. Darcy checked her watch. Her mom was most likely out, picking the loser she was going to take home for the evening. She could be in and out before her mother ever got home.

The smell almost knocked her over when she keyed into her mom's apartment an hour later. Her eyes watered as she tried to breathe through her mouth. The place was a sty, but maybe she'd get lucky and find something that might give them a direction to focus their search.

An hour later, Darcy gave up. The only thing she learned conclusively was that her mom was a disgusting pig and had a matchbook fetish. She looked around the place that had been her prison and wanted to torch it—but that wouldn't accomplish anything except landing her in jail. She pulled the door closed behind her as disappointment filled her, but at least she wasn't standing on the sidelines doing nothing.

⎯⎯•◆•⎯⎯

Ember sat and listened as Charles told all his volunteers that he was pulling out of the race. It was only two weeks since he'd told Trace about Heidi and already he was folding up camp. They had met earlier with her editor for the article she was going to write for *In Step*. She felt sorry for him because he had been a pawn too.

For a man to have to give up his dream because of the actions of another was hard to watch, but he did so with integrity and again Ember found herself admiring him. Vivian looked about ready to spit nails, probably more concerned about how the change in Charles's circumstances was going to affect her social life. Vivian Michaels looked out for herself, though, so Ember had no doubt she would land on her designer-shoe-covered feet.

Ember had started looking into her part of Darcy's case, but because it had happened fourteen years ago, nothing was electronic. Per the hospital, files before 2005 were hard copy only and stored in archives.

"Hey, did you hear that the cops are no longer looking at Seth?" Brandon settled on the corner of her desk, grinning.

"I didn't, no."

"Yeah, he's relieved. I mean he knew they'd eventually figure it out, but now that they have, he's like totally flipping."

"Thank God. I wonder if Trace knows?" Ember thought out loud.

Ember knew that Brandon had a crush on her, which was why she usually found a way to work Trace into their conversation, but that didn't mean she couldn't help him. "I was just talking to my editor about you. You still need to put in community service right?"

"Yeah."

"Well, she thinks she can find a place for you."

His brow furrowed before he asked, "Why would she do that?"

"Because I asked her to."

It took him a minute before a smile spread over his face—a lethal smile. "Sweet."

He noticed her notepad where she had jotted down notes from her conversation with the hospital. A strange look passed over his face. "Are you sick?"

"What?"

He pointed to the name of the hospital that she had scribbled on the pad. "Oh no. I'm trying to get my hands on records that are pretty old."

"Records about what?"

"A friend is looking for someone."

"Oh. Are the records at the hospital?"

"Yeah."

"And you can't just ask for them?"

"That's where it gets complicated, because the records I want are employee records."

"So, what's your plan?" he asked. But she suspected he already knew, and he confirmed this when he said rather incredulously, "You're thinking about stealing them, aren't you?"

"Not steal, but I would like to get my hands on them. The problem is, I don't know how to get access to the archive room or where in the room I would need to look."

"I'll help."

"How?"

"Well, the way I see it, you need information, and there are people who work in the archive room, so why not just ask the people who work in the room to find what you want?"

"Because it's against hospital policy to share employee records. If I could get a copy of my friend's file that would help, but I'm not the patient, so doctor-patient confidentiality will keep them from sharing that with me."

"Why don't you just ask your friend to come and get the file?"

"If I have to I will, but she's going through a really tough time right now. The last thing I want to do is force her into a place where she has some truly horrible memories."

"Fair enough."

Clearly something was on his mind, so Ember asked, "What are you thinking?" But she wasn't sure she wanted to hear the answer.

He flashed her a grin that got her heart beating a bit faster. "I've a way with people."

"Of that, I have no doubt, but this is insane. I can't pull you into this."

"You're not. I'm volunteering," he said, and wiggled his brows at her.

"And the fact that I'm actually considering it means I'm going to hell."

"I can't believe I agreed to this." They were walking down the administration wing of the hospital on their way to—as Brandon so simply put it—ask for the information they wanted.

"Are you sure you can do this?" Ember asked.

He grinned and the sight of it was both disarming and very familiar to Ember. When he noticed her stunned expression, he said, "What's the matter?"

"Nothing, you just looked a lot like a friend of mine for a minute."

The grin turned into a full-on smile. "Sweet." And then he added, "Watch and learn."

Before she could ask him what he was talking about, he strolled away from her and headed to the desk where two women were working. Ember stood off to the side and watched as Brandon turned on the charm; even as a kid of sixteen, he had the women eating out of his hand. She watched as the one woman shook her head no, but Brandon wasn't discouraged. After only about five minutes, the woman headed into the room behind the desk. A few minutes later she came back out with a file, photocopied the contents, and handed them to him. Ember was convinced that she was definitely going to prison.

In the next minute, Brandon turned and walked back to her all loose-limbed and easy. "Piece of cake."

"You are entirely too good at that."

"It's a gift."

"What did you tell them?" she asked.

He shrugged before he said, "That I was looking for my birth mom."

They headed outside to a bench before Brandon handed Ember the file. There had been two nurses in with Darcy when she'd delivered, a Nora Jerkins and a Lacy Shane.

"I wonder if these women still work at the hospital?"

"Do you want me to go back and ask?"

Ember couldn't help but smile—he was just so freaking adorable. "Thanks, but I'll call my uncle."

She reached for her phone and did just that.

"Hey, Ember."

"Can you do me a favor?"

"Sure thing, honey."

"Can you look into a Nora Jerkins and Lacy Shane? I need to know if they still work at Mt. Sinai. And I also would like their home addresses."

"Sure, I'll google them—there's probably an online directory. Is this about Darcy?"

"Yeah."

"Give me a minute." Brandon stood and started to pace around while Ember waited the few minutes before her uncle said, "Okay. Nora died in 2002. Lacy Shane doesn't work at the hospital; she quit in 2004. I have her address if you want to write it down."

She pulled a pen from her purse and jotted it down.

"Let me know what you find out, and be careful, Ember."

"I will, thanks, Uncle Josh."

Brandon was now leaning up against a tree as if he had not a care in the world.

"Find them?" he asked.

"Nora died, but Lacy is still around. I've got her address."

"So let's go talk to her."

"Now?"

"Do you have anything else to do?"

He was right; she had the entire day open. "Okay, and after I'll buy you lunch."

"Good deal."

Lacy Shane lived in a rundown row house in Queens, so if she had been paid off all those years ago, she hadn't been paid much.

"Can I ask what this is all about?" Brandon asked.

Ember stopped midway up the front path to Lacy's house and turned to Brandon. "I'm sorry—of course. A friend had a baby that she was told had died in childbirth, but she recently learned that it was a lie."

He said nothing at first, just studied her. After a minute or two he said, "That really sucks. How long ago was this?"

"Fourteen years ago."

"And your friend, how is she handling it?"

"She's devastated, but wants to find her child."

"Fourteen years is a long time. How does she know if her kid is still around?"

"I don't know, but that won't stop her or the father."

"They're married?"

"No, but they've recently reconnected."

Brandon shoved his hands into the front pockets of his jeans. "Sounds like something on those soaps I see the nuns watching when they don't think anyone is around."

Ember looked at him from the corner of her eye and smiled. "And yet you seem to know enough about the plots to comment."

His grin came in a flash. "Guilty pleasure."

"Let's get burgers at that place you took me to, once we get done with this. My treat."

"You liked it there?" he asked.

"Guilty pleasure," Ember said, and got a laugh in response.

Lacy wasn't what Ember was expecting. She was in her late fifties, heavy, and with enough gray hair to add a few more years to her age. Her home was as rundown on the inside as it was on the outside. She didn't look pleased to see them and Ember suspected that she, like Brandon, liked her soaps and they were intruding on them.

"What do you want?"

How to put it? Ember decided straight up was the best plan.

"Close to fourteen years ago a child was born to a seventeen-year-old girl, a child she was told died in birth, but has now learned survived."

Ember was about to continue, but Lacy's face went completely white. She looked as if she might faint. She opened the door wider before she said, "Please come in."

They settled in her kitchen, but Lacy couldn't seem to keep still and paced in front of her stove.

"I've been waiting every day for this moment. I was in the middle of a nasty divorce back then. My ex was getting everything and then some guy offered me twenty grand to just turn my back once the baby was born. Every day I thought about what I did to that poor girl and that baby, and for what? I quit my job because I couldn't sustain the lie."

"And Nora?" Ember asked.

"She was my contact and the one to forge the documents and slip the baby from the ward. She never told me how much she was offered, but I had a feeling it was significantly more than I got."

"Do you have any idea who approached you?"

"It was a man who arranged everything, but he only ever talked to Nora and she filled me in."

"How were you paid?" Brandon asked.

"At a bar here in Queens—Polly's. A woman called to tell me they had an envelope with my name on it behind the bar." She stopped her pacing to look at Ember before she asked, "Are you the girl?"

"No, but she's a friend of mine."

"I hope she finds him. He was a beautiful baby."

Tears welled in Ember's eyes. "The baby was a boy?"

"Yes."

They started to leave when Ember heard herself asking, "What happened to Nora?"

"Cancer. She died a few months later."

After they left Lacy's, Brandon and Ember went to lunch as promised before she sent him home in a cab. She stood outside the restaurant and reached for her phone. She couldn't get in touch with Darcy, so she called Lucien. He answered on the first ring.

"Ember?"

"Lucien, hi."

"I've got you on speaker. Trace is here."

"Sweetheart, is everything okay?" Trace said.

"Yes. I've been doing some research and I found out the names of the two nurses who were with Darcy when she delivered. The one, Nora Jerkins, died, but I just came from Lacy's house. She never saw the man, but she was paid out of a bar called Polly's in Queens. Twenty grand to look the other way."

Ember heard Lucien swearing softly and she couldn't blame him. Her cussing wouldn't be soft.

"Thanks, Ember. That's the first break we've had."

"I have one other piece of information."

"Okay?"

"It was a boy. You have a son, Lucien."

There was silence over the line for a minute before he spoke, and when he did, his voice was hoarse. "Thank you. I'll call Darcy."

"Okay, I'm going to stop by and see her."

"She'd like that," he replied softly.

"Ember?"

Darcy continued walking down the hall in Allegro toward her friend. Lucien had called and it was the first time they had spoken since their fight. She had been tempted to not answer, but when he told her about their son, her feelings took a radical turn. Her tears were fresh and her heart continued to pound in her chest. Darcy knew she had overreacted to Lucien's protectiveness, but she was unaccustomed to people taking care of her. She'd been looking out for herself for so long that having someone else doing so was going to be an adjustment, but one she was willing to make. They had a son, they were a family, and that trumped everything else.

It took effort to move her thoughts from her son to the reason for Ember's visit. "Lucien mentioned that there were two nurses with me when I delivered. One is deceased, but the other was paid twenty grand to turn the other way." Darcy took the papers and guessed accurately, "And her contact was the other nurse."

"Yes, I'm sorry."

She was angry that someone had so royally fucked up her world but she couldn't help the touch of humor and gratitude she felt before she said, "You guys really are good." She was still eyeballing the paper when she had her ah-ha moment. "Sister Margaret. Why the hell didn't I think of her? That woman knew everything that went on in St. Agnes."

Darcy's eyes turned to Ember and she asked, "Any idea where she is now?"

"Yeah, actually, I do know."

The bellowing coming from down the hall was almost deafening. "Who is making that sound?" Ember asked the orderly who was leading them to Sister Margaret's room.

A mischievous grin curved his mouth. "The woman you've come to see."

If Darcy hadn't been all twisted up inside with nerves, she would have laughed at Ember's expression, particularly when the orderly added, "She's actually pretty calm today."

They walked into her room. Darcy had never truly appreciated how old Sister Margaret was until she saw her looking every one of her ninety-plus years. Darcy had occasionally stopped by to visit the woman, but less so in the past few years—and those years had not been kind to her. She looked frail, as if at any minute her withered bones were going to disintegrate into dust.

"I want hot chocolate, damn it. I'm a dying woman and I want my hot chocolate now!"

And then her eyes turned to the doorway and she speared Darcy and Ember with a look that actually had the hair on Darcy's arms standing on end.

"What do you want?"

"I don't know if you remember me—" Darcy started to say, but was cut off by the angry nun.

"Darcy MacBride. I didn't ask who you were. I said, what do you want?"

"Still as pleasant as always, I see," Darcy replied with such sarcasm that Ember nearly snapped her neck turning to look at her friend.

"You haven't lost that sass about you. Good. Sit. I rarely get visitors."

"It's really one of the mysteries of life, you not getting visitors—being as charming as you are."

At first Darcy wasn't sure what the sound was that came from the old woman's throat. Thinking that she might be choking, Darcy nearly offered to give her the Heimlich. And then she realized that rusty sound was her laugh.

Sister Margaret turned her focus on Ember. "And you?"

"I'm Ember."

"I know. Trace's wife."

A look of disbelief moved across Ember's expression before she asked, "How do you know that?"

"I've my ways. So are you going to sit or am I going to have to look up at you?"

They sat and a minute later a nurse arrived with a chipped china teapot filled with hot chocolate. Sister Margaret's hands were wrinkled, but steady as she lifted the pot and poured the thick, brown liquid into a cup. She looked almost dainty, holding the cup and saucer like a lady having afternoon tea, but then she opened her mouth.

"So again I ask, what the hell do you want?"

"You were the one who brought me to the hospital the day I fell?" Darcy asked and she apparently didn't need to give any more detail because understanding flashed in the nun's beady eyes.

"Yes. I was very sorry to hear about your baby."

The sincerity was so unexpected that Ember stared at the older woman slack-jawed.

Sister Margaret didn't miss a beat when she said, "You'll want to close that. The flies in this place are nasty." Ember snapped her mouth closed.

"He didn't die," Darcy said softly.

It was interesting watching the emotions that moved across her old, wrinkled face. Darcy saw both anger and confirmation.

"How do you know this?"

"My mother told me she was paid to lie. She's been compensated ever since to maintain the lie."

"Interesting."

"You know something. What aren't you saying?" Darcy demanded.

Instead of getting angry, Sister Margaret looked almost pleased before she said, "I will say that I believe what happened with your child was the final move in a battle of wills that has been going on for a very long time. I think to find the answers that you seek, you need to go back to the beginning."

"Meaning?" Darcy was beginning to lose her temper.

"Heidi knew a lot about a lot of people. But how did she find her information and, more importantly, where did she keep all of her information? Blackmail only works when you've actually got dirt on someone."

Darcy was pondering that when Ember chimed in, "St. Agnes's attic."

Sister Margaret looked at Ember like she was her star student. "Heidi lived at St. Agnes and the attic is just filled with stuff. It's the perfect place to hide something."

"That actually explains a lot, like why Heidi was always hanging around St. Agnes and the creepy way she lurked around. But how is Heidi involved in my son's kidnapping?"

"Like I said, start at the beginning. Find out who Heidi was blackmailing and you'll find out what happened to your child."

Anger turned Darcy's voice hard. "Do you know where my child is?" she demanded.

Compassion, which looked completely out of place on the older woman's face, softened the hard lines of her features. "No, I don't, but I think he's closer than you think."

Chapter Eighteen

D arcy slammed the door of the nursing home. "I would like to strangle that woman, but I've known her long enough to know she isn't going to tell us anything more."

"We can go to St. Agnes and take a look around in the attic," Ember offered.

"I'd like to, but I'm too wired to do that now."

"So, back to Sister Margaret's riddle. We know of a few people that Heidi was blackmailing: my husband, Trace's uncle, and one of the Carmichaels, at least."

"Well, we can rule out Trace," Darcy said, earning a smile from Ember.

"And Charles has been very forthcoming about his involvement with Heidi, so that leaves the Carmichaels. Trouble is there are four of them."

"Figures," Darcy huffed.

"I think we can rule out the youngest of them because he was the one to tell us about the blackmailing and had, at one time, been party to Heidi's activities. Maybe if we sat down with him, we could get him to share more about his family," Ember said.

"Do you think he would?"

Ember held her stare and said, "Only one way to find out. Let's ask."

"Who exactly are we asking?" Darcy asked.

"Dane Carmichael."

———◆◆———

Dane had decided to keep a low profile until Heidi's killer was found. As much as it pained him to do so, he had been sober for two weeks. He needed to keep his wits about him if he didn't want to be staring down the barrel of gun.

His father had learned that his competition in the senatorial race had stepped down, leaving the way clear for him to take his fourth consecutive term. Dane really didn't mind. When his dad was happy and busy with work, he left Dane alone.

He was reaching for his water and wishing it was a Scotch, when he felt the hair at the nape of his neck stand on end. A minute later, two women sat down at his table. His first thought was of Lena and how she would misinterpret the situation.

And then he saw that one of the women was Ember Walsh. No, it was Montgomery now.

"I didn't do anything." He immediately turned to look behind him for her husband.

"Relax, Dane, we're here to talk," Ember said, but Dane still kept one eye on the door.

"How did you find me?" Dane demanded.

"I called Lena," Ember said, and Dane made a mental note to not share his whereabouts with Lena again.

"Does your husband know you're here?"

"No."

"Is he likely to show up, misread this, and rearrange my face again?"

An arrogant smile spread over Ember's face. "Keep your hands to yourself and there's nothing to worry about."

"Right."

He really wanted a hit of something mind-numbing. His eyes moved to the other woman and—damn, she was fine. Instinct kicked in. "Hey, how you doing?"

Her reaction was not what he was expecting. She actually rolled her eyes at him. "Seriously? Does that even work?"

Dane took a moment to think on that. "Yeah, a time or two."

The woman responded to that by snorting.

Ember started to talk. "Lena mentioned that Heidi had been blackmailing someone in your family and you suspected it was your dad. Any idea what she had on him?"

He shifted in his chair. The last thing he wanted was to get involved in whatever it was Heidi was doing with his family, but considering his last encounter with Ember, he felt obligated to give her something.

"I don't, but my dad plays a dangerous game of seducing women. Any woman is fair game, even married ones. He is discreet, so most don't know just how much of a player he is, but it wouldn't surprise me that he has secrets he wants to keep quiet."

"And your uncle?"

"He works hard. All the time, in fact. He doesn't like my dad, or me by extension, but I don't think he has time to do anything blackmail-worthy."

"And your grandfather?" Ember asked.

"He's an arrogant, egotistical misogynist who I hate with a passion. I'd love to believe he did something illegal so I could watch him being hauled off to prison. It's my dearest wish to see dear ol' grandpa in county orange. Asshole. Wait. Why do you care?"

The other woman leaned back in her chair and balled her hands into fists. "We're not really sure why we care. I'm trying to find someone, and I was told to investigate who Heidi was black-mailing."

"Who are you looking for?" Dane asked.

He got the sense she wasn't going to answer, but then she did—not that her answer made any sense to him at all. "My son."

"How's your son linked to Heidi?"

"That's the million-dollar question. I was told he died at birth, but I recently found out that was a lie and somehow what happened to him is linked to Heidi."

"Well, shit. My dad could potentially be involved? Kidnapping is a felony, right?" A smile curved his lips at the thought.

"According to a nun who worked at St. Agnes while I was there, there is a link between my son and someone Heidi was blackmailing."

"Wait, Heidi lived at St. Agnes too," Dane said, remembering how Heidi had bitched about living in a place so decidedly beneath her. Who even spoke that way?

"Yeah, she did," Ember confirmed.

Dane put his elbows on the table.

"I don't see why my dad would be interested in the baby of a teenage orphan"—Dane looked at Ember's friend—"unless it's his."

"It's not."

"Didn't think so. Well, I'll sneak around and see if I can find anything that might help."

"You would do that? Why?" Ember asked, genuinely surprised.

"Because despite my behavior the last time we met, I'm not that big of an asshole. I was high and drunk, which I know doesn't make it okay, but I'm not normally that violent or aggressive unless the lady likes it that way."

"Too much information," Darcy said at the same time that Ember did.

"Give me your cell number and I'll see what I can find out. If you're looking at people Heidi was blackmailing, you might want to talk with Todd."

Surprise rang from Ember's voice. "Lena's ex?"

"Yeah, they were hanging together for a while. Maybe he knows something."

———

Lucien walked the familiar streets of his youth in his search for answers. His mind drifted to Darcy. She hadn't been wrong about him acting like a caveman when it came to her. Now that he had her back in his life, he wasn't about to watch her step into danger. If that pissed her off, tough shit. Thinking of Darcy reminded him of one of their conversations. She had asked if someone had helped him to get to where he was. He'd thought on that quite a bit since she'd put the notion into his head. There were countless jobs that he had gotten over the years that he thought himself lucky for getting.

One of those jobs was working for Santucci—the bastard who had let him hang. He had looked into Santucci and knew that the man was still running his operation out of the same gentlemen's club Lucien had visited as a kid. At the time, Lucien had thought that Santucci was one of the big fish, but he knew better now. His operation was small, so small it didn't even warrant attention from New York's finest.

The place was rundown, the years taking a toll on the small brick building. The inside looked exactly the same. Hell, even the red velvet curtain looked as if it were the same one from fourteen years ago. The memory of what he had done behind that curtain soured his stomach, even as his dick started to harden.

He didn't get far before he was stopped by the thugs, which he expected. What he didn't expect was to see his old pal Jimmy. He wasn't the kid he had been. Lots of years of hard living had turned the young-faced kid into an overweight and tired-looking man.

Like Lucien, recognition flashed in those bloodshot eyes.

"Lucien Black. Well, fuck me."

"Jimmy you're looking . . . older."

"I look like shit, but not you. Living the life, aren't you?"

Lucien wasn't interested in walking down memory lane, so he said abruptly, "I want to see Santucci."

Jimmy's smile showed his yellowed teeth, of which he had fewer than he'd had as a kid. "Santucci's busy."

Lucien leaned closer, his voice deceptively soft. "I'm not asking. Unlike you and your boss, I jumped into the deep end of the pool and lived to tell about it. We both know what that means, so stop wasting my time."

The cocky grin faded from Jimmy's face, because he knew that Lucien had made alliances with men who gave people like Santucci nightmares. Even as a legitimate businessman, Lucien didn't turn his back on friends, regardless of what side of the law they chose.

"Follow me."

Santucci looked exactly the same, and like Jimmy, he knew exactly who entered his office. Unlike their past encounter, Santucci stood and came from around his desk to take Lucien's hand into both of his.

"Nice to see you again. Can I get you something—a cigar, Scotch, a woman?"

"No, just information."

Santucci waved to his men, and they all filed out of his office as he gestured to a chair. "Please sit." He returned to his spot behind his desk before he asked, "What do you want to know?"

"The job you offered me—did someone encourage you to offer it to me?"

Confirmation burned in his shrewd eyes. "I wondered if you'd ever figure it out. Same reason I didn't bail you out from jail. I was told not to."

Someone had been playing the fucking puppet master with his and Darcy's lives. Fury burned like a fire in his stomach. "Who was it?"

"You aren't going to believe me."

"Who, damn it?"

"Your very own Sister Margaret."

Lucien didn't know who was behind the curtain, but he sure as hell wasn't expecting that answer. "Are you fucking with me?"

"No, she used the argument that my soul was damned, so I should do something good. She didn't realize the kind of work you would be doing for me and had a change of heart because she didn't think a life of crime working for me was in your best interest. Anyway, being Catholic, I couldn't refuse a nun."

"Son of a bitch."

Lucien was seething by the time he barged into Sister Margaret's room, but before he could peel a layer of skin from the old witch's bones, she brought him up short by saying, "So you spoke with Santucci. I should have expected that."

"Do you think this is some kind of game? This is my life—Darcy's life—you're fucking around with."

"I was protecting you."

"From what?"

"More like who."

"Honest to God, Sister, if you answer another one of my questions with a fucking riddle, I am going to send you to hell myself."

"Keep your skirt on. I watched out for you because I knew you were hurting and people do stupid things when they're emotional. I was protecting you from you. It's why I let you sit in juvenile detention for a bit. Now you need to go; I've had too many visitors for one day."

"What?"

"Darcy and that Ember girl were here earlier. I told them a few things and now you know all that I do."

"Why would you look out for me when you always hated me?" Lucien demanded.

"I didn't hate you specifically. I just don't like children."

"And yet you worked in an orphanage."

"God calls whom he chooses. Sister Anne was there to offer to you children all that I lacked."

Her eyes grew serious before she added, "Sister Anne was the finest person I have ever had the pleasure of knowing. She asked me to look out for you when she was gone. I was merely fulfilling her wishes."

And once again Lucien felt the burning behind his eyes. For this old bitch of all people. She hadn't had to help him, he realized. She could have said one thing and done something else. He walked over to her and pressed a kiss on her paper-thin cheek and was rewarded with seeing a blush bloom there. And for just a moment he could see the young girl she had been, looking up at him like he was the cat's meow.

"Now get the hell out of here before I take my ruler to you."

And just like that, the moment was gone.

Darcy sat in her office, but, of course, she couldn't focus. It had been three weeks since she'd learned about her baby being alive. He wouldn't be a baby, though; he'd be almost fourteen. Was he happy? Did he have a loving home? She had been his age when she'd met Lucien. What did he look like? Was he beautiful like his father? Did he have her hair or eyes? God, she wanted so desperately to hold him in her arms. And yet she needed to be mindful that he may not want to be a part of her life because he was no doubt wondering where the hell she had been. Her heart ached, but even if she didn't have a place in his life, just to see him and to know that he was happy and healthy would be enough. Thinking about all those years they had missed was hard: first words, first steps, first day of school, first crush. It wasn't fair, and there were times that she wanted to rage at the injustice of it, but yelling, though satisfying, didn't accomplish anything.

Lucien was off doing something, but what, she didn't know. He was still trying to protect her, but she could no longer find it in herself to be mad. His focus, like hers, was on finding their son and, even more, he loved her enough that he didn't give a damn if his need to keep her safe pissed her off. It was a beautiful, if somewhat fucked up, gesture. As hard a time as they were going through with their loss, she was grateful to have him back in her life.

She and Ember were making plans to go to St. Agnes to check out the attic. They were going to sign in as guests of Ember's friend Brandon. She wasn't hopeful that they were going to find anything, though.

The sound of her phone was a welcome distraction.

"Darcy MacBride."

"Darcy, it's Josh."

"Oh, hi. Have you found something?"

"I've been looking into the liquor order. From what I've been able to find, that shipment your mom gets is not a credit card transaction, but from an actual bank account."

"That's good. What's the name on the account?"

"Don't know. Whoever set it up did a really good job at keeping it private."

"Where's the bank?"

"Again, I don't know. The account was set up to be anonymous."

"Damn it."

"However, I do have some good news. I've been able to determine that the vodka is not coming from a local liquor store. I've checked sales receipts for twenty stores in the area around your mother's apartment and none of them match the two cases a month delivered to her. So I started looking at bars in the area, and all the places I visited were very helpful except one. I was actually shown to the door."

"Why?"

"I suspect there's some laundering of money going on and they're using the bar to do it, integrating the dirty money in with the legit cash flow of the bar. Paying suppliers for the alcohol with dirty money is a good way to clean it. Your mom's vodka, I'm guessing, is a by-product of the operation."

"So the person who's paying her off is possibly a gangster."

"Or knows one."

"I realize that Lucien associates with a shady group, but when this all happened with the baby, he hadn't yet started that."

"Whoever is doing this isn't doing it because of Lucien's colorful past."

"So we're back to square one."

"Not quite. We know where the bar is located. Fun fact: it's the same place where Lacy picked up her bribe money."

"Well, hell."

"I still don't see why we didn't bring Trace," Kyle said as he, Darcy, and Ember climbed from the cab. They were on Queens Boulevard checking out Polly's.

"Because if he knew we were coming here, he wouldn't have let me come."

"I shouldn't have let you come—either of you."

Ember looked over at Darcy and nodded her head in Kyle's direction. "He's great, isn't he?"

They'd followed the directions given to them by Josh and when they reached the front of the dive bar, Darcy stopped walking so abruptly that Ember walked right into her. The parrot on the sign was the same one from the matches in her mom's apartment.

Ember asked, "Why did you stop?"

"My mom comes here."

"That's interesting. Maybe she started coming here regularly after she made her deal with the devil. At least we know we're on the right track," Ember said.

"Let's see if anyone in there looks familiar, but stay close," Kyle cautioned. "If something happens to either of you, I'm as good as dead."

Darcy stepped into the bar and the smell of grease and alcohol made her think of her mom's apartment. An old scarred bar lined one wall and was packed; not a stool was empty. Floors that were sticky from spilled beer fit in perfectly with the scattered tables that sat mostly empty, except for a few with remnants of meals.

"Nice place," Kyle muttered.

"That table over there has a good view of the bar," Ember suggested before she started over to it. Once settled, a waitress walked over.

"What can I get you?"

"Two bottles of beer and a glass of ginger ale," Kyle said. The waitress barely acknowledged the order before she turned away.

"Beer in a bottle, good call," Ember said before she looked over at Darcy. "Anyone look familiar?"

"Not yet." Darcy didn't take her eyes from the bar when she replied, but after a few minutes she leaned back in her chair. Her disappointment was obvious when she said, "He's not here."

"Well, he's not here now, but we know he's been here," Ember said encouragingly.

"I know. I was just hoping that we'd walk in and find him standing in a spotlight with a large black arrow over his head." She tried for a grin over her silliness, but was feeling too dejected.

"I say we have our drink and give it an hour. We can come back as often as we need," Kyle said.

Darcy tried for optimistic, but failed. "Okay."

They stayed for a little over an hour before Darcy made the call that they should go.

"I need to pee. I'll be right back." Ember was almost halfway to the restroom before Darcy caught up to her.

"I remember peeing all the time."

Ember stopped so fast that Darcy almost tripped on her own feet to keep from hitting her, and when Ember turned to her, there were tears in her eyes.

"I'm sorry. I'm crying all the time these days, but in this case—Christ, Darcy. I'm here if you need to talk."

Darcy felt her throat closing up because she hadn't realized how much she missed having a close girlfriend in her life until that moment. Words wouldn't come, so she simply replied, "Thank you."

Ember took her hand and squeezed as if she understood exactly what Darcy was thinking.

"Okay, I need to pee or this is going to be embarrassing."

Ember took a step away from Darcy, which gave Darcy a clear view of the hallway in the back where there was a picture on the wall; it looked as if it had been taken when the bar had first opened. There were several people in the shot, but one person in particular caught her attention.

"That's him."

Ember was looking down the hall for the person in question. Darcy stepped up in front of the picture and pointed.

"Not what I was expecting."

Darcy's head tilted slightly in Ember's direction. "Yeah, he doesn't look as intimidating now that I'm older, but when I was sixteen, he scared the shit out of me."

"No doubt." Ember tilted her own head. "I think we could totally take him."

Darcy hadn't meant to smile, because the emotions that were coursing through her were intense, but her lips curved up just the same.

A waitress passed by and Ember turned to her and pointed to the man. "Do you know who that is?"

There was definite distrust in the older woman's eyes, but she obviously wasn't that suspicious, since she offered up his name rather easily, "Nick DiNuzzio, why?"

"I think we may have gone to school together," Ember said before turning back to the picture.

The waitress walked away, shaking her head. Darcy leaned closer and whispered, "You do realize that he's twice your age?"

"I know; I panicked."

Ember looked around before lifting the picture from the wall and stuffing it into her bag.

"We can't take her word that his name is Nick, but with his picture, my uncle can find out everything about him."

Darcy would have taken the picture if Ember hadn't, but she couldn't help teasing her friend. "That's stealing, you know that, right?"

"Yeah, I seem to be doing that a lot lately. Maybe I'll turn to a life of crime. I'll be right back."

"I'll come with you."

Darcy gestured to Kyle who had caught her eye and was holding up his hands in the universal gesture for "What the fuck?"

She pointed at the ladies' room sign before she followed Ember into the bathroom.

"With as often as I'm going to the bathroom, I think I might just move a bed into ours. It's crazy." The sound of the bathroom door opening made Ember stop her chitchatting. She finished up and stepped out of the stall to see Darcy looking a bit weird, her eyes shifting to her left, and as soon as Ember cleared the stalls, she understood why. Nick DiNuzzio was standing in the ladies' room.

He opened his jacket to flash the piece at his hip before he asked, "Why are you asking about me?"

Darcy's mind was racing, looking for an answer, so it took her a minute to realize that Ember had taken a few steps closer to Nick. She was studying his face as if it were a painting.

He was just as confused by it when he snapped, "What the fuck are you doing?"

Ember moved her eyes up to his and took a step back. "No, I think I was wrong."

"About what?" Nick asked, and the same question was on the tip of Darcy's tongue.

"I thought maybe you were my father, but I don't think so. I'm sorry."

It took effort for Darcy not to laugh out loud. Damn, Ember was good. She almost believed her sincerity and she knew better.

He looked uncomfortable, as if the possibility that he could have a woman Ember's age as a daughter wasn't too far-fetched. He started backing up to the door. Clearly he didn't want any part of fatherhood. "Easy enough mistake."

The next minute happened in a blur. The door opened and a second later Kyle had his hand wrapped around Nick's neck, pushing him up against the wall so that his cheek was pressing against the tile. In Kyle's other hand was Nick's gun, aimed at his head.

"What . . . how did you . . ." Ember stopped talking and took a few deep breaths before she tried again.

"How the hell did you do that?"

"I ran with a bad crowd in my youth. Long story for another time."

"I can't believe I've known you for almost four years and I didn't know you knew your way around a gun." Ember looked back at Nick. "I also can't believe we're in the bathroom of a dive bar in Queens and my best friend is holding a gun on a man. You can't make this shit up."

Kyle grinned. "What now?"

Ember exhaled on a sigh. "We call Lucien and Trace. Damn, I wish I had cotton balls."

Darcy didn't bother to hide her confusion. "Why?"

An hour later Darcy and Kyle stood in Lucien's office at Allegro after being escorted there by two very angry men. Even Nick seemed to appreciate the situation and didn't refuse when it was suggested to him by Lucien that he join them. Even from her distance, Darcy heard Trace yelling at Ember loud enough to shake the building.

Kyle leaned up against the wall with a slight grin on his face. "Understand now?"

"Yeah, she's going to go deaf."

"Probably, but she totally had it coming."

"It must be nice to have someone love you so much to shout at you until you're disabled," Darcy said almost dreamily.

"I'm doubting Ember agrees with that statement at the moment."

Loud footfalls came from down the hall just before Lucien appeared in the doorway. He looked as if he wanted to kill someone. In two strides he had Darcy's hand and was pulling her out of his office just as Kyle said, "You might rethink your last comment."

Lucien was so angry that once he had Darcy in her office, he put the distance of the room between them. He was fairly sure he was going to murder her. He tried to take a few deep breaths and calm down, but thinking about how that wannabe had threatened her with a gun, he was steadily losing that battle.

"What the fuck were you thinking? Do you have a fucking death wish? He could have fucking shot you! I should put you over my fucking knee."

Darcy stood quietly, watching as Lucien seethed and paced, admiring his very fine form prowling. He was silent for a minute so, seeking to lighten the mood, she asked, "Is fuck your word of the day?"

He pierced her with a look that should have smote her.

"It's not a joke."

"I know. We didn't realize he was carrying."

That wasn't the right thing to say because he turned a dangerous shade of red. She wasn't a fan of getting reprimanded, but her previous sentiment still held. It was nice having someone care enough to yell. She didn't even think as she walked across the room and wrapped her arms around him, pressing herself as close to him as possible. He tensed for a minute and then his arms came around her before he buried his face in her hair.

"I'm sorry," she whispered. "And not just for walking into trouble, but for getting angry that you were trying to protect me. I'm not used to someone caring. I guess I can get used to it as long as that person is you."

He held her until it must have sunk in that she was here and safe before he pulled back and cradled her face in his hands.

He stared as if he was getting his fill. A slight smile touched his mouth. "I'll try to leave my club in the cave."

She smiled in reply, but it faded. "He's the man," she said.

"I know."

"What are we going to do?"

"Find out who he works for."

"He may not be feeling very talkative."

Lucien pressed a kiss on her forehead. "He'll talk, trust me."

———◆———

Trace stood across the room from Ember after having screamed until he'd practically lost his voice. The man had a fucking gun. The fear sliced through him and fed his anger. In the time it took to blink, she could have been lying in a pool of her own blood like Heidi. The very idea of it had him itching to chain her to him.

"I'm sorry. It was reckless."

He didn't know if he would kiss her or kill her if he reached for her. She was his whole fucking world.

She continued to talk, but he wasn't really hearing her words because all he could see in his head was Ember in place of Heidi in front of that diner.

"I know I'm pregnant and I need to think before I do something so careless. I promise, Trace, I won't put the baby at risk again."

"The baby?" He did move to her then, walking straight at her so that she had to back right up against the wall, where he caged her in with his hands on either side of her head.

"You, Ember. It's you I don't want put in danger. I can't live without you. You burrowed yourself so deeply into my soul that I can't exist without you. Don't you get that? It's fucking *you* I need."

Tears sprang to her eyes and she rested her hand over his heart. "I love you too."

He pressed his body into hers, from chest to thigh, where he held her as his mouth captured and conquered. His lips lingered a breath away when he said, "I want forever with you."

She smiled and touched her lips to his. "Forever is a good place to start."

Darcy watched as Trace and Lucien took the man away, but where they were going, they wouldn't share.

"Where do you suppose they're taking him?" Ember gave voice to Darcy's thoughts.

She shrugged her shoulders. "I don't know, but there's one way to find out."

"No, I'm taking you home. I happen to agree with Lucien and Trace on this. We are way out of our depth."

"We don't have to get out of the cab," Darcy said as she started down the hall to the door.

"True, we could just follow them and then go home. What could go wrong?" Ember said sarcastically, which earned her a look from both Darcy and Kyle.

"You know you're just as curious as we are," Darcy said to Kyle, even though she had no idea if that was true. Kyle pulled a hand through his hair. "We don't get out of the cab. Ember, if you have to pee, you pee in the cab."

"Okay."

They walked outside to see Trace and Lucien flanking Nick, who looked smug, as if he didn't truly appreciate the trouble he was in. Trace seemed to be chatting, as if they were all friends, and then his head turned in Ember's direction and the look he gave her rattled Darcy. A few minutes later, Lucien's car pulled up and the three climbed in.

"Come on, before we lose them." Darcy opened the door to one of the cabs lined up outside the club.

"Definitely can't get out of the cab," Ember muttered before she climbed in behind Darcy. Kyle was just closing the door when Darcy said to the cabbie, "Follow the Charger, but be discreet."

The cabbie looked back at them like it was a joke, but met three very determined stares.

"Discreet is extra."

"Whatever, just go," Ember said, then sat back against the seat. "I have to pee."

⟨⟩

Twenty minutes later, Lucien double-parked in front of a popular restaurant.

"So they're meeting someone, I would guess, but who?" Darcy said.

"Whoever it is, he's probably eating something yummy."

Kyle turned to Ember, who was rubbing her belly. "Focus, Ember."

"I'm trying, but it's hard when your stomach is eating itself and your bladder feels like a water balloon."

"We're not getting out of the cab, remember?" Kyle said firmly.

Darcy looked back at the others. "They would never know we were there."

Kyle pointed at Ember. "Not know you are there? She is like kryptonite to Trace. You saw him outside the club. He knows when she's near."

"He might have a point. It is uncanny how he knows when I'm around."

"Then Ember stays in the cab."

"I'm not leaving her here alone and I'm not letting you go in there alone."

"I'll be fine," Darcy said, and smiled.

"Right, that's what we said last time and ended up having a gun pulled on us."

"And we handled it."

"Together, we handled it." Kyle turned to Ember, "Tell her . . . Ember, what's wrong?"

Darcy looked past Kyle to Ember who looked really pale, with sweat beading on her forehead.

"I don't feel so good all of a sudden."

Kyle gave Ember's address to the cabbie before he reached for her hand and held it in his own. It was cold and clammy. "I'm taking you home."

Ember met his worried gaze. "I think that's a good idea."

— · —

Ember heard Kyle and Darcy in the other room, both refusing to leave her until Trace got home. She was going to need to call Dr. Cole tomorrow.

She glanced at the clock—almost two in the morning—and then she heard Trace's deep voice. A minute later he was standing in the doorway of their room and even in the dark she could feel his worry.

"I'm okay."

He moved silently across the room and settled on the edge of the bed.

"What happened?"

"I just didn't feel right. One minute I was okay and the next I felt wrong. There really isn't a better way to describe it."

"And now?"

"Heartburn, but I've had that for a while."

"You're going in to see the doctor tomorrow." He wasn't asking.

"Yes."

He pressed a kiss on her head before he walked from the room. Ember knew he was upset, so she climbed out of bed and followed him into the kitchen.

He had the refrigerator door opened, but he wasn't reaching for anything. He was scared and she couldn't blame him because she was scared too.

"Do you want to talk about it?"

"I want this child, but not at the cost of losing you."

"I promise you that I will take it easy from now on."

He turned to her then and she saw that lost look in his eyes; the sight of it twisted her heart painfully in her chest. "No running off to chase the bad guy. No gunplay, no walking blindly into the fucking middle of danger."

"You have my word."

"Remember that, because you promised me forever and I intend to hold you to that."

———•••———

By the time Darcy got home it was close to three in the morning, but she was so wired that she knew sleep wasn't going to come. Her heart was still not beating right after the gun incident and, though it had been terrifying, it had been exciting too. They were getting close; she just knew it.

She slipped on her nightgown and then stepped into her bathroom to get ready for bed. She washed her face, and as she reached for her towel, a scream climbed halfway up her throat at the sight of Lucien in the mirror just behind her. She had given him a key, but hadn't heard him enter. She was about to say as much, but the wild look in his eyes stopped her. And then he spoke.

"You scared the shit out of me tonight."

"I know."

"The thought of something happening to you . . ." He stepped closer and ran his hands down her arms. "You feel it too, don't you? The need for release."

Darcy's mouth went dry. "I do."

He held her gaze in the mirror as he slowly pulled her nightgown up over her head. He pressed a kiss on her neck and gripped the silk of her panties and moved them down her legs. His hands trailed back up her body, igniting little fires under her skin, and settled on her breasts. Watching him in the mirror, Darcy was mesmerized. His hands were beautiful, and seeing them caress her so tenderly and feeling what that caress was doing was seriously hot. He pressed his hips against her and she could feel him hard and ready. She wanted him naked and as if he could read her thoughts, he took a step back. She started to turn to help him undress, but his soft command stopped her.

"I want you to watch."

He stepped to the side so he was fully visible to her in the mirror and started to unbutton his shirt, one button at a time, until he pulled the cotton down his arms. His tee hugged his chiseled chest and his muscled arms bunched when he reached for the back of it and yanked it forward over his head. Darcy's heart was pounding in time with the throbbing between her legs. His fingers moved to his trousers and she bit her lip watching him slowly move the zipper down over the hard ridge that was tenting his pants in the front. His briefs came off with his trousers and Darcy moaned because the man was gorgeous. He moved his hand down his body to wrap it around his very impressive erection, and then he slid his palm up the length. The head disappeared in his big hand only to reappear a moment later when he slid his hand back down that hard shaft. Darcy squeezed her thighs together because watching him was making her ache so badly it hurt.

She watched as he pleasured himself, but his eyes were on her, moving from her breasts to between her legs. His hand moved faster and his hips jerked in response. She wanted to watch him bring himself to orgasm and then she wanted to pull him into her mouth so she could taste the evidence of his desire. He stopped suddenly and stepped closer, capturing her breasts in his hands again.

"Bend forward and spread your legs."

He moved his feet to the inside of hers, spreading her open even farther before he positioned himself exactly where she wanted him to be. Their eyes were locked in the mirror when he slowly pushed into her. Darcy braced herself on the counter and tilted her ass back to take all of him and felt his heavy sac pressed up against her when he was fully inside her.

He held himself completely still for a moment and then his hips shifted, drawing another moan from her. She watched as one of his hands moved down her body, getting lost in the curls between her legs so that he could stroke and thrust in time. She wanted to close her eyes and savor being so thoroughly ravished, but she couldn't take her eyes off him as he brought her to climax. She had never watched herself have sex, but she seriously loved the show.

His mouth moved to her neck, sucking hard, and she called out his name as she came. His face froze a second later and pleasure rippled over his expression. The orgasm was still tingling her nerves when he lifted her into his arms and started toward the bed.

"You're right. I needed that," she said breathlessly.

"You and me both." He dropped her on the bed. "But I still need more."

Chapter Nineteen

L ucien stopped his car in front of the Pyramid club, but he was wound so tightly, even after exhausting himself with Darcy the night before, that he thought he might just take off. Last night, Nick had not been interested in talking until he and Trace had worked him over. He hadn't given much up, but he did throw around a name meant to intimidate. But it had the exact opposite effect on Lucien.

Lucien knew who Nick worked for, but he still didn't know why he had been interested in Darcy and him when they were younger. They were here to find out.

Lucien glanced at Trace, who was even more quiet than normal. He didn't know if it was because of what had happened last night with Ember or if it was something more, so he asked, "Everything all right?"

There was definitely something going on with him, but he wasn't one to share. So Lucien wasn't surprised when Trace said, "I'm good," and then changed the subject, gesturing to the building. "You think he'll see you?"

"Yeah, sure." Lucien knew he didn't sound very confident, but then, a lot of time had passed since he'd last seen the man.

It was dark and loud inside the club as they made their way through the crowd toward the back, where Lucien knew there were not only offices, but where the man kept a small residence. Once they hit the checkpoint, some men approached, forcing them to come to a halt.

"Your business?" the largest of the group asked. Trace stood silently at Lucien's side, but he felt the air rippling around him, like he was just looking for an excuse to come out swinging.

"I'm here to see your boss. Tell him Lucien Black's here."

Recognition flashed in the man's eyes as he reached for his walkie-talkie.

"Lucien Black to see the boss."

Seconds later the reply came. "Bring him back."

The contrast between the front of the club and the back was like night and day. The walls were painted a muted gold and Lucien noticed that some of the furnishings were antiques. Vivaldi's *The Four Seasons*, a personal favorite of the man they had come to see, pumped over the speakers. They were brought to a sitting room, where a man awaited them by a mantel that Lucien knew to be hand-carved, because it was Rafe who had done it.

At the sound of their approach, the man turned. Looks were definitely deceiving when it came to this slight, elderly man, someone who had run his family's business for close to forty years. Despite his age, Lucien knew he had no intention of retiring any time soon. This was the man who had reached out to Lucien when he'd been a kid and offered him a job.

"Lucien Black, what a pleasant surprise."

Lucien walked over to the other man, who pulled him in for a hug, kissing both his cheeks in greeting.

"Nice to see you again. Trace, I'd like to introduce you to Pasquale—"

"Grimaldi," Trace finished and reached his hand out to the older man. "Nice to meet you."

"Trace Montgomery. A pleasure."

Pasquale gestured toward the small sitting area. "Please, let's sit. That will be all, Frank." After Lucien and Trace had taken a seat, Pasquale said, "So you are here to find out why I asked Nick to pay that visit to St. Agnes." He paused for a moment before he continued, "It was at the request of a business associate."

As much as Lucien liked the man across from him, he was contemplating grabbing him by the throat.

"Who?"

"I know him as Johnny, but you know him as the honorable Judge Jonathan Carmichael."

It took Lucien a minute to let the name sink in, and when it did, rage practically lifted him from his chair.

"The judge asked you to send Nick to Darcy?"

"Yes."

"What the hell for?"

"He wanted to hurt you. It wasn't hard for Nick to say the words that your girl was already thinking. She was young, scared, and trying to do the right thing."

"And if you agreed, what?"

Pasquale didn't answer, but he didn't have to. It was very clear the judge threw cases to keep Pasquale in his pocket.

Lucien practically bellowed, "That smug son of a bitch always ranting about integrity— he's a fucking dirty judge!" He looked back at Pasquale. "So all the shit Nick told Darcy about helping me if she stayed away was a lie."

"It was supposed to be. She wouldn't have stayed away if he hadn't given her a good enough incentive, but I had an attack of conscience and sent Dominic to offer you a job. It probably wasn't necessary since you already had a few people watching your back."

"Sister Margaret."

"Yes."

"Why the hell would the judge care about me when I was younger? He didn't know me from Adam."

"From what I was able to gather, you were the product of a union that he did not approve of."

Lucien felt numb as Pasquale's words slowly penetrated. "Are you saying the judge knows who my parents are?"

The gangster looked almost solemn when he said, "I'm afraid so."

———◆———

Lucien had just gotten home when Trace called about some box of Sister Anne's that Ember had brought home from St. Agnes for him.

A half hour later Lucien stood in Trace's living room looking at the contents of the box. It wasn't much, just some of Sister Anne's clothes and keepsakes.

"It's weird seeing her street clothes. I only ever remember her in her habit." The habit was there too, of course, and seeing it was painful even after all the time that had passed. Under her clothes, Lucien found a small box, and inside was a gold locket, the type a lover would give. There weren't any pictures inside it, just a folded up note with one word on it: "Forever."

"Who do you think that's from?" Trace asked.

"I've no idea." But it was definitely something Lucien planned on asking around about. He wanted to thank Ember, though, for bringing this to him. "Is Ember around?"

"She's sleeping."

"Everything okay with you two?"

"Things between us are great, but the pregnancy is another

story. C'mon, I'll get us some beers." Lucien followed Trace to the kitchen and gladly accepted a cold one.

"I don't understand. I thought you wanted the kid?"

"I do, but I can't shake the feeling that something bad is going to happen."

"I imagine most first-time parents go through that."

Trace rubbed a hand over his head and took a drink from his beer before setting it on the counter next to him. "Maybe, but hers is a higher risk pregnancy."

"I didn't know. I'm sorry, man, but they deliver babies every minute of every day. And Ember's tough; I mean, she reeled *you* in."

The look Trace gave him was comical—both smug and disgusted with the idea of being reeled in, even though it was true and they both knew it.

Lucien took a pull from his own beer and heard the words coming out of his mouth before he realized he intended to say them. "I screwed up with Darcy. I almost lost her again."

"Yeah? What happened?"

"When I heard about the baby, I immediately jumped to the conclusion that she had given him up. I don't even know why, because I know Darcy would never do that. It was like I wanted to push her away."

"You probably did."

Lucien looked over at his friend, confused. "What do you mean?"

"I don't know, but for me, I didn't want to want Ember. I never needed anyone in my life, and I'm not talking about Chelsea because that's different. And then along comes Ember and it was like I was hit over the fucking head and suddenly I did need someone. I needed her. I pushed her away every chance I got and yet she held on because she knew what I was refusing to see."

"What?"

"She needed me as much as I needed her."

"Such words of wisdom, I hardly recognize you," said Lucien jokingly.

"Shut the fuck up or I'll punch you cross-eyed."

"And he's back."

"What are you going to do about the judge?"

Lucien couldn't help his fury at the idea that the one person he truly hated was the one person who knew the secret of his birth parents.

"I don't know. I want to nail him to the wall for meddling in my life and fucking it up so royally, but at the same time I want to know who my parents are. I'm not even sure why, since I made peace with the circumstances of my birth a long time ago. But he knows. How can I not ask?"

Trace nodded his head in agreement before he asked, "What do you think it was that Heidi had on them? It had to be something pretty significant, because the judge is not a pussy."

"Maybe it wasn't just the judge she was blackmailing. Maybe she was extorting all of them. I think I may need to pay a visit to the DA. He should at least know that his father is a dirty son of a bitch."

"Dane thinks she was blackmailing his dad," Ember said from the doorway.

Trace turned to her and when he spoke, his voice was deceptively soft. "Dane?"

"Yeah, he contacted me to give me a heads-up on Heidi and her activities with his family."

"You've seen Dane?"

"Yes, but he was a perfect gentleman."

"Do you not remember the last time you saw him?" Trace demanded.

Ember reached for his hand and stepped into him. "I do, but he's different now. He's clean and remorseful. He reached out to me to help. He's terrified of you, so he'll keep his hands to himself."

"I don't like it," Trace growled.

"Okay, well if I see him again, I'll be sure to bring you."

"Fucking straight."

"You have such a way with words."

Lucien looked down at the floor so Trace wouldn't see his smile, but it was funny watching his friend so easily outmaneuvered. Yep, Ember was tougher than she looked.

She turned her focus to Lucien. "Whose locket is that?"

"I'm guessing Sister Anne's."

"I found love letters in the attic of St. Agnes. I wonder if they're hers too?"

Lucien wasn't sure how he felt about the fact that Sister Anne may have had a man in her life. Thankfully Ember took his mind off it when she said, "What I'm not getting is the connection between Heidi blackmailing the Carmichaels and your son."

Lucien responded, "Let's see what else Dane knows about Heidi's blackmailing."

———•—•———

Dane brought Lena because he hoped that maybe she could run interference if things got dicey with Ember and her husband. He needed to rethink sobriety; it really wasn't all it was cracked up to be.

"Here they come," Lena said, which made Dane turn in the direction of the three walking toward them. Great, the gangster, Lucien, was with them, and just looking at Trace made his face hurt. Man, he wanted a drink. They settled at the table.

"Hi, Dane. Hi, Lena," said Ember.

"Hi, you guys want drinks?" Lena asked.

"No, thanks," Ember said, but Trace and Lucien remained silent.

Dane shifted in his seat before he found his voice and asked, "What is it you need?"

"Have you figured out what Heidi was holding over your family?"

Again he shifted in his chair—talk about a fucking can of worms. But if he had any hope of walking away from all of this, he had to tell them everything he knew.

"My dad has a taste for younger women. I think he slept with the wrong younger woman and Heidi was using that on him. My grandfather is so psychotic when it comes to image that it's possible Heidi threatened to reveal what she knew about my dad to him as well, hoping to get double money for the same juicy tidbit." Dane leaned back in his chair, growing a bit more comfortable with the idea of selling all three of them down the river. "You know they ride my ass about my behavior, but they're no fucking different. Seriously, I should just change my name to Spano and pretend they're not even my family."

Lucien straightened in his chair. "Spano? Elizabeth's case is all over the news."

Dane was surprised at the jolt of pain he felt in response. "She was my mom's younger sister. It's been over thirty years since she was murdered and we still have no idea what happened. My maternal grandfather won't let it go, refuses to allow his daughter's murder to go unsolved. Apparently now there's new evidence on the case, which is why it's back in the news. Maybe we might finally learn what happened to her."

"That's awful, and it takes a toll on a family. It did on mine," Ember said. She added, "My uncle has been in touch with your mom."

"He has? Do you know where she's been?"

"Living with her sister outside of Baltimore."

Dane wasn't sure how he felt about that. She lived fairly close, and yet she had never reached out to him, not once since she'd left. Ember seemed to know what he was thinking.

"My uncle had the sense that she was afraid—enough to not come back for fear of what would happen to you." Ember leaned a little closer before she asked, "Do you think it's possible that your mom knows who killed her sister and that's why she's staying away?"

"I don't know. Elizabeth was murdered before I was born and my mom left when I was around two. Maybe."

Lucien spoke up for the first time since they'd arrived. "Maybe it's time you had a reunion with your mom."

"Yeah." Dane turned his attention to Ember. "Remember when I mentioned that Todd was spending some time with Heidi?"

"Yes."

"I don't know if it means anything, but Todd owes markers to some seriously bad guys, which might be why Heidi was interested in him."

Dane caught the look of suspicion on Lucien's face just as Ember said, "Thanks."

Darcy and Ember were on their way to St. Agnes to check out the attic. Darcy felt a pang of sadness seeing Ember's growing belly, but she moved past it and asked, "How are you feeling? What did the doctor say?"

"I've got proteins in my urine and my blood pressure is up, which are both warning signs for preeclampsia. I've just got to take it easy." Ember changed the subject. "My dad called the other day."

"The man to whom you owe your advice-giving skills," Darcy said with humor.

"One and the same. He's moving in with my uncle; he wants to be closer to me and the baby."

Darcy could tell by the brightness of Ember's voice that this was really exciting news for her. "Ember, that's wonderful. I look forward to meeting him."

"I can't tell you how many times I picked up the phone to try to persuade him to move closer, but his house was the one he shared with my mom. How could I ask him to leave that? But now he's decided to rent it out."

"That's a good compromise."

"Yeah, and he's going to work for my uncle since he's overwhelmed with cases."

Darcy laughed out loud at that. "PI work is definitely your family's forte."

The cab pulled to the curb. Ember looked surprised. "Wow, we're here already. Brandon is going to sign us in as his guests. He's supposed to meet us at the door."

Darcy waited for Ember to climb from the cab before she paid the cabbie and followed. She heard Ember calling a greeting to her friend and turned. As soon as she saw Ember's friend, her feet stopped moving and all the air left her lungs. She was looking at a boy who looked exactly how Lucien had looked in his youth. Hot tears burned her eyes, but she couldn't look away from the boy who was coming down the front steps toward them. It was her son—their son. She'd bet the bank on it.

"Darcy?" Ember's voice held a note of concern.

"That's Brandon?"

"Yes." Ember seemed to understand what Darcy wasn't saying when she exhaled in a gasp. "Oh my God. I didn't even think; I mean, I saw similarities, but I assumed Brandon was too old to be your son."

Darcy struggled to pull herself under control so she didn't terrify the boy. Ember reached for her hand and squeezed, releasing it just as Brandon stopped in front of them.

"Hey, Ember."

Darcy noticed the odd note in Ember's voice, no doubt because she was holding back tears. "Hi, Brandon. This is my friend Darcy."

"Hey . . ." But whatever Brandon was going to say died on his tongue as his eyes grew wide. His reaction was so strange that Darcy took a step closer to him and asked, "Are you okay?"

His voice was strained when he said, "Yeah, just . . ."

"What?"

"Do I know you?" he asked, and suddenly he looked so much younger.

"No, but I would like very much to get to know you."

"You're the one who was looking for her son?" he asked.

Darcy's heart stopped beating. "Yes." And then Brandon's next words sent it into a gallop.

"You were looking for me, weren't you?"

Darcy gave up and let her tears run down her cheeks. "Yes."

<hr />

Lucien and Darcy walked right past guest check-in; with the expressions on their faces, no one dared to stop them. They stormed into Sister Margaret's room. She looked up in shock, presumably at the intrusion, until she saw who it was; then her expression turned to resignation.

"You fucking knew," Lucien hissed. "You knew our son was at St. Agnes the entire time."

"No, I didn't know at first; I only suspected, but when I did learn the truth, I couldn't say anything."

"Why not?" Lucien demanded.

"I was being blackmailed."

Lucien's anger turned to confusion. "Heidi?"

"Yes."

"What did she have on you?"

"It wasn't me. She had information on Sister Anne, and though she was gone, I didn't want her name, or our order's, to be dragged into the dirt. I think you would have approved of the choice I made. It wasn't an easy one."

"That's why you wanted us looking in the attic at St. Agnes. Heidi really did keep her stash there."

"I think so, but I was never able to find it. It explained why she was always around, why she took interest in what everyone else was doing. I wouldn't be surprised to learn that she had been being paid to watch over you."

Darcy's confusion wasn't feigned. "What do you mean by that?"

"How did the kidnappers know when you went into labor?"

Lucien tensed at Darcy's side. "Fucking bitch."

"Anyway, she moved her stash before she started blackmailing me. I think she actually got more dirt on people from rummaging through the stuff up in that attic. Through the years, the Sisters shared with me that Heidi continued to visit St. Agnes, sometimes bringing that boy of hers. I'm sure she was going through the attic looking for more secrets. She was one twisted girl. But there was another reason I encouraged you to go to St. Agnes."

Darcy answered for her. "You knew if we saw Brandon that we would know he was ours."

"Yes, and then the secret would be out."

"And that's why you arranged for me to go to college. It was penance," Darcy added.

Sister Margaret didn't look even slightly contrite. "So to speak."

"Heidi's dead now, so why didn't you tell us when we came to see you last time?"

"I was going to, but then he called."

"He?" Lucien asked.

"Yeah, this guy picked up the blackmail where Heidi left off, so I kept my silence, but tried to give enough hints that you'd figure it out on your own."

"Who is he?" Darcy demanded.

"I don't know. I've never seen him, but he knew so much that I just assumed he was an accomplice of Heidi's."

———⋯———

Lucien lay in bed with Darcy, but his thoughts were on their son. "Brandon has agreed to take the blood test?"

"Yes, but I don't need the results to know. He looks just like you." Darcy lifted her head onto her hand. "When I see him in my head, he's a baby. I know that's silly because it's been fourteen years, but seeing him almost fully grown . . . We've missed so much."

Lucien tightened his arms around her. "We found him, Darcy. We may have lost fourteen years, but we have the rest of our lives to get to know him."

"Do you think he'll want that—I mean, to be a part of our lives now?"

"I wouldn't have turned family away at his age. Would you have?"

Lucien saw the answer in her eyes before she said, "No, I wouldn't have."

"We need to give him time and not push him, but I think he's as eager to get to know us as we are him."

"I can't wait for you to meet him," Darcy whispered.

"I'm not sure how to be a dad."

"I don't know anything about being a mother, but we'll figure it out."

Lucien knew the awe he was feeling came across in his voice. "A family."

Darcy wrapped her arms around him. "Our family."

"Even better," he whispered before his mouth covered hers.

Chapter Twenty

Dane wasn't sure if he wanted to follow through with his plan, but he supposed standing on his mother's front step was the wrong place for a change of heart. Lena and Ember's uncle Josh had accompanied him. He was grateful to the older man for offering to come to help smooth out what was sure to be an uncomfortable first meeting.

He found Lena's hand in his surprisingly comforting. Sober, his perspective had changed and one of the things he was learning was that Lena really seemed to "get" him.

"You ready for this?" she asked.

"I doubt it."

Josh had called ahead to let Belinda know who he was bringing, so when Dane knocked, Belinda opened the door. Tears immediately filled her eyes as she moved back and gestured with her hands.

"Please, Dane . . . all of you . . . come inside."

They settled in the living room—Dane and Lena on the sofa and Belinda across from them in a chair. Josh stood in the back of the room to give them some privacy, but close enough to step in if things weren't going well.

"How have you been, Dane?" Belinda's voice cracked.

Boy, what a loaded question. He answered bitterly, "Well, considering my mother left me when I wasn't even two years old, I'm pretty fucked up. Thanks for asking."

Belinda's face fell and she started to cry. "I'm sorry. I should have been there."

"Why did you leave?"

"Your father was a pig and I couldn't bear watching him parade his bimbos in front of me anymore."

"So you left me."

"I wanted to take you with me, but I couldn't. I was afraid of your grandfather."

"Why?" Dane asked.

"Your family used to be good friends with my parents, the kind of friendship that transcends generations. When my father and your grandfather were younger they'd made an agreement—an arranged marriage to protect their collective wealth. It was really very selfish, but they were both old-school. So one of the Carmichael sons would marry one of the Spano daughters. When the time came, I was the unlucky one, since Lily didn't prefer men, and Elizabeth was too young and immature. It was on my twentieth birthday that I was told I was to marry Nathaniel. I didn't know him well. We'd said hi at the various functions we'd attended with our parents, but we certainly hadn't dated at all and didn't know each other well enough to marry. I fought it, but your grandfather was a very powerful man, even back then. He also had this way with people. He could make them do what he wanted, but made them feel as if it had been their idea all along.

"My parents threw a long weekend party to announce the engagement. Married life at first was wonderful. Nathaniel was very attentive. But when we had a child, he changed. He was a playboy before I married him, and after he grew bored, he went back to being one. When I realized that my husband was sleeping around again, I went to your grandfather and told him I was leaving. I can't believe I had the nerve to do so, but I had something on him. He was livid, but for the first time he was scared too."

"What did you have on him?" Dane asked.

"I'd caught him one night during that long weekend in my sister Elizabeth's room."

"He slept with your sister?" Lena said, horrified.

What his mother said next seemed like a rehearsed answer to Dane, and her eyes, for the first time during their visit, were shifty.

"Yes, and he didn't want that to get out. I didn't understand why, because it wasn't like she was underage. My guess was he didn't want our father to learn of it because he had no intention of marrying Elizabeth. He didn't believe in marriage, at least as it pertained to him, so he let me go, but the cost of leaving was my son and my family's silence."

Uncle Josh moved from his spot at the back of the room. "Your sister was murdered not long after that weekend. Did you ever consider there was a connection between that weekend and her death?"

Dane watched the change in his mother's expression from guarded to resigned and what looked like relief despite the fear in her gaze, "Of course I did, but if he was capable of what I feared, then he was capable of anything. And he's also a judge with a DA for a son, which makes him pretty untouchable. Any attempt I made to expose him would have been taken out on my son."

"Then why speak up about it now?" Dane asked.

"Because there is something worse than the fear of death and that's not being able to look yourself in the mirror. I may be late to the game, but he needs to pay for what he did."

———•◆•———

Dane waited until his grandfather left for the evening before he hunted down his dad. He found him in his bedroom, dressing.

"Can I talk to you?"

"I'm on my way out. Can this wait?"

"I saw Mom." Dane still couldn't seem to get his head around the fact that he had seen his mother. For him, it felt like the first time because he had been so young when she'd left. She was beautiful and when she smiled, he could see himself in her face. For so long he'd harbored animosity toward her, but to learn that she had been manipulated by his grandfather enraged him. Just one more reason for him to hate the old bastard.

His dad stopped straightening his tie and turned to Dane. "When?"

His question jarred Dane from his thoughts. "Yesterday. What can you tell me about her sister, Elizabeth?"

Pain flashed across his dad's face and he settled on the edge of the bed. Suddenly he looked years older.

"She was a good kid and a very talented actress. She thought Belinda was just the greatest, and me by extension. That she was murdered seemed senseless. I think what made it even harder was that her killer was never found. Her father, your other grandfather, put everything he had into finding the murderer and even now, thirty-two years later, he still hasn't stopped."

"Did you ever wonder why Grandfather allowed Mom to leave, particularly with how anal he is about appearances?"

"Yeah, it's crossed my mind a time or two. Why?"

"Mom told me that she saw him with Elizabeth the weekend of your engagement announcement."

Dane watched his father's various reactions to that statement; he was prepared for the verbal lashing he assumed would ensue because he had listened to the whore, as his grandfather often called his mom.

"What exactly did she see?"

"He was having sex with Elizabeth."

Rage transformed his face, turning him an unhealthy shade a red, and then he reached for the closest object and hurled it at the wall. "Son of a bitch." He looked like he was getting ready for a really good rant when he stopped suddenly and turned to Dane.

"Holy fuck, that actually clarifies a few things."

"Like what?"

"After that weekend, Elizabeth was always coming around. I thought, at first, that she had a little crush on me, but thinking back on it now, it wasn't me she became animated around."

"Grandfather."

"Yeah. She must have developed a crush on him. I always wondered, especially with his hatred of Belinda, but it makes sense now it wasn't so much her, but the fact that she was a constant reminder of Elizabeth's unwanted attention."

"Do you think he had anything to do with her death?" Dane asked.

"I think if Elizabeth threatened him . . . yeah, I think he's capable of anything."

— • —

Trace returned home from class to find his wife entertaining two men. Brandon and Seth were settled on the sofa on either side of Ember as they played Wii. She looked up at him just as he leaned over and pressed a kiss on her lips. His eyes found Brandon who looked envious and he winked before he went to the bedroom to change.

He asked, "Are you hungry?"

Before Ember could answer, Brandon and Seth both said, "Starving."

Chelsea came out of her room holding a book and when she saw Trace, she smiled. "Hi, Trace. Seth was just going to read to me."

Trace had sat Seth down after his talk with Charles and told him everything. He took the news really well, but Charles was no more a father to Seth than Douglas had been to Trace, so he couldn't really blame him for his lack of enthusiasm. Seth did seem somewhat excited about coming to live with them, and Chelsea was thrilled to have a cousin. She and Seth had hit it off instantly.

"Let me get changed and I'll whip something up." Trace started from the room and Ember followed after him, closing the door behind her. He turned to her right before he pulled his shirt over his head and dropped it on the bed. He saw when her eyes moved to her name on his chest. He loved that she looked, every time. Her eyes turned to his and he could see that she saw far more than she let on. She asked, "Something is on your mind. What's going on?"

"Just some scheduling conflicts at the school."

"That's not what's putting that look in your eyes."

He moved to her and wrapped her in her arms before he touched his lips to hers. "How are you feeling?"

"I'm okay." She tilted her head and studied him as understanding dawned. "You're worried, still?"

"Let's just say I'll be happy when there's a little Ember in that crib and you are warm and naked next to me in our bed."

She reached for his face. "This is our first child. It's all scary, but everything will be fine. You have to have faith."

"I'd rather have you instead."

"I'm not going anywhere. You're stuck with me. When I'm ninety, I'll be asking you where I left my teeth."

He said nothing in reply, but he knew his face was saying plenty. He watched her face as she realized where his thoughts had gone with her last statement and he grinned in response.

"Oh my God, at ninety? Are you serious?" she said.

"No teeth and that mouth . . ." He glanced down before looking back up at her. "Fuck yeah."

His finger played with her pebbled nipple through her shirt, his grin turning into a naughty smile. "You're saying one thing, sweetheart, but your body's saying something else."

"There are children in the other room."

"Yes, and that's the only reason why you're not flat on your back already."

"Poetry, you speak in sheer poetry."

"I'll give you poetry." He reached between her legs, but she stepped back from him and shook her head.

"If you start, I won't be able to stop."

His eyes burned like fire in response. "I'll call them a cab."

"I promised them food, but after, I'm all yours."

He grabbed her and kissed her hard on the mouth. "Remember that," he said before he strolled off to their closet. "Did Brandon agree to the blood test?"

"Yes. That's why he's here. I think he's feeling conflicted. Excited that he may have found his family, and terrified at the same time. I think he's worried that Lucien and Darcy will be disappointed."

Trace didn't hide his incredulity. "That's impossible."

"Yes, but he's a young kid facing a major life change."

"True, so it's a good thing that he has you in his life to tell him otherwise."

"Isn't it weird how I even know him? I become friends with a boy who turns out to be Lucien's son. It's almost like someone orchestrated it."

Trace walked to her and drew her close. "I wouldn't be surprised to learn that someone did."

"Really? You don't think it could be life working in mysterious ways?"

"I've no idea, but there'll be nothing mysterious about how I plan on working you over later."

He saw lust flash in her eyes along with humor before he said, "Yeah, I know poetry." And then he kissed her.

———•◦•———

Lucien couldn't believe he was voluntarily in the DA's office, but desperate times called for desperate measures. The man himself was sitting behind his desk when his assistant escorted Lucien into his office.

"Lucien Black is here for your three o'clock."

Lucien watched as the older man's head lifted. There seemed to be the slightest hesitation, almost surprise, before he stood.

"Please have a seat."

Lucien heard the door closing behind him as he sat across from the DA. Horace took his seat before he asked, "You mentioned having some information regarding the Elizabeth Spano case."

"Yes, but it's an awkward situation."

Horace leaned back in his chair. "How so?"

"The information I have concerns your father."

Lucien didn't miss the calculated look that flashed in the DA's eyes. "I'm guessing by that look that you aren't surprised to hear that he may have been involved in her death."

"My father is a tyrant who uses his influence to manipulate people."

"And capable of murder?" Lucien asked.

"I can't discuss the case with you, but I believe he is capable of anything, including using his courtroom as his own personal negotiation table. He doesn't uphold the law; he twists and bends it to get what he wants."

Lucien was probably crossing a line when he said, "And he believes that he's untouchable, with one son a DA and another a senator."

There was the slightest gleam of humor in Horace's eyes. "Arrogance can do that. What is it that you know?"

"Your father slept with Elizabeth on the weekend of Nathaniel and Belinda's engagement announcement."

Lucien saw the anger and the pain. He was surprised by the naked response from the older man. "She was a sweet kid and had her whole life ahead of her." His face hardened. "It's an outrage that her murder has been unsolved for as long as it has been."

"But?" Lucien asked.

"All the evidence, however circumstantial, suggested the Grimaldi family was involved. My problem with that angle was motive. Pasquale Grimaldi is a very smart man, but the murder was sloppy. Elizabeth had been strangled, which usually indicates a crime of passion, and the Grimaldis' style is more a bullet to the brain. Even with all the digging I've done, I have never found a link to tie Elizabeth to anyone in the Grimaldi family. It was neat, too neat."

Lucien read between the lies. "You already suspected your dad."

"I'll deny I ever said this, but there have been countless cases that were thrown from the judge's courtroom, cases that when dug into deeply enough, were tied to the Grimaldis. My gut knew it was him, but I never had the smoking gun. It's why I've been splashing Elizabeth's name all over the news with the 'new evidence' ruse. I'm trying to draw my father out, to make him nervous with the hopes that he'll slip and give me something to use against him."

Lucien held the other man's unwavering stare. "You have the smoking gun now."

A wicked grin curved Horace's lips. "And I fully intend to use the very law my father swore to uphold to hang him."

———•◦•———

Lucien stood in the grand entrance hall in the building where Judge Jonathan Carmichael had his office, debating with himself. He had contacted the man's secretary earlier and knew the judge was just finishing a lunch meeting, and Lucien hoped to catch him on his way back up to his office. He wanted to find out who the hell his parents were, but he hesitated seeking out the older man because, with how he was feeling, he was likely to choke the life from the judge before he ever got what he came for. He was still debating with himself when he heard hushed voices coming from a darkened hallway. He moved closer and, though it was dark, he had no trouble making out the two figures: the judge and the senator.

"She was a goddamn kid."

The judge hissed, "Lower your damn voice."

"I can't believe I didn't put it together. All those visits Elizabeth made to the house. I thought she was coming to see me, but it was you, wasn't it?"

The judge held himself to his full height. "You will remember to whom you are speaking. I am not just your father, but I am a goddamn judge. You will respect that and me."

Lucien watched as Nathaniel moved into his father's space so that they were eye to eye. "You've spent most of my life calling my wife a whore because you couldn't keep it in your pants and seduced a fucking college freshman. Was the constant reminder that you didn't actually walk on water the reason you took your failings out on my wife?"

"What the hell do you care? You didn't love her," the judge snapped.

"No, but I liked her and I liked Elizabeth. She was a good kid and didn't deserve—" Lucien watched as Nathaniel ended his point in midsentence and then he walked away as if in a hurry to go. Lucien stepped farther into the shadows as he passed. The judge wouldn't see it, but Lucien did, the smile that spread over Nathaniel's face. And Lucien felt a begrudging admiration for Horace and Nathaniel Carmichael at their perfectly executed setup.

Chapter Twenty-One

✦

Horace was just finishing the paperwork for his father's indictment when his secretary buzzed him.

"Your four o'clock is here."

"Send him in." Horace stood and walked to the cabinet at the far end of his office and poured himself a Scotch. After his brother's visit to their father a few weeks ago, the old man had contacted the Grimaldi family, trying to take a hit out on Nathaniel. As bizarre as his father's actions had been, what was even more disturbing to Horace was that in his gut, he'd known what his father would try to do. Horace had made a deal with Pasquale Grimaldi, the lesser of the two evils, to make the case against his father.

The door opened and he drank the entire contents of his glass before he turned to his visitor.

"Thank you for coming."

"I'm a little unsure why I was asked here," Lucien said as he stood near the door, unwilling to come in any farther. He'd been here once already and wasn't thrilled to find himself here again. DA's offices made him nervous.

"This is not an official meeting."

Lucien relaxed a bit, but he still didn't move farther into the room.

"Will you have a seat?"

"No, I'm good here."

"Suit yourself. I asked you here because I have some information that I need to share with you."

Lucien wasn't sure he liked where this was going. "All right."

"It's amazing how many lives were altered because of the weekend of Nathanial's engagement party. Belinda was only a sophomore in college when she was told she was to marry my brother. Nathaniel's a good guy, but he's not husband material. Belinda seemed scared and rebellious. I couldn't blame her. That same weekend I learned that the woman I wanted to marry wouldn't have me. It wasn't that she didn't love me, but marriage would force her to give up her calling. She'd debated about it for over a year and I really thought I was wearing her down, but she decided that she couldn't. I was devastated because I loved her—still do."

He turned to Lucien. "You're probably wondering why I'm telling you all of this. I'll get to the point. That weekend, Belinda and I shared our pain by sleeping together. It was only one time and we knew it was a mistake as soon as we had. We vowed to never mention it and she went back to college."

He looked down as if the next words were almost too hard to say. "I didn't realize there was a child, not until almost three years later. Belinda was getting ready to marry my brother. She couldn't show up with a child from a brief affair she had with me, and her sister wasn't prepared to care for a child on her own."

He looked at Lucien, who was pacing because he was being bombarded with emotions he was unaccustomed to feeling. Lucien knew his voice reflected his internal turmoil when he said, "Go on."

"I went for the baby because I wanted him. I had a son. I had planned to bring him home and raise him, but then my father learned of him. He went crazy, vowing all kinds of retribution, and I knew even then that he was capable of anything. So I took my son to the one place where I knew he would be loved, where I trusted the one who would be looking out for him. I took him to the one person who would love him as if he were her own, the woman who couldn't marry me because she had a calling to care for children."

An ache in his throat nearly made speech impossible, but Lucien managed in barely a whisper, "Sister Anne."

"Yes."

He needed to move, needed to focus on something, because he wasn't sure what he was feeling right now. Sister Anne had been in love with Horace Carmichael. Horace was his father . . . he stopped moving and looked back at Horace. "I'm a Carmichael."

"Yes."

And then another thought made him almost laugh at the irony. "Dane's my fucking half brother."

"It was my father who sent that man to your girl all those years ago. It was his way of being spiteful over a situation he couldn't control. His motive was to hurt me because my son would be a constant reminder that he, the judge, was no better than the people he put away. It was why he was so intolerant of Dane. He didn't care who he hurt in the process and unfortunately you and Darcy were collateral damage. He's been arrested and he'll pay for what he did to Elizabeth and you."

"Do you think he also planned the kidnapping of my son?"

"What?" Horace took on a look that Lucien recognized because he'd seen it a few times in the mirror. The man was livid. "What are you talking about?"

"Darcy was pregnant. She was told her baby died, but she later learned that her mother had been paid to lie to her."

"How the hell didn't I know this?" Horace said to himself as he paced his office. "I would like to say no, but I'm coming to learn I don't really know my father. Where's your son now?"

"He's been under our noses all along. We're meeting him soon."

His expression softened. "I'm happy to hear that. I'd like to sit with you to document everything you have on the kidnapping and I'll get a team looking into it. If the judge did have a hand in it, it'll be one more nail in that bastard's coffin."

Lucien pushed his hands into his pockets. "Thank you."

"For what it's worth, we're family."

"Now I know why the judge was constantly getting in my face," Lucien said.

"I'm afraid so."

"You've been watching out for me, haven't you?"

"How could I not?"

"And you recruited Sister Margaret?"

"Actually, that was all Anne. She loved you like a son, despite my betrayal. You see, I didn't initially tell her who you were because I thought I was protecting you, but it didn't take her long to know you were mine. She worried about you because of your connection to my family. She trusted Sister Margaret and she asked the old bird to look out for you when she was gone."

"Sister Anne was like a mother to me." Lucien looked down for a moment because he felt that tightening in his chest again. "If you had to leave your son"—he looked back up at Horace—"you left him with the best person you could have."

"It should have been me raising you, but at least you were loved as a child should be loved."

Though he was way out of his depth, a slight smile touched Lucien's lips. He hadn't been forgotten after all. "I don't know how to be a son, but I'm willing to give it a try."

Tears shone in Horace's eyes when he said, "And that's all I can ask."

"But I'm not changing my name from Black."

"I would have fought you if you had tried."

"Did you give Sister Anne a locket?"

Pain turned Horace's voice hoarse. "Yes."

"And love letters?"

"She kept them?"

"Yes, I have them if you would like them."

There were tears in his eyes when he said, "I would, very much."

"You're a Carmichael," Darcy said as she lay next to Lucien that night.

"No, I'm a Black." He pressed a kiss on her head. "I'll always be a Black."

"Black's a good last name. I like that last name," Darcy said, but her eyes avoided his, as if she were nervous, which was so not Darcy. Lucien grinned.

"Well, Darcy MacBride, what are you hinting at?"

"Nothing."

"Are you looking to change your last name?"

"What?" she blushed, which only made his grin turn into a smile. He sat up and turned to her. "Are you asking me to marry you?"

The teasing in his voice made Darcy look over at him. To hide the fact that she was feeling a bit off balance, she hit him in the chest. "No."

"Really? Because it kind of sounds like you are fishing for a proposal."

"I wasn't."

"Oh well. All right, then." He lowered himself back onto the bed and put his hands behind his head as if he didn't have a thought in his mind.

"And that's it? End of discussion?" Darcy stuttered as she sat up, pulling the sheet with her.

"Discussion? You just said there wasn't one." He was being intentionally obtuse.

"And you have no thoughts about our last names?" Darcy could feel her temper beginning to stir.

"I think MacBride is a great name. Why? Don't you like it?"

"I like yours better," she muttered and started to climb from the bed, but he moved, pulling her under him, pinning her with his body.

"What was that?" he asked.

She refused to look at him because he was intentionally making this hard. "I didn't say anything."

"Really, I could have sworn that you said you liked my last name better. Do you?"

"You know damn well I love your last name and I want it to be mine too."

"So you are asking me to marry you."

"No!"

"Very well." He rolled off and away from her, and Darcy was about to make a disparaging comment about his person when he turned back to her. Instead of holding—dare she even think it—a small leather box, he was holding a small silver cross. She recognized it immediately.

"That was Sister Anne's."

"The day we were going to meet, I was going to give this to you. I wanted to give you something that conveyed how I felt about you and this was the only thing I had of value."

Tears filled Darcy's eyes, but they never left Lucien's gaze. "You were going to give me her necklace?"

"It was all I had to give."

She was about to throw herself into his arms. *Oh my God. What a gesture.* But he stopped her. "I'm not done."

"Sorry," Darcy said, but she couldn't manage disgruntled. She was just too damn happy.

"I was going to give this to you as a promise, a promise to never hurt you, to never leave you, to always find my way back to you even when we were pissed off and wanted to kill each other. A promise to love only you as long as I drew breath."

His hand closed over the necklace. "But you didn't show up."

"What?" And then she punched him because he had made her cry again with the most perfect words ever.

He laughed before he unhooked the clasp and secured it around her neck. "I was a kid then." He climbed from bed and returned with a small box in his hand.

He handed it to her. Her hands shook when she lifted the lid to see the sapphire, the color almost the exact shade of her eyes, surrounded by diamonds.

"But the man I've become still loves you as desperately as the kid I was. Marry me, Darcy."

Darcy had fantasized about this moment so many times through the years and, every time, it was the most beautiful and poignant moment: he confesses his love, she confesses hers, and they live happily-ever-after. In real life, it didn't happen quite that way.

"I'm going to throw up," she managed before she stumbled from the room. The sound of her hacking filled the silence.

Lucien sat on the bed, a little dazed at the turn of events. "I can honestly say I didn't see that coming," he said to himself.

Darcy appeared in the doorway, and the look on her face made Lucien concerned. For a minute, he thought she was going to turn him down.

"What's wrong?"

"What are your thoughts on babies?"

It took him a minute and then his eyes moved to her stomach before looking back at her. "Are you serious?"

"Yep."

He jumped up and kissed her. "You have to marry me, now."

"I was always going to marry you, you fool."

"A baby."

She sobered for a minute before she asked, "Do you think Brandon will be upset?"

"He was an orphan, so no, I doubt it."

He kissed her so tenderly that his heart ached. "We've our futures to think about, which includes children," he whispered against her lips.

"More than two?" she asked.

He flashed her a grin. "The more the merrier." He lifted her in his arms. "And think of all the practice."

He carried her to their bed and made his point slowly and with great attention to detail.

Chapter Twenty-Two

D ane scanned the restaurant for escape routes. Lucien Black wanted to have lunch with him. Fabulous. As if he didn't have enough shit going on in his life, he now needed to deal with the mysterious Lucien Black. And he was still sober; he should get a fucking medal.

He didn't need to see Lucien to know he had arrived, since most of the women in the place turned their heads to catch a glimpse of him. Lucien reached the table and sat without ceremony. Dane was tempted to order a drink, but when prompted by the waiter, he asked for water.

Seeming to take his lead, Lucien did as well. "Thanks for agreeing to meet with me."

"Yeah, whatever. So what did you want?"

"I guess you haven't spoken to Horace," Lucien said.

"Only in that you wanted to talk with me."

"Well, as it turns out, we're brothers."

"*What?*" For a practical joke, this one sucked.

"My father is Horace and my mother is Belinda. They had a one-night stand the night of the infamous engagement party and I'm the result of that."

"You're not kidding, are you?"

"Nope. Believe me, I wasn't particularly thrilled to learn I was related to you, but you can't pick your family. I'm willing to try if you are, but with that being said, you ever lay another finger on my friend's wife and I'll kill you and burn the body. In fact, let's branch that out to any unwilling woman. You feel me?"

Dane gulped.

"I'm getting married in a few months and I would like you to be there."

"Huh? Why?"

"Haven't you been listening? You're family."

Dane felt like his head was in a dryer; one minute Lucien threatened his life and the next he was asking him to his wedding. Damn, he needed a drink, but he couldn't help smiling a little. It felt kind of nice to be included. He wasn't going to let the meathead across from him know that, though, so he strove for bored when he said, "Yeah, okay."

One look at Lucien and Dane knew he hadn't fooled him. He was gracious enough to not call him on it and instead said, "Let's eat."

———◆———

"Maybe this isn't such a good idea." Brandon stopped walking, which made Ember reach for his hand to pull him along.

"They're your parents and you know the story because you were helping us."

"I know, but what if they're disappointed?"

Ember stopped walking to look at him. "How could they be disappointed in you?"

"I don't know. I mean, I come from nothing."

"So did they." She started along, keeping his hand in hers, and said, "Let me tell you a story. Once there was a boy and girl who fell in love almost from the moment they saw each other. They planned to run away and start a life together. When she learned she was pregnant, it made it all that much more magical, but the powers that be pulled them apart. They found each other again after fourteen years, were still as wildly in love as they were when they'd first met, and, the icing on the cake, they found the son that had been stolen from them. It isn't possible for them to be disappointed, because you are the result of their incredible love."

Brandon was silent for a minute, though his hand tightened around Ember's. "That's really cheesy."

"Yeah, it was a little, but every word is true."

"Are they like you?" he asked seriously.

"How so?"

"Goofy."

"I'm not goofy."

"You are a little bit, but I like goofy."

"Children today . . ."

"Thanks, Ember."

"You're welcome, Brandon. Now let's move, your mom and dad are waiting."

"I'm so nervous my hands are shaking," Darcy said, which immediately made Lucien reach for one and hold it in his own. He was conflicted because, though he was thrilled to have found his son, it was heartbreaking to know that his son had been so close throughout the years and he hadn't known. Every time Lucien had visited St. Agnes or attended the annual picnic, his son had been there too and he'd never known.

He pushed those thoughts aside. "Understandable. We're about to meet our son. Our teenage son." Lucien couldn't help the smile. Talk about history repeating itself. His son was best friends with Trace's cousin, and they lived at St. Agnes, just as he and Trace had for a time.

"Small fucking world," Lucien said just as the door opened and Ember walked into the small restaurant she had suggested for the meeting. Right behind her was Brandon.

"Doesn't he look like you?" Darcy whispered.

"And you."

They stood as Ember and Brandon approached. Darcy choked on a sob. "He walks just like you. I didn't notice that the last time."

Ember smiled at them before she looked at Brandon. "Brandon, you remember Darcy, and this is Lucien."

"Hey. Nice to meet you." He held a chair for Ember before taking a menu and sitting himself.

"The burgers are delicious here."

Food was the last thing on Darcy's mind; she absently turned her eyes to her menu, but her thoughts were all on the boy sitting next to her. And then he said softly, "I don't know how to be a son, but I'm willing to try."

Darcy's eyes met his as tears rolled down her cheeks. "That's all we can ask," Lucien said. His tone seemed gruff, though Darcy suspected it was because his throat was as choked as hers.

Brandon flashed them a smile that was all Lucien. "Sweet."

◄─•─►

Lucien and Darcy walked just behind Brandon in the open-air colonnade on the Bronx Community College campus as Brandon studied the bronzes of famous Americans. Lucien watched his son, the word feeling strange on his tongue. He was a smart kid and had a love of all things old. Maybe one day, his likeness would be here too.

"I think he's getting more comfortable with us," Darcy commented, pulling Lucien from his own thoughts.

He reached for her hand and, when she looked up at him, he leaned over and brushed his lips over hers. "I think so too."

There was wonder in her voice. "He's our son. We made him."

Brandon had stopped at the Benjamin Franklin bronze. "Are you okay, Brandon?" Lucien asked.

"I did a report on Benjamin Franklin in school once. He was a cool dude."

"Maybe you'd like to take a trip to Philadelphia. We could check out the Franklin Institute, Independence Hall, the Liberty Bell," Lucien offered.

Brandon's eyes lit up. "Could we?"

Lucien felt on top of the world to see the excitement burning in Brandon's eyes. He'd do anything for this boy. "Absolutely."

And then Brandon seemed to sober. It was with genuine concern that Lucien asked, "What's wrong?"

"I shouldn't take up all of your time."

"Why not?" Darcy asked.

He looked so very young when he turned his gaze on them. "Because you have a life outside of me."

"Not by choice. You are our son and we want you in our lives." Lucien's voice was gentle but filled with conviction.

"I'm not cramping your style?"

"Never," Darcy said emphatically.

"I like spending time with you." Brandon's words were barely over a whisper.

"The feeling is mutual."

"I'm not sure about this," Darcy said to Lucien as they walked up the front steps of St. Agnes.

"It'll be fun."

"Fun? I hardly think so."

As soon as the door opened, the scent of lemon cleaner brought back a wave of memories for Darcy. Brandon was just coming down the stairs with Seth.

"I'll sign you in and then we'll get started. Seth is going to play too."

"I may just watch," Darcy said.

The grin Brandon gave her was so much like Lucien's that she felt it hit her right in the center of her chest. "There's no way you're just going to watch." Cocky like his dad too.

Darcy and Lucien had been spending almost every day with Brandon, taking him to museums, the Statue of Liberty, the Empire State Building. It was touristy, which was why Darcy and Lucien were both shocked to learn that Brandon had never seen either the Statue of Liberty or the Empire State building. They went to see a few movies, but today it was Brandon's pick. Darcy was surprised when he'd invited them to St. Agnes for a zombie-killing marathon. Darcy wasn't much for video games and certainly not ones that involved killing zombies, but it was his day, so here she was. Lucien, on the other hand, looked excited at the prospect of blowing out the brains of the undead.

Darcy was happy to see that Seth was joining them. He would be moving in with Trace and Ember once the paperwork over guardianship was approved. Darcy and Lucien were in the process of adopting Brandon, but that was going to take some time. It was nice that the boys had each other while the adults navigated through the legal stuff.

They stepped into the media room. It was a drab room with threadbare furniture and scarred floors, but the flatscreen was new. Darcy took a seat and watched as Brandon set up the machine.

"We can all play. I'll give you a quick rundown of the game and then we'll get started."

Darcy crossed her legs and smiled. As if she was going to play.

"Darcy, we're hungry. Let's go get something to eat." There was humor in Lucien's voice, but Darcy barely registered it because she was in the middle of a herd of dead things.

"After I kill these."

"You said that a half an hour and two levels ago," Brandon said.

"Five more minutes," Darcy hollered as she nailed two zombies with one shot. "Take that, suckers."

"Maybe we should just order something," Lucien suggested.

Darcy immediately replied, "Yeah, that's a good idea."

Darcy stood in her kitchen working the dough for the pie she was baking for dessert. She was making dinner for Lucien and Brandon at her apartment. She was moving in with Lucien, but she wanted Brandon to see what had been hers for so long—to share a little of her past with him.

She heard the footsteps before Brandon's voice filled the silence. "Can we help?"

She turned to see father and son standing just inside her small kitchen and how right it looked to see them there.

"I'm almost done."

"That print you have in the living room, there's one like it at St. Agnes," Brandon said.

"The one at St. Agnes was Sister Anne's print," Lucien offered.

Brandon suddenly took an interest in his shoes. His head was lowered, which made it more difficult to hear his words. "I used to look at that print and wonder about my mom and dad. I'd made up countless excuses for why they'd left me behind. How they were doing what was best for me." His head lifted and a ghost of a smile touched his lips. "It's crazy that the reality is even more way out there than my imaginings."

Darcy burst into tears. She saw Lucien start for her, but it was Brandon who reached her first.

"Sorry, I didn't mean to make you cry."

Darcy shook her head and tried to collect herself. After a minute she wiped at her eyes with a paper towel. "It isn't that. I hung that print because it reminded me of you and your father. Somehow you both felt closer to me when I looked at it. To think that you were doing the same makes me happy and sad all at once."

Brandon seemed to hesitate for a minute before he asked very softly, "Can I call you Mom?"

Darcy lifted her head as tears spilled down her face. "I would love for you to call me Mom."

And then Brandon pulled her into his arms and held her close. "Don't cry, Mom."

Her arms went around him and she savored the moment she had only ever believed would come true in her dreams. After a minute, Brandon took a step back and looked at Lucien. He didn't have to ask and Lucien replied by smiling.

"I'd be honored."

Brandon's smile covered his face and then he said, "Dad and I got you a gift."

Darcy's gaze moved from Brandon to Lucien and back again. She didn't hide her excitement. "Really?"

"An Xbox and *Resident Evil*."

Darcy took a word from her son's playbook when she replied, "Sweet."

———•◦•———

Trace watched as Ember got ready for bed, taking in her very round belly. She was eight months pregnant and, though she was tired all the time, she looked beautiful. His eyes moved higher to her breasts and he couldn't help but smile because only Ember would bitch about her breasts getting bigger. He didn't feel the same. In fact, he was tempted to put his hands and lips on those magnificent breasts, but that would drive him crazy and he'd want to finish what he started. He was avoiding sex until the baby came. Ember didn't understand, had told him repeatedly that it was perfectly safe, but he didn't want to take the chance.

At her last visit the doctors said her proteins were the closest to normal that they had been throughout the entire pregnancy, as was her blood pressure. The baby was in a good position, the uterus looked great, and they were confident that her delivery would be perfectly average. He was happy with the news, but he still wasn't going to chance it by having sex. He knew he was being ridiculous, but he didn't care. Waiting was good; it meant that when they did come together again it would be fucking explosive.

Ember glanced over at him, and the smile that turned into a frown made it clear that she knew what he was thinking.

"You're being silly, Trace."

He walked to her and brushed his lips over hers. "After the baby comes, you'll have to beat me away."

"Promise?"

"Absolutely."

"It's just as well; I don't feel particularly sexy anyway."

His eyes moved over her slowly before he looked back at her. "Why do you think I've been taking so many showers lately?"

It took her a minute, but he saw as understanding moved over her features. "You're in here . . ." She gestured with her hand because she couldn't seem to say the word, which was ridiculous, considering their sex life, but so fucking adorable.

"I'm jacking off four, five times a day, Ember."

"Why?"

"Because I want you."

"Then take me."

He grinned, but it faded before he said, "I want you healthy and whole more."

"I'm fine, Trace."

"I know, and I'm not going to do anything to change that." He pressed his lips to hers again. "Are you hungry?"

"I am."

"I'll make you something."

"Something chocolaty."

"You got it, sweetheart."

He had just reached the door when she said, "Thanks for caring so much."

"That's like thanking me for breathing," he said as he glanced at her from over his shoulder.

She started for the bed and stumbled. He rushed toward her. "Ember."

Her eyes lifted to his, but they were glazed over; her lips parted, but he couldn't hear what she said before she just dropped.

He tried to reach her, but her head hit the dresser before she crumpled to the floor like a rag doll, and then her body started to convulse.

Trace didn't realize he was screaming until Chelsea appeared in the doorway. Her look of horror matched his own.

"What's wrong with her?" Trace was already at Ember's side with a sheet in his hand as he tried to staunch the flow of blood from the head wound.

"Call nine-one-one, Chelsea, now!"

Ember's eyes were white, the irises had rolled into the back of her head. Her body was jerking so violently, he was afraid she was going to break something, but thankfully the shakes started to subside.

"Ember, sweetheart, wake up."

She wouldn't open her eyes. She didn't respond to him in any way and then he noticed the blood between her legs.

"They're coming," Chelsea said from the doorway before she moved to join Trace.

"What's happening to her?"

She was dying. That was Trace's immediate answer. He was going to be forced to watch as his wife bled to death right in front of him. He was still applying pressure to the gash on her head when the paramedics arrived. Trace hadn't even heard the doorbell.

"I've got it," said one of the paramedics as he ran into the room and knelt down next to Trace, replacing the sheet with a sterile cloth from his bag.

"Her pulse is weak and her breathing is shallow. Prepare to bag her."

And then the next words from the paramedic shattered Trace.

"I've got no pulse."

Trace called Lucien from the hospital. His friend answered on the first ring.

"Is it time?" Lucien asked.

"It's Ember; she's in the hospital."

"Trace, what's wrong? Is she having the baby?"

His next words were broken. "I need you to come."

Trace didn't notice when his friends came through the ER doors, because he was wild with grief.

"Where is my wife?"

The nurse was on the phone and put up her finger to Trace, signaling she needed another minute or two while she continued her conversation.

He slammed his hands down so hard on the counter it sounded like a gun blast.

"Where the fuck is my wife?"

"I'll have to call you back." The nurse's hands shook as she replaced the receiver.

"Who, sir?"

"Ember Montgomery."

"The doctors are in with her."

"Where? I want to see her."

"You can't," the nurse said, trying to be firm.

Lucien walked up to Trace. "She's right. You want the doctors focused completely on Ember. You will only distract them."

Trace raked his hand through his hair and felt himself losing control. He gazed back at the nurse. "Can you tell me how she is? What's happening?"

He knew she could see the depth of his despair. She stood. "I don't know, but I'll go back and see what I can find out."

She moved briskly down the hall.

"What the hell happened?" Lucien demanded.

His pain and fear were consuming him. He barely recognized his own voice. "She died. For almost a minute she was gone." He had watched Ember die. The sight was going to haunt him for the rest of his life.

"What?" The word was ripped from Darcy's throat on a sob.

"She was getting ready for bed. She stumbled before she just dropped to the floor, her head hit the edge of the dresser"—tears filled his eyes—"and she just crumbled and then her body started convulsing. They're most concerned about the head wound—there could be brain trauma." He needed a minute to fight for control before he added, "She was bleeding badly from between her legs. The paramedics think she may have ruptured the placenta when she fell."

The nurse returned and she looked so solemn that Trace immediately thought the worst.

"The seizure was brought on by eclampsia, so they're delivering the baby."

"Isn't it too early?" Darcy asked.

"The doctors will have to tell you that; I'm sorry."

Trace walked to the far corner of the waiting room, leaned up against the wall, and lowered his head.

Over the next hour the waiting room filled up and, though it was standing room only, the voices were only a soft hum. Through it all, Trace stood alone in the corner.

Trace's head lifted as Ember's father approached. "How is she?"

"There's no word yet."

"She'll pull through this. You know Ember, she's tenacious."

The room was so silent that Trace's next words hung in the air hauntingly, "I can't live without her."

"You can. Believe me, son, you can, but you aren't going to have to."

———◆———

Two hours after Ember was brought into the ER, Dr. Cole came out into the waiting room. "Trace?"

He lifted his head and moved to her. "Yes."

"The baby's fine, a few weeks early, but she's very strong."

"And Ember?"

"She lost a lot of blood and, unfortunately . . ." She looked down at the chart before she returned her gaze to his. "I'm sorry, but we had to give her a full hysterectomy to stop the bleeding."

"Is she okay?" Trace demanded.

"The seizure was brought on by eclampsia and it isn't uncommon for the patient to slip into a coma. However, with the blow she took to her head, we're unsure if the coma is from the eclampsia or if it's a result of brain trauma. If the trauma to her brain was significant enough to render her unconscious . . ."

"What, damn it?"

"Well, there's a possibility, though unlikely, that she may never regain consciousness. The next six hours are critical."

"And if she doesn't wake up within six hours?"

"There are rare cases that the person can be out for days and regain full function, but, like I said, that is very rare." Dr. Cole reached for Trace's hand. "Ember is young and strong. She'll pull through this."

"Can I see her?"

———◆———

Trace walked down the long corridor, but didn't see anything, didn't hear anything. His feet moved him, but he wasn't sure how. When he reached her room, he stood outside of it for a moment, battling what was raging inside him. He needed to be strong for her even if he felt as if he were being ripped apart, his body being eviscerated by the doctor's words.

She looked like she was sleeping. Her hair had been washed, and he thought how fucked it was that even though she may be lost to him forever, her hair had been shampooed. He moved to the chair next to her bed and reached for her hand and, when he felt its warmth, a tear slipped down his cheek because he had feared it would be cold.

"We have a daughter. You need to wake up, sweetheart, so we can meet her together. Everyone's here, waiting to celebrate with us, but you need to wake up first. I know you're tired, love, you've been so tired, but you can sleep later and I'll hold you for as long as you need. But right now, I need you to open your eyes so that I can see inside you. I need to see inside you, Ember."

He rested his head on her stomach and his next words tore from his throat with his anguish. "Please don't leave me. You promised me forever."

———◆———

Lucien sat in the waiting room with Darcy curled up in his lap because there wasn't another available seat; people were on the floor, leaning against the wall. Everyone that Ember knew, everyone that had been touched by her in some way, was here, including Lena and Dane. Brandon and Seth were getting food and coffee for people. Kyle was keeping regular tabs with the nurses and passing on any news. Rafe was passing around boxes of tissues, comforting while being comforted. Charles Michaels stood with Horace and Nathaniel, all silently waiting. Lucien couldn't put into words how it made him feel to see them there, knowing that the Carmichaels didn't even know Ember; but Lucien was now a part of their family, and Ember was a part of his.

Lucien couldn't imagine what Trace was going through, but it nearly broke him to think about Darcy going through this very same thing all alone.

Trace would survive the loss of Ember. He had friends and family that would help him through it, but why the fuck should he have to? Ember's dad, Shawn, had finally convinced Trace to go see the baby, and Lucien knew he would never get the sight out of his mind for as long as he lived. He had sweet-talked the nurses into letting him into the NICU with Trace so he could be there for his friend. And seeing Trace holding such a small baby, watching the tears that streamed down his friend's face as he looked at her, Lucien knew what Trace was thinking as if he were saying it out loud. If Ember died, her baby was all that he would have left of her. It wasn't fucking right.

Ember had been in the coma for five hours. Except to see his new daughter, Trace never left her side, holding her hand and demanding that she come back to him. Lucien really didn't want to think about what-if, but they may just have to. He looked over at Trace, who was waiting to see Ember while the nurses were in with her, checking her IVs. He looked lost.

"I'm going to go wait with Trace," he said to Darcy as he lifted her from his lap, but he stopped in midmotion. "You are in a hospital."

"And my opinion of them hasn't improved," she said sadly. "Should you take him some food? I don't think he's eaten anything."

"Good idea. Could you ask Brandon to bring him a sandwich?"

"I will."

Lucien pressed his mouth to Darcy's, and they lingered over the kiss, heartbroken for their friend and grateful for each other. He said nothing when he leaned up against the wall next to Trace. He knew his friend well enough to know that if he needed to talk, he would.

"She looks just like Ember," Trace said softly.

"She's beautiful."

Trace looked over at his friend, and the sight of his despair ripped through Lucien. "I can't do this without her. Fuck, I was okay before she came into my life. I learned to be alone and then she came pushing her way into my life and, fuck, how do I go back?"

"You don't. You can't because, even if we lose Ember, she's left a piece of herself with you. She'll always be with you, Trace, and I know it may not be in the way you want and, believe me, I understand, but she will always be with you."

Trace hung his head and his voice broke when he said, "It's not enough, not fucking nearly enough."

———

Two days after Ember was brought into the ER, Trace stood in the corner of the waiting room with Lucien and Rafe. As Lucien looked at his friend, he knew that he was beginning to give up hope.

How did one plan for that? How did someone pick up the pieces and continue on when a part of them was gone? Chelsea was inconsolable, crying on Seth's shoulder, not fully understanding why Ember wouldn't wake up.

What should have been one of the happiest times in all of their lives was some fucked-up nightmare, a nightmare Lucien knew would haunt Trace for the rest of his life.

Trace spoke from his corner, "I was so afraid of this pregnancy, afraid that if something happened to Ember, I would lose my way, fall back into that pit with my demons, but she's changed me. As hard as it will be, I can live a life without her; I can parent our child alone . . ." There were tears in his eyes when he looked over at Lucien. "I can do it because of her. We're her legacy, my daughter and me."

The moment was shattered when an alarm went off down the hall in the direction of Ember's room. Trace was off the wall and running down the hall and Lucien had just caught up when Dr. Cole turned to Trace, crying.

Trace stumbled, falling into the wall as tears streamed down his cheeks. Anguish filled his expression, the sight so raw and heartbreaking that Lucien didn't even realize he was crying himself until he couldn't see the doctor anymore. And then she said, "She's awake."

Lucien's head snapped to Trace who was looking at the doctor, but clearly not hearing her. The doctor smiled wider, "She's awake and asking for you."

The doctors cleared the room and, for a few hours, Trace just held Ember's hand while she went in and out of consciousness. Four hours after she woke, her eyes opened and stayed open. He saw when she focused because a smile touched her lips. If he weren't sitting, he would have fallen to his knees in gratitude. He pressed his mouth to hers and then he just stared into her big brown eyes.

Her voice was hoarse and hardly over a whisper when she asked, "What are you doing?"

"Seeing inside you." His hand wasn't steady when he brushed a lock of hair from her face. "I almost lost you. I can't even begin to tell you what that feels like."

"I—"

But Trace wouldn't let her speak. "I need to say this. I was so afraid that I was going to lose you, that without you I would become the horrible guy I used to be. But you changed me, you're inside me, and I can't find the words to tell you just what that means to me except to say thank you." His finger brushed over her lips. "Thanks for not letting go."

He wiped the tears that rolled down her cheeks before he kissed her, her salty tears lingering on his lips.

"I love you," she whispered.

"Love, sweetheart, is not strong enough a word."

She turned her head and pressed a kiss to his palm. Her eyes were sad when she looked back at him.

"I can't have any more children, can I?"

"We have a child."

The sight of her heartache ripped at him as silent tears streamed down her face. Somehow she managed to ask through her tears, "Have you seen her?"

"She looks just like you."

"Have you named her?"

"I was waiting for you, but I do have a name, if it's all right with you."

"What?"

He touched her face. "Everyone said I needed to have faith that you would come back to me and so it seems fitting that our daughter should be called Faith."

"There's someone here to see you." Ember looked past Trace to see her dad in the doorway, and in his arms was a small bundle. Behind her dad was her uncle, Chelsea, Lucien and Darcy, Rafe and Kyle, and even Brandon and Seth were there.

Shawn walked across the floor and lowered the baby into Ember's arms. Trace watched Ember's face as she looked at her daughter for the first time. Her pain was still there, but a radiance covered her expression, and he knew what she was feeling because he had felt it too. He brushed his finger across his daughter's cheek. He hadn't thought there was room, but his heart swelled looking at his daughter. *His daughter.* He had feared he'd become his dad, but looking into her sweet, innocent face, he knew he was nothing like him. He would fight all the world's armies for her; he would walk right into hell and take on the devil himself for his daughter.

"She's beautiful, isn't she?" Ember said softly.

"She looks like her mom."

Tears that were still fresh in her eyes began to well up and over, trailing lines down her cheeks, but she didn't seem to notice.

Her eyes looked up into his. "Our daughter."

"What's her name?" Brandon asked.

She reached for Trace's hand and they shared a moment before she said, "Faith Amanda Montgomery."

Chapter Twenty-Three

Darcy sat in her office, but her thoughts were on Trace and Ember. Ember was growing stronger every day and, though Darcy knew her friend was heartbroken that she would never have another child, she had Faith and Trace. It was a beautiful sight, seeing the three of them together, knowing how close Trace had come to losing her.

Her thoughts turned to her son. It was just another twist to the tale that they'd only met him because he'd worked with Ember. It was amazing to her how so many lives could be entwined, especially in a place as large as Manhattan. Thinking about that, she wondered: Had it been a coincidence that Brandon worked at the Michaels campaign headquarters?

She had thought about it a lot during the weeks since her reunion with Brandon, and finally her curiosity over whether Charles intentionally brought Brandon into their lives made her want to talk with him. If he had, she needed to thank him, because he had ultimately brought them together. Ember had said that he was still maintaining the headquarters while he tied up a few last things. Darcy had called and explained who she was, and he was very amenable to talking to her that same day. She was supposed to meet Lucien and Brandon at Clover, but she didn't have to be there for an hour.

The headquarters were empty. Apparently everyone had been let go the same time as Ember and Brandon. There was a light in the back where she assumed Charles's office was.

"Hello. Is anyone here?"

She walked toward the office and heard what sounded like a scuffle, but before she could react in any way, the door opened and out walked a woman dressed to the nines. She pointed a gun at Darcy.

Part of Darcy was convinced that she was imagining the bizarre scene she found herself in. Her gaze moved behind the woman to see Charles Michaels out cold on the floor, and immediately she feared the worst. Her first instinct was to run, but the woman looked out of control, her hands shaking as she held the gun on Darcy. Darcy feared if she startled the woman, sheer terror would make her squeeze the trigger.

She asked, afraid to hear the answer, "Is he dead?"

"No."

"What did you do to him?"

"Just knocked him in the head."

She sounded awfully calm for someone who had just rendered a man unconscious and was now holding a gun on a complete stranger. Darcy's fear kicked up a notch and her words were tainted with it when she asked, "Who are you?"

"Oh, sorry. Hi, I'm Vivian. His wife."

She looked like a PTA mom, so why the hell did she have a gun?

"You do know that you have a gun on me, right?"

"Yeah, sorry. Dreadful things, aren't they?"

"Why don't you put it down?"

"Not sure who I can trust."

"Maybe you should start from the beginning?" Darcy suggested.

"Good idea. Heidi . . . Do you know Heidi?"

"Yes."

"Well, Heidi got pregnant with his child."

"And she started blackmailing you," Darcy offered.

Surprise covered Vivian's face. "Yes. For almost two years we were being held hostage by her greed. I wanted to get out from under her control, but I didn't know how to make her stop. And then one day I get approached by someone who offers me a solution."

Sarcasm dripped from Darcy's words. "Let me guess. Kidnap a baby?"

"Exactly. Looking back on it now, it was beyond stupid of me to agree to such a plan, but I wasn't thinking clearly: fear and my own greed clouded my judgment."

"It was Jonathan Carmichael who approached you, wasn't it?"

Darcy didn't miss the look of suspicion on Vivian's face. "How do you know that?"

"It was my baby he took."

"Oh my God. I wanted to return him to you, but I was afraid I would go to jail. I didn't understand why he did it, but he took great joy in separating you from your baby. He never intended to take Heidi's baby; he lied to me and made me his accomplice and then threatened me to keep my silence about the kidnapping or he'd leak it to the press, which would have destroyed Charles's political career." Tears filled Vivian's eyes. "I tried not to think of you and how what we'd done had changed all of your lives. I'm so sorry."

Darcy wasn't about to absolve the woman. Instead she asked, "How is Heidi tied to this?"

"I think it was Jonathan who told Heidi of the botched kidnapping, but I don't think it was to keep me in line. I had the sense he was distracting her. My guess is that she was getting close to finding out something he didn't want discovered, so he set me up and gave Heidi more leverage over Charles and me."

Well, that was certainly true. Heidi must have learned about Jonathan and Elizabeth and somehow put it together that Jonathan was her murderer.

Vivian continued, "The night Heidi died I went to see her. I called her and demanded a meeting. We fought. I didn't mean to kill her. I wanted to kill her, but I didn't think I'd hit her hard enough, and then I heard on the news that she was dead. I panicked; I mean, Charles was trying to run for the senate and here I'm plotting kidnappings and getting myself caught up in a murder. I thought about turning myself in, but then that would still have reflected poorly on Charles. And that's when he called me."

"Who called you?"

"I don't know. He said he'd clean up my mess, but it was going to cost me. Ten thousand a month. I mean, I don't have that kind of money and I couldn't take that amount from our account without Charles knowing about it."

"So you told Charles everything," Darcy finished.

"Heidi had been to Charles's office a few times to taunt him about my indiscretions, including my botched kidnapping attempt, but I shared with him my part in her murder. He's been trying to make it right ever since. Months of fixing what took me years to so royally screw up."

"So, him bringing Brandon here was intentional."

Vivian looked confused. "Brandon, is that your son?"

"Yes."

"So you found him?"

"Only because your husband put Brandon in the same social circle as Lucien." Charles Michaels seemed like a decent man. "Why did you knock him unconscious then?"

"Oh, that. I didn't know it was him. I thought it was the blackmailer. He called me and told me to meet him here."

Dread slithered down Darcy's spine just as a voice spoke up from the shadows. "You shouldn't have done that, Vivian, because now I'm going to have to kill her too."

It was a completely inappropriate emotion to be feeling, but in that moment Darcy was furious. She turned her eyes on the man and asked, "And just who in the hell are you?"

"I'm a friend of the family." He moved closer so that Darcy could see his hazel-green eyes. "I'm Todd."

———◆———

Lucien checked his watch for the sixth time. Darcy was almost an hour late.

"Where do you think she is?" Brandon asked.

"I don't know. She would have called if she was going to be late."

He reached for his phone and called her, but it went immediately to voice mail, so he called Allegro. Tara answered.

"Tara, have you seen you Darcy?"

"Hey, Lucien. Not for a while. She left here about two hours ago."

"Did she mention where she was going?"

"Yeah, she said she was meeting up with you and your son. That's really cool, boss, that you found him and you're all together now."

He didn't mean to be curt, but with each minute that passed, he was getting more and more worried.

"Anywhere else?"

"Oh, wait. She did ask if I knew where that senator dude's office was located. You know, the one who dropped out of the race?"

"Thanks." Lucien hung up. "Do you know the number to Charles's office?" he asked Brandon.

"No, but we could google it."

Lucien called the number, but there was a busy signal. Who had busy signals anymore? He looked over at Brandon. "You know how to get to this office, right?"

"Yeah."

"Let's go."

Darcy stood in what felt like a bad horror movie scene. She wanted the director to call cut and for them to reshoot the scene. She'd forgo being thoughtful and instead head directly to where she wanted to be.

Lucien and Brandon were waiting for her. Would he come looking for her or would he just get pissed and assume the worst because she was late again?

At the shock of seeing Todd, Vivian had dropped her gun, which was bad, but it was made worse when Darcy realized Todd was carrying.

Vivian was crying softly, but without tears, probably because it would ruin her perfectly applied makeup. Todd was pacing as if he hadn't really thought through the rest of his plan.

"So what's the plan, Todd? Have you thought past the entrance? I have to give you credit—that was well done."

"Shut up."

Darcy knew she must be in shock, because she was behaving irrationally; but even knowing it, she couldn't get herself to stop taunting the man.

"How do you plan on taking all of us out of here? Or are you going to just kill us here in the same place you've been sweating profusely? I wouldn't worry about DNA or anything." She rolled her eyes.

And then she realized what she was saying; she was actually wishing she was with someone who knew exactly how to dispose of their bodies. Bad tactic, so she changed it.

"You haven't done anything wrong. So you could just let us go."

His laugh was just on the wrong side of crazy. "Didn't do anything wrong. I fucking killed that bitch, Heidi."

Gone was the ladylike demeanor as Vivian responded, sounding like a truck driver.

"What the fuck do you mean you killed her? You've been blackmailing me all this time, and you killed her?"

"She was blackmailing *me*, sucking me dry. I took money from work that I shouldn't have taken and then lost it gambling. I was paying it back, but I made the mistake of mentioning it to Heidi."

Darcy jumped on that. "How did you know her?"

"I met her through Dane."

It was clear to Darcy that by knowing her, Todd meant in the biblical sense. "So a little pillow talk and you find yourself being blackmailed."

"That's pretty low, even for Heidi," said Vivian. Darcy had to agree with Vivian on that point.

"She was a self-serving bitch. I was in way over my head, so badly that I ended up borrowing the money to pay back my company. Heidi still held it over my head because, despite the fact that I had returned it, I could still go to jail for embezzling it in the first place. I started following her, hoping that maybe I'd catch her in something that would cancel out what she had on me. I saw you two fighting and I saw when you hit her hard enough to lay her out with her head breaking the fall. You walked away, but you never looked back and I thought, hell, I can just finish her off and be free of her."

"So you called nine-one-one before you murdered her."

If Todd was surprised that Darcy knew about that, he didn't let on. "Yeah, I wanted to screw up the timeline and then while she was still struggling, I gave one more slam of her head against the sidewalk and that was all it took. Her little black book fell from her purse when Vivian knocked her over. So I thought, why not take up where Heidi left off?"

"So what happened? Why are you here now?" Darcy asked.

"That fucking DA. He's asking all kinds of questions, and it's only a matter of time before they find Heidi's connection to Vivian and"—he gestured with disgust at Vivian—"if questioned, she'll squeal like a pig. It wouldn't take them long to figure out how I fit into the picture. I was so desperate I even thought to blackmail Dane's dad with what Heidi had on him. Thought instead of money, I could get him to leash in his fucking brother, but the man refused to take my calls."

"So you decided since you're already going away for murder you might as well take as many people with you as you could?" Sarcasm dripped from Darcy's words.

"No, I figured I'd tie up my loose ends and then take off into the sunset with the money I got from my marks. I wasn't expecting him here, or you."

"You came here to kill me? How rude!" Vivian's ladylike poise had returned. At least she was back in character, which meant she wasn't about to flip out and do something stupid.

"Well, I don't want to put pressure on you, but I was expected an hour ago and people knew I was coming here. You're running out of time."

"Damn it."

"Let us go," Darcy said again. "You can make a run for it."

He looked as if he were thinking about it, but then he raised his gun and fired. Vivian crumpled to the floor.

"I'll get farther with a hostage."

Lucien flew through the door of the campaign headquarters and saw the body on the floor. His heart sank as he ran to it, but when he saw that it was Vivian, God forgive him, he sighed in relief.

"Charles is in here. He's coming around from a blow to the head," Brandon called.

"And Darcy?" Lucien demanded.

"Not here."

Lucien pulled out his phone and called 911, and then turned to Brandon.

"Wait here until the cops come, and tell them what you know. They can't know I was here because I need to go after your mom."

At that moment Vivian started to stir.

"He took her."

"Who took her?" Lucien demanded.

"Todd Samuels."

"Shit."

Lucien's head turned when he heard the sirens coming. He stood and walked to his son. "I've got to go or I'll be here all night answering questions. I was never here. You were here looking for your mom. Have the cops drop you off at Trace's when they're done. I know I'm asking a lot. Are you okay with staying?"

"Yeah, I'm good. Go get Mom."

Lucien stopped halfway to the door and looked back at the boy who looked so young in that moment. "I'll bring her back, I promise."

"I'm going to hold you to that."

On the sidewalk, Lucien pulled out his phone. He needed to call in a few favors.

Todd dragged Darcy through the doorway of Polly's.

The events of the evening started to sink in for Darcy: she'd been held at gunpoint, witnessed a shooting, and then been kidnapped. More bizarre, her kidnapper was taking phone calls, even as he held a gun against her ribs. He just chatted away, as if he had not a care in the world. He was either a freaking criminal mastermind or the stupidest person ever. She heard herself asking, "What are we doing here?"

"My bookie works out of the backroom. He called earlier; he's got my money. I'm going to pick up my winnings and then we're out of here."

"What about the money you've made from blackmailing?"

"I've got that stashed."

"Aren't you pushing it by coming here? Won't the people you borrowed from know you're here? I'm sure they know everything about you, including your bookie's hangout and if you are still gambling with their money."

"Maybe, but by the time they learn of it, I'll be gone." He grinned before he added, "They can't collect if they can't find me."

That seemed to Darcy like a really good way to land six feet under, but she held her tongue. She was leaning more toward the idea of him being the stupidest criminal ever.

They passed the bar and Darcy's eyes landed on Nick DiNuzzio, the man who'd changed her life irrevocably, and she almost had to bite down on her lips to keep from crying out at the absurdity of seeing him at this moment. Just fucking poetic. He was probably harboring all kinds of ill will, what with the pounding he had gotten from Lucien and Trace.

She wondered if Todd would just leave her if she curled up into the fetal position and started to cry.

She was tempted to try it, but it was the gun digging into her ribs, pointed at her baby, that squashed that urge.

Nick moved from his spot behind the bar and approached them. Darcy braced for a backhanded slap or some indication that he knew exactly who she was.

But when a move was made, it wasn't from Nick, but another man who was smaller in build, but older. He must have been someone important, because his presence immediately brought a hush to the crowd. He stopped just in front of Darcy and smiled.

"Darcy, let me introduce myself. My name is Pasquale Grimaldi, and your fiancé asked that I keep you safe until he can join us."

She was dreaming. Totally dreaming. Maybe it was Darcy that Todd had shot back at the campaign office, and now she was unconscious and dreaming. But why would she be dreaming this? No, her dream would be of Lucien and Brandon and the baby that was coming. She most definitely would not be dreaming this; couldn't have imagined this scene even if she were tripping—not that she'd ever inhaled.

He seemed to understand that she didn't exactly believe her eyes, and he reached for her hand. Todd panicked as he saw himself losing control of the scene, and waved his gun.

"I've got the gun, asshole. Back off."

Things turned rapidly into a scene from *Lethal Weapon,* with Todd as the comic relief. Seconds later he was surrounded by men, all of them with bigger and shinier guns aimed at Todd's head. Yep, definitely the stupidest criminal ever.

Todd dropped his hand and his head. "My life fucking sucks."

Nick walked over and took the gun from Todd as Pasquale walked Darcy toward a booth. "Shock can make you refuse to believe what your eyes are seeing. I assure you, though, dear, I am very much in earnest. Lucien called me earlier, and told me of the situation."

"Why are you helping us?"

"Our paths have crossed before. Last time, I broke something, and I've been given the chance to mend it." He was so soft-spoken and kind that Darcy was having trouble imaging all the terrible things he had been accused of. And then his eyes turned to Todd and, just like that, the sweet older man was replaced with a killer, his eyes turning dark and empty as a doll's. "Besides, it was an opportunity to talk with Todd, regarding certain payments that he is very behind on. "

Darcy looked back at Todd, who looked like he was about to cry. Nope, he *was* crying.

Darcy felt funny, her limbs turned to noodles, probably the result of profound relief. "It's over?"

"Yes."

"And Lucien is on his way here?"

"Yes, dear."

And then Darcy MacBride did something she had only ever done once before—she fainted.

———◆———

"There she is." Lucien's soft voice drew Darcy completely into consciousness, and when she opened her eyes to see his beautiful worried face, she started to cry.

"You okay?" he asked with tenderness.

"Yeah."

"The baby?"

She smiled. "Fine. How did you know where to find me?"

"I'll tell you, but not now. I want to get you home because there's someone waiting to see you."

"Brandon?"

"Yes."

Lucien helped her to her feet. "I need a minute. Are you okay?"

She pressed her hand to his cheek. "Yes."

He kissed her palm and then turned to Pasquale. "Thank you."

"I'm a sucker for love."

Lucien grinned and turned to Nick, at Pasquale's right. "Thanks."

Nick nodded, and then Lucien knocked Nick flat on his ass with a solid to his jaw.

Nick took it and even acknowledged the hit with a small grin. Lucien reached for Darcy and pulled her up against him. "Let's go see our son."

When they arrived home, Trace was there with Brandon.

Trace's eyes moved over Darcy before he started for the door.

"Thank you, Trace," Lucien called. "How's Vivian?"

Trace turned to him when he reached the door. "Fine. The bullet went through her shoulder. She's already demanding sparkling water and Egyptian cotton sheets."

And then he quietly closed the door behind him.

Darcy's attention was solely on Brandon. She started toward him and, though it had only been a month since they'd connected, it had been a really fantastic month. She stopped just in front of him, but before she could say a word, he wrapped his arms around her and pressed his face to her shoulder. She hugged him back and pretended that she didn't feel his tears on her neck, even as her own tears rolled down her cheeks.

Later that night, Darcy lay in Lucien's arms, grateful that she was there and not in some alley. She shuddered just thinking about it and, as if Lucien knew what she was thinking because he was thinking it too, he held her tighter.

"You came for me."

"I learned that lesson the hard way. I'll always come for you."

She always thought that when her dream came true it would be with great fanfare. But instead it was a whisper. She was ready to soar the skies. She moved closer to Lucien because she didn't want to soar; she was exactly where she was meant to be.

Lucien noticed the look that crossed her face and asked, "Are you okay?"

She looked up at him and smiled, "I'm not a caterpillar anymore."

He touched her face, running his fingers down her cheek, tenderness washing over his face. He pressed a kiss to her lips before he tucked her head under his chin. "You'll always be *my* Caterpillar."

That memory made Darcy think of Sister Anne. "I need to visit Sister Anne tomorrow."

Lucien looked at her. "Why?"

"Her flowers are fading."

He sat up at that. "That was you?"

"She always loved flowers and it was my way to remember her and you."

He pulled her to him and kissed her. "I love you, Darcy."

She smiled up at him. "I know." And then she batted her lashes at him. "Did you mean it?" she asked.

"What?"

"That you'll always come for me."

"Yes."

"Like right now?"

The meaning was clear when Lucien rolled to pin her under him. "Ladies first."

Epilogue

The old tree had never looked more beautiful. White lights were strung around its gnarly branches, and an arbor of white, with pink and yellow roses wound through it, was centered at its base. Rows of white chairs, divided by an aisle of white silk, stretched up the gentle slope of the hill.

Brandon held Darcy's hand tightly as they made their way to Lucien, who stood waiting for her.

"You look beautiful, Mom."

Darcy's eyes met his, but her emotions were making it impossible to speak. She squeezed his hand and knew he understood.

Her eyes moved to those who had come to share this day with them. There weren't many, but everyone here was family. She spotted Ember sitting next to Trace, his hand wrapped around hers while he held their daughter in his arms. How very different that picture could have been. She turned her focus on Lucien. When she reached him, he took her hand into his own before he brushed his lips over her ear.

"You're stunning and late."

It had taken a long time to get them to where they were, but had they not gone through all that they had, they wouldn't truly appreciate what it was they had found. It hadn't been easy, downright awful at times, but it had all led to this moment. She smiled back at him.

"Not late—exactly right on time."

A slight grin touched his lips before he said, teasingly, "So you didn't forget."

"Not then, not now, not ever." She touched his cheek. "How could I?"

His eyes grew dark before he pressed his mouth to hers.

The moment was broken when Sister Margaret cackled, "Get on with it, I'm hungry."

They turned and walked together toward their tree. Lucien leaned down and whispered, "Thanks for meeting me this time." His gaze fell on the small silver cross around Darcy's neck.

"Thanks for waiting."

"I'd wait forever for you."

She looked up at him just when they reached their tree, and smiled. "Luckily for us that forever is starting now."

The pastor cleared his throat. "We are gathered here today to celebrate . . ."

Acknowledgments

I really enjoyed writing this story and being back in the world of *Beautifully Damaged.* As a writer, you can get so lost in your story that days can turn into nights before you even realize it. My kids and husband are so wonderful: tolerating me when I drop off the grid for weeks at a time.

Thank you to my twin sister for being my sounding board and for being so gracious with me even after filling her e-mail with scenarios about fictional characters.

Thank you Krista Stroever, my editor, for your expertise. It is truly a pleasure working with you.

Michelle Hope Anderson, my copyeditor, thank you for your keen eyes.

Krista and Mindy, thank you for your unwavering support. I love you guys.

And lastly, I'd like to thank my dog, Artemis. We rescued her three years ago; an abused dog who was so terrified she would sit in her own pee. And now she is my constant companion and even at four in the morning when I'm still feverishly typing, she is right at my side. You are a beautiful creature and I adore your company.

About the Author

L.A. Fiore enjoys writing to music. OneRepublic, Halestorm, Life-house, Plain White T's, Evanescence, Steve Earle, and Flogging Molly are a few of the bands she listened to while writing Lucien's story. When she's not writing, she's wrangling her two kittens—who can leap like Olympic pole vaulters—and keeping her dog from smothering the little furballs with affection. She loves hearing from readers and can be reached through Facebook.

Facebook.com/l.a.fiore.publishing